MW01252393

Back Flip

▪ Back Flip

■ **Anne Denoon**

back *flip*

a novel

❏

❏

THE PORCUPINE'S QUILL

RARY OF CANADA

IN PUBLICATION DATA

)44−

PRICE: $24.95 (6480/apbkm iovel / Anne Denoon.

ISBN 0-88984-238-8

    1. Title.

PS8557.E5643B33 2002   C813'.6   C2002-901285-6
PR9199.4D47B33 2002

Published by The Porcupine's Quill, www.sentex.net/˜pql
68 Main Street, Erin, Ontario NOB 1TO

Readied for the press by Doris Cowan.
Typeset in Minion, printed on Zephyr Antique laid,
and bound at The Porcupine's Quill Inc.

This is a work of fiction. Any resemblance of characters to persons,
living or dead, is purely coincidental.

Represented in Canada by the Literary Press Group.
Trade orders are available from General Distribution Services.

We acknowledge the support of the
Ontario Arts Council, and the Canada
Council for the Arts for our publishing
program. The financial support of the
Government of Canada through the
Book Publishing Industry
Development Program is also
gratefully acknowledged.

ONTARIO ARTS COUNCIL
CONSEIL DES ARTS DE L'ONTARIO

Canadä

The Canada Council | Le Conseil des Arts
for the Arts | du Canada

This book would not have been finished without the hand-holding, encouragement and commitment of a brilliant editor and steadfast friend, Doris Cowan. Another superb editor and lifelong co-conspirator, Alison Reid, held my other hand and offered essential insights and constant, irreplaceable support. I also thank Tim and Elke Inkster for taking me on, the Ontario Arts Council for its assistance, and Lucas and Richard Magder, without whom I could never have done it.

▪ Chapter One

ON A CARPETED PLATFORM surrounded by easels, the model pulled a well-worn red kimono over her workaday nakedness. Harriet – the name alone dated her – had been around for years. Her hair, once dark auburn, was now an odd pinkish shade, and he could not remember whether she had ever been attractive. Did it sometimes cross her mind that her physical decline had been documented in hundreds, maybe even thousands, of muddy, laborious paintings now mouldering in basements or on parents' rec-room walls? He guessed not; the job itself would probably demand a certain absence of imagination.

The large, cluttered room, full of the pungent smells of art, was emptying fast.

'Um, Mr Willard?' A straggler.

'Yes …?'

'Um, I was wondering … do you think I could just start again? Like, paint over what I did and …'

'No. You've got to have something finished the week after next. There's only two more classes.' Unwillingly, Bob walked over to take a look. It was even worse than he expected. 'But I see what you mean. That leg couldn't possibly.... Maybe just paint over this section and we'll try to fix it up next class. The head, too. And the hands. They're all much too big.'

'Okay.'

They only took this class because it was compulsory. The more sophisticated among them considered painting from the nude a criminal waste of time and their instructor, himself, an out-and-out loser. Or at best, a has-been. He could hardly blame them; he hadn't painted, hadn't put brush to canvas for … oh, never mind how long. Except in the classroom. *Those who can't, teach.* During his own omniscient youth he had spoken those heartless words plenty of times. Now the kids were saying *Never trust anyone over thirty.* And he was nearly forty, irretrievably beyond the pale.

By assuming a preoccupied expression, he got through the crowded corridors and out onto the street without having to talk to anyone else.

He narrowed his eyes against the late-afternoon sun. The air itself seemed pale green and tremulous, and the trees had sprouted a pointillist chartreuse fuzz that almost forced you to gaze vacantly through it to the innocent blue sky above, as if looking for some kind of revelation.

However, the only question to be answered now was where he ought to have his first drink of the evening. Should he turn southwest to the Paramount, or northeast towards the Pilot? The Paramount, on Spadina, was closer and cheaper, but at Yonge and Bloor he'd be nearer home when he eventually had no choice but to go there. Something – maybe it was that poignant, slanting light – made him decide to head uptown on foot, instead of taking the subway.

A few minutes later, dashing through a break in the sluggish rush-hour traffic, he crossed University Avenue. On the west side, just north of Dundas, he turned right onto Edward Street. Then, as he passed the grey slab of the dentistry building, he remembered that the original Angelo's (not yet grown Old) had once stood at the corner of Chestnut. And a bittersweet pang ran through him like a shudder. Nostalgia: the opiate of the disappointed. If you got hooked on it, you were finished. There was no surer sign of failure.

At Elizabeth Street, he turned north towards Gerrard, at one time the area's main drag. In the old days, the only people he considered worth knowing in Toronto – artists, actors, musicians, writers, malcontents and misfits of all kinds – either lived or hung out in what everybody called 'the Village'. Some of them, the doughty pioneers of provincial bohemia, had been there since the thirties. To young Robert Willard, fresh out of Listowel in the spring of 1952, it was almost too thrilling. But people were friendly: the proprietor of Little Denmark, a coffee shop at Bay and Gerrard, had even offered to let him have his mail sent there until he got settled.

Nowadays he rarely passed this way; but when he did, the devastation of his youthful stomping grounds always came as a fresh, demoralizing shock. On some level below rational consciousness, he continued to feel that the whole ramshackle collection of cafés, galleries and studios must still exist. And perhaps it did, if only in the way a place you visit in a pleasant dream can seem more real than the all-too-familiar room in which you reluctantly awake.

Most of the Village's half-dozen blocks had been gobbled up years ago by the parking lots and outbuildings of the hospitals on University, but a few remnants survived the last great wave of demolition in 1963. At the corner of Elizabeth and Gerrard, Mary John's waited humbly for its appointment with the wrecker's ball, and a string of one- and two-storey buildings were still standing on the south side of the street.

But on the north side a whole block had been razed. Somewhere in that paved wasteland, now half full of parked cars, he and Lorraine had lived in a second-floor flat. Those days would probably turn out to be the happiest of his life. And yet he found he could no longer quite picture the house's façade, or even identify the precise spot where it had stood. It seemed that progress, not content with destroying the material evidence of the past, had to demolish memory itself.

The Vanguard Gallery had been ... somewhere over there. Soon after he blew into town he'd met Max Lurie, a wiry, energetic little guy about his own age, but way ahead of Bob: he already had a girl, a weaver with cat's-eye glasses and hair that was too black to be natural. Max and Betty actually lived together, *unmarried,* over the tiny store whose interior they'd whitewashed and filled with their friends' art. Willard's own first one-man show had opened there in March 1953. Fourteen years ago. And even at twenty-four he'd still been dumb and cocky enough to take his amazing luck entirely for granted. How often, he wondered, do people look back and wish they had paused to savour that first easy triumph, instead of letting it slip by on the naïve assumption that it would only be one of many?

He turned up Laplante Avenue and continued north towards College, walking slowly now, drugged by reminiscence. Back then, there wasn't anything like the mass-market, fun-fun-fun rebellion-à-go-go that was happening all over the place these days. Being a bohemian in old Hogtown – the real Orange Order, temperance-pledge, IODE Toronto – actually cost you something. In that Toronto, art was strictly peripheral to the real, cash-and-carry life of the city. And so were artists.

Oh, if you kept your head down and behaved yourself you might get to hang a piece in some Unaffiliated Artists show or maybe in the International Cinema lobby or even Simpson's furniture department. But if you dreamed of recognition or even solvency you had to make a break for it to New York, which only a few had the gumption to do. The rest stayed put, happy to play in their little toy village until the grown-ups decided it was time to tear it down.

Sure, there were some working artists around then: the remnants of the Group of Seven, the guys in the artists' societies, and even a self-confident little coterie that called itself Painters Eleven. But even they had to sneak art into the good burghers' sightlines disguised as interior decoration. And there were a few lone wolves, too; Tom Dale, for instance. In those days he was only a middle-aged adman, making a very nice living and painting on the side. But just like every other hack, what he really wanted was to be taken seriously.

At the time, Bob hadn't thought much of Dale or his work; he'd even tried to talk Max out of giving him wall space at the Vanguard. Okay, he'd been wrong, and Lurie, to his credit, had never once reminded him of that. Or mentioned it to Tom, as far as he knew. But *come on* – considering the warmed-over Theosophist-expressionist stuff Dale was doing in the fifties, who could have ever guessed the guy would make it so big?

Reaching Yonge Street, he headed north. In the early sixties, the avant-garde scene had been driven uptown to the rundown streets north of Bloor. Max had always had a nose for trends, and the Lurie had been one of the first galleries to open up there. That would have been in '62 – the year of Bob's last solo show. The year Lorraine left him.

He passed Wellesley, beginning to tire on the last leg of his trek. All right, artists probably had it better now than he ever had. He was willing to admit that. There were more galleries, sure … but Yorkville was already getting chichi. And the young guys starting out today didn't know what they had missed. Oh man, oh baby, oh you kid, let me tell you sonny, *those* were the days.

TOM DALE did not have a telephone in his studio. He liked being incommunicado while he worked and, not infrequently, drank. Max was always grousing about the inconvenience of not being able to reach the Lurie Gallery's top-selling artist, but as far as Tom was concerned, his success had made isolation more necessary than ever. All kinds of self-important people seemed to think it was great fun to visit a famous painter's studio and watch him work. Or even cut out the middleman and snap up a bargain.

His friends knew he didn't have a phone, so their noses didn't get out of joint just because he didn't feel like lifting the receiver. If they showed up in person, he also reserved the right not to open the door, and he'd had a peephole put in with just such triage in mind. Most people regarded this as the loveable eccentricity of genius. And if he couldn't recall somebody's name or why he was supposed to know them, so what? He'd had more than enough of hop-to-it glad-handing during his years in the advertising business. In the old days, he was always on the ball, never forgot a name or a face. But now he had more important things on his mind.

By six or so in the afternoon, Tom had ingested what he deemed a judicious quantity of Scotch and thereby attained a pleasantly omnipotent state of mind. Glass in hand, he was walking slowly back and forth in front of a large canvas that was probably ... yes, almost certainly ... finished. 'A Sailboat in the Moonlight', the Holiday and Young version, was playing on the portable record player. A perfect marriage of the exquisite and the banal, Tom thought; a real object lesson in how unerring instinct could transform a vapid cliché into something of lasting beauty. It must be thirty years old, and it sounded better than it ever had. Lady and Prez, likely buoyed by a little reefer, floated in tandem through the song, so languorously, so dangerously and deliciously close to falling behind the beat that the corny lyrics somehow seemed profound. Holiday's voice was youthful, teasing, quite unlike the weary rasp of the later, junk-fuelled years. You could almost hear the blissful smile on her face, he thought, smiling too.

As he paced, still studying the canvas in front of him, Tom's head bobbed gently and his shoulders undulated to the beat. He sang softly,

'A chance to drift
for you to lift
your tender lips to mine ...'

Then, halfway through the three-minute song, came Young's meandering solo, ingratiating and insolent at the same time. Ironic yet lyrical. Casual, superb, flippant, sublime.

Well, the painting he had just finished wasn't bad, either. Not bad at all. He backed away and looked at it from across the studio. Yes, it worked, all right: two big rectangles of green floating in a very faintly mottled blue sea, tethered by a sinuous rope of silvery grey. Nothing more, nothing less. The right note, at the right time, in the right place. Yes. *Don't touch it again,* he warned himself. Even at his age, with his experience, he occasionally overworked a piece.

While he freshened his drink, he began to sing again.

'... the things, dear, that I long for are two,
just a sailboat in the moonlight and yo-o-o-ou!'

Waggling his elbows, he took a few sliding sideways steps in time to the gently bouncing beat. As the song ended with a jaunty phrase from Buck Clayton's horn, he glanced at the canvas again and grinned. Then he strolled over to the old leather-covered sofa that sat under the large north-facing windows, placed his topped-up glass on the floor within easy reach, lay down and, still smiling, closed his eyes.

TO THE JAPANESE, Bob thought as he took a gulp of his second beer, the nape of a woman's neck is a focus of erotic longing. He glanced again at Jenny Kosma's dark, close-cropped head, which was bent and turned half away from him as she leaned over to stow her big rucksack under the table. Her hip came briefly into contact with his as she settled herself on the banquette where he, she and – on his other side – Eddie O'Hara were sitting.

O'Hara, a gangly, raw-boned kid with a shock of startlingly red hair and a permanently sceptical expression, had dropped out of art college the year before. But he was doing well; he'd had a couple of things in a group exhibition at the Gonzaga, a new gallery just across the street from the Lurie, and there was even talk of a solo show in the fall. He couldn't have been much more than twenty-two, and his companions – Barnaby Keeler, a performance artist, Sven Jorgensen, a painter, and Jiri, an audiohydrokinetic environment guy who used only the one name – were all about the same age. There was another kid, someone Bob didn't know, with long hair and suspenders – and Jenny.

The Pilot had opened near the end of the war, and retained an aura of daredevil manliness that appealed to its regulars, most of whom at least claimed to be artists or writers. They liked to think of the place as Toronto's answer to the Cedar Tavern, the Greenwich Village watering hole where the he-men of the New York school duked it out and puked it up. Females were tolerated mainly as decorative accessories, and when Jenny first approached their table, the young men had barely acknowledged her. She didn't leave, though, so finally Bob slid over on the banquette to make room for her, forcing Eddie to do the same.

According to Max, she was right out of Winnipeg and determined to crash the Toronto art scene. At least once a week she showed up at the Lurie with her box of slides, trying to get a show. Thus far Max was resisting, but something told Bob that his old friend would soon weaken. Not that the girl was exactly alluring – in both appearance and manner she was dauntingly androgynous. A lezzie, Bob decided, noting that she now had both elbows forthrightly on the table, with a pack of Export A's between them.

'Any of you guys heard about Artquake '67?' she asked. Nobody had. 'You know Quintin Margrave – the guy who runs the Spitalfields Gallery in London?' There were some murmurs of assent to this. 'Well, he's coming over here to put together this huge show – because of the Centennial and all – at the Art Gallery.'

'No shit,' said Jiri after a pause.

'Yeah.' She took a deep drag on her Export A, in no hurry to continue now that she had their attention, then slowly exhaled it. 'And after that the whole show goes to England for a month.'

'Hey,' said Eddie, 'this could be like when Greenberg came here in … what year was it, Bob? You met him, right?'

'Yep. In '57.' Met him … well, not exactly. But they'd been in the same room for a few minutes; Clem and his entourage had swept past Bob as he lurked unnoticed in a corner of the Vanguard. He sipped his beer and attempted an expression of blasé reminiscence. 'No big deal.'

O'Hara glanced at him with what might have been respect, but then the conversation reverted to the present. As time passed and the general level of inebriation rose, nearly everyone at the table agreed that he who could get next to Margrave would be able to write his own ticket in the international art market. A questionable hypothesis, it seemed to Bob, but never mind; why crush the sweet optimism of youth?

Jorgensen, who had appeared to be nodding off, raised his hand to his nose to wipe away the drop of snot that was dangling there. Then he turned his head slowly like a stoned old buffalo and fixed his tiny eyes on Jenny. 'This guy – Margrave – is queer, right? That's what I heard.'

Before she could reply, Jiri spoke up. *He* had a contact in swinging London who knew for a fact that Margrave had been a habitué of the many-roomed, false-mirrored flat of Dr Steven Ward.

'Feel the kiss of the lash as you lie bound by silken cords …' crooned O'Hara.

Then Barnaby Keeler leaned very close to Jenny and stared at her as if seeing her for the first time. She didn't flinch. 'Hey, *you'd* look really sweet in a leather corset,' he whispered loudly enough for everyone to hear.

'Want to lend me yours?' she shot back.

After that, the group grew strangely quiet. Bob guessed that every person at the table except himself was calculating what their best angle would be with Margrave. Yet when he got up to leave he felt oddly light-hearted. He had nothing to tempt the man, whatever his proclivities, and no work that might conceivably interest him. So as far as the big exhibition was concerned, he could immediately, and with a completely clear conscience, abandon hope.

THERE WAS ONE major problem with living alone, Eddie had discovered: you had to go out and, all too often, spend money to find company. By eight o'clock, he had drunk several more beers than he could afford and didn't have enough bread left to order anything to eat. As he watched Jorgensen wolf down a hot chicken sandwich, he began to think seriously about the half loaf of dark rye and the jar of peanut butter in his new place over on Spadina.

Eventually, he pulled himself together and went home. Until a month ago, he'd shared a house on D'Arcy Street with some guys he knew from art college. There, when he didn't feel like painting any more, somebody was always hanging out in the kitchen – maybe even cooking. Often some wine or weed was going around too. Okay, his room had been the smallest in the place and he'd probably been poisoning himself by sleeping right next to his drying paintings, but at least he'd never had to be alone unless he wanted to.

Sandwich in one hand, he rooted with the other through a cardboard box of records, pulled out a Muddy Waters album, and put it on the turntable. At least when you lived alone over a store, there was nobody to complain if you stomped around or blasted the stereo in the middle of the night. Mr Swartz, his landlord and the proprietor of Morris the Hatter, the shop on the ground floor, occasionally poked his head out the door when he saw Eddie coming or going. Once or twice he'd grumbled about loud music during business hours, but his protests were half-hearted and Eddie figured the old guy was just lonely.

While Muddy got started on 'Make Love to You', he dragged a paint-splattered wooden chair across the bare floor to the middle of the room and sat down on it to finish eating. The space wasn't huge – it was only the front parlour of the long railroad flat – but there was enough room for at least one painting on each wall. And it was good to have his own place, with three – count 'em, three – rooms all to himself. Most of his stuff was still in boxes and his bed was just a slab of foam rubber, but as soon as he could get the cash together, he'd bring in some real furniture. At least he no longer had to deal with other people's bathroom stinks, and he could let the kitchen get as dirty as he pleased. One of the gang at D'Arcy Street, a chick, had been a real clean freak, always scrubbing away at the countertop in a permanent state of outrage at the messes the rest of them left.

But Sandra had had her good points, too: in particular a relaxed attitude towards occasionally messing around with Eddie, in his room or hers. These sessions, he had discovered with relief, did not entail any social or emotional obligations. Sometimes, as he sat watching her bustle officiously around the kitchen, he'd even wondered if they'd actually had sex or whether he'd only imagined it. A couple of times they'd also dropped acid together – she, surprisingly, seemed to have no problem at all getting hold of it – but they'd never made a big deal out of that, either.

Still, all things considered, he couldn't really say that he missed old Sandra. Apart from her fussbudget ways, she was nearly invisible, with her pale, freckled skin, washed-out blue eyes, mousy brown hair, long and wavy but lank. And Eddie didn't care that much for pastels; he liked his women, his work, and his life, more intensely coloured.

Anyway, during his last month at D'Arcy Street, he'd been preoccupied, torn between public amazement at his luck in getting a dealer and a private conviction that luck had nothing to do with it. Okay, Bruno Gonzaga was already known to be a little weird and the rest of the guys made it clear they thought Eddie had simply been in the right place at the right time.

But when Howard McNab, who wrote reviews for one of the local papers, singled him out for special praise – actually saying that Edward O'Hara might well become the next Tom Dale – and a rich guy named Zeffler bought one of his felt-pen pieces, even Eddie's friends had had to face facts. He'd put his stuff up on the wall of a commercial gallery and actually *got some bread* for it.

Not enough to live on, though. His old man cut him off when he dropped out of OCA, so he'd been forced to take a part-time job in a store selling art supplies. Along with the few bucks he took home, the employee discount came in handy, because the scale of the pieces he was doing now made materials expensive. And the store was just down the street from his gallery, which meant he could drop in regularly for strategy sessions with his dealer.

My gallery … my dealer. He couldn't seem to stop dragging those phrases into the conversation, and that must have got on his D'Arcy Street buddies' nerves. Well, tough shit. This was real life, not dreamland. And quitting art school was the best thing he'd ever done. He saw now that those two years had been completely wasted. Most of the teachers were hung up on either some Group of Seven mystical landscape vibe or an Académie Julian, *vie-de-bohème* Paris trip. Oh, a few of them had got as far as Rothko and de Kooning, were hip to Rauschenberg and Johns – Bob Willard, for one. But then Willard had his own delusion to feed: the fantasy that he was still an artist himself, when it was obviously all over.

Yeah, he'd only been tying himself in knots at school. Now he could get down to work and back to basics. For instance, the stuff he was doing these days went way back, right back to a toy he'd had as a kid: a black metal board on which you could arrange squares, strips, circles and triangles of wood painted in primary colours that had magnets on their backs. The box it came in showed all the things you could make with the pieces: houses, trees, animals and people, even tidy little tableaux with some of each. But by age five, Eddie had already had his own ideas. No matter how often his mother showed him how to make the pictures, he just jammed all the shapes he could onto the board, moving the pieces around until he had them arranged the way he wanted them.

'That's nice, dear. What is it?'

'A picture.'

'A picture of what?'

'Colours.' Finally she stopped asking.

Nowadays, he made preliminary studies, rough at first, then more precise and on graph paper. But the principle was the same: you took the elements, the shapes and colours, and sorted, arranged and rearranged them until they looked right. That was something you had to recognize. After that you had to decide – no, you just had to *know* – when to stop. Or when to walk away and start all over again, kind of sneaking up on the canvas and slapping something entirely unexpected but totally inevitable onto it.

Right now, only a few pieces in the room were inevitable enough for his solo show, which was coming up in two – well, almost three – months. Pretty soon. And the Spitalfields guy was supposed to be in town just about then. Shit, he really had to get to work.

▌ Chapter Two

B R U N O   G O N Z A G A had asked Jane to write her name, address and phone number on a sheet of paper. Now he was staring at it, as if it might, all by itself, reveal whether he should give her the job. She had printed her last name – H-A-I-G-H – clearly, because she knew from experience that non-native English speakers sometimes got rattled by those Hs, especially the second one. *Jhan Egghuh* – that was what her French boyfriend had called her; not that she had minded.

While she waited for Gonzaga to speak, she looked around the alcove in which they were sitting and, with some practised squinting, brought it into slightly better focus. She was very near-sighted. For walking around in public, she had a pair of prescription sunglasses, but naturally she had removed them for the interview. The narrow space, nearly filled by a long Parsons table, formed a kind of buffer zone between the fashionably austere exhibition area and the cluttered workshop behind it. On the white stucco wall facing her, there was a hectic herringbone pattern formed by dozens of L-shaped frame samples hung diagonally.

Gonzaga shifted in his chair. He was a substantial man, but there was nothing soft or flabby about him. The only words that might have described him – *portly*, or *bull-like* – were terribly old-fashioned. His black hair was slicked back severely from his forehead and glued in place in the style of the 1950s, and though it was only four o'clock, there was five-o'clock shadow on his jaw. He wore a black suit with a white shirt and a skinny dark tie. But his clothes could hardly contain him. From the just-too-short sleeves of his jacket, wedge-shaped forearms emerged, then erupted into remarkably broad and meaty hands. Adrift in the silence, Jane's mind sideswiped another hackneyed but apt word: *ham-like.*

He picked up the cigarette that lay smouldering in the ashtray at his elbow and raised it slowly to his lips. Then, exhaling, he said, 'You know Susan for a long time.'

'Oh, yes. Ever since we were kids.'

Susan, Jane's best friend since the fifth grade, had been Gonzaga's assistant for nearly a year. She had given her notice the day before, and apparently he had taken it hard. But Susan was far too wrapped up in her brand-new husband to worry about that. 'He'll probably hire the first person who comes through the door,' she'd said. So they had made sure that that person would be Jane.

Not that her qualifications were inadequate; two years before, with a surprising feeling of relief, she had abandoned a half-finished degree in art history at the University of Toronto. The accumulation of knowledge had seemed pretty pointless when what she really wanted was experience. Or more precisely, *experiences.* In the Honours Art and Archaeology program, where male students were rare and therefore cherished by all concerned, a girl could be taken seriously if she was prepared to be very, very serious herself, or condescended to if she was not. Neither option had appealed to Jane.

After dropping out, she had clerked in a bookstore, filed for an insurance company and, for two horrible days, hawked cellophane-wrapped sandwiches and doughnuts on a passenger train that ran from Toronto to North Bay. On the third morning, she leapt off the snack-bar car just before it pulled out of Union Station, confident that another job would be along any minute. She had managed to avoid learning to type, but employment always seemed to be available for a presentable girl with realistic expectations as to salary. Her current duties at the university library, checking new books for defects, had seemed quite congenial at first. She had her own desk and could spend the day reading, but lately there had been nothing but East Asian anthropology, and a flirtation with the guy at the next desk had petered out. It was time to move on.

Gonzaga sighed. Then he glanced unhappily past Jane and out into the gallery, where Susan was now flicking a feather duster at some vaguely Brancusian, volleyball-sized blobs of polished stainless steel, each perched on its own black wooden pedestal. Such were the responsibilities of the assistant manager of the Gonzaga Gallery, and the salary, Jane already knew, was tiny. But she was also aware that lots of other arty girls would be more than happy to take the job. So she sat up straighter and tried to look alert and capable.

'Start at ten o'clock tomorrow. We pay fifty dollars a week.'

'Really? I mean, yes. Okay. But I have to give notice at the library. I could start ... next week?'

'All right. Tuesday. Ten o'clock.' He got to his feet, took her hand in a surprisingly delicate grip, and said goodbye.

Jane made her way to the front of the gallery. Three partitions

divided the long tunnel-like space. In the main exhibition area, there were some large paintings, all apparently by the same artist. At close range the big pastel shapes in them looked amorphous, but from farther away they could be identified as the petals of gigantic flowers. According to the labels, the artist was a woman, someone Jane had never heard of, called Winifred Beecham.

At the street end of the room, a huge plate-glass window looked out onto the traffic and provided the only source of natural light. Near it, but tucked discreetly behind a strategically placed wall, there was an imposing teak-veneer desk and a black stenographer's chair in which Susan was now sitting. '*Félicitations,*' she muttered as Jane approached. 'Beware the Royal We.'

'Thanks. Call you later,' Jane mouthed. Then she pushed open the tall black door and, feeling in her purse for her sunglasses, went out onto the sidewalk.

AS SOON AS Jane had left the alcove, Gonzaga sat down again at the table, stubbed out his cigarette and listened. He heard her walk through the gallery, then the murmur of her voice and Susan's, but could not quite make out what they were saying. After the street door had opened and closed, he pulled out the neatly folded white handkerchief his wife provided each day and took a quick swipe at his eyes, which were slightly moist. Then he went into the workshop and started on the set of frames ordered by an old customer who had brought half a dozen Gavarni lithographs back from a holiday in Paris.

As he positioned a sliver of silver leaf on the slender wooden moulding, he felt the tide of emotion within him begin to ebb. Everything was settled now; Susan had been replaced. And he had foreseen her betrayal. When the Englishman had first appeared one afternoon about six weeks earlier, talking of buying some Canadian art for a wedding present, Bruno was instantly suspicious. But he had not really believed that the intruder would carry her off so soon, without purchasing even a print.

His own relationship with Susan had always been strictly proper; she was not that sort of girl and he was not that sort of man. Yes, there had been a single slip. But the instant his hands cupped her face and began to raise it to his, Susan's eyes told him very clearly that he had made a mistake. Laughing uneasily, they had agreed to blame the open but still three-quarters full bottle of Canadian rosé, left over from the previous night's exhibition opening, that they had just shared to celebrate a sale.

A plausible and convenient explanation, but false. He had not been drunk. At that happy moment it had only seemed right that everything within the Gonzaga Gallery should be his for the taking.

But from then on he sensed a condescending intimacy in Susan's manner, as if her discovery that he was a man like any other had made him seem weak and harmless. And maybe she had never really felt the loyalty he had relied on. Perhaps her time at the Gonzaga had simply coincided with what he now remembered as his innocence, before he learned how difficult and unrewarding, in every sense, the work of an art dealer would actually be. Especially in this raw, childish country, where simply having survived the cold for a hundred years was cause for national self-congratulation.

In his own birthplace, the village church had stood for more than eight hundred years on the layered ruins of churches and temples far older. There, as the son and grandson of master carvers and carpenters, he was entitled to a secure and honourable niche. But he knew that he was also fixed in amber, forbidden to aspire higher and always required to be thankful for what little he had. His father's early death – heart trouble, no cure for it – had only strengthened his resolve to get out as soon as he could.

Though still a young man when he arrived in Canada, he had come too late. His skills were not valued or even needed in the Toronto of the early 1950s. The wood-panelled mansions of the late Victorian and Edwardian years were being demolished or converted to rooming houses, and there were no more Casa Lomas to be built. So he had installed plywood kitchens, glued Formica and laid vinyl floors in the strange new houses – 'side-splits' and 'back-splits' they were called – that were multiplying on the outskirts of town. After that, he joined the army of men gouging out the new subway along the city's spine.

On the sad, becalmed Sundays of his first months in Toronto, he found a kind of comfort in the Royal Ontario Museum. He always hurried past the huge totem poles, several storeys high, that stood guard in its dim stairwells. Dark and coarse-grained, they might have been the malign spirits of this wilderness in which he had rashly come to live. But in the European gallery upstairs was a large oak altarpiece, Gothic, swarming with intricately carved figures. Sometimes, if he was alone in the room, his hands moved gently, tracing in the air the gestures that had formed it.

Eventually he also made his way to the Art Gallery of Toronto, a rattling streetcar ride away from the city's core. At the entrance, nose to nose with Rodin's *Adam,* Bruno felt the relief of kinship: here was a man who, like himself, had abandoned what in hindsight might have been paradise. Inside, his footsteps rang on the marble floor of the sunken sculpture court as he approached the fountain, flanked by leaping dolphins, that stood in its centre. All around him rose tall, rounded arches and plaster medallions that carried faint, flattened echoes of Alberti, and from high above his head, through the coffered skylight in the ceiling, a watery illumination fell.

As he walked through the Old Master picture galleries, he was torn between contempt for the paintings on display – how pitiful in number, how inferior in quality – and gratitude that they were there at all. Then he ventured into the adjoining rooms, where the modern art was, and felt the weight of the past begin to lift from him.

After a few years he found a partner, if not quite a friend. Pooling their savings from their indenture in construction, they established a small framing shop in a lane off a busy main street. When the other man decided to return to his own village in modest triumph, Bruno became its sole proprietor. Then, a year ago, he had moved to larger premises and opened the Gonzaga Gallery.

He was aware that his appearance, speech and manner led many people to see him as at best an enigma, at worst a buffoon. But for the present, being underestimated didn't bother him: it would only give him more chances to watch and learn about the tiny, self-conscious Toronto art world, more room to manoeuvre, more time to plan.

TO GET a couple of hours off from the library that afternoon, Jane had had to mention a doctor's appointment. And in fact, after leaving the Gonzaga, she took the subway to the Bathurst station (her usual stop) and then walked a few blocks further west. Behind a nondescript door next to a typewriter-repair shop was a flight of steep and narrow stairs leading to the office of Dr Felix Eisen, purveyor of birth-control pills to (it sometimes seemed) nearly every young woman in Toronto. It was not unusual for two girls who had just become friends and were beginning the customary exchange of confidences to find that they already had Dr Eisen in common.

He was a small middle-aged man with a Professor Waynegartner accent and an inscrutably calm and neutral manner. Unlike the University Health Service doctors, he did not ask whether you were going to be married within three months before handing over a prescription. And unlike Jane's parents' physician, who had treated her case of poison ivy the summer before, he didn't expect to be paid in advance; he would wait until you got your refund from OMSIP.

At first, conscious of the slight furtiveness of the transaction, Jane had been wary of Dr Eisen's complaisance. However, there was no prurience in it. Out of delicacy, inertia or maybe simple prudence – there was no nurse or receptionist in his minuscule two-room suite – he did not perform internals, which was an additional point in his favour. On no stronger evidence than his name, age, accent and air of intractable melancholy, Jane decided that he was a concentration-camp survivor. Yes, it made sense: the horrors Felix Eisen had experienced must have immunized him forever against authoritarian moralizing, and he had then undertaken to do whatever he could to increase the sum of carefree pleasure in the world.

It was nearly six o'clock when she left his office and started for home. Her prescription was in her purse, ready to be filled at Starkman's, where the staff was nearly as blasé as Dr Eisen; the pharmacist's sole gesture towards propriety was to attach a faintly reproachful 'Mrs' to her name on the typed label. But though she had every intention of taking them faithfully, the new batch of pills might well turn out to be just as unnecessary as the last.

It was spring, for heaven's sake – the green buds dangling overhead made that glaringly obvious. She was young, willing, and reasonably attractive, at least when her hair would stay straight and she had eye makeup on. Yet it had been ages since she'd had a … well, a date. Anyway, the word itself, not to mention the courtly ritual it described – dressing up and attending some kind of public entertainment with a person of the opposite sex, at the man's expense – was pretty much obsolete nowadays. Really, the only 'dates' she (a former beatnik who scorned high-school dances, though she wasn't invited to any) had ever had were with older men, who hadn't caught on yet that girls no longer had to be seduced. Three years before, to reduce the possibility of bungling, she had efficiently lost her virginity to one of them, and had never regretted it.

But young men, at least those Jane considered desirable, took it for granted that she would acquiesce without any preliminaries, even walks in the park or insincere flattery. Too arrogant and self-absorbed to waste time wooing, they gave up at the first sign of coquetry or resistance. The

❑ 22

most you could expect was an impromptu late-night drop-in, and Jane hadn't even been granted one of those for some time. She was definitely in a rut, and the library was a tomb, romantically speaking; but maybe at the Gonzaga she would meet some new prospects. And at least, thanks to Dr Eisen, she would be ready if she did.

At the end of Jane's street, where it intersected with Bloor, stood a pair of ornamental stone gateposts, relics of the area's former grandeur just after the turn of the century. Her place was on the third floor of a large house that, like nearly all the others on the street, had been divided into apartments. She went up the steps to the front porch and opened the door into the vestibule. There was no sign of her landlords, an elderly Portuguese couple who occupied the main floor. Apart from the occasional whiff of baccalau, she was hardly aware of their existence, except on the first of each month when the rent was due. The mail was left on a shelf over the radiator to be picked up by the tenants, herself and a pair of married and eerily quiet graduate students who lived on the second floor.

There was a letter for her: a pale blue, nearly square airmail G. Lalo envelope with a Paris postmark. The big one-franc stamp on it was also squarish: a two-colour reproduction of an Ingres bather, seen from the rear. The model's spine was so sinuous that she seemed to be cowering. One of her arms covered the nipple of her exposed breast but left its peachlike roundness visible. A striped turban like a knotted dishtowel clung precariously to the back of her head as she turned to look, not quite at the viewer, but somewhere off to the side with an expression that combined sadness and apprehension. Though that could just have been the effect of the wavy postmark across her forehead. Jane stuffed the letter into her purse and started up the stairs.

The door at the top, which she opened with a key, was painted a bright shiny red, a little drippy in places. High-gloss enamel had been more difficult to handle than either Jane or her roommate had expected. Inside, the walls were stark white and the doors cornflower blue; right after they moved in, the two of them had painted the whole place. But she had it all to herself now: Debbie had moved on to a rural commune somewhere out west, and on the whole Jane actually preferred living alone.

Compared to her former roommate, who attracted men of all ages and also claimed to experience spontaneous orgasms in her sleep, Jane had often felt inhibited and envious. But now that she was the apartment's sole tenant, her standard of living had fallen dramatically. The rent, a hundred and twenty dollars a month, ate up almost all her salary from the library, and she would be earning slightly less money at the Gonzaga.

She took off her coat, put on her glasses, went to the phone in the living room and dialled Susan's number. Although it was nearly seven, there was no answer. Perhaps she and Eric were having dinner out; maybe at this very moment he was drilling her in the proper use of cutlery, correcting that appalling North American habit of switching the fork from one hand to the other.

Since her marriage, it seemed to Jane, Susan had become a two-dimensional, monochrome version of her former self. In the past, the two friends had theorized endlessly about love and sex – especially the summer they were in Paris together and both had French boyfriends. But they had never talked of becoming wives. Oh, no – they both wanted to be the soulmates, or muses, of fascinating, brilliant, creative and, if possible, beautiful men. And of course to be adored by them.

But then, quite unexpectedly, Susan had married Eric and developed a bizarre interest in housework. At the newlyweds' place, Jane sometimes had difficulty making herself heard over the vacuum cleaner. And when Eric – a sandy-haired, almost handsome Englishman who did something at an international bank – came home, he was no more than civil to Jane. Beneath the *Goon Show* routines he often launched into without warning she sensed distaste, and possibly even fear. He seemed to consider her a threat to well-ordered domesticity and soon it was tacitly agreed that she would schedule her visits to coincide with the absence of the man of the house.

After twelve rings there was still no answer. Jane hung up and went into the kitchen. She opened the refrigerator. Debbie had been all for painting it black, as they had the table and chairs, but Jane, fearful of the DaSilvas' reaction, had talked her out of it. Inside, on the middle shelf, there was a small carton of milk that felt almost empty, an open can of baked beans, its turd-toned surface congealed and cracked in places, and a single wizened orange. An antique package of wieners, a hint of verdigris visible through its plastic wrapper, had somehow found its way into the crisper.

The shelves over the sink yielded a tinned Danish camembert, a half-empty box of Saltines, and a bottle of Paarl sherry, medium dry, with an inch or two of liquid in it. The sherry, even then only half full, had arrived with a young man Jane had invited over for dinner and pointedly asked to bring wine. And quite apart from its moral taint (everybody knew apartheid *had* to be boycotted), it had not been a fitting accompaniment for the beef Stroganoff from the *James Beard Cookbook* she had prepared.

Impulsively, she pried open the camembert, slid some crackers onto a plate and dumped what was left of the sherry into a glass. It all turned out to be quite palatable. Afterwards, she tried Susan's number again. When there was still no reply, she lay down on the daybed that served as a sofa and, through the window that led to the fire escape, watched as the sky gradually darkened to purple and finally to black.

She got up then and switched on the overhead light. In its pitiless glare, the room leapt into horrid focus. With her glasses on she could not help seeing that the royal-blue carpet remnant from Honest Ed's was threaded with long hairs and seeded with a repellent mixture of fluff and grit. She went to the hall cupboard and pulled out a dustpan and a straw broom that was worn down to a lopsided nub. Returning to the living room, she began to drag it vigorously back and forth across the carpet, which had also started to fray badly along its raw, unfinished edges.

WILLARD LIVED on Tranby, a few blocks north of Bloor and a few doors west of Avenue Road, just above the cockroach line (or at least where he had understood it to be in 1962). The street was packed with narrow red-brick row houses where, in the old days, the working people who served the mansions in the district must have lived. Some had already been done up as cunning bijou residences. But Bob didn't own the house he lived in, and there was no way in the world he could have afforded to buy it. He had just rented the upstairs flat for ... had it been five years already?

The place was small but fairly cheap, and at the back there was a sunroom with windows on three sides that he used as a studio. In winter it was so cold that ice formed on the inside of the windows, and in summer so stifling that spending more than ten minutes in it was unbearable, so the creative season was inconveniently short. Nevertheless, a collection of desiccated paint tubes, mangy brushes and cans of long-departed Varsol had accumulated there, along with some canvases that Max had tactfully but firmly resisted showing. However, the mere presence of these things was heartening, which was probably why Bob never bothered to clean up the mess.

Housekeeping standards in the apartment had definitely slipped since the spring of '65, when his last wife left. Ha. *My Last Duchess.* Who'd'a thunk he'd ever have more than one? His first, Lorraine, a statuesque blonde with a loud but seductive laugh and big brown eyes, had waltzed into his life during his first show at the Vanguard. It had been love at first sight, joyfully reciprocal, and within a week they were shacked up. The money Lorrie earned in the hosiery department at Eaton's College Street covered the rent and most of their bills, so he could paint all day in the living room while she was at work. And in the evenings (if they weren't out at the House of Hambourg or the Second Story) she worked away in the kitchen at her potter's wheel.

Eventually, under pressure from her parents, surprisingly well-heeled squares much too accustomed to calling the shots, they got married at city hall with Max and Betty as their witnesses. Instead of the conventional gold band, Lorrie picked out (and paid for) a hammered silver ring at the Interesting Jewellery Shop. He often wondered if she still wore it – in Ibiza, or wherever she went after that.

Lighting another cigarette from the butt he was holding, he glanced across the living room to the beat-up sofa where Margie, wife number two, used to sit of an evening, her legs crossed at the knee, one foot swinging ominously like a disgruntled cat's tail. When he first met her, she'd been a cute small-town girl, impressed by his status as creator, certified bohemian and wild man of the world. However, the glamour of marriage to an artist had soon worn off. Less than three years later, she decided she'd had it with supporting them both on her salary as a secretary at the CBC. She could have got him a job in the design department, she claimed, and she was sick of hearing that commercial art would have ruined him as a real painter. 'Look at Tom Dale,' she always said, as if that really clinched it.

There was no way to explain, at least no way she might have understood, why he simply couldn't do as she wanted. Or to describe the poisonous, paralysing certainty he was just beginning to feel that every damn thing he'd produced in the past was derivative garbage.

Then, near the end, he saw contempt in her eyes. And he found out about a certain razor-coiffed, horn-rimmed producer who with a wave of his magic wand had transformed her from typist to production assistant. Though Margie didn't admit it until she was actually packing to leave, she'd even been skewered by the wand itself during a series of lunchtime trysts at the Town and Country Motor Inn.

It hadn't been nearly as bad as losing Lorraine. Money was tight without Margie's salary but he wangled a temporary job at OCA, filling in for someone on sabbatical, and had been teaching part-time ever since. Max kept his name on the gallery roster, saying he was always willing to look at new work if Bob produced any. But they both knew that whatever talent he had once had, it hadn't been enough to go the distance. There was no point in either of them lying about it.

After all, the Lurie wasn't a charitable institution. If your stuff didn't sell, your dealer didn't make any money. And Max wasn't the kind of chiseller who put on vanity shows where the artist had to pay all the costs, plus, without knowing it, a bit extra, so the gallery could make a few bucks without risking anything. He had too much integrity for that. Besides, now that he had Tom Dale, generating commissions that back in the Vanguard days would have been unimaginable, Max could well afford to be high-minded.

Bob, on the other hand, was simply getting by. It was just about all he had ever been able to do, and maybe that was why both his wives left. Almost six years now since Lorrie's sudden bolt, and two since Margie had thrown him. It was time to get back on the horse, but the sort of women who'd be happy to have him – battle-weary spinsters and divorcees – only filled him with dread. He stubbed out his cigarette in the ceramic ashtray shaped like a palette that Lorraine had made for his twenty-fifth birthday. Somehow he had managed to hang on to it, surreptitiously, right through the Margie regime. He was hungry now, and fortunately he knew how to scramble a decent egg – a far better one, really, than either of his wives had ever produced. By some weird coincidence, and no matter how many times he told them how to do it right, they'd both been careless, chronic overcookers.

THE NEXT DAY, Jane gave her notice at the library. Her supervisor, a remote but not unkind man, took it well. He didn't even seem to mind that she wanted to leave in just three days. That same afternoon, a letter of reference addressed 'To Whom It May Concern' appeared on her desk while she was down in the staff lounge having coffee. It concluded, 'Overall, Miss Haigh's performance could be rated above average.' After thinking about that 'could be' for a while, Jane tore it up. She already had another job, anyway.

It hardly seemed worth doing any more work from then on. None of the books in the pile waiting to be checked looked at all interesting, and the desk beside hers was empty. George (who until recently had always been available for idle conversation) was over on the other side of the room, talking to the new girl who had just started the week before. Then she remembered the letter from France. It was still in her purse, unopened.

She had met Bertrand in the Tuileries the previous summer. That day, a migraine had confined Susan to their attic room in a historic but austere students' residence just around the corner from St.-Germain-des-Prés. So Jane had been sitting alone in a rented wrought-iron chair, resolutely keeping her nose in her Livre de Poche (*La Vagabonde,* by Colette) and ignoring the Algerians who kept stopping to whisper at her.

But just as she was about to retreat, a different sort of man appeared at her elbow. He carried his own paperback, *For Whom the Bell Tolls,* and a pocket French-English dictionary. 'Excuse me, miss,' he said, very nearly bowing. 'You will be more tranquil if you will permit me to take the chair beside you.'

He was right, and Jane hardly had time to wonder whether she was sliding from the frying pan into the fire. Young, of medium height, neatly though shabbily dressed, dark-haired, long-nosed, small-mouthed, sallow and generally knobbly, he was a student at the École des Hautes Études Commerciales, and indisputably *français de France.* He lived, it turned out, with his widowed mother in a small apartment in a narrow, more or less art deco building that clung like grim death to the southernmost edge of the sixteenth arrondissement. It also turned out that he possessed deep reserves of ardour, which were soon poured unreservedly upon Jane.

Her French was more than adequate for romance, but not fluent enough to reveal much of herself. There was no danger of cleverness or cynicism breaking through the mask of language at the wrong moment. Bertrand found her sweet, natural and just intelligent enough, and said he'd make it his business to enlarge her French vocabulary and improve her idiom.

However, the affair was constrained by the lovers' living arrangements. The widow was rarely absent from the apartment with the good address, where, in any case, Bertrand's bed sat in a niche attached to the *salon.* And the student residence where Jane and Susan were staying permitted no males to penetrate beyond the ground-floor waiting room, which itself was monitored by a large, contemptuous woman with violently hennaed hair.

Besides, Bertrand had no confidence in the Pill. It had not yet been legalized or distributed in France, and therefore could not in any meaningful sense be said to exist, even if Jane had two full disc-dispensers in her possession. Chivalry and patriotism, he stated, did not permit him to risk sending her back to Canada with a French citizen inside her. However, in August the parks of Paris provided a lot of seclusion, and Bertrand was surprising. He seemed content with kissing and caressing, and Jane discovered that prolonged stroking of her bare foot could render her quite woozy with pleasure. New vocabulary: *bander, baiser (dans les deux sens), jouir.*

The letter inside the envelope with the Ingres stamp was just like the dozen or more she had already received. It was poetical (sometimes Bertrand even copied out verses by French writers like Pierre Louÿs) and highly flattering to herself – quite the antithesis of the treatment she received from the men she knew in Canada. She liked getting these letters, but answering them was a chore. However, it provided excellent practice in French composition, a useful skill for a Canadian in this year of enlightened bilingualism.

George was still talking to the new girl. He didn't seem to have any intention of returning to his desk that afternoon, and even if he did he'd probably just stick his nose in the dog-eared copy of *Tropic of Cancer* that he kept in the bottom drawer. It was nearly a quarter to five. Why shouldn't she leave early? She didn't really work there any more.

▪ Chapter Three

DR MEREDITH was running late, which was not unusual, because an obstetrician always has emergencies to deal with. However, it meant that patients like Eleanor Zeffler, neither pregnant now nor likely to be so in the foreseeable future, had to wait. And wait. Maybe he wasn't in the office at all; the receptionist was politely evasive about that, and Eleanor was pretty sure there was a second, back entrance to the small but nicely decorated suite in the Medical Arts Building.

Well, at least the magazines were reasonably current. She had already seen all the *Vogue*s and *Harper's Bazaar*s – she subscribed to both – so she was catching up on how the other half lived by reading *Chatelaine*. The ads, for things like Norforms and Does-she-or-doesn't-she hair bleach, evoked a style of life that to Eleanor seemed ... well, rather pathetic. And the food! She could just see Jerry, the connoisseur, gagging on those Kraft-infested concoctions if she ever tried to serve them to him. On one page there was even a calendar with suggested menus for every meal of every day of the month, like the lines a prisoner might scratch on the wall of her cell to mark the passage of the days.

Nearly every issue also had an article about the difficulties and disappointments of marriage. In the magazines Eleanor usually read, the bliss of Amanda and Carter Burden was taken for granted, and though there must have been a Mr Holzer somewhere in the background, he did not cramp Baby Jane's style in any appreciable way. But as she looked at a quiz that was supposed to help you figure out just how bad things were, she was struck by its almost uncanny relevance to her own situation.

Do you tend to take innocent remarks as personal criticism? Yes, naturally. *Can you resist saying, 'I told you so'?* Rarely. *Are you happy to listen to your spouse chat about his/her special interest just because you enjoy his/her enthusiasm?* Of course not, after nearly twenty years of marriage.

Sometimes she actually wondered whether she had *ever* been in love with her husband. Back in 1948, when they met, he'd been handsome, intelligent, ambitious – what, her mother had demanded, was not to love? Even Eleanor had to admit he was still all those things, so maybe it was she herself who had changed.

Do you enjoy sex with your spouse? Yes, but … These days, it was almost embarrassing to admit that Jerry was the only man she had ever slept with. Her virginity had been a kind of prize awarded as much by her family as herself to the worthiest of her suitors. And she hadn't really started to appreciate the sexual thing until much later, when she was in her thirties and had given birth to Rebecca. Once self-consciousness was routed by familiarity, she had entered a purely physical zone in which unexpected things began to happen. But as everyone knows, familiarity also breeds contempt, and by that time she had almost come to dislike her husband.

The door at the end of the tiny hall behind the receptionist's desk opened, and a very pregnant woman waddled out. But no one else was called upon to enter.

For a brief period before Becky was born, Eleanor had been infatuated with Dr Meredith. Her regular prenatal appointments had seemed like assignations, for which she dressed and made up with special care, and in the stirrups, as his deft hands probed her, she'd felt relaxed and happy. But when – finally – she understood what the sex-fuss was all about, her fixation on Dr Meredith had evaporated. Now the internal was just an internal, and when she saw him – sooner or later – this afternoon, they would simply discuss in a desultory way the possible reasons for her failure to conceive a second time. She never told him, or anyone, that she didn't really want to, which made it easy to accede gracefully to fate.

But she *had* begun to wonder what sex would be like with a man she was madly in love with, who was also absolutely crazy about her. Everything she heard or read suggested that she would not really have lived at all until she experienced that. So, with an increasing sense of urgency as forty gained on and easily overtook her, Eleanor had been keeping a lookout for a likely person. She was fairly sure that when she found him, she would know what to do.

The door to the inner sanctum was opened again by an unseen hand and again half a dozen heads turned towards it. This time, no one came out. But then, after few tantalizing moments of silence, Eleanor heard the receptionist speak her name. She closed her magazine, replaced it in the rack provided and got up from her chair.

ON HER FIRST DAY at the Gonzaga, Jane was early. It was still only five minutes to ten when she emerged from the subway. But when she was still half a block away from the gallery she saw though her prescription sunglasses that Bruno Gonzaga was waiting for her.

Leaning against the door frame, one leg bent slightly at the knee, he looked like one of those stock figures carried over from classical sculpture into Renaissance art. A shepherd with a crook leaning against a tree in a pastoral scene; or a soldier, spear in hand, lounging callously on the sidelines of a Crucifixion. As she got closer, she realized that the object Gonzaga was holding in one hand was a broom. Seeing her, he took a last drag from his cigarette, tossed it to the sidewalk and ground it out with his foot. Then, with one swipe of the wide industrial broom, he shot the butt into the gutter.

After they had greeted each other and entered the gallery, Gonzaga said, 'We keep the floor clean every morning. The first thing we do.'

He then demonstrated the finer points of the process, including the use of an oil-saturated, strong-smelling cloth that, pushed around the floor with the broom, attracted dust and gave a faint sheen to the black-painted concrete. It was clear to Jane that in this instance the first-person plural pronoun was not royal at all but actually indicated the second person singular. As soon as she had hung up her coat and put her purse into the largest desk drawer, the rag and broom were ceremoniously transferred to her hands and Jane officially began work as the Gonzaga's assistant manager.

By eleven o'clock, she had explored all the drawers of her desk, limbered up her hunt-and-peck technique on the typewriter and repeatedly tested the hold button on the telephone. It had not rung yet, so she had not had a chance to say 'Bruno Gonzaga Gallery' in the energetic but calm tone she had rehearsed the previous evening. If and when someone did call, she wondered how she would communicate with Bruno, who was now out of sight in the workshop. From her station near the door, she could hear muted clattering and tapping.

Apart from these distant sounds, and the muffled swish of traffic in the street outside, the gallery was deathly quiet. By noon, the only person who had passed through the door was the mailman, who greeted the appearance of a new face behind the desk with a smirk that clearly conveyed his opinion of the Gonzaga Gallery and all it contained.

Finally Jane put on her glasses and inspected the current exhibition. The flower paintings, with their big, loopy shapes and pale colours, were pretty; so were the fluttering petals of pastel tissue-paper that nodded gently from the smaller-scale collages. But they were all kind of innocuous. She had pictured herself surrounded by more muscular, challenging and maybe even offensive art, the kind of thing that a year or two before had caused another gallery just up the street to be raided by the police. On the bulletin board just inside the gallery door, there was a biography of the artist. Winifred Beecham was incredibly old – born in 1913! – but she'd only shown in a few group exhibitions, all at libraries and churches, all within the last two years, and there were no review clippings. A list of gallery artists was also tacked up on the board. Tibor Czerny was the guy who did the stainless steel sculptures, but the only other name Jane knew was Edward O'Hara's. According to Susan, he was the most up-and-coming of the up-and-comers who were starting to show at the Gonzaga.

Suddenly the door from the street crashed open and a man strode past her. Jane only caught a glimpse of a plaid shirt before he disappeared behind the central partition. Whipping off her glasses, she dashed back to her desk, sat down in her chair and listened. Quick footsteps, then a few muttered, indecipherable words. Was he talking to Bruno? There was no answer from the workshop. It sounded as if the visitor was making a rapid circuit of the gallery, keeping close to its walls like a cat tracing the perimeter of a strange house.

Then he reappeared and advanced on her. He was compact, wiry and tanned, dressed in tight-fitting grey flannel pants, oddly short around the ankles and noticeably grubby, and a brown-and-black plaid shirt under a pin-striped vest. On his long, greasy hair sat a black beret, rusty with age. He stopped in front of her desk.

'So *this* is modern art,' he said. His accent was foreign but unidentifiable, his tone rhetorical, his expression haughty.

She took a deep breath. All right, the Beechams were a little soft, stylistically. But her job was to interpret the work shown by the gallery in a knowledgeable yet friendly manner, and ideally to sell some of it. 'Well, this artist's work does have a symbolic element. Think of Georgia O'Keeffe,' she said with sudden inspiration. 'A very feminine aesthetic ...'

The man only stared fixedly at her.

'And,' she went on, feeling her way, 'her paintings are very sensual, don't you think?'

'Blobs and smears. A child could do better.'

A not unpleasant sensation, a heady blend of outrage and condescension, passed through her. Obviously the guy was just your garden-variety, run-of-the-mill idiot. 'Oh, but –'

'Parliament of harlots,' he said. 'Vengeance is mine, saith the Lord.'

Then again, he might be dangerous. Leaning forward, he put his face very close to hers. He smelled bad, and his expression, she saw now, was not haughty but crazed.

'Well,' replied Jane as she got to her feet, '*chacun à son goût* and all that.'

As she ran towards the back of the gallery, she almost collided with Bruno, who was making his way without haste to the front. 'That guy ...' he muttered, shaking his head wearily.

As soon as he saw Bruno, God's Critic slipped quickly and quietly out onto the street. Jane returned to her post, and for a few moments Gonzaga stood in front of the window, almost daring the man to return. Then he came over to the desk and rested one hand on it. Leaning there, as if momentarily drained of energy and emotion, he ran the other hand over his face.

'Who was *that?*' she asked.

'Nobody.' He tapped one finger meaningfully against his temple. 'He comes in here ever' so often. Goes to all the shows. Let me know if he comes back.' He glanced around the gallery, making sure that all was in order. 'What We are doing here,' he said, and now the pronoun was certainly regal, 'many people don't understand. But We are just beginning. One day, they will understand.' He turned and stared sternly out the window, as if ranks of doubters were massing on the sidewalk. 'But that one, he's just a crazy guy.' Then he reached into his pants pocket and jingled some change. 'How you take your coffee?'

'Um, just cream.' Gonzaga nodded and went out. For the first time, Jane was alone, the solitary and entire We.

But not for long; only a minute or two later, the street door was flung open again. The person who came in this time was a middle-aged woman wearing a beige silk-shantung suit, unfashionably long in the skirt. However, her shoes were visibly expensive, as was the handbag slung over her shoulder. She passed Jane without a glance, then began to walk around the gallery with a proprietary air. Finally she came back to the desk.

'You're not Susan.'

'She got married. I'm replacing her.'

'I see.' It was clear that she would not require additional details. 'Is Mr Gonzaga in?'

'He's ... just stepped out for a moment.' *Gone to the greasy spoon to get coffee for the two of us* did not seem an appropriate response, somehow.

The visitor turned and strode purposefully to the rear exhibition area. Then she came back. 'The glass on the watercolours is absolutely *covered* with fingerprints,' she said. 'Please be sure to clean it every morning.'

Jane gaped at her. *Two* maniacs on her very first day? This lunatic's indignant pink face had perhaps once been pretty, though age and insanity had made its features soften and sag. She didn't look dangerous, though, so Jane decided to tell her where to get off.

At that moment, Bruno reappeared carrying a brown paper bag, and the woman's manner became more cordial, almost girlish. 'Well, Bruno,' she said, 'I thought I'd better come in and keep an eye on you.'

For an instant he seemed flustered. Then he put down the bag containing the take-out coffees on Jane's desk.

'Ah … Mrs Overton.'

'Now, Bruno. Remember that within these walls I am Winifred.'

'Winifred. Please come and sit down.' He began to usher her towards the rear of the gallery, then came back to retrieve his coffee. Thinking better of it, he muttered to Jane, 'Go to the Rancho. Get another one for Mrs Overton. Regular.'

BRUNO NOW BELIEVED the Beecham exhibition had been an error, though not a serious one. According to information he had obtained, Mrs Overton represented what passed for nobility in this place. Overton was her married name, Beecham her maiden and professional one. And there had been a third name, that of a previous husband, now long gone, or so he had heard. On the day her show opened, she had finally told Bruno to call her Winifred. He tried to do this, but sometimes failed.

Her demeanour was strikingly similar to that of a contessa with advanced intellectual interests for whom Bruno's father had built many bookcases. Mrs Overton was imperious, but also wished to charm those she commanded. Though now well into middle age, substantially older than himself, she was not physically unappealing. Her body, in what he recognized as a costly but unostentatious silk suit, was slim and straight, her face still pleasing though no longer beautiful. He glanced at one of her hands, slender, fine-boned, capable, holding the cup of coffee he had sent Jane to get, and for an instant imagined his head bent deferentially over it, his lips gently brushing its pale flesh.

Bruno felt no nostalgia for the nearly feudal setting of his childhood, but at least it had provided a rough map by which an ambitious man could get his bearings. Because the privileged had not always bothered to behave well in the presence of their inferiors, he had also acquired a useful pessimism about human nature. That, he believed, might be his most powerful weapon in this new world where nearly everyone pretended to be equal and honest.

Here it was harder to find out who was actually important, or from whom financial patronage – the other kind was all too common – could be expected. Until recently, he had hoped that Mrs Overton would bring her wealthy and cultivated friends to the gallery – connoisseurs ready to invest in contemporary art. But they were quite satisfied with their Lawren Harris, or the little Krieghoff that Grandma had left them. Winifred's show would close in two days, but only two of her smallest pieces had sold. His forty per cent share of the proceeds would not cover a fraction of the gallery's rent for the two weeks the exhibition had been up.

'I *am* rather disappointed, I must admit ...' she said, looking at him with an expression that demanded consolation as well as an accounting.

He batted her words away into the air with one hand. 'We look to the future. Not everyone understands what we are trying to do. We are far ahead ...'

'Yes,' she said, evidently satisfied by his answer. 'I suppose one must simply accept that, keep working and wait for the others to catch up. Or so Tom often tells me.'

That was something else about Mrs Overton that interested him. She was a friend of Thomas Dale, Canada's foremost abstractionist. Naturally, Dale already had a Toronto gallery. It was right across the street. Its proprietor, Max Lurie, even dropped in at the Gonzaga from time to time, and his friendly, interested manner was reason enough for Bruno to mistrust him. Dale himself had attended the Beecham opening, slightly intoxicated and alone, and Dr Overton, visibly ill at ease, had left early. So Bruno, a man of the world, reached certain conclusions about the two artists' relationship, and felt all the more astute for it.

'How is Tom?' he said, smiling.

'Oh, quite well, I imagine.' She looked faintly displeased now.

'When will he have another show?'

'Heavens, I wouldn't know. You'd have to ask him that. Or Max – they've been great pals for ages, you know.'

Well, she was the one who had brought up Dale's name. But Mrs Overton didn't matter any more. He would not offer her another show.

He was gathering a stable of new artists now, opinionated, confident young men for whom he had great hopes. Jorgensen, for instance – his exhibition, the last of the season, was opening next week – and a couple of artists from Quebec. And Edward O'Hara, the young unknown he had discovered, the one Howard McNab was already comparing to the great Dale. O'Hara's one-man show was already scheduled for the fall.

When she got up, he rose too and shook her hand, refraining without the least difficulty from kissing it. However, she seemed in no hurry to leave, and lingered for a few minutes, walking around the gallery. Finally she stopped at Jane's desk, and he heard her say, 'Please remember what I told you about the glass.'

Then, a moment later, Mrs Overton was gone. Her coffee still sat cooling on the table, almost untouched, though there was a scallop of pink lipstick on the rim of the cup. Frowning, Bruno carried it to the sink in the workshop and poured it down the drain.

THERE DIDN'T seem to be anybody around at first. But then Eddie heard footsteps coming from the back of the gallery and a girl appeared, carrying a dust rag and a spray bottle of Windex. When she saw him, the pissed-off look on her face faded a little.

So this was Bruno's new assistant. She was slightly less attractive than the other one – Susan – who had left. Not bad-looking, though, in a standardized kind of way. Her straight, blondish, shoulder-length hair, parted in the middle, framed a blurred baby face, in which only the eyes, heavily outlined in black, really stood out. Beneath the teal blue scoop-necked sweater she wore, small but strenuously uplifted breasts pressed insistently forward. All in all, your basic, run-of-the-mill arty girl: cute, kooky and desperately eager to be awed. Although … when those black-rimmed eyes met his, he suddenly felt he could be wrong about that last thing. In fact, the cool assessment in her glance kind of stalled him for a second.

'So,' he finally said, returning that look without blinking, 'you must be the new art chick.'

She sat down at the desk, yanked one of the drawers open and shoved the cleaning stuff inside it. 'Uh-huh.'

He took another drag on his cigarette and squinted at her through the smoke he slowly exhaled. 'Handmaiden and amanuensis to the great Bruto Godzilla…'

She cocked her head, taking her own sweet time to decide whether that merited a laugh. Well, he didn't feel like just standing there until she made up her mind. 'Is our leader around, by any chance?'

'I think so. Is he expecting you?'

He realized that she had no idea who he was. 'Always.' He flicked two fingers across his brow in a casual salute, then turned and walked as slowly and unselfconsciously as he could towards the rear of the gallery.

When he stepped into the workshop, Gonzaga looked up with the slightly panicked expression he always wore when caught off guard. But then, recognizing his star artist, he smiled and put down the curved knife he had been using to carve the ornate moulding on the work table in front of him. As he came into the alcove, Bruno called out to the new girl – Jane, it turned out her name was – to go next door to the Rancho and get them coffees.

By the time she placed the two cups in front of them, Eddie had laid out the whole Artquake scenario, and he could tell from the way Bruno's silences grew longer and more intense that he had instantly twigged to the importance of Margrave's visit. Godzilla hated to give anything away. But boy, you could practically hear the wheels turning inside that big Brylcreemed head. He was a fast learner; he'd probably never even heard of the Spitalfields or Quintin Margrave until five minutes before. Sure, the guy was a real weirdo – but definitely no fool.

THE SUN was already well over the yardarm, it seemed. From the landing, Win could hear music, some popular song from the thirties, and Tom's voice singing along with it.

'Now I know why Mother –'

At the sound of her knock, he broke off, and she heard him coming across the large room.

'She meant me for someone exactly like …' There was another brief pause, and when he finally opened the door he looked remarkably pleased with himself.

Yes, sure enough, the quart of J&B on the paint-splattered table already had a fair dent in it. Tom cleared her a space on the old brown chesterfield that sat under the row of north-facing windows. Then he turned down the volume on the record player and busied himself with finding a more or less clean glass for her. Eventually he came up with a chipped blue coffee mug, which he rinsed out in the grimy sink in the corner before half-filling it with whisky. They clinked receptacles convivially, and each took a rapid gulp.

'I needed that,' she said, leaning back and crossing her legs decorously. 'I've just been trying to have a sensible conversation with Bruno Gonzaga – not to mention getting down that vile coffee he always presses on people.'

'And?' He looked at her expectantly.

'Oh, some of my friends have bought. The Women's Committee girls, you know. But he's obviously disappointed. We only sold two of the collages. And I suppose it's really you he's interested in.'

He smiled. 'Max and I still get along just fine.' They both knew the very idea of Tom being represented by Gonzaga, who had no track record and no connections, was preposterous.

She took another, more delicate sip from her mug, hesitating. 'In fact, I get the distinct impression he thinks I am your *maîtresse en titre*, or something of the sort.'

He snorted, almost spewing Scotch into the air.

'*Maîtresse en titre?* You mean like Madame de Pompadour and Louis the Whatsis?' He laughed again. 'I like the sound of that.'

'Well, I don't,' she replied primly, conscious that she was not telling the whole truth. Such a rumour – unfounded, of course – could only enhance her own reputation, both as an artist and a woman.

'Aw, who cares?' he growled.

Win said nothing to this but took what could only be described as a swig from her mug.

She wondered if any such insinuations had ever reached the ears of Tom's wife, a sensible person whose staying power Win rather admired. Joan Dale, very much the little-brown-hen type, was the sort of woman positively cut out to be the helpmeet of genius. And certainly Joan had had quite a lot to put up with over the years. She'd quietly done her duty as a bourgeois wife and mother while Tom was in advertising, and then, at a fairly advanced age, learned to cope with the necessary egotism of the artist – not to mention the ever-rising tide of Scotch. Nowadays, she also had to deal with the lionization that came with success, because Tom finally had both kinds: financial and *d'estime*. And even someone like Joan must find that galling at times, for as somebody-or-other once said, No man is a hero to his valet.

But when it came to sexual fidelity, Joan Dale likely didn't have to worry much. True, success is an aphrodisiac, artistic success an especially potent one. And Tom had retained a little-boy-lost quality that probably appealed to a certain type of woman. But he seemed far too dependent on reliable domestic comfort to indulge in casual infidelities. And too preoccupied with painting to invest the time and energy that a real, passionate affair would demand.

But … sometimes Win had caught him looking at her with an intense though not precisely identifiable expression. Could it be…? Surely not – heavens, they'd known each other for close to forty years. They were barely teenagers when they met – Lismer's classes at the Art Gallery, wasn't it? Then, much later, Tom turned up again, working for her first husband Alec's agency, Newsome and Biggars. The two couples had not moved in quite the same circles, but she and Alec had occasionally socialized with the Dales in that era. Though she hadn't seen much of Joan since Alec's death and her remarriage to Eliot.

But now, looking back, it did seem that Tom had always been unusually attentive. Hadn't he also praised her rather uninspired cooking excessively, on the few occasions he'd tasted it? That was years and years ago, of course – strange how time began to accelerate after one reached a certain age. These days it was her painting that Tom praised. But was there something more to it than mutual respect?

She sipped her Scotch. The idea was not entirely unappealing, and she was not without experience in such matters. She'd been married twice – happily, for the most part, in each instance – and there was also that discreet affair one summer up at Go Home Bay. Alec, like most husbands of the era, had stayed in the city during the week. She'd been in her thirties then, knocked off balance by the unexpected sexual urges that had hit her in what at the time she had thought of as middle age. Now that she really was middle-aged, such impulses were rare. Though not, perhaps, completely extinct.

Tom had wandered away and was looking at a huge canvas hanging on the other side of the studio. Yes, she thought daringly, they might be quite good together at the actual physical exertions, once they got to them. But there lay the difficulty. She found it impossible to imagine how they would reach that point. Perhaps they had been friends too long. Sometimes they even bickered gently, like any long-married pair. And they were awfully alike: proud, fond of being in control and yet fundamentally shy – despite her secure social position and his hard-won patrician manner. They had each found a way to keep one foot in bohemia and the other in Rosedale, at least metaphorically – the Dales actually lived farther north, in Hogg's Hollow. Maybe that was why she and Tom understood each other so well, why he could accept her as an artist without visible scepticism, even when no one else could.

For that alone, she loved him. But perhaps less romantically than with … what was it the Greeks had called it … *agape?* He turned and glanced at her from across the room. They smiled at each other. *At this moment, we are happy together,* she thought, maudlin and fearless from the Scotch.

Tom came back and sat down beside her. 'That one's a winner, I think,' he said, indicating with his glass the serene blue-and-grey painting on the opposite wall.

'Lovely,' she said truthfully.

He took a gulp of his drink and then, resting the nearly empty tumbler on his chest, leaned back and closed his eyes. His thigh was only a millimetre from hers as his arm slipped casually along the sofa back, just behind her shoulders. Win stared steadily into the distance.

She knew from experience that between affection and passion lies a vast and perilous landscape. The road that winds through it passes by coyness, coquetry, arch hints and meaningful looks, sighs, revelations, endearments, declarations and promises. Then, at journey's end, nakedness, urgency, irrepressible sounds and irresistible convulsions … and very probably regret.

Suddenly, the very idea of traversing that terrain and reaching that destination with Tom filled her with a self-consciousness so acute that it was indistinguishable from dread. She got up from the couch, leaving her empty mug on the floor beside it, and walked quickly towards the canvas on the far side of the studio.

'Oh yes, it's really marvellous,' she said, throwing out her arms to emphasize her admiration, but not daring to look back at him.

∎ Chapter Four

'OW!' SAID JANE. 'Don't be so rough,' she added, trying to sound good-natured. Her left ankle had just been given a twist that really hurt.

'And don't you be issuing so many instructions,' replied Barnaby Keeler, pushing her foot even higher above her head. His tone was playful, yet fundamentally unfriendly.

They lay entangled on a mattress that sat right on the bare floorboards of the cavernous space where he lived, in a nearly derelict industrial building at the eastern end of downtown. Jane's enthusiasm for Barnaby was fading fast. His whimsical, flirtatious manner had been shed along with his speckled corduroy suit, pale green shirt and Liberty-print tie.

Normally she hated whimsy, but in this case she had made allowances, imagining that at least Barnaby would be a tender, gentle lover. Instead, as soon as she had abandoned her pro forma show of reluctance and they were both naked, he had begun to arrange and rearrange her limbs as if he were setting up an uncooperative deck chair.

She was not in any danger, she told herself, and the remnants of the desire she had felt when he first touched her would certainly carry her through this. He appeared to know exactly what he wanted to do, but seemed uninterested in her reaction to these manoeuvres. Then, satisfied sooner than she had expected, he immediately got up to ignite a postcoital joint. He tilted it perfunctorily in her direction, clearly not very eager to share. When she shook her head, he lay down beside her again and sighed deeply, as if after a job well done.

A few days before, Allison, Barnaby's wife, had taken off unexpectedly with their Volkswagen van, heading out to the West Coast but leaving no forwarding address or explanation. Or so Barnaby said. The story had elicited Jane's sympathy, and anyway she already found him attractive. He was tall, fair and bearded – something like that Dürer self-portrait, the one with the hat. Naked, he reminded her of a centaur, with hindquarters that seemed too powerful for the narrow, hairless chest above them.

It hadn't come as a great surprise that Barnaby had turned up at the

Jorgensen opening; the circle of young, arty people in Toronto was small. But now she realized that the best part had been over long before they'd reached the mattress, or even entered the loft. He was a great kisser, at least; the taxi ride from the gallery had been even more intoxicating than the wine that she had drunk at the opening. She had already tasted a few of those above-average kisses in the stockroom of the bookshop where both of them had worked for a few months the previous year. Allison was still around then and Jane had felt uncomfortable about that; she usually avoided married men. But Barnaby had never seemed – or acted – like anyone's husband.

Then this evening she had heard about Allison's defection and received the definitive summons to the mattress. With hindsight, she recognized that that was what it had been, a summons. And now it seemed that she was about to be dismissed. Though it was past midnight, Barnaby was giving her the impression that he was a man who had better, and pressing, things to do.

After waiting on the deserted sidewalk for a quarter of an hour, Jane caught a westbound King streetcar. Barnaby had not offered money for a taxi. She had enough in her purse for one, but with the whole rent to pay, she could not really afford to spend it. As she walked home from the subway station she tried not to dwell on the disappointments of the evening. She had made rather a fool of herself that night, in more ways than one. Though she'd pretended not to, she had seen the dark looks Bruno directed at her as she knocked back glass after glass of thin, acidic rosé, bolstering her courage for, but soon forgetting all about, her duties as hostess and salesperson.

And then came the awful letdown of sex with Barnaby. He hadn't even bothered to say he'd call her, though she was pretty sure he would. But to him she was probably nothing more than a toke that had drifted obligingly into his lungs and then out again – with minimal effort on his part. She wished she could talk to Susan, who had flown off to Paris the week before and hadn't even had time to send her address yet. Or even to her old roommate Debbie, who for all her popularity could be pretty scathing about the shitty behaviour of men.

THE NEXT MORNING, Bruno arrived early. He set his coffee on the table in the alcove, lit a cigarette and went back into the gallery to look at the Sven Jorgensen exhibition. In the light of day he saw that it was mediocre at best.

The opening had been like a bad dream. A handful of potential buyers were present, but his new assistant had ignored them. Instead, she spent the whole evening drinking and flirting with a young bearded man who was an obvious freeloader. And Sven had been surly. Jerry Zeffler, who seemed interested in Jorgensen's work, tried to engage him in serious conversation. But after a few moments he turned away, shaking his head. Perhaps, Bruno had thought then, there was something to be said for dealing only in the work of artists who were safely dead. Zeffler's wife, a spoiled beauty, had stood off to one side and surveyed the gathering with undisguised boredom. The couple left early, and Bruno resolved to keep Jorgensen away from possible customers in future.

Jane wouldn't be in for another half hour. He sat down at her desk but found nothing incriminating in its drawers, just a letter with a Paris postmark. Sliding the flimsy airmail paper out of the envelope, he unfolded it carefully. Though it was in French, he could tell that it was only a love letter, so he put it back, shaking his head at the foolishness of youth. But he stayed sitting at the desk, smoking.

The summer months, when no one of importance was likely to be around, could be filled in with a group exhibition. It would not include any of the second-rate stuff that he'd had no choice but to show when he'd first opened the gallery. He'd already packed up those shiny coffee-table blobs and told Czerny to take them away. They'd had only a verbal agreement and, given both parties' tactically imprecise English, that was easy to ignore. Besides, he was almost certain that Tibor, an argumentative crank who disapproved of the gallery's new direction, had been selling work out of his studio all along.

Yes, a group exhibition would fill in nicely until September, no opening, no announcements, no wine, no freeloaders, and then in the fall, Michel Bontemps (extruded plastic multiples, very up-to-date) and after that the O'Hara show. Fall was an auspicious time for it. The sprawling village that people here called a city would be at its brief best as the trees turned red and gold. Rich people like the Zefflers would surely be looking for cultural diversions, but their appetites would not yet be jaded from the social activities of the winter. Acquisition committees would meet again, refreshed and adventurous after spending summer at the lake. And this Margrave guy, the one Eddie had told him about ... he'd be in town, too.

Bruno felt as comfortable with Eddie as he could feel with anyone, even if a lot of what O'Hara said went right past him. He listened carefully, anyway, though he would never have given Eddie the satisfaction of admitting it. But he felt that both of them had seen something in the other – a streak of steel, perhaps – and realized that they might go further together than either could alone.

Margrave, the curator from England. That was the kind of information he still had to get from Eddie. Bruno rarely entered the Pilot, and so missed hearing things, but he preferred to keep his wits about him. Alcohol, by inducing intense but transient emotion, might cause him to act against his own best interests. Besides, he sometimes had difficulty following the rapid flow of gossip and boasting in the tavern. That was only partly due to his still imperfect English. It was also because he knew that life was both simpler and more serious than any of those talkative fools could ever imagine.

Though he paged slowly through the art magazines – *Artforum, Studio International,* nearly five dollars a copy! – he didn't really try to understand the words. He just studied the pictures with intense concentration, training himself to look, to judge, to decide, willing his mind to recognize what was serious, important and in demand. Postpainterly, hard edge, shaped canvases, Pop, Op, colour field, minimalist, maybe even a few ... what were they called ... installation pieces, environments, happenings ... that was what the curators liked. For it had dawned on Bruno that public institutions were the most likely purchasers for the new, up-to-date art he wanted to show. And perhaps a few wealthy people who also read those magazines, who wished to prove they were more sophisticated than their neighbours.

When he looked at his watch he was startled to find that it was already five after ten. He got up and unlocked the door, then went back to the alcove to drink his cold coffee and wait for Jane.

HUNG OVER and contrite, Jane listened humbly while Bruno rehashed the Jorgensen opening. However, he did not seem quite as annoyed with her as she had expected. Maybe he had already identified in her fecklessness some advantage for himself, a debt to be collected later. Anyway, it wasn't her fault that Sven himself, the supposed star of the evening, had been blasted on something much more powerful than wine, and as far from personable as a human being could be. But no one seemed to like his paintings very much, either.

Last night she'd overheard a sandy-haired middle-aged man say to

Eddie O'Hara, 'Now, why does this show make me think of *A Streetcar Named Desire?*'

'I dunno, why?' said Eddie, already grinning.

'Ste-e-ella, Ste-e-ella!' the man replied, and then the two of them had clinked their glasses of rosé together and drained them in unison.

This morning, Bruno's expression was even more mournful than usual. She guessed that he already regretted taking Jorgensen on. During the preparations for the show, Jane herself had come to dread Sven's arrival. Sometimes he'd sidle up and stand leering complacently at her, then walk away chortling. Or he might pass her without a word or glance, sit down cross-legged on the floor in front of one of his masterpieces and contemplate it in silence. There was no sign of him today, though. Thank God.

At lunchtime, because Howard McNab had promised a review, Bruno went out to get the paper. After spending the best part of an hour alone with it in the alcove, he emerged and beckoned to Jane. With an accusing finger he indicated the line that read 'ambitious in scale but more decorative than imposing'. Nevertheless, he still seemed to hope that McNab's verdict was neutral, or even mildly complimentary. When Jane gingerly explained its dismissive nuance, he slammed the offending paper down on the Parsons table.

'Huh!' he said, glaring at it. On Bruno's lips, the syllable could convey surprise, wonder, satisfaction, disappointment or anger. Now Jane recognized in it something close to pique, because ever since McNab had praised Eddie, Bruno had counted on him as an ally.

Late in the afternoon, Sven came in, but Bruno was nowhere to be found. That was odd, because he always told Jane when he was going out. Eventually Sven got tired of hanging around and lurched out onto the street. Jane walked to the back of the gallery, stood at the door to the workshop and said softly, 'He's gone now.'

A moment later, Bruno's head popped up from behind the work table. As he got to his feet, dusting himself off, he seemed quite unembarrassed.

'You want coffee?' he asked, jingling the change in his pocket.

'UNREQUITED LOVE is the perfect love,' said Eddie. 'No mess, no fuss, no cleanup.' He passed the joint to Bob.

'Your hands never touch it.' Bob took a quick drag and handed it back. 'I take it a certain damsel is unresponsive?'

Eddie didn't answer, but his face gradually assumed an expression of Olympian detachment. Then his eyes, kindly and vacant, slid in Bob's general direction.

'Why think of it in such literal terms, my friend? Responsive ... what does that mean?' Again he paused for what seemed an awfully long time. 'Does it matter? That's what I'm asking myself. What I'm trying to tell you. Consider the difference, distinction, differentiation ... all of the above, I mean, between a regular, available chick and a ... a ... well, I guess I'd have to say *muse*...'

'Muse? Will this Daisy you speak of be any good at musing? Or even want the job?'

Eddie's lips pursed delicately around the joint, then clenched in a determined grimace as he sucked in smoke and air.

'Matters not a whit, my friend. She doesn't have to ... that's the point. The beauty part. Muses don't volunteer, they're *apprehended,* in a moment of blinding revelation ...'

'Stop calling me "my friend", will you?'

'Okay.'

Bob had been walking down Spadina, on his way to Switzer's, when he saw Eddie and invited him to join him. But O'Hara, who was unlocking the door to his studio, had insisted he come up and get the royal tour. The entrance was next to a men's hat shop, in whose flyspecked windows dusty Homburgs and fedoras sat on stands draped with faded satin, like the relics of some extinct civilization. Eddie led the way up a steep flight of stairs to a string of cramped rooms off a narrow, windowless hall. The place was stifling, and Bob kept an eye out for cockroaches, which he still hated and feared, even after all the years he himself had spent in dumps just like this one.

After he had inspected the pieces O'Hara was working on for his solo show with Gonzaga, and had made the required noises of approval, they went down the hall to the kitchen. There, from a cupboard over the ancient refrigerator, Eddie took a coffee can with a plastic lid. And from the baggie of grass inside it, he hospitably rolled a joint for them to share. It wasn't Bob's poison of choice, but he didn't say no.

Now they were back in the front room, perched on a couple of straight-backed wooden chairs. O'Hara's stuff wasn't bad, he allowed, as his mood grew more genial and receptive. The kid had some colour sense, and his composition was solid enough. But Bob didn't really dig the whole masking-tape, acrylic-on-a-roller routine that Eddie was into.

Where was the emotion, the turmoil, the struggle, the love and hate, the lust and disgust? Take Pollock or de Kooning; now, those guys knew how to put a dame – muse or not – up on the wall, take her apart and rearrange her so she stayed rearranged.

'Well,' he said, glancing at what was obviously the best piece, a diamond-shaped expanse of robin's-egg blue bisected by a chevron slash of acid yellow, 'just promise me one thing.'

'Okay.'

'Don't do a Kokoschka on me. He got so hung up on some broad that after she left him he built a life-size doll of her. Carried it around with him everywhere. You know, what's-her-name … Alma … Mahler … um, let's see … Mahler, Gropius … Gropius … and …'

'James, James, Morrison, Morrison, Weatherby George Dupree,' said Eddie.

'Took great care of his mother, though he was only three.… Let's see, Alma Mahler, Gropius, *Werfel* … yeah, Mahler, Gropius, Werfel … remember that Tom Lehrer song?'

Eddie shook his head, more glassy-eyed than ever. It figured; Lehrer's brief moment of popularity was before the kid's time. Though at least he seemed to have heard of Kokoschka, and possibly even Mahler and Gropius. 'Well, anyway, he chopped her, I mean the doll's, head off. Threw a party for the occasion.'

'I dismember Alma …'

Once again Bob accepted the joint Eddie held out to him. 'So you're pretty hung up on this one.'

'Hmm?'

'The muse, the chick.'

Eddie seemed to think for a moment. 'No-o-o-o, no-o-o-o, not at all. Far from it. I mean I'm content to admire her from afar. That's the beauty part, that's the …'

'Ah. A *belle-dame-sans-merci* deal, your basic *princesse lointaine?*'

'Yeah, yeah … it's the emotion that matters – pure, raw, uncut, unmixed, unadulterated. Free-floating. Looking to attach itself to something, and that's cool. I put it into my work, slap it right up there on the …'

'Good thinking, man. If your muse wants you, who needs her? Just like Groucho said.'

Eddie looked blank. Then he grinned. 'The club he wouldn't want to join, right?'

'*R-i-g-h-t!*' The Marx Brothers' movies were big with the kids right now.

Eddie had turned his head in the direction of the blue-and-yellow piece, and seemed to be studying it through half-closed eyes. For another long interval, he said nothing. However, there was no evidence of thought on his face, which somehow gave the impression of being both rigid and slack.

Bob wondered, idly, if his own face looked that way too. Surely not. If it did, he wouldn't be feeling what he had just that moment discovered he had felt for some time: that he couldn't stand another minute of this elliptical tedium or the sweet-musty-acrid smell of pot. He might have been at O'Hara's place for hours, or maybe only a few minutes; he wasn't crazy about not being sure which.

Worst of all, as he listened as politely as he could to Eddie's sophomoric maundering, he watched his own thoughts flutter back to the woman he had seen at the Gonzaga the week before. She'd stood a little apart, elegant, remote, yet somehow familiar ... and at any moment he might start blathering about her. All at once he longed for impersonal camaraderie, powerful air-conditioning and the bracing feel of a cold glass in his hand.

'Hey.'

'Yeah?'

'Eddie.'

'Bobby.'

'What say we go out and have a beer? Get something to eat.'

'Good idea. I'm starving.'

'Okay, then.'

'Okay.'

'Let's go.'

'*EN TANT QUE FRANÇAIS,*' Bertrand had written, '*je tiens à te présenter mes excuses. Quand les grand-pères deviennent gâteux...*'

Jane reached for her trusty *Cassell's Compact French-English-French Dictionary*. Gaspiller ... gastrique ... gateau ... gâter....

Gâteux (n.,m): idiot; (adj.): idiotic.

'*... on devrait les enfermer pour les empêcher d'aller faire du scandale chez les voisins!*'

The letter was dated two days after Charles de Gaulle had loomed up in the midst of the country's Centennial euphoria like the bad fairy at

Sleeping Beauty's bassinet. In the next paragraph, after commending her progress in written French, Bertrand reproached her for the tepid sentiments it conveyed. He was right; Jane's supposed love letters were prosaic and evasive. But, child of the Enlightenment, heir to a tradition of rational thought, he had a theory to account for her reticence: *'C'est simplement un des traits du caractère anglo-saxon. Tu es une "fille du Nord" et j'essaie simplement de te faire prendre la liberté d'expression des "gens du Sud", des Latins.'*

It had never occurred to him that emotion itself might be lacking. But, to be fair, she didn't have a clue what was going on in his head, either. Both of them had simply played their assigned roles in a time-honoured tradition – the cross-cultural summer affair. And now, from this distance, Bertrand was almost completely theoretical – just the disembodied voice of romance. That sound was still absent from her present existence, because all the men she knew were real *garçons du Nord*, and stubbornly uninterested in falling in love.

Take Barnaby. At regular intervals, she decided to break off with him. But by the time he showed up again she was always too bored with life to stick to that resolution. Besides, how can you tell someone you don't want to see him again, when you don't even know for sure when or if you will?

She also knew that the occasional overtures made by male visitors to the Gonzaga were only impersonal, Pavlovian responses to her long, laboriously straightened hair, heavy eyeliner and uplift bra. There was no point in taking them seriously, and anyway, lots of the men who flirted with her were terribly old – for instance, the sandy-haired guy she had overhead talking to Eddie at Sven's opening, whose name turned out to be Bob Willard. His presence almost always drew Bruno to Jane's desk, where he would stay, making mildly threatening conversation, until Willard decided to leave.

'Don't talk too much to that guy,' Bruno instructed her, and Jane sensed that in some much-too-weird-to-even-think-about way, he was jealous. Not of *her*, but of any attention paid to her, which he considered should be directed exclusively at himself. Besides, since Bob was a painter and represented by the Lurie Gallery, Bruno considered him a potential spy. According to Eddie, though, he hadn't had a show in years. 'Probably wants to go with us now,' Bruno said in a satisfied tone that clearly designated Willard a nuisance and a failure.

Bertrand's de Gaulle letter was now nearly a month old and still unanswered. Denied any encouragement at all, he might stop writing. He'd expect her to say something about the *vive-le-Québec-libre* thing, but she really couldn't have cared less about the old fart and his four little words. She looked around the empty gallery, searching for material or inspiration. In summer, fewer people than ever came in, and the days seemed endless. Well, maybe something would happen in the fall.

▌ Chapter Five

ONE MORNING in early September, Bruno got into his car and drove directly from his home in the northwest part of the city to Eddie's studio downtown. It was Monday and the gallery was closed, so he felt he could safely be absent for a few hours. But even at ten o'clock traffic was heavy, and it took him some time to find a parking space. Finally, he left the car a block away from the hat shop that Eddie had described. The day was already hot.

When O'Hara buzzed the door open in response to his ring, he climbed the stairs and arrived in the dark hall at the top slightly short of breath. After shaking hands with Eddie, who looked a little rumpled and bleary-eyed, Bruno took out his handkerchief and mopped his brow. Then he surveyed the place approvingly. The dingy rooms seemed appropriate for a young painter on his way up.

Artists were like spoiled children, Bruno believed; troublesome creatures whose ability to create precious, significant objects won them freedom from bourgeois responsibilities and (within reason) the right to certain carnal and chemical indulgences. Like children, too, they craved attention and approval but actually required discipline. They didn't need money. Material things were the consolation of less fortunate beings, like himself, who had to toil ceaselessly for a living.

As far as Eddie's work was concerned, he was more than satisfied. It was accessible but not insipid, attractive but not prettified. Most important, it resembled the art his research had established as fashionable in New York and London, the kind he now knew he wanted to show. He looked carefully at the canvases that were hanging on the walls, then sat down heavily on a paint-splattered kitchen chair, lit a cigarette and watched Eddie wrestle with the other paintings that had been stacked against the walls. These they examined together, one by one.

Bruno indicated his responses with a series of minutely calibrated shrugs, grunts and sighs. Generally, he liked what he saw, particularly a blue-and-yellow piece, hung diagonally. Occasionally he shook his head with a severe expression, or waved his cigarette dismissively. He did not attempt to justify or elaborate on his reactions, because he didn't trust

artists' opinions when it came to their own work. He even made a point of telling them so, for he had begun to relish the awesome power that his vocation allowed him. The artist was the creator, true, but was there not also something godlike in the man who could say of that artist's work, 'Let it be (or not be) seen?'

EDDIE HAD BEGUN the day with a therapeutic joint to preempt the jitters he knew he would experience during Bruno's visit. The night before, he had already winnowed out the weaker pieces and stashed them in the bedroom, but considering the cost of materials he had no choice but to show Godzilla most of what he had done. As they looked at the work, he watched his dealer's face covertly but made no attempt to influence Bruno's choices. Once the guy's mind was made up, he was impossible to argue with anyway.

When he had picked out enough paintings for the show, Bruno stubbed out his cigarette in the tin can on the windowsill, wiped his face again with his handkerchief, shook hands with Eddie and started down the stairs. From the bay window, Eddie watched him emerge onto the sidewalk below, pause for a moment to light another cigarette, then walk slowly up Spadina. Once he was out of sight, Eddie fished out the second joint he had kept in his shirt pocket throughout the morning, as a kind of talisman, and lit it. Then he sat down on the chair that his dealer had just vacated, took out his notebook and waited for some ideas for titles to arrive.

He always had trouble coming up with names for his stuff. But Bruno believed that people didn't find works of art that were called *Number 8* or *Composition V* very exciting or fun to talk about – or to buy. Sweating in the heat, drained from facing scrutiny of his work at this ungodly hour (it wasn't even noon yet) but growing more tolerant with each inhalation, Eddie admitted that maybe there Godzilla had a point.

Procrastinating, he thought of Daisy, remembering her eyes looking up at him from beneath the false lashes she wore. But despite that bad-girl smile of hers, she played hard to get. In fact, she pretty much ignored him. But what the hell; the emotion was useful in itself.

Willard obviously agreed with that theory. Over at the Embassy the other day, after they'd had a few beers, he'd droned on and on about the care and feeding of the female of the species – booze always made old guys talk like that – as if his advanced age and two failed marriages made him some kind of expert. 'Treat 'em rough, lad,' he'd advised, his head held unsteadily high, his lips moving with exaggerated precision.

'Don't call me "lad", okay?'

'Shertainly, m'boy.' Then he'd started to sing under his breath, 'Daisy, Dai-sy, give me your answer true ... I'm half cra-zy, all for the love of...'

Thank God they'd been alone at the table. But Eddie managed to swing the conversation around to the romantic exploits of Clem Greenberg. And sure enough, Willard had plenty to say on the subject, eventually expanding his thesis to cover both the Jackson/Lee/Clem and Bill/Elaine/Harold triangles. After that, the guy just wouldn't shut up. He got onto the topic of collectors and started to jaw about the Zefflers, who had actually, back in the Stone Age, bought some of Willard's stuff. Road-company Sculls, they had agreed. But for some reason Bob kept saying, as if anybody gave a shit, that Mrs Z was much better-looking than Ethel Scull would ever be.

He wiped his brow on the sleeve of his shirt, sat down again and returned to contemplating the yellow-and-blue piece. He ran his hands through his hair, tipping his chair back and teetering. Now, what the hell was he going to call it?

THINGS DID pick up a little in September. For the first two weeks of the month, the Gonzaga showed a Montreal artist, Michel Bontemps, a very presentable young man with soulful brown eyes and a nice head of hair. He created, or rather *caused* to be created in a factory (the distinction, Jane soon found out, was significant philosophically as well as materially), thick worm-like shapes in extruded candy-coloured polystyrene. These *Coordinateurs*, as they were called, could be arranged and rearranged in various ways on the wall, and snapped together with their integrated vinyl grommets. This gave the viewer, or more strictly speaking the purchaser, a chance to participate in the creative act. And thus, Michel explained in charmingly accented English, the artist (so called for want of a more modern word) succeeded in separating himself almost totally from exhausted Beaux-Arts ideas of craftsmanship, expressiveness and sentiment. On the contrary, he attached himself to the vitality of the modern industrial world, co-opting and interrogating its dehumanizing techniques of mass production.

Bruno, to Jane's surprise, appeared to grasp all this with ease, nodding sagely as Michel spoke. She herself felt an inner resistance to such notions but did not even for a second consider voicing it. Even though Michel politely but firmly rebuffed her attempts to speak French to him, he was nice to have around.

The opening was quite festive; too; all the pink, yellow and silver translucent bubbles on 'the walls made the gallery look like the setting for an elaborate children's party. There was a smallish crowd with only a modest proportion of indisputable freeloaders, for most of Michel Bontemps's friends were in Montreal.

Jane had added the names and addresses that Win Beecham had supplied for her own opening to the mailing list, and some of them actually came. The Lurie had had a successful group exhibition of Quebec artists a few months before and anyway French Canadians were rather chic. The artist's *beaux yeux* and dis-and-dat accent seemed to charm many of the Women's Committee ladies, who ignored his faintly patronizing manner.

Michel had also produced some mini-multiples, small versions of the larger *Coordinateurs,* and these sold surprisingly well. Bruno grumbled at first because they were too inexpensive to produce any meaningful profits for the gallery, but when the Zefflers reserved a complete twenty-four-piece set of the minis in pink he conceded it was better than no sales at all.

Mrs Zeffler came to pick them up on the last day of the show. She left her car – a black Mustang convertible – idling on the street outside and paced back and forth near the window, keeping an eye on it, while Bruno wrapped the minis in brown paper. She refused coffee, but while she was waiting she told Jane she was going to hang them in her teenage daughter's room, which she was completely redecorating with new furniture from Karelia and a really up-to-date 'groovy' theme. Jane agreed, as Mrs Zeffler seemed to expect, that this was not only a good but an original idea. As she helped her carry the packages out to the car, she wondered if the stiff little cap-sleeved dress Mrs Zeffler had on was a genuine Courrèges or just a copy. Probably real, she decided, but it was hard to be sure.

BRUNO NEVER liked having people around when he was hanging a show, not even the wife or girlfriend of the artist. And because he expected great things of the O'Hara exhibition, he was even more on edge than usual. When Jerry Zeffler, probably attracted by the lights and activity in the gallery after closing time, tapped on the window, Bruno sighed irritably. He was up on a ladder adjusting a spotlight, with Eddie watching critically from below. Artist and dealer exchanged glances, and after a moment of silent calculation, Bruno nodded. It might be good for business to let him in for a few minutes. So Eddie went to unlock the door.

Recently Zeffler had started to drop in fairly often during business hours, and to display a somewhat proprietary attitude towards the gallery. Not that he had any right to; except for the O'Hara drawing and the mini-multiples his wife had selected from the Bontemps show (less than two hundred dollars' worth of art all told) he'd yet to buy anything substantial from the Gonzaga. But if he did, it could well be one of O'Hara's new paintings.

Bruno clambered down off his perch and they took a break while Jerry looked around, carefully casual yet not missing anything. He paused, Bruno noticed, in front of the blue-and-yellow piece that Eddie had decided to call *Back Flip*. It was already in place, hanging on the central partition that faced the window. When, after completing his tour of the gallery, Zeffler returned to it, Gonzaga walked over and stood beside him.

'You like what you see?'

'They're strong, very strong.' Jerry turned to Eddie, who was leaning against the far wall, smoking. 'I see progress, real progress.'

'Thanks,' said Eddie. 'Are you going to be here tomorrow night?'

'Absolutely. Without fail.'

'Good,' Bruno said. He swayed slightly on his feet, tilting closer to Zeffler, who then had to take a step back. 'You will see everything then. Now we have work to do.'

Jerry raised both his hands in front of him and lifted his shoulders in a gesture of surrender. 'Okay, okay, I'm going.' He clapped Gonzaga on the back, apparently eager to forgive his rudeness. Bruno followed him to the door, and observed that as Zeffler went out, he turned to cast one last – and, it seemed, covetous – glance at *Back Flip*.

THE HAND that held Jane's did not respond to her feeble attempts to pull it away.

'Lovely,' Howard McNab said.

He was half sitting on her desk, right next to her chair, with one of his knees pressed insistently against her thigh. Apparently, he was talking about the silver ring on the little finger of Jane's left hand, but she could not help wondering what attraction such a commonplace trinket could hold for a man with his highly developed aesthetic sense. And yet he seemed fascinated by it.

Finally he let go of her hand. But before she even had time to breathe a sigh of relief, he began a close examination of the matching necklace she was wearing. Her thoughts skittered, half amazed, half indignant, around the perimeter of the situation, as McNab's fingers began to wander – no, stroll – boldly yet casually over her neck and breastbone.

Flâner was the verb that sprang to mind, probably because her brain was still gallicized from the mental effort involved in answering Bertrand's latest letter, which had arrived in late August, weeks ago. And now the thrifty, laboriously filled aerogramme she had just folded and sealed was most likely being crumpled by McNab's oblivious rump. He himself was quite exceptionally repulsive. The angle of his inclined head exposed a small bald spot beneath trailing strands of limp brown hair, and his pale, long-fingered hands felt slightly clammy.

Though his touch was revolting, it was McNab's nonchalance that truly disgusted her. She was already well accustomed to the sensation of determined hands exploring her flesh. But such expeditions were usually undertaken in an atmosphere of urgency, of spirited resistance or happy surrender. In either situation, she felt extremely important. And even if the pleasure she experienced was minimal, she always had the satisfaction of knowing that she was taking part in an activity that was daring, healthy and modern.

However, as McNab's hand continued its relentless itinerary, Jane did not even experience that gratifying sensation. Something that should have been wrenched or wheedled from her in a secluded place was now being calmly pilfered in broad daylight, a few feet from a door that opened directly onto one of Toronto's main streets.

Languidly, his fingers inched downward towards her breasts, which were propped up on a hidden shelf of wire and lace, a segment of their upper halves highly vulnerable above the scooped neckline of her dress. It was unbearable. She thought of propelling herself out of his reach in her wheeled stenographer's chair with a swift kick to the underside of her desk. But that would have sent her zooming into the small O'Hara that was hanging on the wall behind her. And McNab, she was sure, would only be amused at getting such a rise out of her.

She noticed that his eyes occasionally strayed to the rear of the gallery, where Bruno had been cornered by Jenny Kosma with her slides.

It was strange, with the O'Hara show opening that very night, that Bruno was keeping a critic waiting while he wasted time with an artist he had no intention of taking on. Maybe he just wanted to punish McNab for the Jorgensen review. 'Bruno will be out any minute,' Jane said in a meaningful voice, as loudly as she dared.

At that moment Jenny emerged from the alcove and strode to the door with a perfunctory nod to Jane, apparently not recognizing Howard McNab. As she passed, he let go of the necklace, and the back of his hand made one last lingering sweep across Jane's chest. But his knee remained firmly wedged against her.

In Jenny's wake sailed Bruno, holding out his hand with every appearance of friendliness. 'All the young artists, they come to Us!' he bellowed congenially, transforming the expected apology for keeping the great man waiting into an apparently guileless boast.

This was just the kind of mysteriously effective tactic Bruno had begun to employ on the many self-important yet insecure persons who, he judged, needed to be disarmed or bullied for the good of the Gonzaga Gallery. Affability and truculence, deference and menace were deployed in unpredictable and disorienting proportions: it was complicated, but it worked like a charm. Jane had not been able to figure out how much of Bruno's act was spontaneous and how much strategic. Sometimes she even wondered whether it was an act at all.

McNab chuckled indulgently and his knee finally lost contact with her thigh as he rose to shake hands with Bruno. She watched as the two men walked through the gallery, making sounds of mutual ingratiation, and entered the alcove. After a few minutes, there had been no call for coffee, and their voices seemed to be coming from the workshop itself. She heard the clink of glasses, which meant some leftover wine had been poured.

Jane gathered up a handful of mail that was sitting on her desk (Bruno reserved its ceremonial opening for himself) and carried it to the alcove. As she placed the envelopes on the Parsons table, she paused. Bruno was saying, 'This Margrave guy … you know him?'

'Only by reputation,' McNab replied. 'But I'll be meeting him very soon.' His voice took on a mid-Atlantic tinge at the very thought of being in proximity to the important visitor. 'I expect I'll be taking him around the local galleries next month, as a matter of fact.'

So, not during O'Hara's show. She heard Bruno grunt non-committally, and knew that he was disappointed. But then McNab said,

'Dieter should be here any moment; we were to meet at three.'

The photographer from Howard's paper did arrive a few minutes later. After he had taken a dozen or so installation shots, his eye fell on Jane, and he asked her to pose with one of the paintings, to add 'scale and human interest'. Bruno looked at Howard, who shrugged as if to indicate that he had no control over the man with the camera. So Jane did her best to look attractive, intelligent and absolutely riveted by the work of art beside her.

▪ Chapter Six

'WELL, that purse must have cost at least fifty bucks.' Jerry Zeffler jerked the steering wheel of the Mustang to the left and accelerated, shooting past a Volkswagen in the curb lane.

Eleanor said nothing, but glanced down at the object he had just mentioned, a navy-blue quilted Chanel bag. It wasn't the real thing – that would have cost more than the seventy-five dollars she'd paid for it. Still, it was good quality, with a nice solid clasp, a full suede lining and the essential thin strip of leather twined through its gold-chain shoulder strap. Often that important detail was missing in the fakes.

After a moment Jerry said, 'The O'Hara is only three-fifty, and cheap at the price, because I don't think Gonzaga realizes yet how good Eddie is.' He braked violently behind a cab that was making a left-hand turn off Yonge Street onto Rosedale Valley Road.

Eleanor's hand shot out to brace herself against the dashboard. 'Careful!' she said.

He hit the horn, eliciting an obscene gesture from the taxi driver. When they started moving again, she said, 'So – *only* three-fifty?'

'Yeah.' He turned his head to look at her. 'Tell me something – do I follow you into Creed's or Clarrod's –'

'Harridge's. And for heaven's sake keep your eye on the road.'

'*Harridge's* ... do I follow you there and tell you you can't buy something you want, that it isn't worth the money? Do I?'

She didn't reply.

As they passed Ridpath's he pointed at its half-timbered façade. 'And what about ye olde fifteen-hundred-dollar chesterfield you just had to have from Anne Hathaway's cottage over there? Did I refuse to pay for it?'

More silence.

'Well, *did I?*'

'All I'm saying is there are lots of other things we could spend three hundred and fifty dollars on. Where are we going to put it, anyway? From the way you described it, it's probably too strong for the dining room, and we have no wall space anywhere else, since you've been buying like a drunken sailor.'

'Guess what, babykins, drunken sailors usually blow their dough on broads and booze, not art. But you wouldn't give me that much credit. Anyway, I'm getting rid of the two Willards, so we'll have lots of space. Max says we won't get much more than we paid for them, but who cares? I don't buy just for appreciation.'

After a while Eleanor said, 'But I *like* the Willards. The green one, anyway. It goes with the curtains in the living room. Remember how we chose the fabric to match that big square patch in the middle? I want to keep it. You can get rid of the brown one if you want. I've always thought it was depressing.'

'You have? Funny, you never told me that. Those were the first two pieces we bought together. I even remember you telling Max that you were in awe — those were your exact words — *in awe* of my eye when it came to art. And you were going to learn from me.'

'That was many years ago, and I was very, very young.'

'Anyway, I might even pick out another O'Hara tonight.' He ignored her exasperated gasp. 'I didn't see everything last night, because they hadn't finished hanging the show. And Bruno's very secretive. The guy more or less threw me out.' He chuckled, clearly pleased by the image of virile camaraderie implied by the phrase 'threw me out.'

During the next long silence they both kept their eyes on the road. Finally they pulled into the parking lot around the corner from the Gonzaga Gallery. As they got out of the car, Jerry said, 'Bob Willard will probably be there tonight, so don't say anything about those two pieces of his, okay?'

'You really think I'm a complete idiot, don't you?'

He didn't reply, but Eleanor found the way his chin jerked up was quite eloquent. Then, in silence, side by side, but keeping a two-foot gap between them, they walked down the street to the gallery.

A FEW MINUTES before seven o'clock, Eddie began stalking up and down the still-empty gallery. Each time he passed Jane on his measured but compulsive rounds, she smiled brightly at him, and he nodded absently in response.

Between five and seven she had dashed home to eat, apply more eye makeup and change into her party clothes. These consisted of a short black skirt, black fishnet stockings and a white satin blouse with a long droopy collar and spherical pearl buttons. Feeling that to be found seated at her desk when visitors arrived would create an unsuitably businesslike impression, she was standing uncomfortably next to it. Her new shoes, black patent with a grosgrain ribbon bow on the toes, had been on sale and were a size too small.

The first to arrive were, as usual, the freeloaders: Jenny, Jiri, Sven and four or five other young people, evidently friends of Eddie's, judging from the jocular way they greeted him. Hardly glancing at the paintings, they went directly to the cloth-covered table in the alcove. Bruno poured the first dozen glasses with relatively good grace. Barnaby, accompanied by a long-haired girl in a purple minidress, slipped through the door around seven-thirty, smiled blandly at Jane as he passed her and also made straight for the bar. Soon afterwards, Bob Willard came in alone.

By eight o'clock, the gallery was packed. Jane observed a gentle frisson passing through the crowd when Tom Dale arrived, accompanied by his wife and a couple of unidentified hangers-on. When Bruno advanced to greet them, Dale was gracious. He inspected the exhibition attentively and exchanged a few encouraging words with Eddie. Then he withdrew to a corner to hold court in a tactful way. Win Beecham was there, too, looking quite presentable, Jane thought, considering her age, in a black sheath dress and a heavy silver necklace.

When the Zefflers arrived, Jerry greeted Bruno like a long-lost friend, but his wife merely nodded distantly and melted into the crowd. Then Jane watched Zeffler and Gonzaga begin to edge in the direction of *Back Flip*, which was hanging quite near her desk.

'Great stuff, Bruno,' said Jerry. 'This kid has really got something.'

She saw Bruno nod, without saying anything.

'Now, this one is exceptional,' Zeffler went on. He shook his head as if in astonished wonderment.

Bruno smiled. Then he pointed at the painting's wall label, on which a blue dot was visible.

'Fantastic!' said Jerry, throwing one arm around Bruno's shoulder. 'You must have read my mind!'

Still smiling, Bruno reached into his pocket and withdrew a small box. From it he removed a bright red sticker and placed it carefully over the blue one.

'Hey, where's Eddie?' Zeffler demanded. 'I want to talk to him. I'm going to pick out another piece.'

LEGGY, that was the word. Bob took another surreptitious look at the

woman standing next to him. Not bad, not bad at all for someone of ...
what? ... maybe forty? Very few women that age could wear a skirt as
short as the one Eleanor Zeffler had on, but she looked wonderful in it.
His eyes moved down the long string of pearls around her neck – real
ones, probably – right to the point where they disappeared beneath her
silk blouse. Just the faintest hint of cleavage was visible there. Those
pearls, and the flash of diamonds on her right hand when she lifted her
wineglass to her lips, reminded him that this woman was not a merely a
dish but a matron of means.

He'd noticed her at the Jorgensen opening last spring, and only later
realized she was Jerry Zeffler's wife and that he'd known her for years.
She and her husband even owned a couple of his paintings. They must
have bought them ten – maybe it was twelve – years ago. He was in his
austere, geometric period then, highly influenced by Ben Nicholson,
and still selling fairly regularly. He'd even been in their house once – a
first-night party for a play that Zeffler and Lorrie were both involved
with at the time. Little theatre was a great way to get off with dames,
Jerry had confided in an undertone. After that, Bob had not been able to
stop himself from wondering if his Lorraine was, or might ever be,
among the got-off-with. For the rest if the evening he had watched for
any hint of untoward attention from their host but had observed nothing suspicious.

He also recalled being impressed by the size of the Zefflers' house,
though disappointed in the quality of their Scotch. Probably the good
stuff had been squirrelled away somewhere out of reach. Still, he'd been
naïvely proud to see *Forest* hanging in the living room. And that pride,
he remembered, had only been slightly muted by the chicken-or-egg
debate he'd had with himself over its relationship to the curtains.

'so I said, right then, no Yankee scribbler is going to come up here
and tell *me* what to paint. A lot of us felt that way. If we wanted to be
New Yorkers, we'd have moved there. We used to call him *le douanier,*
y'know, because the guy actually worked as a customs agent.'

God, who cared what happened ten years ago? If it was even true.
Eleanor was only pretending to listen to Bob Willard for Jerry's benefit.
It was pleasant to imagine his unease when he saw them talking. Not
that she expected him to be jealous – he no longer seemed interested
enough in her for that – but he'd certainly worry that she might be
indiscreet about the disposition of their two Willards. He liked to

remain on good terms with everyone in the art world, even people as unimportant as Bob.

Her eyes, breaking contact with Willard's almost pathetically eager ones, panned across the crowded gallery. Just over his right shoulder, she could see Tom Dale, surrounded by a small group of admirers. He was still quite a handsome man, though he'd be well into his fifties now. And it was awfully nice of him to come to O'Hara's opening – especially since, according to Jerry, the boy's work was already being compared to his own. He was even chatting, amiably enough, with the person who had made that comparison in print, the loathsome Howard McNab.

Of course, Howard never bothered Eleanor any more. Not since the time, years ago, when he had gently squeezed one of her buttocks at some crowded party. Turning quickly, she had pretended to stumble, in the process stepping hard on his foot and spilling her martini on the crotch of his trousers. But Eleanor had always, since puberty, been adept at repelling such crude advances. Whatever her parents' limitations, they had given her a high opinion of her own value.

For a moment, she thought Tom Dale was going to look back at her. Jerry had snapped up a small early Dale at auction a few years ago, just before his prices started to get really ridiculous, and she had met him a couple of times. Once she'd even engaged his dowdy wife in conversation while Jerry was busy glad-handing Tom and Max Lurie. But before she could catch Dale's eye, a middle-aged woman in a black dress touched his arm familiarly and he began to talk to her.

Eleanor felt a strange, nearly painful sensation. Envy. She wished she could be in that woman's place, with Tom leaning towards her, listening attentively. His rosy, gently lined face seemed so intelligent and kind. Even his silver hair, falling boyishly across his forehead, and the slightly tremulous movement of his lips as he spoke appealed to her, although she could not hear anything he was saying.

It came to her then that Tom Dale, as well as being madly successful and very probably a genius, was *lovable*. And even more important, *loving*. She felt – no, somehow she knew – that he would accept love with grace and return it with tenderness. *More than anything in the world, that is what I need,* she thought as she saw her husband elbowing his way through the crowd towards her.

EDDIE FIGURED he had now run through just about every emotion an artist could expect to feel at the opening of his first solo exhibition. Yeah, the whole fucking gamut, right from excitement to apprehension to hope to self-consciousness to panic to relief to pride and finally (since the show was obviously a success) punch-drunk euphoria. And he had to admit that regardless of how lame he had once considered many of the people present, they all seemed amazingly perceptive tonight. McNab, Zeffler, Willard – even Tom Dale, for God's sake – every one of them thought he was the greatest, or at least were willing to say they did.

Howard had interviewed him for an article that was going to appear in the paper on Saturday. So what if McNab himself had done most of the talking? And Zeffler had actually put his money where his mouth was by reserving two pieces, *Back Flip* and *Tusk*. He seemed as excited as hell about it. Well, there was no denying the guy had a good eye, because they were definitely the best things he'd ever done. So far.

Willard, ever the sardonic onlooker, played it cool, but Eddie could tell he was impressed. 'Welcome to the big time, m'boy,' he said, as if he'd ever been there himself.

Tom Dale simply seized Eddie's hand in a firm, manly grip and said, 'Good work.' He seemed totally sincere. Now why had he ever thought the guy was a self-satisfied old coot?

Win Beecham was standing right next to Tom, and she smiled almost sweetly as she whispered, 'You must be very proud.' That was a surprise; Eddie couldn't remember her ever paying the slightest attention to him before.

Man, even Godzilla was happy tonight. His big face was red and glistening with sweat, but he wasn't bothering to wipe it with his handkerchief any more. He just wandered from one group to the next, giggling with delight at every word anyone addressed to him. And once, catching Eddie's eye, he actually winked.

Now that the party was finally breaking up, everything would have been just perfect, if it hadn't been for two minor details. Or rather, two chicks: Sandra and Daisy. Sandra had showed up with the D'Arcy Street gang; there was no way he could have prevented that. But he didn't much care for the idea of her intruding on his professional life. He'd had to ignore her tonight, because he didn't want her getting any ideas. To be brutally honest, he had an image to keep up now and she was not good-looking enough to be his girlfriend.

Daisy, by contrast, was all too beautiful, but she was with that prick Barnaby Keeler. They had just left together, maybe for the tavern around the corner, but possibly (how he hated the thought) for Keeler's place downtown. Willard and some of the others were leaving too, insisting he join them at the Pilot. He wanted to go and celebrate, but on this night of all nights – especially if Keeler and Daisy did turn out to be there – he ought to have a girl with him. Someone he might later take back to his place.

Anyone. But not Sandra.

Over by her desk, Jane was slowly putting on her coat. She took her purse out of one of the drawers and slung the strap over her shoulder, but it didn't look like she was in any hurry to leave. She wasn't bad; certainly not an embarrassment to be seen with. And she'd turned out to be less crabby than she seemed the first time he met her. Eddie decided that if she looked at him within the next thirty seconds he'd ask her to go for a drink. If she didn't – well, maybe it was better not to mix business with pleasure.

Just then the Zefflers stopped to say goodbye and Bruno came charging from the back of the gallery to pump everyone's hand one last time. McNab, still hanging around, told Eddie he'd see him over at the Pilot in ten minutes. Willard was holding the door open and saying, 'Come on, wonder boy, we're all waiting for you.' When Eddie glanced over at the desk again, Jane was gone.

ALL IN ALL, Bruno considered that it had been a successful night. Several wall labels now had red or blue dots on them. In addition to *Back Flip*, Jerry Zeffler had reserved *Tusk*, an acid-green triptych linked by a slash of pure scarlet, priced at five hundred dollars because of its size.

At ten o'clock, an hour after the time specified on the invitations as the end of the opening, one solitary, nearly empty bottle of wine sat on the cloth-covered table as a signal to the freeloaders that it was time to go elsewhere and start paying for their drinks.

Tom Dale, Winifred and their group were already gone; they had stayed only the half hour that courtesy demanded. The Zefflers, he flushed and ebullient, she subdued, hung on to the end. But after Jerry had shaken Bruno's hand numerous times and slapped Eddie repeatedly on the back, they went, too. At nine forty-five, Bruno told Jane that she could go home. When she left, she was still quite steady on her feet, he noticed with approval. Then Eddie, in a state of visible but controlled elation, went off to join his friends at the Pilot.

Now only Howard McNab was left, taking a last, leisurely tour of the gallery, wearing a contemplative expression. He paused in front of *Back*

Flip. Then he stepped into the alcove, where Bruno had started tidying up.

'A most encouraging evening,' he said, sitting down at the table without being asked.

After he had folded up the tablecloth, Bruno took a seat opposite him and held out his package of cigarettes. When McNab shook his head, he lit one for himself. 'We are happy,' he said.

'I only wish,' McNab went on, 'that Quintin Margrave were going to be here in time to see this show. He arrives just a few days after it closes, unfortunately.'

Bruno tried to think. Could he somehow hold Eddie's show over? No, he'd already made all the arrangements, sent out the invitations and placed the newspaper ad for the next exhibition. And Jiri had warned him that they'd need at least three days, maybe four, to get his total kinetic environment up and running.

'However, Edward will certainly be one of the young artists Quintin will want to meet. And I'll bring him here, too, naturally.'

Bruno inclined his head slightly, saying nothing. Some sign of gratitude was called for, but justice as well as strategy required that it be muted. For just where and who would Howard McNab be if there were no art, no exhibitions, no galleries, for him to write and talk about?

'But I'll make sure he gets to O'Hara's studio – take him myself, if need be.'

Bruno smiled, but he felt his chest grow tight at the thought of this man – or anyone – entering one of his artists' studios behind his back. Such visits could only be furtive attempts to see and buy objects that ought to be controlled exclusively by himself. And artists could not be trusted. Even those who weren't actually selling out of their studios were all too ready to pauperize their dealers by giving paintings away to friends, lovers and creditors.

Yes, McNab was capable of treachery; the Jorgensen review had proved that. At Eddie's studio, he would be snooping and meddling, and the English curator would be with him. Bruno forced himself to breathe normally. There was no way to prevent their visit, or any of the others he knew took place every single day. And in the end it would surely be good for business, good for the gallery, good for himself.

McNab must have noticed his quick gasp for air. He reached over and patted Bruno's arm encouragingly. 'Yes,' he said, 'it *is* exciting, isn't it?'

JANE HAD TROUBLE falling asleep that night. She'd made a point of remaining relatively sober, but even a modest amount of wine could create an agitated longing for company. Although she hung around until almost everybody had left, no one invited her to the Pilot, and she couldn't go alone. Barnaby's arrival and departure with that girl in purple had caused her unexpected distress, but she felt she had succeeded in hiding it. Her own relationship with him was too undefined to justify any possessiveness. But then what was the point of it, she kept asking herself as she tossed and turned, if its limited pleasures could be so casually withheld from her?

Well, anyway, she was happy for Eddie. Two paintings definitely sold, and a huge turnout. Even Tom Dale had been there. With, she now remembered, Win Beecham at his side, looking all flushed and happy. God, was it possible? She had never bought the idea, once hinted at with some embarrassment by Bruno, that those two ...

No, no, they were both far too old! Love was for the young and attractive. Oh, you could see evidence on any street corner that the ugly did somehow manage to reproduce, but that was something else entirely, and nowadays, thanks to the Pill, could be staved off indefinitely. But passionate love, urgent desire – did such turbulent emotions still throb in the withered breasts of elderly parties like Win and Tom? Impossible! The image of those two silver heads together on a pillow, except possibly for a chaste afternoon nap, was just too laughable.

All right, maybe she should stop feeling sorry for herself. Things could be worse: although she was alone and adrift, she was still young and reasonably good-looking. Therefore something, some*one*, eventually had to turn up. Then, a few minutes later, lulled and comforted by that thought, she drifted off.

▪ Chapter Seven

WINIFRED'S SUMMER had been quite enjoyable. At Go Home Bay with Eliot and her sons, she had given what she had decided would be her farewell performance as a dutiful wife and mother. Away from the studio where lately she had been spending so much time, free of the irritable preoccupation that painting induced in her, she had probably seemed just like her old self: the reserved but loving caretaker of her boys' childhoods. And the gallant young widow Eliot had wed.

But now, as she sat in her attic studio on a lovely, bright morning, she was the self *she* wished to be. A large, primed, empty canvas hung ready on the wall, Glenn Gould's recording of the *Goldberg Variations* rippled from the stereo, and on the work table some oolong tea was steeping in a small, exquisite Japanese pot. Through windows framed by curtains of pale yellow silk she looked down over her back garden. In the fall it was quite beautiful in a valiant, elegiac way.

For years, she'd poured much of her energy and talent into it. Then, one hot August afternoon in 1962, toiling doggedly on her all-white perennial border, she realized even Vita Sackville-West at Sissinghurst had sometimes had other things, such as love and literature, on her mind. Now a man came four days a week in spring and summer, and Win much preferred directing him to scrabbling around on her own knees.

From then on, she devoted most of her time to the Art Gallery's Women's Committee. And at some function – it would be almost five years ago now – she had run into Tom Dale. He was starting to make a name for himself as a painter, though still working full time at the ad agency where he'd finally become a partner. They'd greeted each other with all the delight that well-preserved, successful middle-aged people feel when they encounter a similarly situated person, known from a happy period of their youth.

So a year or two later, when Win decided that she wanted to spend the rest of her life as an artist, she had naturally turned for advice to Tom, who by then was nearly famous. And now they were artists together, he in his big untidy loft in downtown Toronto, she in her neat, airy studio in what he liked to call 'darkest Rosedale'.

During the summer, away from the city, freed from the anxiety that his physical presence had lately begun to evoke in her, Win had thought a great deal about Tom. At times, the prospect of something not quite platonic occurring between them seemed preposterous, even repellent; at others, logical and appealing.

When they'd met the previous week at the O'Hara opening, they had not seen each other for almost three months. And far from being dismayed to find Joan at his side, Win had felt relieved. With Tom's wife present, there could be no uneasy, indecipherable meetings of eyes, no brief, glancing, possibly accidental touches of hands. In the Dales' combined company, there was only the gratifying sensation of being a privileged member of an inner circle. Naturally she had been entitled to the same feeling, socially speaking, all her life, but never before as a recognized participant in the more free-and-easy, egalitarian world of art.

This new pleasure almost, but not quite, compensated for the distinctly less enjoyable experience of seeing Bruno Gonzaga again. In the interval since her exhibition, he had acquired a markedly different manner, one that suggested he thought he had come up considerably in the world. Oh, he was civil enough but radiated none of the simple, unaffected warmth she had appreciated at the start of their professional relationship. Nor did he make any overtures about another Beecham exhibition for the 1967–68 season, now in full swing.

Nearly all the pieces from her first show had found their way back to the studio, at her expense. They now occupied most of her special custom-built sliding storage racks; she would have to have additional ones installed to accommodate the new work. It had proved far more difficult than she had anticipated to conquer the art world. And she was not used to failure; every other challenge she had set herself, she had always been able to meet. In hindsight, it seemed that she had tested her strength mainly by marrying exacting men, and then with enormous effort making the marriages work. However, the creation of domestic order – the raising of children, the supervision of help and the discreet management of infidelity (almost certainly on both sides, though she had never really wished to be sure of that) – had only dissipated her true talents.

When Alec died – so suddenly! – there had been no time to prepare or accept, only the awful, indisputable fact of his absence and the need to recover quickly for the sake of the boys. She had loved him, but she pressed on and soon found her next demanding project in the person of Eliot Overton.

She still thought of Eliot as her 'new' husband, though they had recently celebrated their tenth anniversary. But if he had seemed a saviour in the addled, desperate time of her bereavement, it was now clear that he did not understand the first thing about her. And during those ten years, her dear little sons had grown into taciturn strangers who were just as uninterested in her true self as Eliot. So she had ended up saddled with not one or two but *three* uncomprehending males who in their wisdom unanimously viewed her art as simply the rather embarrassing expression of change-of-life 'blues'. Well, the boys were both away at university now, and her husband's demanding practice and emotional remoteness had lately begun to seem a blessing in disguise, limiting his interest and interference in her new life.

Tom, however, understood her perfectly. But, circling around and around the idea of him, she had finally collided with the fact that he could easily turn out to be the most difficult project she'd ever taken on. His egotism, though well concealed, was certainly substantial; otherwise he would never have been where he was today. He might be more than a match for her.

And perhaps simple romantic attraction was not the only cause of the sudden impulse that had drawn her so disconcertingly towards Tom. Wouldn't we all like to rewrite the story of our life, to rearrange its haphazard jumble of events into a more meaningful, more aesthetically pleasing pattern? To retrace our steps, following the trail of breadcrumbs back to some fork in the path that, at least in retrospect, seems ominously significant? Oh, we say to ourselves, everything might have been different if only I had gone that way instead. And for a woman, another question nearly always arises: who would I have become if I had chosen him, if he had chosen me? I might have had a whole other self, different and perhaps better than the one I assumed blindly, carelessly in youth.

As she poured the first cup of oolong into an old, nearly translucent Wedgwood cup, she looked at her hands. They had begun to show unmistakable signs of age: veins in high relief, knuckles crowned with puckered pillows of skin ... but at least there were no brown spots. Yet. She lifted the cup to her lips and drank.

By the time it was empty she had made up her mind, with mingled regret and relief, that she was far too old to go on believing in the irresistible power of love. Art was the only thing that really mattered to her now. She slipped into her smock, selected a brush and a tube of paint and approached the blank canvas. The sun pouring through the windows was beautiful. But the days were growing shorter now. *Ars longa, vita brevis.* It was time to get to work.

JANE NOTICED a different atmosphere in the Gonzaga Gallery during the run of the O'Hara exhibition. There were not only more visitors than usual, but a lot of them, having read Howard McNab's piece, came specifically to see the exhibition. She did not have to explain to these people that the paintings on the gallery walls were not 'of' anything, were not meant to 'look like' or 'represent' or 'mean' anything, but that they were simply interesting and significant objects in their own right.

A few aesthetic rubes still stumbled in off the street, ready to argue this point, but Jane now dealt with them quite severely. A little of the glamour attached to Eddie and the Gonzaga had rubbed off on her. The informed gallery-goers even treated her with a certain amount of respect, as if she herself had had some role in bringing O'Hara's talent to light. And a picture of her standing next to *Back Flip* was published in the paper.

'Like Betty fucking Furness with a refrigerator,' said Eddie when he saw it. He came in almost every day. Although he didn't pay a lot of attention to Jane and spent most of the time drinking coffee with Bruno in the alcove, she felt they had become friends of a sort. In the small back section of the gallery, some of Eddie's watercolours were hanging. A writer for *IN Toronto*, a monthly magazine devoted to trends in food and fashion, decided to mention them in a forthcoming article for the December issue on culturally conscious and patriotic Christmas shopping. She also invited Eddie to contribute a short piece for a feature tentatively entitled 'The Art of Christmas', in which figures in the artistic field would describe their Yuletide rituals.

He declined, claiming (untruthfully, as it happened) to be Jewish on his mother's side – the side that really counted. After the flustered lady reporter had left, Eddie told Jane that he actually spent Christmas day at his parents' house in Rexdale, where the tree was decorated with ornaments lovingly preserved from the 1940s, and a 78 of 'Santa Claus Is Coming to Town', sung by the Andrews Sisters, played and replayed on the automatic record-changer.

'Oh, my parents have that record, too,' Jane said.

'Far out!' said Eddie. 'Maxine, Laverne and ... who was the other one?'

She shrugged.

'But hey, have you ever noticed that when you're totally stoned, they sound exactly like the Chipmunks?'

Actually, she hadn't; but she laughed anyway.

BRUNO KNEW he should have been happy during the O'Hara show. But he could not shake the feeling that good luck inevitably carried in its wake envy, ill wishes and potential sabotage. Despite the increased number of visitors who passed through the gallery during working hours, he was also rather lonely. This new success distanced him even more from the wife he kept tucked away in a solid brick house in a remote, unfashionable cul-de-sac. She had not yet questioned anything he did, but it was wiser not to test her understanding by trying to explain it. No one in his working life had ever met her, and he himself saw less and less of her as he spent more and more time at the gallery, often staying on for hours after Jane had gone home.

When he had locked the front door after her and turned off the lights, he usually went back to the workshop to take care of the framing jobs that still paid the rent, but that he now preferred not to be seen doing. Later, sometimes long after midnight, he prowled around the gallery in the semi-darkness, not wanting to attract the attention of passersby by putting the lights on again. He could make out the colours and shapes quite clearly by the street lamps outside the huge, uncurtained window.

The night before the O'Hara show was due to close, he rolled the chair from Jane's desk to a position directly in front of *Back Flip*. And the longer he sat there with the smoke rising unnoticed from his cigarette, the more significant, the more beautiful, the more desirable *Back Flip* appeared. But what exactly was there about it that made everybody – Zeffler, McNab and, not least, himself – immediately identify it as the best piece in the show? Could it be simply the knowledge that it was admired and desired by others that gave it such power?

For the rest of them, perhaps. But not for him. *His* relationship to this painting was very different from theirs, closer, deeper and stronger. Stronger even than O'Hara's, he realized with a certainty that shook him. Eddie, arrogant, careless, treating everything as a joke, was merely the unwitting agent by which objects like this one came into the world.

Then, like any other child, he forgot about them and moved on to the next amusement.

So he, Bruno, had to be the custodian. He got to his feet and paced, shaking his head and muttering. He stood looking out onto the empty street, where the silence was broken only by the occasional car, accelerating recklessly from the traffic lights a block to the north. For a while he stared at the darkened window of the Lurie Gallery. Then he returned to the chair and sat down again in front of *Back Flip*. How long he stayed there, whether it was hours or only minutes, he couldn't have said. But the painting seemed to grow until it filled his whole vision. Finally it began to speak to him.

Don't let me go, it said. *Don't let me go*.

TOM DALE DAWDLED as he passed the glass display cases containing selected luxury items designed to appeal to the customers of the Park Plaza Hotel. He had to fight a perverse urge to examine every pair of sheepskin slippers, every tartan scarf, every cashmere twin set, every attractively packaged box of maple fudge, and to read in full the discreet cards that indicated at which nearby shops they were available. He felt a powerful reluctance to continue with the undertaking that had brought him to the hotel on this bright but cool October afternoon. He ought to be in the studio, taking advantage of the clear autumn light. What the hell was he doing here?

As he approached the registration desk, he looked around quickly but mercifully saw no one he knew. Damn it, he felt like a teenager with his first girlie magazine. How had he managed to reach the advanced age of fifty-four without mastering the niceties of a situation like this? Actually, nothing could be simpler, he knew from overhearing the exploits of others. The gentleman arrives first, books a room for which he pays in advance, and shortly afterwards the lady joins him, having obtained the room number by calling him on the house phone. *Onward, then*.

But just as he met the desk clerk's eye, it struck him with a combination of pride and terror that of all living Canadian painters he was probably the only one whose face and name might, just might, be recognized by a hotel employee. Again, he had to wrestle a nearly overwhelming impulse to bolt. *No*, he told himself, there will be no turning back. Suppose the young fellow facing him unexpectedly did turn out to be an art lover? Surely he, Tom, would be neither the first nor the last well-known person to turn up wanting to register, without luggage, in midafternoon.

Besides, this was the only way. He smiled (urbanely, he felt) at the clerk, who looked back with a touch of impatience in his expression. The studio was certainly not a suitable or convenient place to stage an adulterous liaison. The old leather sofa was paint-splattered, cracked and slippery, and you could hardly expect a woman like –

'Tom! What are *you* doing here?'

He turned just in time to see Howard McNab emerge like a grinning river troll from the depths of an armchair not ten feet from the desk, holding out his hand. Tom shook it, trying to think quickly but failing.

Fortunately, McNab went on, 'Are you here for the same reason I am?'

'And what would that be?' Tom managed to ask.

'Quintin Margrave. Alan is tied up with an acquisition committee meeting, so I said I'd look after him. The Gallery people booked him in here, for some reason, but I've got him a room at the Windsor Arms. He'll feel much more at home there, don't you think?'

Tom mumbled his assent, his mind still searching desperately for something, anything ... then, all at once, he had it. 'Ah, yes ... yes, but I'd heard he was going to be staying here, and I thought I'd stop by and take him up to the Roof for a welcome-to-Toronto drink. This can be a chilly town, in more ways than one –' here he chuckled casually '– when you arrive and don't know anybody. Why don't we all go?'

McNab hesitated. Tom guessed he was torn between reluctance to relinquish exclusive custody of Margrave and eagerness to be able to take credit for bringing him together with one of the big guns of Canadian art.

'Since I've never met Quintin,' Tom went on smoothly, 'it'd be nice if you could introduce us. And have a drink on me.' Those last hasty words would probably cost him a Chivas or two, because McNab was known to be a leech with expensive tastes. But what the hell. It would be well worth it to get quickly out of this mess. He couldn't go on standing in front of the registration desk for much longer.

'What a good idea,' McNab finally replied. 'Quintin is in the men's room, freshening up ... oh, here he is.'

A tall, horse-faced, straggly-haired man was coming towards them, looking around through half-closed eyes. To Tom, his expression indicated either utter contempt or severe jet lag. He wore a pearl-grey, double-breasted suit, nipped in at the waist and knees, but flaring out at the ankles over black flamenco-style boots. An emerald-green-and-purple silk foulard tie erupted from beneath the large collar of his pale lilac shirt. Despite his style of dress, he seemed to be in his late thirties or early forties.

After McNab had introduced them, Tom repeated his invitation, and Margrave accepted with a dulled passivity that seemed to clinch the diagnosis of jet lag. It was quickly arranged that Margrave's luggage would be left at the desk until further notice, and the three of them entered the elevator to the Roof Lounge. As they ascended, McNab droned on, outlining the artistic delights he had lined up for the visitor, undaunted by his British captive's glassy-eyed silence. Tom, also a prisoner, also mute, but speculating frantically about the likely whereabouts and frame of mind of the woman he had arranged to meet, cursed his ill fortune all the way to the eighteenth floor.

BOB COULDN'T BELIEVE his luck. Even from the back, she was instantly recognizable. He noticed her legs first: long, slim, one slightly bent and extended like a model's in an Avedon – no, make that David Bailey, to be up to date – fashion shot. Then his eyes moved slowly upwards, over her behind, waist, shoulders, neck, until they lit on the receiver of the hotel's house phone, pressed to one side of her glossy silver-blond head. He was just close enough to hear Eleanor Zeffler say, 'You're sure? Would you check again?' Then, after a short silence, 'He's not registered? I see. Goodbye.'

Bob scuttled away, not wanting to be caught eavesdropping. After she had hung up, Eleanor stood very still for a moment, facing the wall. When she turned around and began to walk away from the phone, he stepped quickly out the door onto the driveway where the taxis pulled in off Avenue Road.

So their paths crossed quite naturally, he coming in, she going out, and before she had time to ask the doorman to get her a cab, he was able to greet her with plausible surprise. Only a certain rigidity in her lovely face betrayed what Bob felt sure was disappointment or humiliation.

She seemed to shake it off easily, though, and agreed with almost frightening eagerness to his impulsive, only semi-serious suggestion that the two of them pop up to the Roof for a drink. That was where he had been heading, anyway, it being payday and a beautiful one, too. He'd felt entitled to a modest splurge: a translucent, tinkling gin and tonic in the golden autumnal daylight, instead of his usual soapy, sloshing draft beer in some windowless beverage room. They walked in silence to the elevator, and as the car started to go up, he took a deep breath of Eleanor's perfume. It seemed to fill the tiny cubicle, but for the moment he could not identify it.

By the time they disembarked in the vestibule that separated the bar from the restaurant on the top floor, he had it: Sortilège. The same perfume Lorrie had worn, and at the beginning, at least, he'd thought she had a lot of class. But even in soft-focus retrospect, she had not been half as good-looking as the woman beside him. Feeling suddenly bold, he gently placed the fingers of one hand between Eleanor's shoulder blades to steer her into the bar.

It was the best place in town to drink on a fine fall afternoon. There was even a large outdoor terrace, the only one in Toronto, which commanded a view southward over the city. It was closed now for the season, but the bar's neoclassical Syrie-Maugham-meets-Napoleon interior was bathed in sunshine. And now he even had his dream girl miraculously at his, side. This was definitely the life – talk about your *luxe, calme et volupté,* your *bonheur de vivre!* It so happened he'd spent the better part of an hour that morning trying to explain Matisse to a roomful of students, some of whom had seemed startled by the revelation that sex had been enjoyed as early as 1905.

Only two or three tables were occupied, and the Roof's two bartenders were polishing glasses behind the bar. They were known for their encyclopedic memories, which allowed them to greet every regular customer by name and produce his preferred tipple without prompting.

Since he could rarely afford to patronize the Roof, Bob was not in the encyclopedia, but he secured a nice table by the window and ordered two gin-and-tonics. Eleanor did not seem to care what she drank, saying she'd leave it up to him, and when the gin arrived she gulped it down. But after mentioning that she'd been having lunch in the Prince Arthur Room with a girlfriend from out of town, she only answered his attempts at further conversation with nods or monosyllables. A smooth, curving lock of hair fell over part of her face, which she kept turned slightly away from him. He felt cheated; he had hoped to gaze into Eleanor's eyes as the gin stole through him. Then he noticed that now and again she glanced quickly out from beneath the curtain of hair, not at him, but towards the other side of the room.

When he followed the direction of her eyes, he saw that she was looking at a table where three men were sitting. He knew Dale and McNab, but he'd never seen the man between them before. Dressed like some kind of Edwardian dandy, he was evidently, even from a distance, in a disoriented state. McNab was jabbering earnestly at him, and from time to time he nodded distractedly. But though Tom Dale sat staring silently into his drink, he appeared to be the host of the party. He was the one who signalled for refills, all the while keeping his head down and avoiding looking around him. Maybe he was embarrassed to be seen socializing with McNab. That made sense. But who was the other guy?

Suddenly it came to him: it had to be Margrave, the director of the Spitalfields Gallery, the guy the kids at the Pilot had been talking about last spring. Well, maybe he ought to take advantage of the chance dumb luck had placed in his path. And Eleanor did seem unusually interested in that table.

'Hey,' he said to her, 'look who's sitting over in the corner.'

She only nodded from beneath her hair.

'Shall we go over and join them?'

Her head moved furiously from side to side. Then one of her hands crept across the table and her long, pearl-tipped fingers gently touched his. 'Oh, no,' she said softly, looking into his eyes at last, 'let's stay where we are. Just the two of us.'

He abandoned any thought of crossing the room.

FINALLY, Tom was able to escape. By the time he, McNab and Margrave left the Roof bar, dusk was falling and Eleanor and Willard had disappeared. As soon as the elevator reached the lobby, Tom said goodbye quickly and went out the hotel's south entrance. He crossed Bloor Street at the light, hurried past the Chinese tomb and took the steps down into Philosophers' Walk. On his left, the back wall of the Museum rose like a towering Romanesque fortress; on his right, ahead and through the trees, he could see the utilitarian red brick of Varsity Arena; and from behind him a contralto voice, singing scales, floated out of a high window in the Conservatory.

Too late, he remembered that after dark the secluded path was a known haunt of pansies. He began to walk even faster. Since his sex appeal when it came to the ladies was evidently increasing daily, who knew what lurkers in the shadows might also find his tired old body irresistible? Although they'd probably have to know a little something about Canadian art in order to become really aroused by it. For surely his success was the only possible explanation for the sudden appearance of Mrs Zeffler at his studio door the previous week. Expecting it would be Win, he was taken so aback by the sight of Eleanor's only vaguely familiar face in the peephole that he'd let her in without giving any thought to why she had come.

It had been a little early in the day for Winifred and anyway, now that he thought of it, she had not dropped in since ... back in the spring. And the last time they met was two weeks ago, at the O'Hara opening. He missed her visits, but felt a certain relief as well. He had been able to open some doors for her, but he could not grant her the recognition she longed for and might never get. And lately he had begun to feel that she expected something else from him. Something personal.

He and Win had known each other for years – they'd been no more than kids when they met in one of Lismer's drawing classes. Even then she'd been a looker. And later – oh, it would be twenty-odd years ago now – she'd turned up again, the wife of a partner in the ad agency where he was working. From that era he could recall a mildly resentful awareness that she was not for the likes of him. And that, he admitted, had made becoming her artistic mentor all the more satisfying.

Lady Winifred was still quite a piece of work, though: blue blood throbbing in her veins, silver spoon firmly clamped between her good strong teeth, high horse always saddled up and ready to ride. Those Family Compact genes were as tough as weeds. Still, there was a kind of pathos in her, too; in the world he had conquered with sheer talent and determination, she was self-conscious and unsure. If he took her in his arms, he believed, she would be passive, disarmed, utterly his. And now that her beauty, which had once made him shy, was only a faint, haunting pentimento, his affection for her was at long last a little condescending.

Yes, he supposed he could have had an affair with Winifred, if he had wanted to. But it had never happened – he and Joanie were faithful to each other, always had been. Though, to tell the truth, he had never been much interested in sexual conquest. What was important was showing his chops in the great cutting contest of twentieth-century art, jamming with the big boys – Matisse, Mondrian, Picasso, Pollock – who-the-hell-ever, bring 'em all on – and just maybe, in the eyes of posterity, coming out on top.

He reached Hoskin Avenue unmolested and headed west. It might do him good to go on walking; perhaps it would relieve the stress of the last few hours. At the next phone booth he passed, he'd call home and make some excuse for missing dinner. He wasn't ready to face Joan just yet. If he continued in a general southwesterly direction, he'd eventually end up at the studio, and maybe stop there for a bit.

But it hadn't been Winifred at his door last Friday afternoon. It was Eleanor Zeffler, a woman he hardly knew. When she arrived, he'd been well into his second J&B, more or less at peace with the world and ready for company. Eleanor had accepted a drink in the blue mug that Winifred always used, and explained that she wanted to get his honest opinion of Eddie O'Hara's work. First her husband had bought a little drawing – she didn't mind that – but now he also insisted on having two paintings from the solo show, and she feared that he was moving too fast, compromising the integrity of their collection with inferior pieces. They were weeding out previous mistakes – for example, a couple of early Willards – and thinking of moving into the American market...

That kind of talk made Tom uncomfortable. He avoided the business end of the art game like the plague now that he didn't *have* to think about it. Besides, he considered the modern masters, preferably dead ones, his sole competitors, and was only willing to discuss his contemporaries in the most noncommittal terms. In fact, he always encouraged younger artists to join the fray, provided of course that he could stay well ahead of them. And damn it, he *knew* he could.

'Oh, honey,' he'd said, 'you're asking the wrong fellow. I'm not a critic or a curator or a dealer – thank God. I'm just a painter, that's all.'

Then he'd turned his back on her and stared uneasily out the window. He had just begun to chide himself for being rude when he felt her arms come around him from behind. She pressed her face against his neck – she was as tall as he was, he thought irrelevantly – and clung there, wordlessly.

Fear, confusion, embarrassment, amazement, delight, pleasure, lust ... in a fraction of a second he felt them all crash through him. What in God's name had brought *this* on – surely not that single meaningless endearment? He placed his hands, which he suddenly realized were covered with paint, over her manicured ones and lifted them gently so that he could turn around. But when they were facing each other, she said nothing, and merely looked steadily at him.

'Whoa, now, girl,' he'd said. 'What's this all about?' He must have sounded as if he was talking to a goddamn horse.

'Do I have to draw you a picture?'

He had to laugh. 'Isn't that supposed to be my job?'

She smiled wanly. Then, when he touched her cheek, she closed her eyes, and he'd thought she might start crying.

Well, what else could he have done, without coming off as a heartless boor? He had to give her a kiss, didn't he? After that, things had got rapidly out of hand, and they had ended up grappling awkwardly but thrillingly on the old Newsome and Biggars waiting-room couch.

Touching Eleanor, he had felt something quite different from the proud, headlong urgency he remembered from his youth. With her he was slow, deliberate, even clumsy, slightly stunned by his own actions, and easily sidetracked by every scent, sight and sensation. Even her underwear fascinated him: stockings that apparently stayed up all by themselves, their elasticized tops gripping the smooth flesh of her thighs just as his hands did, minuscule panties of paisley-printed silk that barely covered her, a matching brassiere with half hoops of wire that passed under her breasts, leaving pink U-shaped indentations in her flesh that were almost unbearably touching. Clearly there had been many aesthetic and technical developments in the field of female underwear since his last impromptu excursion of this kind.

As he was pondering these, she had slid away from him, pulling her clothes back into place even before he had begun to remove his own. Then it had seemed obligatory to arrange a rendezvous at the Plaza for the first afternoon of the following week. She appeared to assume that he was a seasoned philanderer, familiar with the hotel routine, and at the time that in itself had seemed awfully flattering.

It was nearly dark when he turned south on St. George Street. Lights were still burning in the boxy International Style building where the history and theory of art were taught to University of Toronto students. Night classes in classification and analysis, he supposed. Thank God he'd never been touched by the dead hand of Academe. He'd more or less taught himself to draw as a kid, absorbed what art history he knew out of sheer enthusiasm, learned commercial illustration on the job and then become a real painter over countless solitary weekends and evenings. He never said so publicly, but Tom had very little time for the armchair quarterbacks – characters like Margrave and McNab. Most of them were parasites, mere barnacles on the slow, majestic, unsinkable ship of Art. Though, to be fair, Howard had been awfully kind to him lately in print. But from now on, the guy would be forever linked in his mind to the fiasco at the Park Plaza.

As for Eleanor ... what was he supposed to do about *her* now? And what the hell had *she* been doing in the bar with Bob Willard, a man whose paintings she planned to remove from her – or rather her husband's – art collection? The Zefflers had bought a few things from the Lurie Gallery, so he could get her number from Max, even if it was unlisted. But did he dare to – did he *have* to – telephone her? Since he was not even sure which of them had really stood the other up this afternoon, he had no idea what he ought to say, or what she might answer. Would she be willing to speak to him? And even if she was, would he ever get to stroke those firm, slender thighs again?

■ Chapter Eight

IT WASN'T AS IF he intended to cheat anybody. In due course, Eddie would get his share of the proceeds from the show, including his cut of *Back Flip*. All he was doing, Bruno told himself, was preserving a rare, exceptional work from O'Hara's early period for posterity. Or perhaps for later sale, when it would be worth much more than it was today. This was prudent management of a young artist's career, nothing more. One day Eddie would thank him for his foresight. And recognize that Bruno Gonzaga was not like other dealers, whose only thought was for a quick profit.

As for Zeffler ... well, he didn't deserve to own *Flip*, anyway. He'd be just as happy with *Tusk*, which was bigger, flashier and, best of all from Bruno's – and Eddie's – point of view, more expensive. The lawyer had been so puffed up with pride, believing he'd snapped up *Flip* from under everybody's nose, that it had been almost too easy to induce him to buy *Tusk* as well. Or, as he would soon discover, *instead*. Thinking carefully back over their conversations, Bruno realized that he had never actually promised to reserve *Flip* for Zeffler. The blue sticker simply indicated that someone had asked him to hold it ... and Zeffler had never specifically done so. One of the few advantages of being considered a simple, guileless peasant was the fact that no one paid very close attention to what you said.

However, he could not reveal to anyone that he had decided to keep *Back Flip* for himself. He had barely allowed the idea to settle comfortably in his own mind. But one thing he knew for certain: he would look like a fool if it came out that he, just starting out as a dealer, had begun to hoard the very objects he was supposed to be inducing people to buy. And since O'Hara was not yet well known, a false red sticker might seem more a matter of desperation than confidence.

No matter how much money they made, Bruno thought as he wrapped the painting neatly in brown paper, dealers were only glorified shopkeepers and always had been, ever since antiquity. It was not the role he really wanted, but he had had little choice. Without talent, he could not create; without money, he could not collect; without education, he could not pontificate, and so had ended up as a humble go-between. He was better off now than as a labourer, but all the same he hated the odour of subservience that clung to his new profession.

Although *Back Flip* was just over four feet square, Bruno had some difficulty manoeuvring it down the narrow stairs to the basement. He was breathing heavily as he slid the package into the storage cupboard under the stairs, pushing it right to the back and arranging a few framed prints and the mop and broom in front of it, then swung the door closed. The three sections of *Tusk* were wrapped and ready upstairs. They would be picked up the next day by the local art shipping company, Lister Fine Art Transport.

Hank Lister still liked to drive the van himself whenever he could. He was garrulous and had an honest-workingman manner that many people found disarming. Maybe he would be the best person to break the news that he was delivering just one work of art, not two, to the Zeffler residence. And by then Bruno would have figured out a way to deal with the situation.

AT FIRST, *Bay Blues* had hung on the landing of the front stairs – not an inconspicuous location, really, since you had to pass it every time you went up or down. Then, as Tom Dale's reputation grew, the painting had begun to migrate, first moving to the hall, facing the front door, where it remained for a some months. Now that its creator had achieved international recognition, it had come to rest in a prime position over the fireplace in the Zefflers' living room. This had necessitated the removal of *Forest*, by Robert Willard, to *Bay Blues*' former spot on the stairs. Although the Willard was larger than the Dale, it fitted. Just barely.

The Dale, the Willard.... Eleanor had often thought how funny it was that paintings and sculpture were talked about like that. As if, each time an artist sent a work out into the world, he was subdividing himself. Like that Sorcerer's Apprentice sequence in *Fantasia*. People didn't refer to other kinds of art – books, for instance – that way. Nobody ever said, 'I was reading a Proust the other night.' Although they did say, 'an Agatha Christie'. Now that was interesting. But when she'd pointed this out to Jerry he'd just looked at her as if she were a fool.

Anyway, *Bay Blues* was tiny compared with the gigantic pieces Tom was producing, and selling like hot cakes, these days. Back in the forties, he had still signed his work on the front, with the very same fluid, looping signature that now appeared on the reverse of his canvases and in pencil on his serigraphs. It was clearly visible in *Bay Blues'* lower right corner, along with the scribbled date 8/47. There were a few identifiable landscape elements in the composition: a pale orange oval that could have been either a sun or a moon floated in the upper left quadrant, above a horizontal mass of wavy, grey-blue brushstrokes that suggested a body of water. But as Howard McNab had told Jerry, *Bay Blues* also contained clear intimations of Tom's mature, colour-field work, and as Jerry had repeatedly told Eleanor, it was therefore becoming more important and valuable every day.

Stretched out on the chesterfield, with a copy of *Harper's Bazaar* in one hand, she stared at the painting, as if it might hold a clue to the workings of Tom Dale's mind. Of course, *Bay Blues* had been painted long before she and Tom had ever met. A whole day had passed since their aborted rendezvous at the Park Plaza, and Eleanor still had not been able to come up with a plausible scenario that would account for how they had each, separately, ended up in the Roof bar in the company of others. She couldn't even explain to herself how she had come to be there with Bob Willard, of all people, except that she'd been momentarily disoriented by the discovery that Tom had apparently cancelled their tryst.

Dusk was falling when she finally got away from Willard. It was easy, though; all she had to do was look with feigned horror at her watch and mutter something about collecting her daughter from school. He, obviously childless, had not seemed to realize it was already far too late for that to be true. Then she'd rushed out of the restaurant, abandoning her half-eaten shrimp cocktail, and leapt into a down-bound elevator just as the doors were closing. She took a cab downtown to the Simpson's parking arcade, where she had left her car, thinking that if she had to, she could account for any missing afternoon hours by saying she had been browsing in the Room. But she didn't really expect to need an alibi; Jerry had left Monday morning on a business trip – some corporate client in Montreal – and would be gone for a few days. That had made this week the perfect time for the start of her new life.

But somehow, everything had gone wrong. Last week, in his studio, after a momentary and terrifying hesitation, Tom had finally responded more or less as she had hoped. However, the episode on the couch had disappointed her. She had assumed that a man of Tom's stature would take her in hand with ease, perhaps even gently overpowering her, like the violinist in those advertisements for Tabu. But he'd been far too grateful, too tentative, too *awed* (it was the only way to describe it) by her surrender. As he lay gasping, his hand on her breast, it had occurred to her that he might not turn out to be much of a lover – perhaps not as good as her own husband.

The sound of the front door chimes interrupted this unpleasant thought. Putting down her unread magazine on the coffee table, she got up and went like a sleepwalker into the hall. When she opened the door, Hank Lister was on the porch, leaning against the stone balustrade, his hands in his pockets. Seeing her, he straightened up and touched the peak of his grimy, battered yachting cap in an old-fashioned yet somehow unconvincing gesture of servility.

'And how is Mrs Zeffler this fine day?'

'I'm well, Hank. And you?'

'Couldn't be better. Got three pieces for you from Gonzaga's, Mrs Z.'

'Three?'

'Yes, ma'am.'

Had Jerry completely flipped? 'Shouldn't there only be two?'

'Let's see ...' He fished his glasses out of one shirt pocket and put them on slowly, one earpiece at a time. Then he pulled a crumpled waybill from the other, smoothed it out and examined it with exaggerated care. 'Well, what we got here is *Tusk* ... oh, that's a good one ... acrylic on canvas, three parts, each thirty-six by forty-two ...'

'Oh, yes ... the triptych. But then there was another painting, wasn't there?'

'Wouldn't know about that, ma'am. *Tusk,* by Ed O'Hara – say, nice kid, isn't he? A real up-and-comer, too, I'm hearing. Yep – three pieces is what Mr G. gave me.'

What did she care, really? Jerry could sort it all out when he got back on Thursday. 'All right. You can bring them in. Here, I'll sign for them.' She took the unappetizingly chewed ballpoint Hank held out and, holding the waybill against the wall, scribbled her name on it. 'You can leave them right there, in the hall, okay?'

Afterwards she went slowly back to the living room and lay down again. Becky was due home from school any moment now, but she rarely paid any attention to her mother and was quite happy to eat TV dinners, as they nearly always did when Daddy was away. So Eleanor would have plenty of time to think about Tom and decide what she ought to do next.

BOB WILLARD STILL wondered what had actually been going on that day at the Plaza. And why his cosy dinner with Eleanor Zeffler – a crazy, gin-inspired idea to begin with – had ended so abruptly. Fortunately, when she bolted, they had just given their steak orders, so he'd had time to cancel them. The wine hadn't been opened, either. In fact, the waiter was just approaching the table, bottle and corkscrew in hand, when Bob stood up and waved him away, mumbling about an emergency. Otherwise he would have been out a minimum of forty bucks. Blessing his quick reflexes, he'd dropped a ten on the table, stuffed the last two shrimps from Eleanor's cocktail into his mouth and dashed after her, as if they were leaving together.

But by the time he screeched to a halt in front of the elevators, still chewing, she was nowhere to be seen. He'd felt the coat-check girl watching him attentively from her booth until the doors opened on the next car down. When it reached street level, he headed for the exit on Prince Arthur. As he walked through the long ground-floor corridor that led there, he glanced out the windows into the courtyard and saw the doorman putting Eleanor into a cab. He paused, but after a second's thought ducked behind a pillar and let her go. And he didn't even start to regret that until he got to his apartment, a good five minutes' walk away.

Finally he decided it was all for the best. There was really no likelihood of anything happening between him and Eleanor. A kind of invisible equation, he believed, governed all dealings between the sexes. In any given couple, each of the two parties' cumulative scores, based on looks, brains, accomplishments, social status and cold hard cash, plus a number of other less easily quantifiable attributes, had to add up to something roughly equal. Otherwise, they were doomed to make each other miserable, regardless of either one's intrinsic worth as a human being. Eleanor Zeffler was out of his league; he accepted that. Or maybe he was out of hers.

More to the point, she was married. She already belonged, legally and morally, to somebody else, and he had never allowed himself to get into that kind of trouble. If he did, he'd be no better than that little CBC bastard.

QUINTIN MARGRAVE'S first visit to Tom's studio was just a formality, because it pretty much went without saying that there would be a Dale, or maybe two, in both the Toronto and London Artquake shows. All the arrangements had already been made through the Lurie Gallery, and Tom preferred it that way. He was happy to leave all mundane financial and logistical matters concerning his work to Max.

Long after he should have recovered from jet lag, Margrave still had the mild, detached demeanour that Tom had noticed at the Plaza Roof. He came accompanied by both Alan Burnham, the curator in charge of the Toronto exhibition, and Howard McNab, whom he evidently had not been able to shake off. And without anybody actually saying it in so many words, it was crystal clear to Tom that Howard had really started to get on the poor guy's wick.

Margrave's accent oscillated gently between Bradford, where he had been born and attended grammar school, and Cambridge, where he had read art history on a scholarship. Tom's ear only picked up those little shifts because his own father, now long deceased, had immigrated to Peterborough from Sheffield around the turn of the century. But how had the fellow ever got that fancy first name? An ambitious mother, perhaps.

Listening to Margrave, Tom gave posthumous but heartfelt thanks to his old man for removing himself and his yet-to-be-born son from the rigidly layered, snakes-and-ladders England of his birth. He wondered where he himself would be today if he'd had to make his way in a country where one misshapen vowel could send you zipping down the scaly slope. He'd have been too old – *was* too old – to make his mark in the post–Festival of Britain years as an impudent barrow boy like Hamilton or Hockney.

But the odd thing was, he and Margrave really seemed to hit it off – maybe because their Artquake business was already completed and neither one of them needed anything from the other. While Burnham and McNab were talking, Quintin asked Tom in an undertone if he'd mind if he dropped in again sometime during his stay in Toronto.

'Not at all,' Tom said just as quietly, adding that the late afternoon was the best time to come so as not to interrupt his work. And two days later, Margrave was at the door with a bottle of duty-free Glenfiddich.

Quintin didn't match Tom drink for drink, but that was all right. And to Tom's relief, they talked hardly at all about art. But they did discover a shared fondness for early Fats Waller and middle-period Pee Wee Russell. For much of the time they simply sat in companionable silence, sipping their Scotches and listening to Tom's records.

'Extraordinary how potent cheap music is,' Quintin said softly, as

Mildred Bailey sang 'More Than You Know.'

'You've put your finger on it,' Tom replied. And for quite a while after that, neither of them said another word.

SITTING IN THE semi-darkness, Jane heard the little bleep indicating that someone had activated the first electronic eye and entered the Total Kinetic Environment. Then there were two more bleeps. When the three men rounded the partition near the door and paused in front of her desk, their faces were briefly illuminated by the flash of the overhead strobe they had just set in motion. She recognized Howard McNab at once, but not the other two. It was early in the day; only half past ten, she saw when she checked her watch by the light of the small gooseneck lamp that allowed her to type and see the phone dial. But Howard said Bruno was expecting them.

So she led the little party through the minefield that was Jiri's masterpiece. Electronic music burst out here and there, and more lights flashed inside Plexiglas cubes, but no one stopped to press the little buttons that would have set certain pulleys and levers in motion. When they reached the back gallery, she pushed aside one of the shiny silver PVC curtains that now closed it off, and they emerged from the darkness into the track lights.

Bruno came out to greet the visitors. One of them turned out to be Alan Burnham, the new curator at the Art Gallery, an American who was reputed to be unfamiliar with the local scene. That, apparently, was Howard McNab's excuse for trailing him wherever he went. The other guy was Quintin Margrave, the curator from London who was putting together the big Artquake exhibition Eddie had been talking about.

When he shook hands with Margrave, Bruno seemed unable to decide whether the Englishman was more likely to be brought to heel by obsequiousness or intimidation. So, as Jane cringed from the sidelines, he gave him a few doses of each. But Margrave appeared serenely indifferent to both techniques. Despite his mod clothing and shaggy greying hair, his manner was uncannily like that of the Duke of Edinburgh touring a model widget factory in some remote, backward corner of the Commonwealth. But still, even with that long upper lip and those heavy-lidded fried-egg eyes, he had a strange, *joli-laid* appeal, if you could say that about a man.

While Howard engaged Bruno in conversation, Margrave slipped back through the silver curtain and spent a few minutes in the

Environment. When he returned, he took a package of Gitanes out of his breast pocket and lit one. As the smell of Paris filled the air, Jane felt a sudden pang of mingled nostalgia and guilt and resolved to answer Bertrand's latest letter that very day.

In the rear gallery, Bruno had just put up a temporary group exhibition that included a couple of pieces by each of the artists he considered would be most likely to interest Margrave. And as everyone had expected, the painter who interested him most was Edward O'Hara. After examining the two works of his that were hanging, he stated his intention to follow up with a visit to O'Hara's studio.

Bruno, obviously prepared for this, endorsed the idea at once. He even offered to drive Margrave there himself immediately, pulling his car keys out of his pocket with a jangling flourish. But then Howard McNab stepped forward and announced that the arrangements had already been made: Eddie was expecting them – himself and Quintin, that was – that very evening. Nobody suggested that Bruno come along.

There was a brief silence during which a muscle twitched in Bruno's cheek, Alan Burnham surreptitiously checked his watch, Margrave calmly inspected a monoprint by Sven Jorgensen, and Jane noticed that McNab was staring at her breasts. Slowly, Bruno brought his cigarette to his lips and took a deep drag on it, then slowly exhaled. After a long pause, he shrugged as if the matter was of no importance.

'Tell Eddie to keep working hard,' he said. 'We need more paintings. Everybody wants to buy.' Then he giggled in a way that Jane supposed was meant to be affable.

'JUST TO LEAVEN the lump a little.' Those were the words Margrave had used the previous evening when he called to ask Tom to go with him to young O'Hara's place. As usual, Howard had managed to horn in on the visit. Quintin said he hoped Tom wouldn't mind his ringing him at home; he'd remembered that Tom didn't have a telephone at the studio and Max Lurie had been kind enough to give him the number.

Tom *was* a little annoyed, but he hesitated to explain his reluctance to comment on other artists' work to his new friend, who after all earned his living by doing just that. So against his better judgement he agreed to meet Margrave and McNab in front of Morris the Hatter's at seven.

Eddie buzzed them in and stood waiting at the top of the stairs as they climbed them in single file. At the sight of Tom bringing up the rear, Eddie looked surprised but pleased, and Tom felt a qualm. It was impossible not to have mixed feelings about someone who'd been designated in print as the next *you*. Though he knew of no other reason to dislike O'Hara, he reminded himself to make it clear to the others that his presence was not to be taken as an endorsement of the kid's work. He was only there as a personal favour to Quintin.

After Howard had introduced Margrave to Eddie, they all trooped into the front room and looked dutifully around. O'Hara had just started a new series of paintings that in Tom's opinion were going to need a whole lot more thought and work. Black, white and grey squares and rectangles had been precisely outlined on oddly shaped, long and skinny canvases, some of which were six times wider than they were high. Their smooth, unblemished surfaces held no hint of emotion or spontaneity.

McNab didn't miss a beat. 'Now,' he said, taking charge, 'these are new, and quite, quite different from the pieces in his first show.' Ignoring Eddie entirely, he directed his remarks to Margrave, who had already begun to pace the room contemplatively.

'I was starting to feel I was getting too hung up on colour,' Eddie said to no one in particular, 'so decided to eliminate it. I figured it was time to concentrate on structure....'

'The proportions are quite arresting,' McNab put in, the moment Eddie took a breath. He was still talking to Quintin, but since Margrave's back happened to be turned, he caught Tom's eye instead. Tom looked away. 'Eddie's show with Gonzaga was quite a success,' he went on in a louder voice, as if Margrave's inattention was a matter of deafness. 'That gave him a chance to draw a line, as it were. To start afresh, with new ideas.'

Eddie was still talking. '... but these are just the first few of a series, and I haven't fully developed my ideas, I'm just playing around with them right now...'

Margrave paused, listening to Eddie.

McNab didn't stop. 'This is what I always feel is so important for a young artist. He must find his own way, through endless experimentation. And this young man, I can promise you, has all the qualities required for a long and brilliant career.'

Still Margrave seemed not to hear him. 'So your exhibition last month was rather a triumph,' he said to Eddie.

'Yeah, it worked out pretty well.'

'Have you any slides of work from the show?'

'Oh, yeah. Just a minute.' Eddie left the room and reappeared a moment later carrying a plastic slide box and a viewer, which he handed to Margrave. Then he pulled a paint-spattered chair over to the bay window so that the Englishman could sit down. Margrave balanced the slide case on his knee for a moment as he reached into the breast pocket of his pearl-grey suit jacket for his Gitanes. He offered them around, but only Eddie accepted one. Then he lit another for himself and started slipping slides into the viewer.

After a few minutes' silence, he looked up at Eddie, who was slouched casually against the window frame beside him. 'What can you tell me about this one?' he asked, holding up the viewer.

'Oh, that's *Back Flip*. Wait a sec.' Eddie went out of the room again and came back with a newspaper in his hand. 'Here it is. It was on the front page of the Saturday arts supplement. You can get an idea of the scale from the chick in the picture. Too bad it couldn't be in colour, though.'

'I'd very much like to see this piece.'

'Well, I think it was bought by someone who lives in Toronto, Jerry Zeffler. Maybe you could see it at his place.'

'Splendid. Perhaps I'll do that. Do you know him, Tom?'

'Oh, yes,' Tom replied quickly, wondering if his face was getting red. It felt as if it was. 'The Zefflers. Serious collectors.'

'Would they be willing to lend it for the London exhibition, do you think?'

'I'd guess so. Yes, most likely. Nice couple. Jerry … a lawyer, I believe … and … and … Eleanor,' Tom babbled, compelled by some perverse impulse to pronounce the very name he most wanted to banish from his mind. 'They also have an early piece of mine, I understand.'

'Excellent,' said Quintin. 'Let's go together. You'll be the ideal person to introduce us. Lurie will have their telephone number, I expect.'

Tom nodded miserably. Damn it, Margrave was pushing it now. Even though Quintin had at first seemed a hell of a nice fellow, Tom told himself he ought to have known better than to start fraternizing with the enemy, cosying up to the scribblers and theorizers. Damn it and damn it. These days, it seemed, his well-ordered, harmlessly self-centred existence, which allowed him to devote himself without distraction to his art, was constantly being disrupted by the whims of others. Once again he was being placed in a very uncomfortable position through no fault of his own, except kindness and good manners. But whose fault *was* it?

Well, if Winifred – for some reason or other that he couldn't fathom – hadn't stopped coming to the studio he wouldn't have been looking for company around the cocktail hour. Then he would never have got so chummy with Margrave in the first place. And he probably wouldn't have tumbled Eleanor Zeffler on the couch, either. *Oh, damn it all to hell.*

▮ Chapter Nine

EVEN AFTER what had happened at the Park Plaza, Eleanor continued to think about Tom. She knew she ought to stop. Nearly a week had gone by without any word from him – no apology or explanation – so it was becoming difficult to sustain the necessary belief that he passionately desired her. And yet it was even harder to give up on him. Amid the drab, monotone details of her existence – now that she had discovered just how meaningless her life really was – he alone seemed bright and distinct, and only the thought of him brought joy.

Well, that wasn't completely true. She did experience some fleeting moments of happiness. She was awfully proud of Rebecca; in fact, she had told herself so often that her daughter was the best thing to come out of her marriage that the thought had become a kind of mantra. But Becky didn't really need her any more. She had even begun to respond to her mother's helpful hints on fashion and deportment with sullen silence or hurtful remarks.

Ever since her own pampered adolescence, Eleanor had found reliable refuge from despair in Creed's, Holt's, Ira-Berg and the St. Regis Room. There had been a brief hiatus after Becky was born, but once the very mixed pleasures of early motherhood had passed and her clothes were safe from drool and sticky fingers, she began to shop seriously again. And no matter how many outfits she bought, or how many others were hanging in her closets, every new purchase brought at least a temporary sense of renewed possibility.

Hoping to raise her spirits a little, she had made the rounds that afternoon, but startled the salesgirls by leaving every store she visited without buying anything. In front of the flattering mirrors in the large, well-lit dressing rooms, she had felt no elation. Instead, she found herself wondering how Tom would react to the clothes she was trying on. Would he find them alluring, or would she just look out of place in his world – too rich, too fashionable, too superficial and materialistic?

The trouble was, she didn't even know what sort of woman Tom found attractive. According to the discreet research she had conducted, he was faithful to his dowdy wife – at least if you discounted some mild speculation about his relationship with an elderly Junior League type who painted. On the way home from the O'Hara opening, Jerry had only shrugged, then sighed, in response to her attempts to find out what he might know. She wasn't sure whether he was scoffing at the very suggestion of Tom's fooling around, or at the dogged triviality of her mind, which was always more interested in prurient gossip than great art.

Eleanor had never paid any attention to Tom's wife, but she was certainly more Ada MacKenzie than Ira-Berg, more Maidenform full-support than Lejaby underwire. However, the appearance of a man's wife, the mother of his child (a grown-up daughter) was probably irrelevant when calculating the odds of his availability. If Tom were to undertake an adulterous liaison, surely he'd look for an entirely different sort of woman. Or, on the other hand, would he perversely seek out the familiar? Eleanor realized that she didn't have the faintest idea.

She had just come home empty-handed from the shops and was in the kitchen making herself a cup of tea when the phone rang. It was Jerry.

'Hi, doll.' His voice was friendlier and less peremptory than usual. He had returned from Montreal a couple of days before, but was too preoccupied by the case he was working on, which was going badly, to be very angry about the mix-up with the O'Hara paintings. He'd said only that he'd get after Gonzaga as soon as he had time and straighten it out. 'Guess who's coming by for drinks tonight?' he went on, sounding positively happy now. 'I invited them to dinner, but they couldn't make it.'

Thank God for that, she thought, but said only, 'Okay, who?'

'Well, first of all, Quintin Margrave.' After a moment of silence on her end, he added with a trace of his customary impatience, 'The curator from the Spitalfields, in London. He's putting together that big show here, remember, and it's going on to England afterwards? And get this – he's interested in our O'Hara. Can't wait to see it. So I suggested he drop by tonight, about sixish.'

'All right.'

'I told him about our early Dale, too. Tom's going to be in both shows, and the two of them seem to have become quite palsy.'

'Oh?'

'Yeah – so Quintin's bringing Tom with him. I'll be home by five-thirty. Get some hors d'oeuvres from the Vieux Paris. And wear something nice.'

They both hung up without another word. As soon as she had replaced the receiver securely in its cradle, Eleanor let out a shriek. According to the clock on the stove, it was already after three. She called the caterer and told him to send over the usual. Then she dashed out of the kitchen to the hall mirror and, after pausing there for a moment, ran up the stairs to the second floor.

DESPITE the natural enjoyment he derived from thwarting a man like Jerry Zeffler, Bruno did not really look forward to meeting him face to face. He had settled on the word 'misunderstanding' to explain what had happened with *Back Flip*. The truth was, he had never promised the painting to Zeffler. Since Jerry had telephoned that morning to say he wanted to talk to him, Bruno had again gone over in his mind what had been said at the O'Hara opening. He was satisfied that he had not slipped up. Every word he had uttered had been completely ambiguous. And so, armed with the knowledge that the object Zeffler desired was safely hidden in the basement, only a few feet below the spot where he was now working, Bruno felt quite capable of dealing with him.

Still, when he heard Zeffler's voice coming from the front of the gallery, he experienced a twinge of doubt. The man was one of the few adventurous collectors in the city; someone who, as well as being a reliable client himself, might influence others to buy. Until Bruno was in a position to deal exclusively with institutions, he needed a least a few private customers.

Quietly, he moved closer to the door between the workshop and the alcove. The tone of Zeffler's conversation with Jane was calm. It was friendly. She even laughed at some remark he made. Next came the sound of approaching footsteps. Then, from the doorway, Jane said, 'Mr Zeffler is here to see you.'

He took his time wiping his hands on a rag, which he then tossed on the work table behind him, but he didn't take off his varnish-stained apron. Zeffler might be more malleable if he felt comfortably superior, dealing with a humble artisan. Then, after pausing for a moment to take a deep breath, he stepped into the alcove, where Jerry was waiting.

'How are you?' he said, holding out his hand.

'Well, Bruno, very well.'

With some surprise, Bruno took in his visitor's buoyant mood. He waved Zeffler into a chair. 'You want coffee?'

'No! But thanks anyway.'

Bruno sat down, pulled out his cigarettes and offered one to Zeffler, who shook his head. He lit one for himself, took a puff and then slowly exhaled. With an innocent expression he asked, 'How you like your painting?'

'Great! Just great. We haven't decided where to hang it yet. At least permanently. We did some shifting around and we have it in the dining room for now. I moved the Willard – you know, *Earth to Earth*, the brown one – to the back vestibule. But I'm keeping *Bay Blues* – an early but important Dale I picked up a few years ago – in the living room.'

Bruno nodded sagely. He refrained from pointing out that since he had never been invited to the Zefflers' house, their hanging arrangements meant nothing to him. And it was time to broach the subject of *Back Flip*, before Zeffler could bring it up himself.

'About that other piece ...'

'You mean the smaller one you were pushing?' Zeffler smiled indulgently. 'What was it called?'

'*Back Flip.*'

'Oh, yeah. I –'

'It was sold.' The words had rushed out unconvincingly, but he forced himself to look Zeffler right in the eye. 'To another collector. Anonymous.' Jerry was still smiling, but instead of relief, Bruno felt apprehension.

'I'm glad to hear that. It's a fine piece. I almost bought it myself. But you know, Bruno, *Tusk* is really the stand-out from the show. I know now that I made the right decision, taking it instead of the one you thought I should buy. I've got an eye, you see, and it hasn't failed me yet.'

So Zeffler wasn't going to complain. He was proud of himself and his 'eye'. But *Flip* was the better piece, Bruno was still sure of that. God help him if he couldn't trust his own eye. So everyone was happy. Nevertheless, there was something unnerving about Zeffler's high spirits. Now he was actually leaning forward in his seat with an unpleasantly triumphant expression.

'And guess what?' he demanded.

Bruno waited for him to continue but said nothing.

'Quintin Margrave wants *Tusk* for the Artquake exhibition! Here and in London. Tom Dale, no less, told him I'd bought the best piece from O'Hara's show. He's coming over tonight to see it. Tom will make the introductions. By the way, did I mention that I have an important early Dale? He and Margrave are dropping by the house tonight for drinks.'

So that was why Zeffler was so full of himself, why he had so quickly changed his mind about *Flip*. He was picturing the words 'Collection of Mr and Mrs Jerome Zeffler, Toronto, Canada' in a catalogue put out by the prestigious Spitalfields Gallery of London, England.

'Well. That's great.' Bruno felt his smile was fairly convincing. And it *was* good news that at least one of the artists in his stable would be represented in the London show. 'Great,' he repeated more loudly, as if he really meant it.

MARGRAVE HAD SAID he'd pick him up at the studio in a taxi about six-thirty. From there they were to go together to the Zefflers'. So when Tom heard the knock at the door, he knew who it was. He didn't risk going to the peephole to make sure but stayed stretched out on the sofa. He looked longingly at the half-empty glass sitting on the floor beside him, but he couldn't risk making a sound.

The first tentative tap was followed by a series of firmer knocks that finally turned to pounding when there was still no answer from within. Tom willed himself to remain silent and motionless. From where he was he could see that the deadbolt was on. Given the high prices Dales were fetching these days, Max had finally talked him into getting a decent lock installed.

Not that Quintin was likely to break down the door. He was too scrawny, for one thing; also much too polite. Maybe there was some truth to the rumours floating around that he was a fairy. With Englishmen it was hard to tell. The most limp-wristed ones sometimes turned out to be formidable ladies' men.

Of course, whatever Margrave was didn't make one iota of difference to Tom. He was broad-minded; hell, he'd have to be, after all these years in the art game. Live and let live had always been his credo. Still, the thought that Quintin might have a more than comradely affection for him was unnerving, and strengthened his growing inclination to avoid the guy. And there was another thing: when he'd repeated that clever observation of Quintin's about music to Joan, she'd hooted. Then she'd said, in a tone that hinted he ought to have known as much, that it was a direct quotation from Noel Coward – *Private Lives,* she thought.

Tom's eyes moved from the bolted door to the big half-finished canvas hanging on the wall opposite the sofa. It was coming along nicely; he might have finished it today, if the visit to the Zefflers' hadn't been weighing on his mind. Damn Margrave for roping him into it. Well, at least he'd be returning to London in a few weeks, right after the opening of the Toronto Artquake show. In the meantime, Tom decided, he'd simply have to keep lying low.

On the other side of the door, Margrave said, 'Bloody hell.'

Tom closed his eyes and turned his thoughts resolutely to art. By the time he finally heard Margrave's footsteps retreating along the hall and down the stairs, he had just about made up his mind that tomorrow, in the far left corner of the canvas, he would lay down a nice big chunky wedge of ochre, to nudge the broad veil of greyish green falling from the upper edge.

Once all was quiet, he opened his eyes and peered at his watch. It was starting to get dark now, but the Roman numerals on its old familiar face were luminous, glowing pale green in the dusk. When the spindly second hand had made five complete revolutions, he reached for the glass on the floor and drained it. Then he got up, slipped into his old Harris tweed jacket and – without turning on any lights – left the studio, making sure to lock the door behind him.

AFTER NEARLY an hour in front of the full-length mirror, Eleanor decided on the very short black suede skirt she had bought a couple of weeks before at Harridge's. She knew she had the legs for it but, assailed by new, unfamiliar doubts, had wondered if she was getting too old to display them so brazenly. Eventually she had succumbed to the salesgirl's insistence that you didn't have to be sixteen to wear it, not at all.

Anyway, now there was no time for hesitation; the suede skirt was it. With diamond-patterned grey tights, suede Mary Janes with Louis heels, a silver chain belt draped around her hips and a grey silk blouse with a ruffled collar and great number of small buttons with loops, the top five or six of them left undone. That blouse, luxurious and vaguely Edwardian, would bridge any style gap between sixteen and forty-two.

Sitting at her dressing table, she put on, and then took off, her pearls. They were too traditional, too ... *motherly*. In fact, Jerry had presented them to her on the day of Becky's birth. After taking one more tiny sip of her vodka and tonic, she started to dig around in her jewel box. Finally she pulled out a pair of earrings, simple rectangles of translucent blue stone that dangled almost to her shoulders and picked up the colour of her eyes.

In the bathroom, she applied powder, blusher, silvery eyeshadow, black liner, false lashes – no, too insincere – black Fabulash, Softshell

Pink lipstick, blotted, then reapplied. The heavy base of the vodka glass clanked on the sink. Her hair was clean, washed that morning, thank God, and thank Him again that she had hair that behaved. Drawing a strand of it down across her cheek so that it pointed to her perfectly painted mouth, she made a moue and then bared her teeth at her reflection. Throwing her head back, she mimed a spontaneous, carefree laugh, observing the effect out of the corner of her eye. Then she tried it again, this time smiling mysteriously and keeping her chin flirtatiously low.

Her lips moved silently. '*So nice to see you again....*' No. Avoid the word 'again'. She splashed Sortilège on her neck and temples. Not behind the ears, the old-fashioned way – there was too much oil or sweat or something there – apply to the pulse points.

'*Hello, Tom. How have you been?*' No. Why would I care how he's been?

She saturated a cotton ball with perfume and shoved it down into her bra, between her breasts. The vodka glass clanked again. She looked herself squarely in the eye.

'*Hel-lo-o-o ...*' Slowly, imbuing the single word with infinite meaning without revealing too much, her eyes speaking silent volumes ...

In the mirror, she saw her daughter standing in the doorway.

'Yes, sweetie?'

Becky seemed to recoil from the endearment. 'Are you going out tonight?'

'No, some people are coming for drinks.'

Becky groaned. There was that sullen expression again. 'Does that mean I have to appear?'

Eleanor's eyes moved back to her own reflection. 'Only if you want to.'

'Who's coming?'

'Oh, Quintin Margrave, a curator from England. And ... Tom Dale, the artist. He's the one who did the little painting over the fireplace ... he's quite well known actually ...'

'M-u-u-m, I *know* who Tom Dale is.'

'You do?'

'Sure. He's English Canada's first truly great modern painter.'

Eleanor turned and looked closely at her daughter.

'That guy who writes the art reviews? You know, he's sort of creepy? He was here with Dad one night. He told me all about *Bay Blues* and

Tom Dale when Dad was down in the cellar getting some wine. I remember because just as he said that about him being the first truly great, he put his hand on my ...'

Eleanor took a deep breath. 'He put his –'

At that moment Jerry's voice boomed up from the front hall. 'Hey, where are those gorgeous Zeffler girls? I've brought some Krug up and I need an ice bucket right away. Our guests will be here any minute!'

TOM GOT HOME about a quarter after seven. Joan had dinner ready, and they were just about to sit down when the phone rang. He left her putting the food on the table and went into the hall to answer it.

'Tom? Margrave here. What happened?'

'Quintin? Where the hell are *you*?'

'At the Zefflers'. I came to the studio at six-thirty, as we arranged, but you weren't there. Did we get our wires crossed?'

'Looks like it. You were supposed to pick me up here.'

'Surely not. I distinctly –'

'Nope. I came home early and I've been sitting here all along, wondering where the hell you were. If I'd known you weren't coming I'd have stayed and got some work done.'

'Damn and blast. What a balls-up.'

Tom noticed that despite his best efforts to make Margrave take the blame, he wasn't falling for it. He was a tougher cookie than his languid manner suggested. Some of his sort were. 'Well, never mind. You found your way there all right, I take it?'

'Yes, no problem, but why don't you come over and join us? Jerry's opened some champers in our honour, it appears, and it's all rather jolly.'

Jolly? Tom frankly doubted it. 'Oh, I don't think so, Quintin. I'm feeling a little under the weather, anyway. Touch of flu. Think I'll have an early night. By the time I got there you'd be ready to leave, anyhow.'

'You're quite sure?' Margrave's voice was plaintive. 'Sorry about the mix-up.'

Now that he'd got his completely undeserved apology, Tom felt mischievous. 'Oh, you'll have fun, don't worry. Champagne Jerry isn't such a bad guy, you know. And have you noticed that Mrs Z is quite attractive? A regular stunner, I suppose you limeys would say.'

Margrave made a sound like an amused cough. 'Since you mention it, yes, I had noticed, and she is, rather. Bye for now.'

'Bye.' Tom hung up, smiling, and went back to the dining room, where he tucked into Joan's chicken divan with gusto. That made her glance fondly at him. It had always been his favourite dish, from the earliest days of their marriage.

ELEANOR hovered, rearranging the almond-stuffed olives and the Twiglets that she had laid out ten minutes earlier in a divided glass dish. Tom wasn't coming, that was clear. This – eavesdropping on Quintin Margrave's telephone conversation with him – might be the closest she would ever get to him now.

The two men were on a first-name basis, apparently. But Tom was obviously resisting Margrave's suggestion that he join them. However, the mix-up about where they were to meet sounded genuine. Probably. And it had been Margrave's fault, because she heard him apologize. Then he made a strange noise, as if he were chuckling and clearing his throat at the same time. She glanced surreptitiously at him.

'Since you mention it ...' he said, his face getting a little red, '... yes, I had noticed, and she is, rather.'

She ... is ... rather.

Eleanor's brain, dulled by anxiety and vodka, laboriously processed each individual word and slowly arrived at an inescapable conclusion. Personal pronoun, feminine, present tense of the verb 'to be'. Becky was hiding out in her room. So there was only one female person presently, personally present. *She. Her. Me. I. Eleanor.*

'Bye for now.'

As Margrave hung up the kitchen extension, she gave him the sultry, meaningful smile she had prepared for Tom. And then remembered with a sickening lurch that this was not the first time they had been in the same room.

But either he did not recall seeing her at the Plaza Roof or had guessed that it would be unwise to mention it. He looked slightly less odd now than he had that afternoon. In fact, he was rather attractive in a repulsive kind of way. When she'd hung up his coat, a worn but genuine Burberry – she checked the label – it smelled intriguingly like French cigarettes.

Since you mention it ...

Briskly, she picked up the glass dish and led him back into the living room, where Jerry was opening the champagne.

'Let's drink to Art,' he said, pouring the first glass with a flourish. In the early days of their marriage, Eleanor had admired her husband's sense of occasion, but now it seemed tiresome and self-aggrandizing. Why did he always have to make such a big production out of everything?

'Well, this is a quite unexpected pleasure ...' Margrave said as they all watched the bubbles rise rapidly to the rim of the crystal goblet and then gradually subside.

Jerry filled the second glass for Eleanor and the third for himself. 'Art!' he said. Margrave and Eleanor merely raised their glasses.

I had noticed...

Noticed what?

After everyone had taken a sip of champagne, Jerry asked, 'And what about our friend Tom? Is he coming?'

'Alas, it appears he has a touch of the flu.'

'That's too bad. I thought he might enjoy seeing that painting over there again. See it, above the mantel? I picked it up at auction not long ago. Done in 1947. It was tucked away in a private home – little old lady, widow of an old-school collector – for years.'

'Oh, yes? Let's have a closer look. Yes, yes, quite fascinating, really.'

'There are definite foreshadowings of his current work, don't you think?' Jerry said. 'For that reason alone it's quite an important little piece, I've been told.'

She is, rather.

Rather what?

'Mmm.' Margrave drank the last of his champagne. 'Nice passage there on the lower left,' he said, gesturing at the painting with the empty glass.

Jerry stepped forward at once to refill it. Then he looked meaning-fully at Eleanor. When she stared blankly at him, he said, 'How about some nibblies?'

She went quickly back to the kitchen. The hors d'oeuvres had been delivered at five o'clock. Henri, owner of the Vieux Paris, tolerated the short notice because the Zefflers were good customers. Now the smoked salmon canapés were sitting on a silver platter in the refrigerator, each glistening red oval decorated with a little sprig of dill. All she had to do was carry them in. Surely she could manage that.

Since – you – mention – it – yes – I – did – notice – and – she – is – rather.

When she returned with the platter, the living room was empty.

She heard the men's voices coming from the dining room.

'An ambitious piece, certainly,' Margrave said.

'The three parts really work together as a whole, don't you think? Everybody's doing modules and multiples these days.'

'Urh. Though the triptych, as a form, has quite a venerable history. But this – *Tusk* – is it the only O'Hara you've acquired thus far? Just the one?'

'Yeah, and I almost had to tear it away from Gonzaga by force, you know.'

'You don't say. Unusual fellow. I met him briefly the other day.'

'Weird, actually, but don't underestimate him. I'm closer to him than most people, because I picked up the good vibes on the gallery right from the start. Got in on the ground floor with a nice little O'Hara drawing – it's in my office and I get a lot of comments on it – and some Bontemps multiples for my daughter's room. Bruno and I understand each other. I know how to handle him and he knows how to pick 'em; I'll give him that. Take O'Hara ... he'll be one of the great ones, mark my words, Quintin. I'm talking Stella, Rothko, Noland – you know, the biggies. Smart, articulate, too.'

'Seems a bright lad, yes.'

'So you've met him?'

'As it happens, I visited his studio just the other day with our friend Dale.'

The name yanked Eleanor out of her torpor and into the dining room, carrying the tray of canapés.

'Well, here comes some food at last,' said Jerry pointedly. 'Quintin, I think you'll find that our Canadian salmon stands up quite well against the Scottish stuff. Try some. Meanwhile, I'll get us some more bubbly. I prefer the Krug. But our government doesn't allow us to have it.' He paused, enjoying Margrave's puzzled expression. 'Only the province is allowed to sell alcohol in Ontario, you see. And only a small selection. In some ways we're still quite backward here. So I go to Century Wines in Rochester – just across the border, in the States. You'll have another glass, won't you?'

'With pleasure.'

'Good. I'll be right back.'

Eleanor held out the platter and Margrave's hand hovered for a moment over it. He seemed to be deciding which canapé was the most compositionally pleasing, which minuscule frond of dill had been placed most artfully against its salmon background. When at last he made his selection and his lips closed around the delicate, rippled, dark red flesh, his eyes met Eleanor's. He chewed and swallowed with deliberate slowness. Then, speaking so quietly that she only just made out the words, he said, 'Yes, I *had* noticed that Mrs Zeffler was rather a stunner.'

And there they stood like a couple of statues, looking into each other's eyes, neither of them saying another word, until Jerry came hurrying back with two more bottles of his Rochester Krug.

▪ Chapter Ten

SLOWLY but relentlessly, the door buzzer penetrated Eddie's brain. As he reached consciousness he also became aware of the hardness of the floor beneath the thin slab of polyethurene foam, especially at the pressure points, where in the course of the night his shoulder and hip bones had burrowed nearly through to the linoleum. There was a faint smell of stale beer in the room, and when he rolled over, his elbow hit an empty and sent it clattering, then spinning, across the floor. *Shit.*

He opened one eye and looked around for the Westclox he had buried under a pile of clothes the night before in a vain attempt to muffle its thundering tick. By stretching out one leg he was able to kick the clothing aside, but the clock, though still clacking away, was face down. He tried and failed to turn it over with his toes, then sat up with a mighty groan and crawled towards it, his eyes half open now. A quarter to eleven. Who the hell would be at his door at this ungodly hour of the morning?

He decided to stay put. It was probably Mr Swartz, complaining about noise again, or – wait a minute, it was Friday, but what was the date? – looking for the rent. He pulled the tangle of bedclothes up to his neck and buried his face in his lumpy, stale-smelling pillow. Finally, after a few minutes, there was silence. Groaning, he got up and staggered to the bathroom to relieve his bladder.

Afterwards, he strolled naked into the front room and out of curiosity went to the bay window. From the sidewalk below a tall man in a long, tightly belted raincoat was looking up at him. The second after Eddie had jumped back out of sight, he realized that the guy down on the street was Quintin Margrave.

He dashed into the bedroom and grabbed his jeans, hopping and swearing frantically as he put them on. By the time he got to the street door, barefoot and shirtless, still buttoning his fly, Margrave was half a block away. As Eddie started to sprint after him, the cool autumn air hit his bare chest like a bucket of cold water, but he kept going.

When he got close enough he stage-whispered, 'Hey there,' having remembered at the last moment they hadn't ever got on first-name terms.

Margrave turned around. 'Good Lord!'

'Were you looking for me?' Eddie asked.

'In point of fact, I was.'

Eddie's teeth were chattering now, so he only jerked his head in the direction of the studio. Together, they ran back to the open door and up the stairs.

Once Eddie had got Margrave settled on the wooden chair in the front room, he slipped into the bedroom and rummaged on the floor for a shirt. Then he brought another chair for himself from the kitchen, stopping to put the kettle on.

Margrave was lighting a Gitane when he returned, looking at the paintings from the grey series that were on the walls.

'I'm making coffee,' Eddie said, 'but it's only instant.'

'That's all right. Have a fag?'

Eddie took one. He couldn't figure out why Margrave had deigned to enter his humble quarters without escort or advance notice. However, the best course of action would likely be to say as little as possible and let him reveal his purpose when he was ready.

'Sorry to appear at your door so unexpectedly,' Margrave finally said. 'I'd hoped to get your number – you do have a phone, I suppose?' Eddie nodded. 'Yes, well, I had hoped to get your number from Tom Dale this morning and give a you a ring first, but he doesn't seem to be at his studio today, or at home. So I thought I'd just chance it and drop in.'

'No problem.' It seemed highly unlikely that Tom Dale would have had his telephone number to hand, but Eddie let it pass. If Margrave believed he and Tom were buddies, so much the better.

'And I didn't want to ruffle feathers at the Gonzaga.'

'Yeah. Bruno can be a little paranoid. He thinks everybody is selling out of their studios.' He grinned. 'But since they all *are,* maybe *paranoid* isn't really the right word.'

Margrave chuckled in a friendly enough way.

Keep cool, Eddie reminded himself.

In the kitchen, the kettle let out a preliminary squeak and then started to wail in earnest, building to a screeching crescendo that could not be ignored. Eddie excused himself and came back in a few minutes with two mugs full of a hot, dark liquid that smelled slightly like coffee.

Margrave took a sip of his without showing either pleasure or distaste. For what seemed like hours to Eddie, he continued to look around the room without saying anything. Then, finally, he spoke.

'I like your work. But the thing is, I visited the Zefflers last evening and it seems they don't have your *Back Flip*. It's another, three-part piece they have – *Tusk*. It's a lovely thing, too, but I really prefer *Flip*, at least what I've seen of it. At this point, I couldn't possibly fit as large a piece as *Tusk* into either of the shows, in any case. I've already gone rather overboard.'

He smiled as if to say *I've been a naughty boy* and puffed on his Gitane. Then he went on, 'I very much want a picture of yours in both exhibitions, but I feel it must be *Flip*. It would be a marvellous addition to the group I've already selected. I want it in both shows, certainly. But there is a slight difficulty. Without knowing who owns it ...'

The surge of elation that rushed through Eddie when he realized that he was as good as in the Artquake shows, here and in London, was so powerful that he almost laughed aloud. It blew the top off his head like a monster hit of primo weed, and he knew he was grinning at Margrave like a stoned, lovesick fool. Forget the rumours that were still floating around about the guy. Right then Eddie felt like throwing his arms around him, queer or no queer, out of sheer gratitude and pure, undiluted, straight-from-the-tube joy.

THE BED was in a shallow alcove, surrounded on three sides by just slightly dingy wallpaper in a beige-and-cream Regency-stripe pattern. Lying on it, Eleanor felt as if she were in a train compartment, or perhaps a ship's cabin. Not that the room's decor could have been described as either streamlined or shipshape. The small, chintz-covered armchair over which her clothing was draped was faded on the side that faced the window. On the light brown wall-to-wall carpet, old enough to be pure wool, the room's innumerable previous occupants had worn a path from door to bed to bathroom. Framed prints hung here and there on the walls. Some had obviously been clipped from magazines a couple of decades ago, but a few were real, if foxed and buckling, nineteenth-century engravings.

Quintin said the Windsor Arms reminded him of the sort of small, genteel hotels to be found in London. The Wilbraham for instance, where, he added casually, he ran into Cyril Connolly once in a way. Eleanor had no idea who this Connolly person was, but nodded as if she did. Nearly everything Margrave said and did impressed her to the point of near terror. No, perhaps 'impressed' was not the right word. Amazed, confused, disoriented? Yes. But she was also, to be honest, a little frightened. She had not fallen for Quintin as she had for Tom. In fact, she found his pale horsy face, shaggy hair and large, yellowy-grey teeth very nearly repulsive. Yet beneath and between all these conflicting emotions trickled a perverse, slightly sickening excitement.

The agitated misery that followed the Park Plaza Incident (as she now thought of it) had left Eleanor ready for anything. Finally she had had to face reality: Tom had made no effort to contact her and might actually be trying to avoid her. He had even ducked Jerry's invitation to drinks at their house. It seemed that she had been definitively brushed off. But instead of being chastened by Tom's rejection, she felt even more reckless than before. She had made a complete fool of herself, so why not go for broke? The brief, violent storm of longing that Tom had inspired made her life with Jerry seem more intolerable than ever.

In a peculiar way, Quintin's lack of physical allure and his oddly detached yet recognizably prurient manner were quite magnetic. Besides, he would be leaving town, maybe forever, in a matter of weeks. And perhaps doing something completely insane with a man she knew to be Tom's friend would blunt the jagged edges of her humiliation. Tom might even find out about it and be jealous.

So when Margrave telephoned the day after his visit to the Zefflers', she had immediately accepted his invitation to afternoon tea. They arranged to meet in the Windsor Arms's cosy parlour on the following Friday afternoon. There, sitting side by side on a velvet-covered love seat, they were served tiny sandwiches and pastries by a woman dressed in a black-and-white maid's uniform.

'Will you be mother?' said Quintin to Eleanor after the waitress had placed the teapot and strainer on their small round table. She wondered if he was assigning her a role in some Oedipal pantomime to be enacted later, upstairs. But then he had held out his cup to be filled and said a little peevishly, 'I believe this is the only decent tea to be found in the entire city.'

'Yes,' said Eleanor, 'a real English high tea!'

That made him laugh, not particularly indulgently. 'But, alas, not a single kipper,' he muttered, and she didn't have the nerve to ask him what *that* meant.

Eleanor was too nervous to eat much, but Quintin certainly had a healthy appetite. He ate nearly all the sandwiches. Then, after he had finished off the last miniature éclair and wiped his lips delicately with his snow-white napkin, he said, 'Shall we go up?'

'All right.' She was thankful then for the Valium she had taken just before leaving home.

Once they were in the room, she had expected the kind of hungry, feverish grappling – buttons popping, end tables toppling – that went naturally with forbidden lust. But Quintin only stroked her hair gently and calmly suggested that she undress. When she was naked, he contemplated her for a moment, very much as she had seen him look at *Bay Blues* and *Tusk*. Then he took her hand and led her over to the bed.

He never removed his own clothes, except for his suit jacket, which he hung carefully in the closet. She thought of that famous French painting by Monet or Manet (she could never remember which) – the picnic scene where the women were nude and the men dressed. However, afraid of blundering again – why had her remark about high tea had been wrong, exactly? – she decided not to mention it.

But now he was touching her in ways and places that were undeniably pleasurable. And becoming more so every moment. From her vantage point, she couldn't see whether there was a reciprocal bulge in his trousers. Surely there had to be.

Should she tell him that she was on the Pill? Dr Meredith had agreed to prescribe it, despite her supposed infertility. If she *were* to become pregnant unexpectedly, he'd said with a commiserating smile, she was far too old now to have another healthy child – remember those poor little Thalidomide tots. From the doctor's expression she'd also understood that, even if she did somehow manage to bring forth a normal infant, it would be quite unseemly of her to procreate at the advanced age of forty-two.

But mentioning procreation to Quintin might turn out to be yet another faux pas. And he seemed quite content simply to recline between her parted legs. For a moment it almost seemed she was back in Dr Meredith's stirrups. Yet this was so very, very different. She felt a distant tremor begin. At that very moment Quintin paused and raised himself on one elbow.

'Having fun, darling?' he asked.

Eleanor, dragged unwillingly back to reality, only nodded, lifting her head feebly. It would be foolish to deny it, with the evidence on his fingers. As if from a distance, she toyed with the idea of getting up and leaving. And then, in a gesture that she found oddly tender, Quintin laid his cheek against her thigh and began to stroke her again.

'You are lovely,' he said after a while. 'A pity your husband doesn't appreciate you.'

'Hah-hummm ...' she replied, focusing with difficulty on these true but unwelcome words.

There was another interval of quiet, broken only by Eleanor's occasional murmurs. Then Quintin's hand began to move more rhythmically and insistently as he whispered, 'I saw at once that you aren't happy together.'

She felt a far-off, half-hearted urge to defend herself and Jerry. But why did she have to be reminded of him now? She grunted noncommittally.

'Well, if you were, you wouldn't be here, would you, darling?'

Her head rolled impatiently from side to side. 'Uhhmmm.'

'Quite. And this is doing you a world of good, isn't it? You've been needing it dreadfully, haven't you? Absolutely longing for it!'

'Aahh!' Struggling, twitching, Eleanor felt a surge of anger, whether at Quintin's smug, plummy, superior voice or at the thought of Jerry, she didn't know.

And oh, Tom ... Tom ... oh darling. Ooohhh ...

Then the anger turned to nearly unbearable sadness, and she felt tears trickle from her half-closed eyes. She seemed to hear herself groan. And then, irresistibly, she shot up into space and dangled there for a moment, triumphantly free of Jerry, Quintin, Tom and even herself.

THEORETICALLY, Jane was not allowed to read novels during working hours. However, she didn't believe Bruno really cared very much how she spent her time, once her work was done. He was only interested in preserving the *bella figura* appropriate to his position as employer and impresario. So she continued to read novels and write letters, usually concealing her book or notepaper inside approved reading matter such as *Studio International* or *Artforum.* But she kept her top drawer slightly open so she could slip illicit materials into it when she heard Bruno coming.

Nowadays, she had Saturdays off instead of Mondays. Bruno represented the change as a kindly gesture on his part. But Jane knew him well enough now to suspect that he didn't like sharing the limelight with his assistant on the gallery's busiest day and evidently considered that her station near the door conferred an unfair advantage. She had got to know many of the regulars and often chatted with them during their Saturday art promenades. So Bruno had put a stop to that.

To Jane, working Mondays meant only that she had another largely uneventful day to fill. On weekdays, once the dusting and sweeping were done and she had laboriously pecked out a few letters on the typewriter, her only remaining duty was to answer the phone. But it still rang very rarely. So on Friday afternoon, when Eddie O'Hara bounded through the door, she was happy to see him. After hastily marking her place with an emery board, she put her book away in the drawer. But Eddie only paused for a moment to ask, 'Is he back there?' She just had time to nod, and he was gone.

'Hey,' she heard him call out as he reached the workshop, 'want to hear some good news for a change?'

Bruno's reply was inaudible, but after a few minutes he called out to Jane, asking her to bring the sales ledger. This was a black binder containing loose-leaf pages on which she typed as neatly as she could the titles, prices and purchasers of each work of art sold by the Gonzaga Gallery. So far, there were very few pages in it, even though the entries were widely spaced.

She handed it to Bruno, and he opened it with a flourish. When he found the page he wanted, he shoved the open binder across the table to Eddie. 'There it is,' he said.

'*Back Flip*, by Edward O'Hara, three hundred and fifty dollars,' Eddie read aloud. 'Sold to ... Anonymous.' He turned and grinned affably at Jane. 'Okay, anonymous who?'

'The collector did not want his name known,' said Bruno. His expression was bland, but Jane noticed that he wasn't meeting Eddie's eye.

'I know what the word means. But who was it? Who bought it? I *painted* the thing. I should be able to find out who bought it.'

'I can't tell you.'

Eddie laughed uneasily. His eyes moved from Bruno to Jane and then back again. '*What?* Let's stop fooling around.'

'The collector made it a condition. He had to stay anonymous if he was going to buy the painting.'

'*Fuck* his conditions. Don't you get it? I have to find that painting. Margrave wants it for the Artquake shows. Whoever bought it has to lend it. And I've got to let him know right away that it's available. And when.'

Bruno shook his head. He seemed to be mastering strong and conflicting emotions.

Eddie stared at him.

Jane looked from one to the other, but both of them seemed to have forgotten that she was there.

Bruno shrugged. 'I can't help you,' he said. Then he got up and disappeared into the workshop.

For a second it seemed that Eddie would go after him. He reared forward in his chair, then fell back again and just sat there with a stunned look on his face. Finally he got up.

'You are really out of your fucking mind!' he yelled. 'Everybody told me you were a nutcase, and man, were they right!' He looked at Jane as though he was seeing her for the first time. 'And I never got the money for it, either, so I guess that makes him a thief, too, doesn't it?' he said loudly enough to carry to the far reaches of the workshop. Then he turned and started to stalk through the gallery.

Jane picked up the sales book and trailed silently behind him.

They were about halfway to the door when Bruno came barrelling after them. 'Hey!' he bellowed. 'You want your money?'

Jane and Eddie turned around just in time to see him reach into his pants pocket and pull out a thick roll of bills. With deliberate slowness he peeled off two fifties, five twenties and a ten and tossed them one by one into the air. As they fluttered jerkily to the ground he roared, 'Take it and get out!'

Eddie's reflexes were faster than Jane expected. His arm shot out and caught the ten in midair, and he scooped up the other bills as soon as they hit the floor. Carefully, he smoothed and folded them and stuffed them into the back pocket of his jeans. Then he walked quite slowly to the door, yanked it open and went out onto the street.

Bruno muttered something inaudible. Perhaps his lips were only twitching. His face was slick with sweat, and he was breathing heavily. He glanced around the gallery as if he wanted to make sure that its walls were still standing. 'Son of a bitch bastard,' he said, clearly enough this time for Jane to hear each syllable, though he avoided looking at her. Without another word, he turned away and began to walk slowly towards the workshop. As he rounded the central partition, he lurched slightly.

Jane sat down at her desk and stared straight ahead for a moment. There was nothing but silence in the empty gallery, so she opened her book and started to read.

NOW, THAT was amazing, Eddie thought as he quickly put as much distance as he could between himself and the Gonzaga. Even in the heat of anger, supposedly gripped by Vesuvial emotion and outraged honour, Bruno had still been able to calculate his commission to the dollar. Forty per cent of three hundred and fifty came to … let's see, three and a half times forty … one hundred and forty. That left … two hundred and ten dollars for the artist.

When the traffic lights at the corner forced him to pause, Eddie eased the folded bills out of his jeans pocket. Yep, it added up. Back at the gallery, he'd only made a show of counting the money, just to make it clear that he was cool, calm and collected. And now that he actually was starting to simmer down, he realized there had always been something weird going on with *Back Flip*. On the night before his show opened, it had seemed a foregone conclusion that the Zefflers were going to buy it. And, at the opening itself, there had definitely been a red sticker on it. He remembered making a last, triumphal circuit of the show, counting red and blue dots, his elation only marginally dampened by the sight of Daisy leaving with Barnaby Keeler.

After the show closed, and Eddie pointedly mentioned his need for cash, Bruno muttered vaguely about customers being slow to pay. But he'd agreed to give him a couple of hundred on account. At the time, that had seemed like a lot, and all the more valuable because it was the first decent bread he had ever earned from doing something he actually wanted to do. Somehow it was worth more, dollar for dollar, than the money from any of the temporary, dead-end jobs he'd held down in the past in order to paint.

However, he was still broke. Now that he wasn't sharing with anyone and ate out most of the time, life was expensive. He was hungry right now, because there had been nothing to eat in the studio that morning, just enough instant coffee for the two cups he and Quintin Margrave had left unfinished. Whatever fantasies Eddie might entertain about quitting his job at the art-supply store, he knew he couldn't do it yet. The stretchers for his new *Cloud* Series pieces had to be custom-made because of their unusual proportions. It seemed that any money you made from one exhibition was instantly devoured by the cost of materials for the next. And now he had to wonder when and if he'd even have another show, at least at the Gonzaga.

He hurried on, with no particular destination in mind, except maybe Murray's over at Avenue Road, where he could get something cheap to eat. It took him a moment to recognize the woman he'd just passed, a slender, well-dressed and good-looking blonde wearing big black sunglasses. When he turned to look again, she'd shoved them up on top of her head and was peering into the window of the Gold Shoppe. Then she glanced around as if she was afraid she was being followed.

Zeffler's wife. He couldn't think of her first name, but she'd been at the opening of his show. That night he'd registered the fact, more or less subliminally, that she was kind of a bitch. However, today Mrs Z's mouth looked a little less disapproving and sulky. It was softer, looser and ... what, exactly? There was something kind of spaced-out about her.

When he spoke to her, she looked blankly at him for a moment, with a touch of unfocused panic in her eyes. And before she got the sunglasses back in place, he noticed that her mascara was smudged. Then she seemed to recover and recognize him. 'Oh ... hello,' she said, with almost no enthusiasm, and he was pretty sure that behind the black lenses, her eyes were still darting around.

QUINTIN HAD SAID it would be best if she left the hotel alone. Just before he shut the door after her, he kissed her lightly on the cheek. That was the closest they had come to anything even vaguely normal. As she stepped off the creaking little elevator on the ground floor, Eleanor realized that her first adulterous assignation had turned out to be even stranger than she had expected. Satisfyingly strange, on the whole, though Quintin's rather condescending tone still rankled a bit. But she felt sure he had found her beautiful; at the very least, a superior object of aesthetic value. Anyway, she had not been counting on love. But the point was, had she committed adultery or not?

Preoccupied with that question, she almost didn't notice Howard McNab lurking near a row of mullioned windows. From there, he had a full view of the lobby and must have seen her emerge from the elevator. If she claimed to be coming from the tearoom or the bar, he'd know she was lying. He was right next to the double doors that led to the street and escape. She decided to pretend she hadn't seen him. Just as she reached the door, he spoke her name, but she looked straight ahead and kept on walking.

If she hadn't been afraid of turning to find him a step or two behind her, Eleanor would have stopped at Georg Jensen to browse. But she only glanced quickly into the display window as she hurried past the store and around the corner onto Bloor Street. Once she was out of sight of the Windsor Arms, she felt more at ease, and had paused at the Gold Shoppe's window to look at a heavy antique rope necklace, when she heard someone say, 'Mrs Zeffler'.

Edward O'Hara. Tall, redheaded, lanky. Not unattractive, she decided, somehow feeling that as an adulteress, or near adulteress, she should consider this. Or maybe it was only the lingering sensations in her body. Was this how men felt, walking around with a kind of sensor between their legs, ever alert to the slightest provocation? Perhaps it was just the Valium. But the way Eddie had addressed her reminded her he was only a kid. She slipped her sunglasses back on, thankful that at least it hadn't been McNab, following her.

'Oh ... hello.'

As he stood there, evidently searching for words, she glanced quickly back in the direction of the Windsor Arms.

'Um, Mrs Zeffler ...'

'Eleanor.'

'Eleanor, do you have a minute?'

'Not really.' She looked pointedly at her watch. 'I have to pick up my car at the lot on Yorkville.'

'Well, can I walk along with you?'

'All right, if you want to. Let's cross here.' She stepped off the curb and he reached out and grabbed her arm.

'Hey, don't get yourself killed, Eleanor.'

'Okay.' She tried, but failed, to suppress a giggle. Was there really something different about her now, something this boy could sense? She took his hand. 'Come on, let's make a run for it.'

They wove through the traffic, followed by honking horns, and reached the north side of the street slightly out of breath. At least, she was.

'I was wondering about that painting of mine,' Eddie said as soon as they were safely on the sidewalk. '*Back Flip*. Didn't Jerry buy it?'

'He wanted to.' Eleanor disengaged her hand from his without much difficulty. 'But I think Gonzaga talked him into buying a bigger one – that three-piece one with the red stripe. *Tusk*.'

Then she saw them, right across the street. Quintin and Howard McNab were strolling along, deep in conversation. She started walking rapidly towards Yonge, with Eddie still at her side.

'The thing is ...' he said. 'You know Quintin Margrave, the curator from the Spitalfields Gallery?'

Eleanor blessed her sunglasses again. From behind them, she searched Eddie's face for slyness, but his expression was innocent and he seemed too engrossed in what he was saying to have noticed the two men making their way slowly along the south side of the street.

'He was at my place this morning, and he wants to put *Back Flip* in the Artquake shows.'

Eleanor was nearly trotting now, but Eddie had no trouble keeping up.

'Well, I was just at Gonzaga's and he claims some anonymous, secretive guy bought it. I thought maybe you might know what happened to it.'

'I haven't the faintest idea.'

Then, as in a nightmare, she saw Tom Dale coming right towards them, less than half a block away. She shut her eyes, certain that when she opened them, he would have disappeared like a mirage of water on a blacktop country road. She'd imagined, longed for, just such a fortuitous, casual meeting so often that it now seemed utterly impossible. But when she opened her eyes, he was still there, getting nearer and nearer. And the last person in the world she wanted to meet at this moment, with the possible exception of her husband, was Tom.

She ducked quickly around the corner onto the side street that ran north from Bloor, with Eddie right behind her.

'But why don't we discuss it over a drink?' she said. 'How about this place?' She pointed at a door from which people were emerging, blinking at the late-afternoon light.

'The Embassy? It's a little rough.' His hand went to the back pocket of his jeans, and his expression brightened. 'But we could go over to the Windsor Arms; there's a nice bar there. Or how about the Plaza Roof?'

'I like this place better. And you'll protect me, won't you?' she whispered, taking his arm and looking up at him as fetchingly as she could manage under the circumstances.

EDDIE WAS astonished (and a little frightened) by the way Mrs Zeffler knocked back the first two drafts. For a moment there, when she first dragged him into the place, he'd almost thought she was putting the make on him. She was definitely giving off some strange vibes, what with the hand-holding and all. But before he had time to decide how he felt about that, she stopped being flirtatious. Now conversation had ground to a complete halt, though from time to time she sighed heavily, with a dazed and dissatisfied look on her face. But at least she was working her way through her third glass of beer a little more slowly. Eddie began to wonder how and when he could escape to continue the search for *Back Flip*. It was obvious that Eleanor Zeffler knew nothing and cared even less about its whereabouts.

Suddenly, she placed both hands on the table, shoved herself upright and got unsteadily to her feet. 'God, I really have to pee!'

'I think it's over there....' Eddie pointed at a door on the far side of the room, and she picked up her purse and lurched off in that direction. Wrestling with a nearly overpowering desire to run, he stood up, then sat down again, held by fear rather than chivalry. He wasn't dealing with your regular, run-of-the-mill juiced-up matron here. He couldn't just abandon Mrs Jerome Zeffler in the Embassy Tavern.

On the other hand, given the condition she was in, she probably wouldn't remember any of this. Or who she'd been with. But then again, she might remember very well. No, he couldn't afford to alienate Jerry Zeffler. He'd already as good as lost his dealer this afternoon. And if he didn't get his hands on that painting, and soon, he could very well lose his first – and maybe last – chance at international recognition. *Shit. Shit. Shit.*

He stood up again and looked desperately around the room. There was no sign of Eleanor. Maybe she'd left. That would be good. Or maybe she'd passed out in the john. *Fuck it.* He might actually have to go in there and drag or carry her out. He shuddered, sat down and drained his glass. Then he heard somebody calling his name.

'Hey, Eddie!'

The voice came from somewhere near the entrance. Then it asked, 'Have you got one? A lady? A woman? A broad? A chick?'

Bob Willard was alone, which accounted for his question. The Ladies and Escorts side of the tavern, marginally less grungy than the section accessible through the Men's entrance, was off limits to males who didn't have a female in tow. Willard obviously hadn't managed to latch on to one, for he kept on signalling doggedly.

As Eddie hesitated, not sure whether he wanted to acknowledge him, Mrs Zeffler returned to the table. She'd taken a stab at reapplying her makeup, and although accuracy had been heavily compromised by beer, she looked better. Just as she flopped into her chair and put her elbows on the table, Bob came towards them, wearing an incredulous but pleased expression.

'Well, well … this is a surprise,' he said in a debonair tone that sounded painfully corny to Eddie. Eleanor's head turned slowly sideways, and her eyes moved upward, taking in Willard's arrival. A faint smile crossed her lips, now generously repainted with lipstick.

'We really can't go on meeting like this,' Bob said, grinning. Eleanor just shook her head, several more times than necessary.

The two men's eyes met for a moment. Then Eddie got up and they took a few steps away from the table. 'She's blasted,' Bob whispered, with a hint of reproof in his voice.

'I *know*.'

'Well, what's going on? You know who she is, don't you?'

'Sure, sure. But she was the one … she dragged me in here. I met her on the street outside and I was walking her to her car. It's parked up on Yorkville. I was only trying to find out about that painting of mine that her old man was supposed to have bought, and then …'

'And then what?'

'Well, she knocked back three drafts in fifteen minutes, and …' They both glanced at the table where Eleanor was sitting. Her chin was propped on her two hands as she stared into her half-empty glass. As they watched, she began to list gently to the left. 'I was just trying to figure out how I could get away.'

'She can't drive, that's for sure. Somebody has to take her home, drive her car for her.'

'Well, *I* can't do it,' Eddie said quickly. 'I don't have a licence. And I've got to split. Really. Margrave was at my place at the crack of dawn this morning and he wants *Back Flip* for the show, and it's missing, or anyway Bruno won't tell me where it is and – Oh, *shit,* I have to work at the store tonight.' He dragged a hand across his face. 'What time is it?'

Willard checked his watch. 'Getting close to five.' They didn't speak for a moment. Then Bob patted Eddie on the shoulder. 'Okay, kid, why don't you run along?' he said. 'I'll take care of this.'

▮ Chapter Eleven

BRUNO SAT STEWING in the workshop until six o'clock. When Jane came to the back of the gallery to tell him she was leaving for the day, he pulled himself together enough to rattle the unfinished frames on the work table in front of him and give the table itself couple of sharp raps with a hammer to create an impression of activity. Then he called out, in a voice that was fairly calm, 'See you Monday.'

Once he had heard her lock the street door, he slipped quietly into the exhibition area. He couldn't have explained even to himself why his movements were so stealthy. But caution, cunning, dissimulation now seemed more essential than ever. He made his way to the stairs that led to the basement. The door was right behind Jane's desk, and with the instinct of a mother animal that stays away from the nest when she senses the presence of predators, he had avoided going down there until he was alone. Much as he would have liked to believe that Jane was steadfast and credulous, he could not, dared not, confide in her.

He switched on the basement light and, closing the door behind him, went down the steps. Satisfaction surged through him as he dragged the canvas out of the cupboard and peeled back a corner of the paper in which it was wrapped. Now the decision to keep it for himself seemed more logical and justifiable than ever. Finding out that Margrave wanted *Back Flip* for the exhibition – not *Tusk*, however much Zeffler wished to believe that – only confirmed Bruno's own shrewdness, prescience and eye. And now the painting was legally as well as morally his, bought and paid for, cash on the nail. He had only to wait, and the great Margrave would come to him.

FROM A DISCREET distance, Bob watched Eleanor drive the Mustang into the garage attached to her large, vine-covered pseudo-Gothic house. She was steering with the infinite care of the seriously inebriated. Then, even before the automatic door had finished closing behind the car, he walked away without a backward glance.

After she'd taken his place behind the wheel at the corner of her street, he'd decided to stick around long enough to make sure she wouldn't crash into the side of the house. Though what he would or could have done if she had, he didn't know. On the walk from the Embassy to the parking lot on Yorkville, she'd leaned on him for support, but at first resisted surrendering the car keys. Eventually he'd talked her into handing them over, but when he suggested that they stop at his place until she sobered up – 'felt better' was the phrase he actually used – she had adamantly refused. So his half-formed plan to reenact the shower scene from *My Man Godfrey* had had to be shelved. Like Carole Lombard, Eleanor managed to retain at least a portion of her allure even when sloppily drunk – but Lombard had only been acting.

As he strolled along Ava Road, he asked himself whether he'd ever want to live there, assuming some previously unknown relative died and left him a quarter million or so. You could probably pick up one of these dumps for a paltry fifty thousand, he guessed, but the rest would go on furnishings, gardeners' salaries, pool upkeep and a quality motor vehicle or three to occupy the garages. The residents of this neighbourhood probably travelled exclusively by car. He met no one on foot, except for a couple of gloomy middle-aged women carrying tote bags and wearing sensible shoes, who could only be live-out domestics heading home at the end of their working day.

And now kind-hearted old Bob, Good Samaritan, superannuated Boy Scout and rescuer of distressed gentlewomen, was on his way home, too. He'd done his good deed for the day and wished he could say that he looked for no recompense. It would be nice, though, if a grateful, sober and (why not?) amorous Eleanor were to turn up at his door the next day to show him just how much she appreciated his gallantry. Yeah – and maybe Hell *would* freeze over this year.

More likely, she wouldn't even remember him driving her car up Avenue Road and turning left at u cc to plunge fearlessly into the wilds of Forest Hill. He'd had a rough idea where the house was from the one occasion he'd been there, all those years ago. Eleanor sat in the passenger's seat like a zombie, staring straight ahead and not saying a word. However, by the time they were in the right neighbourhood, she had come to enough to give him directions. Then, just before she got behind the wheel, she leaned over and kissed him quickly on the corner of the mouth.

She'd probably been aiming for his cheek and missed. But just for the sake of argument, let's say it hadn't been a mistake, a slip between cheek and lip, a spatial miscalculation. Suppose Eleanor had intended to – had actually *wanted* to – kiss him? And if he'd had time to imbibe some Dutch courage himself, he might have turned that impulsive peck into something more significant. Why not? Eleanor was obviously unhappy. Otherwise, she wouldn't have been getting soused in the Embassy with Eddie O'Hara.

Yes, she was unhappy, and the main reason that women were unhappy was that old devil called L-O-V-E. Since she was beautiful and rich, what other reason could there be? That meant that her marriage was in bad shape, perhaps even a marriage in name only. Oh yes, he thought, warming to his subject, she was just another *objet d'art* for Jerry the collector. A bird in a gilded cage. He himself, on the other hand, was as free as one – a bird, that is. So if he and Eleanor were to … well, they wouldn't really be hurting anyone. Right there you had a entirely different situation from Margie and Mr Razor Cut – who, if he remembered correctly, had kept a wife and kids tucked away in Don Mills.

Lights were coming on in the mansions now. It was getting chilly, too. He stuffed his hands into the pockets of his jacket as he hurried on. There was probably no chance of picking up a cruising cab in this neighbourhood, he realized. He might have to hoof it all the way over to Bathurst to find one.

THAT NIGHT, Winifred Beecham dreamed of her first husband. Alec's manner towards her was fatherly, even though in the dream he was younger than she was, younger than he had been when he died. He took her hand, smiled at her more sweetly than he had ever done in life and apologized for dying. She didn't remember saying anything in return, but upon waking she knew that she had let him know she had forgiven him. And though she had always been certain he had never known of it, he in turn forgave her for that long-ago summer adultery. It was a calm reconciliation, as if they had been separated by a civilized and amicable divorce rather than wrenched apart by cruel, capricious death.

The moment she opened her eyes on Saturday morning, the scene began to slip away. Sunlight sliced in through a crack where the linen curtains, in a green-and-cream William Morris willow pattern, had not been pulled completely closed, but the room was quiet. She and Eliot had agreed it was best to sleep apart, now that the change of life was causing Win so many restless, sweat-drenched nights. She turned her head languidly on the pillow to look at the bedside clock. He would have left for the hospital by now, anyway, she thought; he liked to make early rounds on the weekends.

In her dream they had sat at a table surrounded by weeping willows – she could remember that much. On the table was a white, footed bowl of fresh figs, purple and bulbous. Why figs? She never ate them. And there had been three people at the table. Alec, herself and … another man. Asleep, she had known who it was, but now, awake, she didn't. Logically, it should have been Eliot, to take her hand from Alec's and draw her back safely into her present life. But Alec and Eliot had never met – not that such details mattered in dreams. Alec *had* known Tom, however, and as far as Win was aware, had approved of him. So the person sitting with them among the willows could have been Tom.

She got up slowly and went to the bathroom to use the toilet and wash her face. She did not look in the mirror any longer than necessary. It was odd, but she had only become vain when it was no longer useful or appropriate. Surely she had never cared as much about her looks as she did now, had never asked herself whether she was beautiful until she began to understand that she once had been but was no more. Nor ever, she thought lugubriously, would be again. *Quoth the raven.*

Resolving to be very stern with herself about such thoughts, she returned to her bedroom to put on her pale blue silk kimono, the one that matched her eyes. Before the full-length mirror in the bedroom, she held out her arms so that its long, square Japanese sleeves hung straight down on either side of her. With the *eau-de-Nil* walls and the leafy chintz of the bedroom curtains as a background, she looked rather like one of the pale, columnar and matronly goddesses pasted awkwardly onto the faded, funereal landscapes of Puvis de Chavannes. The thought reminded her that the willow trees in her dream had swayed over a gently flowing stream. She decided to go directly to her studio and capture the atmosphere of that scene on paper as soon as she had had her breakfast.

TOM SPENT most of the weekend at the studio. Joan was happy to see him go, he could tell. She always knew when he was about to start bouncing off the walls and preferred to have the house to herself when he was feeling like that. Perhaps she'd invite some other solitary wife in for coffee. He guessed that most of the other breadwinners in their neighbourhood were on the golf course, savouring the last hours of green time before the snow started to fall. Yesterday had been Joan's forty-ninth birthday, and he'd shown his mate he was as good a provider as any of the hole-in-one types. He'd wined and dined her at La Scala, and then, after they'd had their zabaglione, he brought out the antique rope necklace from the Gold Shoppe and fastened it around her neck.

When he got to the studio late Saturday morning, the unfinished canvas was waiting for him. He rummaged through his records looking for something suitable, selected a Fats Waller reissue LP, slapped it on the turntable and set to work, humming. By noon, he had laid down the block of colour he'd envisioned while hiding out from Margrave. He stepped back and grinned at the nice fat triangle of yellowish ochre pressing amorously up against the broad swath of mouldy grey just to the left of centre. Yep, just as he'd thought, it did the trick. He went to the record player, flipped the long-playing disc over and dropped the needle on it.

'You great big babykins,
I wish that I were twins
So I could love you twice as much as I do....'

Singing along, he backed away to the far side of the studio to get a better look at the huge canvas. Yeah. Okay. What next? He strolled back and forth, considering. Maybe something down there on the right ... a patch of red, say, to goose the grey a little from the other side. Yes, a nice tomato-sauce red would do it. The middle section was still just lying there, getting much too comfortable.

Well, he couldn't say the same for himself, he thought as he started to mix the red. He'd managed to beat off some of the distractions, disengaging from Margrave and sidestepping a potentially complicated misunderstanding with Winifred. But he'd only escaped from that hotel tryst with Eleanor Zeffler by the skin of his teeth. Saved from debauchery by McNab, of all people! He couldn't help chuckling at that. Still, he wasn't out of the woods yet. Margrave would be gone in a few weeks and Winifred was keeping her distance, but Eleanor ... hell, he might have to hide out from her for the rest of his natural life.

The horror of nearly bumping right into her on Bloor Street on Friday afternoon had only been compounded by the sight of Margrave *and* McNab a few minutes later. Couldn't a man even buy a birthday present for his wife without having to fight his way through a horde of people he didn't want to see? But ... Eleanor had almost seemed to be trying to avoid *him*. And wasn't the fellow with her the O'Hara kid? He had even thought for a moment that they were holding hands. Good God – was she robbing the cradle now? Had she pulled the same sort of stunt with Eddie that she had with him?

He was surprised to find himself feeling annoyed by the idea. But just because Eleanor and O'Hara had ducked around the corner together didn't mean they were … well, it didn't mean anything, surely. Besides, it wasn't any of his business, just because for a brief period – a *very* brief period – he'd had illicit designs on her himself.

Anyway, most people would say he was entitled to a little fling. Years ago, in his agency days, he'd known several guys, some of them fairly close friends of his and all of them happily married (or so they said), who cheated whenever they got the chance. Pretty indiscriminately, it had seemed to Tom, they'd pursued other men's wives, secretaries in the office and the occasional female artist, although those were rare in the old days.

But he'd always wondered what the Lotharios really got out of these dangerous and often quite unappetizing dalliances. They all had presentable, faithful and, at least to the naked eye, loving wives. And once a man had found his mate – a fond, steadfast spectator at the unfolding drama of his life and work – he was all set. Why look for more trouble, for turmoil and distraction? Well, from the way those fellows talked, they had extramarital affairs simply because they *could*. Supplemental, illicit sex was just one of the perks of success, a reward for ability and hard work, like a fancier car, a bigger house or a solid gold Rolex.

In that case, he himself was overdue for an adventure. Hell, he was the best painter this country had ever produced. That's what people kept saying, anyway. He wasn't one to boast, but why indulge in false modesty? And nowadays there was a whole army of uninhibited, undemanding young girls who made the free spirits he'd known in his brief bachelor youth look like nuns.

Thank God his own daughter had passed through adolescence in a safer, more innocent time. Now she was nearly twenty-six and married, securely, he supposed, to a dull but reliable engineer. They lived in Vancouver and Tom didn't have – good Lord, didn't *want* to have – a clue about their sex life before or after marriage. Other than paying for the wedding, he hadn't experienced one moment of worry about Nancy. But then, he realized, he knew almost nothing about her.

Maybe that was the trouble. He was out of touch. Everything was different these days. Why should he settle for Winifred, lovely as she'd once been, now that she was as old and decaying as himself? Or even for Eleanor Zeffler, a beauty to be sure, but forty if a day and, he suspected, slightly unhinged? If he did indulge in a touch of hanky-panky – and he wasn't saying he was going to, mind you – surely he could find someone fresher and less troublesome than either of them.

He set to work again. In late afternoon, he stopped to fix himself a little liquid refreshment and to reassess the situation. Bingo! Bull's-eye. The red did it. The whole thing was shifting, stirring, coming alive. At least as far as painting was concerned, he still knew exactly what he was doing. That was something. Hell, what was he thinking? It was *everything*.

PURPLE, PALE GREEN, perhaps a touch of acid yellow, glazed with a silvery sheen. Bulbous, swelling forms shaped like little minarets, one of them sliced open to reveal a glistening golden interior, cradled in a simple white porcelain bowl. Ancient, biblical, Mediterranean, succulent and very faintly suggestive.

Win's sable brush swept confidently over the thick, creamy sheet of handmade watercolour paper on the table in front of her. Once she had worked out and captured the nature of the fig – not just its appearance, but its essence, its resonance – she would begin to abstract that essential figness into a larger composition in which the uninformed eye would recognize no reference to any identifiable fruit. When transferred to the six-foot-square canvas that was waiting in her storage rack, the two figs (she had decided on two) would become two great mauve teardrops, each nearly as tall as herself, suspended in a huge ivory sling. And an intimate, domestic still life would be changed into something universal, mysterious and heroic.

Small-scale domestic observation did not sell. Not that Win really needed to be concerned with sales, except perhaps as a purely objective measurement of artistic acceptance. But she did want, passionately, to be taken seriously. And none of the painters people took seriously were doing easel painting any more, or recording the objects or characters of everyday life. There was Pop Art, true – those tedious soup cans, or the ten-foot-high frames from comic strips, and the rows upon rows of celebrities' faces or car wrecks, methodically drained of emotion – but even that much specificity could only be tolerated when mechanical and ironic.

As for symbolism or spirituality – they could be no more explicit than Rothko's resolutely inscrutable and sombre epiphanies. The clichés of Surrealism – those pliable clocks, bathing-suit torsos and floating bowlers that had seemed quite daring in her youth – were now so debased that only LSD-addled youngsters or slick advertising people thought they had meaning. Even the advertisements used them rather ironically. How she detested that smirking flight from the past and from all elevated emotions, everything sublime! She could not accept the relentless levelling of perception and experience. Some individuals simply were more sensitive than others, whether the less privileged wanted to admit it or not. And if art had to be impersonal, accessible to everyone, what on earth was the point of it?

WHAT STILL amazed Eleanor was that Jerry actually believed they were happy. As far as he was concerned, their marriage was a success. On Saturday they went out to dinner at Mr Tony's, and while their waiter was reciting the menu, Jerry reached over to stroke the back of her neck.

'You look great, doll,' he said, smiling proudly, 'not a day over thirty.'

She guessed that was a compliment.

'I'm a lucky man, Sal.' Jerry always made a point of knowing waiters' names.

'Yes sir, Mr Zeffler,' replied the dapper little man standing by their table, without looking at Eleanor, 'a very lovely lady.'

Jerry had the veal piccata, and Eleanor had the chicken cordon bleu. There was the usual fussy consultation with the sommelier, as Jerry insisted on calling him, about the wine. For dessert, they both had the house specialty: *gâteau Saint-Honoré*, golf-ball-sized puff pastries lacquered with shiny caramel glaze, hacked with a flourish from a two-foot-tall pyramid that was rolled over to their table on a trolley by the ever-attentive Sal.

Later, in the restaurant's second-floor smoking room, they drank ten-year-old Armagnac, and Jerry lit a cigar. Eleanor slid the band of the Montecristo onto her right ring finger, next to the diamond eternity ring. Then Jerry let her take a puff and she gagged playfully. That always made him laugh. He tipped his head back, watching the costly smoke float towards the ceiling, and sighed contentedly, placing one hand proprietarily on Eleanor's thigh. All in all, they were the picture of affluent, up-to-the-minute domestic bliss.

But how, Eleanor asked herself, could her husband have failed to notice that everything between them was different now? And how could she ever again be the same woman, wife and mother? Yet it seemed that at the moment she was. From within the confining but comfortable walls of her marriage, everything that had taken place at the Windsor Arms with Quintin Margrave looked utterly implausible.

Some details were definitely hazy, especially what had happened after she left the hotel. But she *thought* she remembered sitting with a young man in a … could it have been a beer parlour? And was it … Eddie O'Hara? Yes, it was coming back. She could almost smell the musty-metallic air of the place and see the waiters rushing through the gloom carrying huge circular trays loaded with overflowing glasses. In the washroom, where the aromas of urine, mildew and disinfectant fought it out, she had fished another Valium out of her handbag and gulped it down with a handful of tepid water from the tap. There had been no paper cups, and the cloth hand towel had hung off its roller mechanism, sodden and tangled. She'd had to use the flimsy toilet paper to dry her hands. It had stuck, and then immediately disintegrated. That was the last thing she could recall about the afternoon.

▮ Chapter Twelve

JANE LOOKED around for Eddie, but there was no sign of him. She took off her glasses, put them back into her purse and sat down on the wooden bench in the middle of the Old Masters gallery. Then she got them out again to make sure the madman with the beret, the one who had shown up at the Gonzaga on her first day there, hadn't followed her inside. He, or at least someone who looked like him, had been hanging around the entrance. However, he wasn't in any of the small groups of people moving slowly from painting to painting, talking in the hushed tones the setting imposed. Only the giggles of restless children disturbed the contemplative atmosphere.

The painting in front her probably accounted for a lot of the kids' embarrassed laughter. It looked just as she remembered it. The central figure was, at least nominally, female: a completely naked, though strangely slender and boyish Venus, approximately life-sized. Her long limbs were folded into an odd triangular position, not quite sitting or kneeling or lying. She was really only a pyramid of luminous flesh pressed up against the picture plane, filling most of the canvas and float-ing illogically in space. A lanky, pubescent Cupid, his bare behind jutting lasciviously at the viewer, was wrapped around her. With a drugged yet meaningful expression on his face, he was kissing her, his mother, on the lips and tweaking one of her nipples between his fingers.

On one side of this pair, a plumper, younger cherub with a maniacal grin was winding up to pitch a fistful of rose petals at them. On the other lurked a half-concealed figure with a mask-like face and a screaming crone whose flesh was a putrid green. Behind the cherub there was a girl with a serpent's tail and hands that seemed (though it was hard to tell in the jumble of limbs) to be attached to the wrong arms. And across the top of the canvas, behind them all, the sinewy arm of an old man held out a curtain of rich, brilliant blue. Ambiguous, sinister, large enough to climb right into, this painting had always seemed to speak of incomprehensible delights and terrors. As a child, Jane had been almost too afraid to look at it. But she had. In the Toronto of her youth, there had not been much nudity on public view. Male genitals, in particular, were always tucked safely away beneath loincloths or fig leaves.

Brotherless, and with a vigilantly modest father, she seen almost no penises before she reached puberty. The only one she remembered seeing had belonged to a neighbour boy who took it out to urinate in front of her. His, pencil-like and puny, had not been substantial enough to produce awe or fear. She had felt as much surprised as embarrassed. It wasn't until years later, in a restaurant kitchen in Greece, pointing out what she wanted for dinner, that she saw its like: okra. Funny, she'd never encountered another similar one since then. Perhaps it was because the boy next door was only a child. And, she thought, looking at the tiny, budlike extrusion on the cherub in the painting in front of her, he must have been circumcised. The kid in the picture was not. Anyway, it had turned out that the organs of grown men were not like okra at all. Her first real lover, a crude but cheerful sensualist ten years older than she was, had thought it was funny to strut around his apartment with a hand towel draped over his erect member....

'Now that's kinky.' Eddie took a seat on the bench beside her. 'Man, it's got everything! Voyeurism, nudity, pedophilia, incest ... what more could you want?'

'I can't think of a thing,' said Jane, whipping off her glasses.

She'd been just as startled on Friday afternoon when she heard his voice on the phone. 'Is Bruto within earshot?' he'd asked right off. When she said no, he went on, 'Okay. Listen, I want to talk to you. Not at the gallery. Someplace else. Soon. But I have to work at the store. tonight and tomorrow. Maybe tomorrow night?'

Saturday night? Night of romance? When a girl was supposed to have a date? Or, taking present realities into consideration, when at the eleventh hour, she might get a better offer? 'I can't tomorrow. Maybe on Sunday afternoon ... how about at the Art Gallery?' When she'd suggested that they meet in front of the Bronzino, he was silent for a moment, as if the idea was too silly for comment. But then he'd said okay. So here they were.

Eddie got up and walked over to the painting. 'The scale is important,' he said, spreading his arms as if he were measuring the canvas like Leonardo's circle-and-square man. 'She's life-size, at least. I bet if she unfolded herself and stood up, she'd be nearly six foot. That's tall for a sixteenth-century chick.'

'Yes. It's sort of as if she's squeezed into the frame. But just floating there, too.' Jane had never had this sort of conversation with Eddie before. It was hard to talk about the art shown at the Gonzaga in any terms other than the obligatory *Wows*. 'Did you know this is a copy of a painting that's in the National Gallery in London? I was just reading a book that –'

'Yeah?' He seemed to have lost interest in it. Sitting down again close to her, he said, 'Listen, do you have any idea what happened to *Back Flip*?'

'Well, I thought Mr Zeffler was going to buy it, but I guess he didn't. I heard him telling Bruno that *Tusk* was a much better painting and how he was glad he'd picked it instead. And then Bruno told me to put Anonymous in the sales book for *Flip*.'

'But where is it? Where was it shipped?'

'Who knows? Maybe Hank Lister picked it up after hours, when I wasn't there. Sometimes he comes late. Bruno hangs around the gallery all the time – he's almost always there before I am. Just to make me feel guilty for being late, I think.'

'So you don't have any idea where it is?'

Jane shook her head.

Eddie was already on his feet. 'I've gotta go. See y'around.'

BOB HITCHED his pyjama bottom up over the incipient paunch that he was definitely going to do something about. Daily sit-ups, starting tomorrow, he resolved as he poured himself another cup of coffee from the pot that was still stewing on the stove.

It was Sunday morning, and he'd spent a ridiculous number of the past twenty-four hours thinking of Eleanor, imagining and re-imagining what the reeling, delicious plunge into her embrace might be like. 'Darling,' she'd say, simply, *sweetly* twining her arms languorously around his neck. And as she opened herself to him he'd say – What *would* he say? 'I've been meaning to do this for a long time ...' *No. God!* Block that cliché! Everything he imagined was hopelessly corny, utterly inept. And the thing about adultery, as he understood it, was that at some point you had to say *something* about what was going on. You couldn't just, by mutual, silent agreement, slip casually into sexual congress, as he seemed to remember doing with Lorraine, and even with Margie. Surely the madness, the willed wrongness of what was about to happen had to be at least alluded to? But maybe not. It might be best not to say a word, thereby avoiding lies that would come back to haunt you. But whichever way he handled it, he suspected Eleanor might find grounds for displeasure and possibly even scorn.

The weekend was already half over, but thank God his first class on Monday wasn't until two in the afternoon. Life drawing again: the usual roomful of blasé nineteen-year-olds sketching droopy old Harriet, supervised by paunchy old Bob. The whole procedure would be more of a *memento mori* than a glimpse of the pleasures of the flesh. But all the better, perhaps, to approach the human body as pure form, which was what the students were supposed to be doing. A tough proposition at their age and difficult even at his, as he was discovering.

He decided to put her out of his mind. It wasn't all that hard, but he still felt a distant inner twitch, a kind of subterranean rumbling in his brain. He stepped into his sunroom-studio, which now, in autumn, was habitable for a few weeks. As he flipped through the dusty canvases that were stacked there, he admitted for the first time that Max was right. They were no good. But maybe he could do better – and suddenly he wanted to try.

After some determined rummaging he unearthed a pad of 20-by-24 cartridge paper, its top few pages tattered, smudged and yellowed. But a couple of sheets down, it was still usable. A few minutes later, he'd dredged up a box of oil pastels. Most of them were just stubs. That was okay. He was only fooling around, working out a few random ideas that had started percolating. He ended up spending most of Sunday in the studio.

'WELL, NOW, that would be confidential,' Hank Lister said. 'But as a friend and off the record I can tell you, Eddie, that I don't recall shipping that particular piece, unless it was from your place – you're on Spadina, am I right? – to Mr Gonzaga. Maybe, now that you mention it, we did take it over with all the others.... That would be back in September, now. Fine show, by the way. But there was maybe a dozen pieces, if I recall correctly, that went from your place to the gallery at the time, and we didn't have every title down on the list, y'see ...'

Eddie shook his head. He already knew he was wasting his time. 'I mean *after* the show closed. When you shipped the work out of the Gonzaga.'

'Well, y'see, that's my point exactly. I can't tell you from memory, and I couldn't be showing you every waybill for every job I do. Lots of folks wouldn't want their private dealings discussed. Other artists. Other dealers. And some of those collectors – they're demanding. Finicky. It'd be ol' Hank's neck on the chopping block if I talked about some of the things I've seen. No, that wouldn't be at all professional. And Lister Transport is professional, y'know. Why, some very important people entrust us with their prize possessions, don't they?'

Hank could jaw until hell froze over *and* the cows came home if you let him. But he'd never tell Eddie what he wanted to know. The dealers, and the public galleries that might entrust Lister Transport with whole exhibitions were Hank's bread and butter. Not artists, who had no money. And much as he loved to gossip, Lister would never bite the hand that fed him. If he even knew where *Flip* was. It could be stashed away in the Lister warehouse down on the waterfront, or still at the Gonzaga. It might even be inside the truck that Hank was leaning against right now. Or orbiting the earth in a spaceship, or hanging halfway up the Guggenheim ramp.

'Now, Mr Lurie ... Max, he's a fine fellow,' Hank continued as if on cue, gesturing towards the back door of the Lurie Gallery. 'A true friend of art and a gentleman to boot.' His voice dropped to a confidential whisper. 'Gave me my start in the business ... not many people know that. And today he asked me to take a couple of pieces by a very well-known individual – and a darn nice guy, too, not stuck up, like you might expect – over to the Art Gallery. There's one by a young lady, too. Both going to the big show that English fella is putting together. That much I can tell you, but no more. It wouldn't be ...'

'Professional,' said Eddie under his breath. He felt like socking Hank in the jaw just to shut him up. Instead, he muttered, 'Yeah, Max is the greatest,' and started to walk off down the alley, raising one hand in farewell. 'See ya.'

So the show was already being assembled. Tom Dale – big surprise, big secret – had *two* paintings in it. And some chick from the Lurie Gallery was in it too – could it possibly be Jenny Kosma? None of the guys had believed her when she claimed Max was taking her on. When Eddie paused at the end of the lane and glanced back, Hank was leaning on the buzzer at the Lurie's rear entrance. *Shit*, he had to come up with something. Fast.

'UNETHICAL?' Bob cocked his head at Eddie. 'Are we talking about painting? The creation of *be-yew-tee* itself?' He raised his glass. '"Beauty is truth, truth beauty, that is all ye know on earth.... And all ye need to know ..."'

Eddie grimaced and looked away, and Bob felt a little guilty for teasing him. But for no plausible reason, he was happy. He'd been feeling pretty good even before he finished the first of several beers. Okay, tossing off a few sketches on paper was a long way from getting something on canvas, and light-years from actually putting a show together. He knew that. And he had no intention of telling anyone he met at the Pilot, including – maybe *especially*, O'Hara – that he was working again. But he was strangely buoyed up by the effort itself.

'Okay,' he said to Eddie. 'What you're talking about, if I understand you correctly, is making another version of one of your own paintings. What's the big deal? Reworking an idea ...'

'Well, not reworking ... not a *version*, exactly. A copy. An exact copy. So that Margrave won't know the difference. So he believes it's the same painting that was in the Gonzaga show.' Eddie was perched on the edge of his chair, like a heron ready to take flight at the slightest disturbance in the vicinity. He'd barely touched the glass of beer in front of him.

Bob took a sip from his own glass. Then he pulled out a pack of cigarettes, extracted one, lit it and took a drag. 'Why the hell not?' he asked, exhaling.

'I don't know. It just doesn't seem ...'

'Honest?'

'Maybe.'

'It's your own stuff, isn't it? Margrave is just running you through the gears, anyway. I know his type, probably a failed artist himself, into that "my exhibition is a creative act, far greater than the sum of its parts" routine, blah, blah, blah.... Couldn't the guy find *one* other piece from your show that he likes? And as for Gonzaga –'

'I could do it. Easily. I've got the sketches, the slides....'

And the masking tape, Bob added silently. One thing about that hard-edge stuff, it was quick and easy to duplicate when the need arose.

'Matter of fact, I could probably finish it tonight.'

'Then what are you waiting for?' Bob reached over and gave him a comradely slap on the shoulder. 'Beat it and get to work!' Out of the corner of his eye, he'd just seen Jenny Kosma come in. She was alone, though she seemed to be looking around for someone.

'The thing is, I'll have to take it over to the Art Gallery myself. I don't want that asshole Lister involved. He costs – and talks – too fucking much. If I can get a van, could you do the driving?'

Bob shrugged. When and how had he become O'Hara's free taxi

service? Oh, well, ferrying Eleanor Zeffler across town had paid off, even if not in the way he would have preferred. 'Sure,' he said, 'give me a call when you're ready to go.'

'First thing tomorrow? It has to be there by tomorrow night.'

'I've got a class in the morning. I could make it in the afternoon, though.'

'Great. Thanks. I'll call you.'

Once he was gone, Bob deftly transferred the contents of Eddie's nearly full glass to his own. Then he looked around the room. Jenny was sitting by herself two tables away. Apparently she wasn't a dyke, after all. He'd heard from Max, who had decided to give her a show and had even placed one of her pieces in the Margrave exhibition, that she'd lived with Mike Orley in Winnipeg for nearly a year. Monumental Mike, whose factory-made ten-foot-tall cylinders of cold-rolled steel were considered the absolute latest by all up-to-date curators. But they'd broken up just before she came to Toronto.

After staring fixedly at her for a couple of minutes, he was able to catch her eye. He pointed at her, then at the empty chair beside him. She looked around the room, as if she thought he might be gesturing at someone else behind her. Or maybe she was only assessing her chances of finding more desirable company. But finally she hoisted her knapsack onto her shoulder and came over to his table.

JANE COULDN'T quite make out his face in the darkness and, strangely, their bodies hardly seemed to be touching. Stranger still, she felt an exquisitely sweet sensation that quickly spread through all her deliciously lethargic limbs. She knew everything, understood everything, and so did her partner. He was perfect, she was perfect, the act was perfect and they both knew it; absolutely, certainly, definitely. They smiled fondly at each other, both hovering weightlessly in space and yet crucially joined, mortar and pestle, socket and plug, quiver and arrow, lock and key ... why hadn't she realized before how simple everything was, how effortless, how inevitable ...?

She found herself hanging over the side of her bed with one arm dragging on the floor. She tried to crawl back into the dream. But she couldn't, because there was a horribly irritating sound nearby. Her eyes moved reluctantly around the room, blinking at the harsh daylight that was pouring through the window, taking in the daisy-printed sheet that was tangled around her legs and coming to rest on the alarm clock squalling on the bedside table. She swiped at it, silenced it, and fell back on her pillow.

As she began to recall the dream, she instinctively reached down to check for physical evidence of arousal. There was none. The dominant sensation in the area was an urgent need to pee. She tried to ignore it. Which *was* the mortar, and which was the pestle, anyway? She could never keep it straight, and resolved to look it up that very day.

Eddie was ... *Eddie?* She sat up. What on earth had *he* been doing there?

She had never consciously considered him a potential lover. However, it *had* been Eddie in her dream. Not that dreams actually meant anything, but it only made sense to pay attention to your unconscious. You couldn't share a moment of such transcendence, imaginary or not, with someone without looking at that person differently – even though (thank God) Eddie would never – not in a million years – find out about it. But she resolved to keep an eye on him, discreetly, from now on. Just in case.

Then it hit her. She wouldn't get the chance to observe Eddie O'Hara from the underbrush now. After that ugly scene with Bruno, he'd very likely never darken the Gonzaga's door again.

WINIFRED HAD firmly decided to renounce all romantic illusions, especially those pertaining to one Thomas Reginald Dale. But her resolve crumbled at regular intervals. She did not reproach herself for that, however. Nor did she blame her unconscious, which she had never considered reliable when it came to practical as opposed to artistic decisions, for summoning him repetitively into her thoughts.

As the firstborn of a family that included two much younger brothers, she was neither awed by men nor fearful of them – unlike many women of her generation. The Beechams had had servants, but Win had liked helping Nanny with the boys. And if, as a girl of eight, you have changed the diapers and dried the tears of a little lad of two, you can never see men as either truly intimidating or dignified. Thus she had been well prepared to raise her own sons and had rarely had much difficulty managing the adult men in her life. The way to deal with tantrums and defiance, she believed, was simply to ignore them.

And so, once Win realized that Tom had always been rather in love with her, she came to accept his furtive devotion as no more than her due. Though she did sometimes wonder why she had never noticed it until recently. Now that they saw each other less often, she chose to ascribe his slight coolness when they did meet to pique at her own elusiveness. Oh, she was sufficiently in touch with reality to recognize that her days as an object of lust or romantic longing were probably over. But for that very reason an admirer of such long standing as Tom was especially valuable. Surely he would grant her what you might call retroactive credit for the beauty that once had been hers. *Time cannot wither, nor custom stale*... that sort of thing.

THE VAN Eddie had mentioned turned out to be a beat-up, two-tone, lime-green-and-white Chevy station wagon, spotted with rust and at least ten years old. It was parked in front of a house on D'Arcy Street. When Bob showed up there as instructed, Eddie was already on the front porch, talking to a long-haired girl in an Indian-print gauze dress. From the sidewalk, Bob observed that they kissed briefly on the lips after Eddie pocketed what had to be the keys to the car.

'Girlfriend?' he asked when Eddie joined him.

Eddie tossed the keys over. 'The heap belongs to her brother.'

Bob restrained an impulse to kid him about her, wondering if she was the chick he'd talked about, the one he was so stuck on. Daisy. Probably not, he decided, glancing back at the girl on the veranda. Though presentable, she was no beauty – hardly the type you'd conscript as a muse.

Surprisingly, the Chevy started on the first try. As they pulled away, the girl waved goodbye. Eddie ignored her, but out of kindness Bob waved back. In a couple of minutes they were cruising by Eddie's place. Bob found a parking spot only half a block away and eased the station wagon into it.

The brand-new *Back Flip* was sitting in the hall at the top of the stairs. 'My, my,' said Bob, 'a veritable pea in a pod.'

'You think so?'

'I couldn't tell the difference, kid. But let's hope we can fit it into the wagon. And you'd better wrap it up, because we may have to do some manoeuvring.'

'Yeah, I've got some P V C here. I just wanted you to see it first.'

Once they'd got the plastic on, secured with masking tape, the two of them carried the painting down the steep staircase and out onto the street. Then they walked it along the sidewalk to the car. At first it looked as if the canvas wouldn't fit, but finally they managed to wedge it in diagonally, with Eddie crouched underneath it, bracing it with both hands.

It occurred to Bob that it would have been a lot simpler just to carry the damn thing the few blocks to the gallery. Although, he supposed, there would be a certain unbecoming humility attached to an artist who delivered a large-scale piece to a supposedly prestigious institutional show on foot. Questions about its provenance might even arise, and that was something Eddie would want to avoid under the circumstances. Although whether *Back Flip*'s arrival in this low-riding, rust-speckled near-antique would be any more impressive than hand delivery was a good question in itself. But he didn't say any of this; he just slid into the driver's seat of the Chevy and started her up.

Before pulling out into traffic, he glanced into the back of the wagon. Eddie took one hand off his masterwork to give him a thumbs-up sign. 'Okay,' he said happily, settling himself back into position under the painting, 'let's go.'

'ONE MOMENT, PLEASE.' Jane jabbed the hold button and put the receiver back in its cradle. The call had come through while Bruno was next door at the Rancho, getting their afternoon coffees. She had been about to say 'I'm sorry, Mr Gonzaga is not in the gallery at the moment,' when she heard the street door open and he came in. He put her coffee down on the desk beside the typewriter.

All day Monday and Tuesday he had seemed quite calm. He even wore a slightly pleased, almost sly expression that Jane found pretty odd after that big, maybe irreparable blow-up with the Gonzaga's most successful artist. He had not said anything about it or about the whereabouts of the painting in dispute. Naturally she hadn't mentioned her rendezvous with Eddie, either – the one in the Old Masters gallery. About the other, imaginary encounter she would never, ever breathe a word to a living soul.

'It's Alan Burnham.'

'Burn-ham?' He gave both syllables equal emphasis and aspirated the *h* with care, although Jane had not done so.

'From the Art Gallery. The contemporary curator. Remember, he's working on the Artquake show with Quintin Margrave?'

'What does he want?'

Jane took a deep breath. 'Well, it's weird. He wants to know ... what the credit line should be for the O'Hara painting that's in the show. It

was delivered today, he says.' She looked down at her desk as she continued. 'And it's called ... *Back Flip*.'

When she looked up, Bruno had half turned away from the desk and
was contemplating a point in the air somewhere on the far side of the
gallery. In profile, his expression was impossible to read.

'So I guess that's where it is,' she said.

He made a sound that was something like a giggle but continued to
stare off into the distance.

'Maybe I should ask him to call back?'

'No. No, I'll talk to him. On the other phone.' Then, without meeting
Jane's eye, he walked slowly towards the back of the gallery.

She peeled the lid off her cup of coffee and took a sip of the pale
brown liquid. So Anonymous was lending *Back Flip* to the Artquake
exhibition. Wouldn't Eddie be happy about that? And wouldn't Bruno
be, too? Getting into important institutional shows was what everybody
wanted. But why would Bruno keep it a secret from Eddie? It had been
obvious the other day that Eddie himself had no idea where the painting
was. Maybe she should tell him, just to put him out of his misery. He *had*
asked for her help. But she couldn't very well phone him from work,
where Bruno might overhear. She'd make the call from home tonight.

∎ Chapter Thirteen

THE MOMENT Bruno's foot touched the top step, the narrow passage seemed to tilt crazily. He had to grab the door frame to keep from falling. Through tightly closed eyes he saw himself sprawled on the concrete floor at the bottom of the stairs, bleeding, unconscious, maybe even dead. He pulled the door closed and turned back to sit down heavily in Jane's chair. There was really no need to check to see that the painting was still in the cupboard. He knew it was. How could it not be?

To calm himself, he began to root through the desk drawers. He turned up only a jumble of pens and pencils, elastic bands, paper clips, push pins and many, many crumpled-up address labels. There were no personal letters this time, but he found a library book called *To the North.* Jane had stuck an emery board into it to mark her place. He shoved the book and the spoiled labels into the wastebasket, then crossed his arms on the desk and laid his head down on top of them.

After a moment he lifted it again and leaned to one side to pull his cigarettes from his pants pocket. When he had one lit, he tried to consider the situation rationally. First, the phone call. He'd handled Burnham well, he thought, not letting anything slip, acting as if the arrival of *Back Flip* at the Art Gallery was perfectly normal and that he was fully aware of it. After an amiable chat, they'd settled on a credit line that read 'Collection of Bruno Gonzaga'. Burnham didn't question his claim that the anonymous owner preferred it that way. He hadn't been able to bring himself to let it just say 'Private Collection.' So, in a way, he had got what he wanted. If only he could enjoy it. But he knew that sooner or later he had to go down to the basement again.

He realized with increasing dread that he wasn't even certain what he hoped to find there. Had the painting, *his* painting, been stolen and handed over to the Art Gallery? That was impossible. But it was preferable to the only other explanation. If *Back Flip* was still in the cupboard under the stairs, wrapped in brown paper, just where he had left it, that meant that the painting Burnham had called about was … was … well, not what it seemed. A fake? A copy? Another painting entirely?

Whatever it was, Eddie O'Hara was certainly behind it. But in that case why had he been so frantic, so insistent on finding the painting only a couple of days ago? And why would Burnham have telephoned the Gonzaga if the piece came from Eddie? He moaned softly. Why? Why? *Why?*

He didn't know, and any attempt to find the answer would entail a loss of face. If he called Burnham back or tried to reach Margrave at his hotel, he'd be as good as admitting he'd been outfoxed by O'Hara. And if he turned to Eddie after ordering him out of the gallery, he'd lose control of him forever, become dirt under the son of a bitch's feet – just when it seemed that O'Hara might be on the brink of real success. Success for which he, Bruno, was solely responsible.

And there was another thing. Whatever the wall label in the exhibition said, he might not be able to take credit for *Back Flip*'s inclusion in the Artquake show. Margrave, or Eddie, or Burnham, perhaps all of them, must know what had actually happened. So that even though the painting, the real one, was still his, the glory had somehow been snatched from him.

He dragged himself to his feet, intending to toss the butt of his cigarette into the tall ashtray that stood on the floor near the central partition. But for a moment he was unable to move and could only stand there, swaying slightly. He felt lightheaded and short of breath. Leaning on the desk, bracing himself with both hands, he made the decision not to go downstairs just yet. He had to be completely in control, stronger, faster and cleverer than his enemies, before he opened that cupboard again.

WHEN IT CAME right down to it, Jane didn't have the guts to telephone Eddie. First of all, she'd have to be insane to place herself between him and Bruno, knowing that they would cheerfully tear her to pieces to get at each other. And there was one more minor detail: she depended entirely on Bruno for her livelihood. As it was, she was barely getting by, and she had no savings. If she lost this job she might even have to go back to living with her parents.

Who was she kidding, though? The real reason she didn't want to call Eddie had nothing to do with Bruno, or keeping her position at the Gonzaga Gallery, or moving back home. Ever since the night of the dream she had not been able to think of him in the same way. The fact that he knew absolutely nothing about this was irrelevant. It was still completely out of the question for her to telephone him after office hours, and that was that. She would just have to wait until the Artquake exhibition opened to find out what was happening. In the meantime, she had to decide what she was going to wear. After the opening at the Art Gallery, there was going to be a party at the Old York Factory, a restaurant downtown.

When she arrived at work the next morning, Bruno was not there, but it wasn't long before she found her book and the cache of spoiled labels in the garbage. Since emptying the wastebasket was one of her duties as assistant manager, she took that as a sign, and not a particularly good one. She had intended to smuggle the labels out of the gallery in her handbag, but had never got around to it. She retrieved *To the North*, dumped the remaining contents of the basket into a plastic bag and transferred it to the larger garbage can in the workshop. Then she resolved that in future she would be, or at least appear to be, a more conscientious employee. When Bruno showed up a few minutes later with their morning coffees, she already had all the dusting done and was sweeping the floor near the front window, looking as cheerful as possible.

WHETHER IT WAS a blessing or a curse, Bob had never quite figured out. Sometimes he felt his tendency to be detached and analytical was a bad thing. It could well have been a factor in the failure of both his marriages. If he had been a different kind of person he might not have *allowed* Lorraine to run off to Ibiza. Maybe a heartfelt profession of love, an abject, tearful appeal to everything they had shared – their ideals, their dreams, their very *youth*, for God's sake – would have done the trick. But at the time, younger and prouder than he was today, he just hadn't been able to bring himself to say any of those things. Goddamn it, he'd raged to himself, if she didn't know by now how much he cared for her – all right, *loved and needed* her – she didn't know much of anything at all. A woman *that* stupid was not worthy of his love, so let her go, man, let her go.

And perhaps his analysis of the situation had been accurate. Maybe Lorraine really hadn't been any more intelligent than her successor. Right from the start, he'd seen Margie for what she was: a cute, affectionate, easily impressed birdbrain with a weakness for 'creative' men – a small-town girl. He, born in a near hamlet himself, was something of an expert on the type. So it shouldn't have come as a surprise that little Margie couldn't tell the difference between him, a serious

artist, and some buttoned-down hack whose watery creative juices drib-
bled only onto TV quiz panels and variety shows. But it had; he'd felt so
superior to his wife that he hadn't noticed any of the signs. Eventually,
though, he'd been able to understand, by the clear-eyed application of
logic and reason, that it was an open-and-shut case of good riddance.

However, he was having trouble applying the same logic to Eleanor
Zeffler. Sure, there were lots of things about her he didn't like. She was a
brittle, self-centred beauty with no appreciation of art beyond simple
acquisitiveness. But what did that matter, when she herself was no more
to him than a superbly formed but essentially frivolous object, the
human equivalent of a Fabergé egg?

All he felt towards Eleanor was simple, uncomplicated lust. All right,
not simple, not uncomplicated. You didn't have to crawl into an orgone
box to figure out that lust made the world go round in all kinds of
twisted, subterranean ways. And when it was yanked out of the abstract
and applied to a specific individual, there were plenty of complications.
For example: your reckless lunge might be unspeakably repugnant to
the lungee. Lots of guys didn't care much about that, but Bob did, and he
wasn't likely to change, not at his advanced age. Then you had to look at
the competition, for wasn't sexual performance always tied up somehow
with the challenge of 'better than'? Even if Eleanor's romantic life with
her husband was dormant, he recognized something in her demeanour
that suggested she wasn't doing without sex.

So she and Jerry still ... it wasn't out of the question. Anybody who'd
been married knew it was possible to have adequate, even satisfying sexual relations with someone who irritated the hell out of you. Or maybe
Eleanor was already involved in an extramarital affair. But with whom?
He cast about half-heartedly for a likely name and, with a shaming sense
of relief, failed to come up with one.

At times like this, he envied the innocent egotism of youth, the kind of
obliviousness he saw in a kid like Eddie O'Hara. Or in Jenny Kosma,
whose self-confidence was positively unnerving in a girl barely out of her
teens. When you were young, other people's motives and emotions
seemed not only cartoonlike but static. The awareness that they might
well be every bit as contradictory, illogical and fluid as your own only
dawned slowly with age. Or from experience. Like the moment you discovered that someone you thought you knew as well as – maybe even
better than – yourself could change beyond recognition right under your
nose. Always, forever and our-love-is-here-to-stay not-withstanding.

Oh, he was old enough to see that even if he thought he had Eleanor pegged, he could still be wrong. All he could say with certainty was that her existence gave him pleasure. Something about her, or perhaps just the idea of her, had galvanized him, got him working again. For that he was grateful. Naturally, he would sleep with her if he ever got the chance. And that, he felt, was a reasonably objective assessment of the situation.

IT SEEMED STRANGE to Eddie that he hadn't heard anything from Margrave or Burnham. But he wasn't going to call either of them, even though a week had passed and the exhibition was scheduled to open in two days' time. He didn't want to talk about where *Back Flip*, Version Two, had come from and how it had got to the Art Gallery. He and Willard had just left it on the loading dock and made their getaway without even asking for a receipt. He'd printed the title on the crossbar of the stretcher and signed and dated the painting on the back, but it had been Bob's idea to stick a strip of masking tape on the plastic sheeting they'd used to wrap it and write on that 'For Artquake '67 Exhibition'. So there was no way it could have got lost. Was there? Well, he'd only know for sure when the show opened.

He decided not to think beyond that night. It was scary enough. For one thing, it would be the first time he'd see one of his paintings hanging in a public institution. Unfortunately, he'd also be forced to see Gonzaga again. Bruno would probably freak out when he saw Version Two hanging there. But at least there'd be onlookers who might, if he was lucky, prevent Godzilla from tearing him in two with his mighty hands.

If he started to think about life after Artquake, he'd have to figure out what he was going to do about the Gonzaga Gallery, about the paintings from his last show that were still in storage there and about Bruno himself. Right now, he'd have been happy never to see his dealer again. Maybe the guy really was insane.

And maybe the *Cloud* series had been a huge mistake. Or, as one kind-hearted instructor from his art college days always used to say when faced with some godawful mess, 'a failed experiment'. Yeah. Well, Bruno had hated the grey paintings. He'd dismissed the idea of a *Cloud* show for 1968 with a grunt that left no room for argument. And Margrave, in his ever-so-frightfully-tactful way, had said nothing at all about them when he came to the studio. Even Willard, who as far as Eddie could see had no axe to grind, had gone all tactful on him, resorting to the dread word 'interesting' when he took a look at the *Clouds*. Then he'd said, 'I thought you were one of those colour guys.'

If he was going to capitalize on the Artquake show, especially after the London exposure, he had to find another dealer. And in order to get one, he needed some work to show. Good stuff. But the *Clouds* were lousy. Empty, academic, embalmed. He needed something to kick his head loose, get the old creative juices flowing ... force him to look at things differently.

It was getting on for five o'clock. Jorgensen might be rolling into the Pilot just about now. He'd be the guy to see – he was always yakking about the mind-blowing trips he had taken. Eddie grabbed his coat and galloped down the stairs to the street.

ALTHOUGH HE WAS never overbearing, Max could be pretty eloquent when he wanted to. And his argument in favour of Tom's attending both the exhibition opening and the party after it was starting to sound quite persuasive. Naturally Tom had not revealed to Max the real reason for his reluctance to go. His cowardice in the face of Winifred's, Eleanor's and Quintin's possible expectations was hardly compatible with the congenial, self-assured persona he usually showed to the world.

But now Tom found himself growing susceptible to his dealer's line of reasoning, based as it was on an up-to-date interpretation of *noblesse oblige*. The two of them were sitting in Max's private office at the Lurie. It was Wednesday afternoon, and Artquake '67 was scheduled to open on the Thursday evening.

'Remember,' said Max, 'all the younger artists look up to you.' He poured them each a couple of fingers of Scotch from the bottle he kept in the bottom drawer of his desk. 'You're really the only internationally recognized artist in the show.'

True, thought Tom, accepting his glass with a nod of thanks. Perhaps these days he *was* something of an elder statesman. His presence might add a certain lustre to the proceedings.

Max continued, 'Don't you think you owe it to the other guys – the young ones coming up – to be there? To show your support, underline this show's importance, make sure people here and abroad know that things are really happening here – that Canada is no longer an artistic backwater.'

All right, maybe it was his patriotic duty to go. He *had* been something of a pioneer, clearing the dense forest of provincialism, uprooting *The Jack Pine*'s stump once and for all. He sipped his Scotch thoughtfully. A blend, but an acceptable one. Yes, he'd done his best to blast a broad highway through the rocky Canadian Shield, opening the wilderness to the world beyond and all its influences. 'You may have a point there.'

'As a matter of fact, when Artquake goes to London, we may be able to set up a commercial show for you at the same time. Quintin's going to put me in touch with some people there. He has a lot of influence and he's a big fan of yours, you know. I think he'll be pretty offended if you don't show up at the opening.'

Dear me, poor Quintin's feelings might be hurt. We can't have that, can we? Tom took a gulp of his drink, nearly emptying the glass. Could be he'd been too hard on Margrave. The guy had his job to do. And Max nearly always knew what he was talking about. A London dealer ... a base of operations in the Mother Country. How that would have tickled his dad! A trip a year, largely tax deductible. Bond Street, Liberty's, Burlington Arcade, Simpson's in the Strand ... Joan would really enjoy it all. And so, honestly, would he. There might even be a European connection eventually ... Paris, most likely. Tom felt the last of his resistance evaporate.

'Oh, I guess maybe you're right.' He took another sip from his glass. 'I suppose I really ought to put in an appearance.'

Max nodded approvingly and raised his own glass to his lips. But he wasn't finished. 'Another thing is, apart from all those considerations, we also ought to support the people from our own stable. Artquake '67 will be good not only for you and the Lurie but also for our other artists. You know Jenny Kosma has a piece in the show. Try to make sure she gets a chance to talk to Margrave. It's her first real break and the association with you won't do her any harm. Especially with her show here coming up in a couple of months.'

Now that was a bit much. However benevolent Tom felt in theory and at a distance towards the younger generation, up close he found them pretty hard to take: arrogant, undisciplined, soft, proudly ignorant of history yet self-importantly determined to remake it. The Kosma girl, especially.

Not that he had anything against the fair sex, or female artists, for that matter. Far from it – look what he'd done, or tried to do, for Win. But Winnie was an old friend and an entirely different sort of woman. Besides, her work was excellent in its own way: lyrical yet organic, occasionally veering unpleasantly towards the gynecological and at times a tad too prettified, but on the whole a fine and normal expression of the female sensibility. Frankenthaler out of O'Keeffe, you might say. And there was a place for that sort of thing, definitely.

Kosma, on the other hand, thought she could just go ahead and try to paint like a man. Why, you might even mistake her big, aggressive canvases for the work of some guy of the second rank. And both her appearance and manner seemed to Tom utterly charmless. The girl was devoid of flirtatiousness or deference, and in his opinion a woman without either could hardly be considered female at all. For all her airs, Winifred never allowed him to forget how much she admired him, both as an artist and a man. And he admired her, too. Mind you, in the reverse order, woman first and artist second.

The thought of Win's informed admiration – leaving aside the question of whether he wanted to do anything about it – was a comfort. As he finished the last dregs of his drink, he chided himself for his faintheartedness. He had nothing to fear from Winifred. Whatever he decided or wished to offer her, she could only be grateful. And she would certainly be kind.

Max was saying, '... by the way, did you hear that Howard McNab wrote some of the entries for the Artquake catalogue? And part of the introduction, too, although of course Margrave's name is on it. Apparently Quintin lost interest in it, and Burnham, in turn, got fed up with Quintin and refused to carry the can. Then Howard volunteered to step in and finished it right on deadline. So they're both in his debt.'

'And I'm sure he'll collect, eventually.'

'Oh, you can bet on it. It's also a feather in his cap. You might even have to start being nicer to him now.'

Tom guffawed. 'Hell, I hope not,' he said cheerfully, holding his glass out for a refill.

JERRY WOULDN'T hear of it. He greeted Eleanor's calculated boredom at the prospect of attending the Artquake opening with annoyance so excessive that it shattered the temporary atmosphere of good will created by their sexual encounter the night before.

That, to her surprise, had gone like clockwork, despite all her recent transgressions. Feeling contrite, she had tried not to think of Tom, or anyone else, during her exertions with her husband. She had almost succeeded. There was a brief period in which Tom, Quintin and, for some reason, young O'Hara had each briefly appeared, but then she immediately and violently crested the wave. A few moments later, Jerry was finished too. And before their brains were fully functioning again, the two of them had even shared a few fleeting moments of tenderness.

But now he was saying, 'Are you nuts? Everybody will be there. How could it possibly be a bore? And if you feel one of your so-called migraines coming on, take a pill. I'm not going alone.'

'Okay, okay. But I don't find all those artsy people as fascinating as you do. Besides, you always leave me to fend for myself while you run around glad-handing everybody.'

'*Glad-handing?* What's that supposed to mean? "Those artsy people," as you call them, respect me as a connoisseur. Anyone but you would consider it a privilege and an honour to meet internationally recognized figures like Tom Dale and Quintin Margrave. Because and *only* because you're my wife, you get that chance ... and what's so damn funny about that?'

'Oh, nothing.'

Eleanor had never had the slightest intention of missing the Artquake opening, but she didn't see why she should allow Jerry to take her presence there for granted. She hadn't yet decided whether to make another run at Tom, or just pretend not to see him, and she was merely curious about how Quintin would behave. At least, that was what she told herself. With the party still a full twenty-four hours away, it was easy to act brave. She'd probably be a nervous wreck when it actually came time to go. She lifted her hair off the nape of her neck with both hands and held it against the back of her head. After a few moments she said, 'I really haven't got anything to wear, though.'

Jerry rolled his eyes in a hackneyed pantomime of exasperation. 'Oh, for God's sake go and get yourself another damn dress, if that'll make you happy.'

JANE'S MACHINE was nearly an antique, a 1930s model she had inherited from her mother, who had long ago lost interest in sewing. It still ran well enough on straight seams, as long as you didn't rush it. But if the needle started racing along beyond a certain speed it sometimes produced a tangled knot of thread that could take hours to extricate from the mechanism. So Jane was going slowly. The long zipper she was inserting was tricky; she was going nuts trying to get the seam that ran around the dress under the bustline to meet precisely at the back when the zipper closed. And she really wanted the mauve-and-blue-paisley print to match along the back seam, too. Now it looked as if the whole thing would have to be ripped out.

It was nearly midnight, but she was determined to get that zipper in before she went to bed. So far the dress had turned out all right. She'd deepened the scoop neck a little when cutting out the pattern and altered the straight, tight sleeves so they flared out like trumpets at the wrists – a kind of pre-Raphaelite look. Then she'd faced the sleeves up to the elbow with satiny material that matched the teal blue in the paisley. She'd have to turn up the hem the next day, in the interval between work and the opening. In the same couple of hours, she would also have to wash, dry and then laboriously straighten her hair with the curling iron, praying that it wouldn't rain that night.

Getting ready for a gala occasion like the Artquake party was almost like setting off on a trip. Jane liked to assemble all the elements of her outfit well in advance. Dark blue fishnet tights, still miraculously intact after a couple of previous wearings, a navy blue lace push-up bra and a matching foot-long half slip were already laid out on the mattress that still sat in what had once been Jane's bedroom, before she took over Debbie's bigger one. Nowadays, Jane used the room for sewing, ironing and general clutter.

A pair of Italian-made blue-metallic-patent pumps with Minnie Mouse toes and spool-shaped heels that last summer had cost thirty bucks (more than half a week's salary but well worth it) were sitting beside the bed. Now all she had to do was finish the dress. She sat down cross-legged on the floor and, with a pin, began to pick out the tiny stitches along the edges of the zipper, one by one.

▮ Chapter Fourteen

THE ACID really made the twenty-minute walk from the studio to the gallery ... interesting. Before setting out, Eddie had reminded himself to be extra careful when he crossed the road. But he forgot all about that as soon as the streetlights began to radiate spiky auras that reminded him of... something. Oh yeah ... that Van Gogh thing. *The Night Café.*

Hey. Wow.

Every few seconds, those dazzling rings buzzed and spat against the saturated blue of the sky at dusk. They looked like the sparklers he used to drag through the suburban-spring darkness as a kid on Victoria Day. When he heard an indignant clanging behind him, he tried to shake it off by waggling his head, but it didn't stop. Whirling on the sound just in time, he saw the blunt beige snout of a streetcar bearing down on him, its huge glassy eyes alight, ready to nose him out of the way. As he leapt off the tracks and onto the sidewalk, he saluted the gesticulating maroon-clad figure trapped in one of those monster eyeballs. From then on, he kept to side streets as much as possible and stayed close to the buildings, far away from the curb.

When at last he reached the gallery entrance, he kept his eyes averted from the bronze Adam standing there, because he knew as well as he knew his own name that it would start to writhe gently if he looked at it. He concentrated instead on the double doors that, glimmering gently in the dusk, would lead him to his moment of triumph. Still, in a far corner of his mind one fear lurked, now and then popping its gleaming cubical head out from the underbrush. It was possible that *Back Flip* would not even be hanging in the building he was about to enter. Three hours ago, it had seemed like a good idea to festoon that heavy, all-too-solid doubt with the complex and fanciful decorations provided by LSD.

And it more or less did the trick. As he prowled through the show, he kept having to shake off the beckoning tendrils of other people's work. They clutched at him, forcing him to stop again and again in front of some mediocre yet temporarily entrancing piece. But by then he was having just as much trouble disengaging from the faces, the hair (if long enough) and even the ties (if brightly coloured) of the people he saw in the crowd. He had to force himself to look beyond, into the distance, to scan the endless walls and partitions for *Back Flip*. There it was, at last, way across the room. Transfixed, he pushed his way through the jostling mob, and after a brief interval that seemed like years he was standing in front of it.

The painting vibrated, the descending triangle of yellow plunging like a fiery sword, stake, cock ... into a velvety bed, ocean, cunt, of bottomless, poignant and mesmerizing azure blue. A pulse was beating steadily at the point of entry. He nearly staggered back, awestruck and proud. A feeling of warmth, an effusion of heat, a gently pulsing orgasmic glow started to work its way through him, and he realized, understood, *knew* that the painting was better, far better than he had ever suspected.

A far, far better thing... Dirk Bogarde on the scaffold ... *than I have ever done...* A masterpiece, by gum. *We who are about to die salute you...*

Hey, wait a minute. *No.* Hold it.

He pressed his forehead against the wall and closed his eyes. When he opened them, the first thing he saw was a neatly printed label. It was pinned to the wall, right opposite his chest. He took a step away and looked at it.

Edward O'Hara (Canadian, b. 1946)
Back Flip, 1967
acrylic on canvas

Yeah. There it was. Perfect. But then all the letters from the next line floated up from the cardboard rectangle, danced jauntily in space for a moment, reformed themselves into words and hit him, *pow,* right in the kisser.

Collection of Bruno Gonzaga, Toronto

ELEANOR STAYED CLOSE to Jerry at the exhibition. In protective custody. At the entrance, all her false bravado had evaporated in a moment of sheer panic. Conscious of the still unretrievable hours that had followed her visit to the Windsor Arms, she had decided not to take any Valium tonight. Her new dress, a little shift covered all over with sequins – every one hand-sewn, the saleslady had assured her – would have to supply the needed confidence.

So here she was: the lovely Mrs Zeffler, right beside her dynamic husband. A woman who clearly could do no one harm; a mother, to be sure, but she had never, would never, ever, let herself go. Still a fashion plate, still with the looks to carry it off. A patron of the arts, but far from stuffy. She was now, today, with it, in the groove, baby. Even Jerry glanced at her approvingly from time to time, though more as if he were calculating the effect she might have on other people than admiring her appearance himself.

Faced with the possibility of encountering Quintin or Tom, or both of them at once, she suddenly understood just how far out of her depth she was. She hadn't the slightest idea what either of them thought of her now. Or if they ever thought about her at all.

TOM AND JOAN DALE made their way through the crush arm in arm. Their progress was slow, because people kept stopping them, wanting to chat. The Dales had an unspoken agreement about their strategy at such events: as long as the interactions remained primarily social, they stuck together. They made a good team. Joan always remembered faces and names, which was useful because Tom tended to smile at everyone indiscriminately and sometimes forgot to be especially nice to certain people who considered themselves important. However, when it was a matter of professional recognition, Joan would fade instantly and amiably into the background so that he could deal with the glory alone.

'But,' Tom told her as they entered the exhibition, 'tonight isn't really *my* night. Artquake '67 belongs to the kids getting their first break.' Hell, he'd been around long enough to take this kind of thing in his stride, if not entirely for granted. His work was already in all the important permanent collections, and Max said there was even talk of a National Gallery retrospective, which of course would be quite a thrill.

Still, he couldn't have been left out of Artquake. The work he was doing nowadays was as vital and contemporary as that of the young unknowns that Margrave had plucked out of obscurity. Which just showed to go you that 'youth' was all a matter of perception.

'But then,' Tom went on, 'to a guy like Margrave, everything I've produced and, by the way, *sold*, over the past fifteen years might as well have been painted in a cave. Right there you have the British imperialist mentality in a nutshell. Luckily the Yanks are a little more on the qui-vive.'

Joan smiled her agreement to everything he'd said and then squeezed his arm. That meant he should pay attention because some bigwig was heading their way.

BOB WONDERED why he'd bothered to come. He spotted Eleanor at once, but she seemed to be glued to her husband's side, so he decided to bide his time. Meanwhile, he was keeping an eye out for Jenny. Their tête-à-tête at the Pilot the other day had been quite pleasant.

He'd timed his arrival well, just missing the few well-chosen words that Margrave and Burnham must have said to mark the exhibition's opening. Given the absence of booze and the vaguely inhibiting atmosphere, these institutional do's were never much fun. Even if you happened to have something in the show being celebrated, there was always that Chardin or Rembrandt (studio of) hanging in the next room to mock your own white-knuckled hold on immortality.

But maybe he, always the cock-eyed pessimist, was the only one who saw it that way. Most guys probably loved to see their work hanging in such august company, feeling sure that they themselves were about to join the pantheon. However, when you knew that one of your own early masterpieces was languishing permanently somewhere in the vaults, it was tougher to be optimistic about your chances. He'd never forget the glorious moment – late in September '57 – when Max had called to say that *Composition III* had been purchased the Art Gallery of Toronto. But the painting had never, as far as he knew, seen the light of day since.

Besides, there were always far too many people at these things; you couldn't see the art for the bodies. That was true of all openings, but he preferred the more intimate setting of commercial galleries. There, the background hum of money being made or lost added a certain piquancy to the proceedings, and the free, if invariably cheap, wine created at least the illusion of a low-budget cocktail party. As for entertainment, you could usually count on somebody, usually a friend or lover of the artist, behaving badly.

Although he wouldn't exclude the possibility of some kind of floor show taking place tonight. He looked around for Eddie. He was starting to feel positively avuncular about the kid and he could hardly wait to see whether the second *Back Flip* would actually be up on the wall. A minute or two before, O'Hara's red head had been visible, bobbing above the crowd on the other side of the room, but now he'd disappeared. Bob wondered if Bruno Gonzaga had shown up yet. If those two happened to meet in front of *Back Flip*, it could turn out to be an interesting evening.

JANE WAS ALSO keeping an eye out for Eddie. It would have been a lot easier if she'd been wearing her glasses, but that was out of the question. Beyond a small zone of clarity, everything was a blur, and she moved through the exhibition as if in a bubble. However, she was used to that sensation and didn't really mind the social passivity it imposed. Strategy was impossible when you could barely see, and in a way it was relaxing not to have to mingle purposefully. You simply had to wait for people to come close enough to be recognizable and then deal with them. Besides, she'd read somewhere that the dilated, myopic eye was rather seductive.

The main problem was the danger of coming face to face with undesirables when it was too late to escape. She spotted Sven Jorgensen just in time. He had his back to her, so she was able get away unnoticed. His natural belligerence would probably be increased by the fact that Margrave hadn't picked any of his work for Artquake, and she didn't see why she should have to deal with it outside working hours. As Jane moved away from Sven, Win Beecham strode past her with only a brisk nod of recognition, and she was grateful for that, too. Being saddled with her on an occasion like this would be kind of like going to a party with your mother. The visibly impatient old guy trailing after her must be her husband, Dr Overton.

Eventually Jane got to the edge of the crowd, then began to work her way around the room, sticking close to the walls. If she couldn't find Eddie himself, at least she could see if *Back Flip* was here. After about five minutes, she saw it. Bruno was standing in front of it, looking closely at the wall label. Then he turned to her with a slightly dazed expression.

'So,' he said, 'We are in the show.'

'Yeah, it's great.' She started to ask if he had seen Eddie, but thought better of it. Anyway, she wasn't going to spend the evening making polite conversation with her boss. At that moment, fortunately, Max Lurie came up to them. He smiled vaguely at Jane, deftly avoiding the issue of whether he knew who she was, and seized Bruno's hand.

'Wonderful show,' he said buoyantly. 'It's a fine night for our young stars, isn't it?'

Bruno was forced to agree. He chuckled amiably enough, but to Jane his expression revealed that he was searching for the hidden, sinister meaning beneath Lurie's friendly greeting. Seeing a chance to escape, she took a couple of quick steps backward and melted into the crowd.

AS SOON AS he saw him, Eddie ducked behind the nearest partition and tried, with very little success, to brace himself. Right now, meeting Bruno would be a serious downer and at least as unwise as walking into traffic. From previous experience he knew that when you were on acid, any hateful thoughts rattling around in your brain would be instantly animated and transformed into relentless, unstoppable cartoons. That was why you were only supposed to drop in a benign, harmonious setting.

He realized now, when it was already much too late to do anything about it, that the Artquake opening was just about the worst place he could have chosen. Carefully, he looked around the edge of the partition. Bruno was still there. His hair was giving off oily bluish glints, and even his black suit looked faintly slimy as, beetle-like, he crawled around in front of *Back Flip*. Eddie felt himself laugh and shudder at the same time. What a corny, bargain-basement metamorphosis. With his unconscious, he ought to be able to come up with something better than that. And what a fucking idiot he was. *Shit.*

Without risking another glance at Bruno, he set off quickly in the opposite direction, fixing his eyes on the floor. The beige industrial carpeting had a herringbone pattern that rippled gently under his boots like the sandy bottom of a shallow lake. When he got to the men's john, he pushed the door open a crack and peered through it. The room appeared to be empty, so he slipped inside. Without looking at the row of mirrors over the sinks, he went directly to the nearest cubicle, entered it and locked the door behind him.

IT WAS a good thing he always kept a clear head, Bruno thought. If he'd been in the habit of drinking to excess, or drugging himself the way degenerates like O'Hara did, he'd be in very deep trouble now. But even stone cold sober and hyper-vigilant, he was not one hundred per cent sure he was in control of the situation.

When Lurie was finally gone, he tried to collect his thoughts, glad to be left alone. After his telephone conversation with Burnham, finding *Back Flip* in the exhibition had not come as a surprise. No, it was not the sight of the painting, or rather its double, that troubled him – or even the fleeting glimpse he'd caught of O'Hara sneaking around near it. What really unsettled Bruno was the urgent, passionate sensation that was now gripping him: the almost overwhelming desire to believe the canvas in front of him really was *his*. If only he could forget all about the other *Back Flip* – the one he'd hidden in the broom closet – and simply claim ownership of this one!

But then, why shouldn't he? He *was* the person responsible for O'Hara's success. He had discovered him, believed in him and given him a chance when no one else would. And this was the thanks he'd received. *Ingrate, traitor, thief ...* When a couple of strangers looked at him curiously and started to edge away, he realized that he must have spoken the words aloud. He turned his back on them and pretended to study *Back Flip*.

The thought came to him that Eddie was the only other person in the world who knew that two versions of the painting existed. But O'Hara didn't know where the first one was. Only he, Bruno, knew that. If he simply disposed of the original, this copy would be the 'real' *Back Flip*, and he its real owner. Why, look at the credit line, right there on the wall label: 'Collection of Bruno Gonzaga'. Each time he saw them, those words seemed more beautiful.

IT WAS ONLY Margrave, Tom realized. The gentle but insistent pressure of Joan's fingers on his forearm had simply been a warning that the Englishman was within earshot, close enough to overhear himself being mentioned in not entirely flattering terms. Well, Tom didn't really care if Quintin had heard his basically good-natured grousing, and he raised his eyebrows at Joan to show her as much. There were times when she was a little too protective. Her intentions were good, but a woman had to know when to give a man his head. With an effort, he pasted an affable grin on his face as he turned around to greet Margrave.

Jenny Kosma lobbed that smile back to him as if it had been meant exclusively for her. Tom had to repress a snort of indignation; so this was the timid fledgling Max had asked him to take under his wing! Judging from the almost proprietary way she was looking at Margrave, she wouldn't be needing his – or anyone's – help. Though it might be interesting to find out whether the Englishman was actually susceptible to feminine – or at least female – wiles.

'Well, well, the man himself,' said Margrave.

Tom kept smiling. 'Evening, my dear fellow,' he replied, pronouncing the last three words in an approximation of a British accent. *Mah deah fellah.*

'Do you know Jenny?'

Tom managed a nod.

'You've seen *Duo,* I imagine,' Margrave went on in a confidential tone. 'Looks splendid, doesn't it? I thought it needed a spot all to itself. And *Pee Wee's Place* is wonderful, too.'

Tom continued to smile blandly. 'Haven't made the tour yet, as a matter of fact. We just got here.'

WIN'S BAD TEMPER was only partly due to the fact that her work had not been chosen for Artquake. She was quite aware, thank you very much, that she was no longer a member of any 'younger generation', and if it hadn't been for the inclusion of Tom Dale's two paintings, she wouldn't have given the snub a second thought. But the inescapable fact that Tom – almost exactly the same age as she – was deemed a credible representative of up-to-the-minute art had suddenly begun to rankle.

She hadn't succeeded in securing a private audience with Quintin Margrave, although she'd heard Tom mention his name in a way that suggested he and Margrave were on quite friendly terms. Then why on earth hadn't her dear friend and admirer spoken up for her? She'd hardly expected Gonzaga to push her work forward; it had become abundantly clear that he didn't understand or appreciate it. Besides, he was far too busy promoting O'Hara, who was now considered quite the Young Turk. But surely Tom … it was a grim thought, but perhaps he had actually been avoiding her. Perhaps the gradual tailing off of their friendship had been his, rather than her own, tactful decision.

She was unpleasantly aware of the long-suffering expression on Eliot's face, even though she avoided looking at him. No doubt he had conveniently forgotten the hundreds of deadly hours she'd wasted hob-nobbing with his colleagues and their wives.

And now, from only a few feet away, she had to witness the chummy little group clustered around Tom, who seemed determined to avoid meeting her eye. Well, if that was the way he wanted it, she was hardly the sort to push in where she was not welcome. Casually, she glanced over at them: Margrave, Lurie (whose gallery, she had often thought, would be so much more suitable for her work than Gonzaga's), Joan

Dale (of course), and – right in the middle, simpering gleefully at them all – that dreadful Kosma girl.

ELEANOR HAD NEVER really looked at Jenny Kosma before; there was no reason why she would have. Jerry said he couldn't understand why Max had brought Kosma into the Lurie stable. Everybody seemed to agree that with very rare exceptions, women artists were usually second-rate. Anyway, Eleanor couldn't see why any girl who was attractive would want to be a painter, especially nowadays when art itself was so muscular. But then Jenny was quite the tomboy type, to put it mildly. Well, she'd have to be to move those great big canvases of hers around. Poor thing, she probably had to do her own lifting; she was hardly the type to elicit acts of chivalry. Eleanor certainly didn't envy her that.

However, she did resent the fact that Jenny had ended up tucked between Quintin Margrave and Tom Dale. She looked very much at ease there. As the two men conversed, her head swivelled attentively from one to the other. Eleanor was too far away to hear what they were saying but she could see that every so often Jenny's mouth opened and her lips moved. So she wasn't being ignored or excluded from the discussion. Max, who was also in the group, kept smiling encouragingly at the girl and drawing her into the conversation.

Eleanor glanced at her husband, who was half turned away from her. *Back Flip*'s being chosen for the exhibition instead of *Tusk* had come as a blow, but Jerry wasn't the kind to admit disappointment in public. Anyway, O'Hara's star was rising, that was the main thing. And he had that felt pen drawing – it would become an 'early O'Hara' any day now – and *Tusk* to prove he hadn't been asleep at the wheel.

McNab had attached himself to them, and he and Jerry were immersed in an unbearably boring discussion of the show. She had stopped worrying that Howard might say something about seeing her at the Windsor Arms. Jerry wasn't the jealous type; it probably never occurred to him that other men might look at his wife with more than theoretical admiration. To get his attention, McNab would really have to spell out the implications of her presence at the hotel.

Saw your lovely wife at the Windsor Arms the other afternoon. She'd been upstairs. Guess she must be having an affair, eh?

Maybe you're right, Howard. But it's certainly news to me.

You know, Jerry, I've always thought she was quite a cold fish.

Oh, you'd be surprised....

No, that wouldn't happen. Anyway, when it came right down to it, she decided, McNab was not very interested in the deeds or misdeeds of women. To him, they were just slabs of more or less malleable flesh. But was Quintin really any different? Was Tom?

Despite these sombre reflections, she was still alert enough to sense Bob Willard hovering about five feet away from her. Even without looking directly at him, she could tell that he was trying to catch her eye. She moved closer to Jerry and slid her arm through his. He turned his head to look absently at her but went on talking.

BOB WASN'T absolutely sure, but it seemed that Eleanor had deliberately avoided seeing him. Maybe that was just as well. Anyway, it was pretty obvious that for the moment, she did not require rescuing. It wasn't as if he and Eleanor actually had a relationship. The romantic urges she had roused in him had been merely speculative. Without encouragement from her they would never spur him to decisive action. As for the vascular stirrings taking place in more southerly locations – well, he'd never allowed those to lead him into places where he wasn't truly welcome.

But it was pleasant to discover that he wasn't entirely past it in that respect. There might be life in the old depressive yet. His thoughts about Eleanor had been exploratory, a kind of enjoyable doodling, not unlike the sketches he'd been doing lately. Still, they suggested that maybe life did begin at forty, like the man said. And maybe he'd even start painting again.

Drifting casually away from the Zefflers, he spotted an intriguing group just in front of him: Max, Dale, Margrave and Jenny, who, wearing makeup and a dress, looked unusually girlish. What the hell, why not? He stepped resolutely forward and laid a comradely hand on Max's shoulder. For a long and dreadful moment his old friend seemed to hesitate. Then finally he turned and drew Bob into the circle.

AFTER A WHILE, he had no idea how long, Eddie opened his eyes and peered around the men's room through the gap at the bottom of the stall. All was quiet and no feet were visible. And he was definitely feeling much better. With some difficulty, he pulled himself upright and leaned against the cubicle wall for a few seconds. Then he opened the door and stepped out.

The lights were painfully bright, and the face that looked back at him from the mirror over the sink was only vaguely familiar. In some odd way that he couldn't quite put his finger on, he seemed like a different person; a stranger, but on the whole, he decided, not an unfriendly one. When he lifted his hand and pressed it against the glass, his twin's hand rose, too. As their palms met precisely on the smooth, cool surface, the other guy's eyes gleamed meaningfully at him.

'Okay, pal,' he said to him, as if they'd known each other for years, 'let's blow this dump.'

▪ Chapter Fifteen

SOMEHOW OR OTHER, Bob got separated from Max and the rest of them when the general exodus from the Art Gallery began. The lobby was packed, because everybody seemed to have decided at the same moment to go over to the York Factory. As he stood in the lineup for the coat check, he saw Eddie come up the steps from the sculpture court. The kid looked a little strange, smiling in self-absorbed way and keeping his eyes firmly on the floor. He seemed to be in an awful hurry to get outside. On a sudden impulse, Bob went after him. But by the time he got to the door, O'Hara was already on the other side of the street and heading rapidly west. He'd catch up to Eddie at the restaurant, he decided. Although, right now, O'Hara seemed to be going somewhere else.

When Bob went back to the spot where Max, Tom, Margrave and Jenny had all been standing, they had vanished. But at least the line was shorter now and he got his coat almost immediately. He had hoped to catch a ride over to the party with somebody in the group. It hardly seemed worth taking a cab, and after a quick, discreet check of his wallet, he realized he didn't have enough money on him anyway. So it looked as if he'd have to walk.

JANE TOOK the new University subway southbound to King Street. From there it wasn't far to the Factory. The restaurant, a refurbished nineteenth-century industrial building, was already filling up by the time she arrived. Its décor – a kitschy Edwardian mix of red velvet brothel and Wild West saloon – had been fun a few years ago, but looked a little passé now. There was a large central area, rather like the nave of a basilica, flanked on both sides by aisles marked off by rows of pillars. Right in the middle, a patch of floor had been left uncarpeted for danc- ing, and the strobe lights aimed on it were already flashing. Elsewhere in the restaurant a more muted light was cast by the frosted glass lamps that hung low over the tables. Judging from the noise level, quite a few of these were occupied. After dropping off her coat, Jane ducked into the washroom to check her appearance, which proved to be satisfactory.

Then she made straight for the bar, where a long line had already formed.

BRUNO DID NOT anticipate enjoying the Artquake party any more than he had the opening itself, though he felt duty-bound to go. But the unpredictable and mysterious nature of such festive events made him uneasy. The thought always weighed upon him that every person present came armed with his or her own agenda, some or all of which might be in direct conflict with Bruno's own best interests. In these circumstances his attempts at jovial good humour rang false even to himself.

As he put his car in gear and prepared to pull out onto the street, he silently admitted that what made the prospect of going to the Old York Factory especially unpleasant was the near certainty that Eddie O'Hara would be there. With care, he'd managed to avoid a face-to-face confrontation at the exhibition, but he was less sure he could do the same in the more fluid atmosphere of a party.

Not that he was afraid of O'Hara. He chuckled scornfully at the very thought. Aloud, it seemed, because Howard McNab, who was in the passenger seat, turned his head to look at him. Affecting absolute concentration on the road, Bruno ignored him. When they'd met just outside the Art Gallery, Howard indicated that he was looking for a ride over to the Factory and, after a second's thought, Bruno was more than happy to oblige. It was now clear to him that McNab's status was less secure than he had at first assumed, and he therefore felt more comfortable with him. Anyway, the man could still be useful to the Gonzaga Gallery. As he drove south, following his passenger's directions to the restaurant, Bruno's mood began to improve and he resolved to make the best of the evening.

THE CAB SLID to a halt in front of him, startlingly close, at the exact moment when Eddie realized he was going in the wrong direction. The relief of getting outdoors, the blessed sluice of cool air that ruffled his hair as he rushed along the street, had somehow made him lose his bearings. And now, after walking for … it was impossible to say how many blocks … he felt suddenly drained of all energy.

He knocked on the taxi window, feeling with his other hand for his wallet. He had enough money. Just as the driver nodded and waved him into the front seat, the traffic light turned green and the car behind them honked. As they pulled away, the cabbie gave it the finger and after a moment, grinning, Eddie did too. They had already travelled a couple of blocks, still in the wrong direction, when the driver finally glanced at him quizzically and said, 'Well, where to?'

The guy had an interesting face – cheeks pitted with acne scars like the surface of the moon and a single dark eyebrow that hung low over his glittering eyes. There was something kind of pirate-like about him. A buccaneer. *Avast, me hearties. Shiver me timbers. Swab the decks. Pieces of eight. All that glitters is not.*

'Hey, pal, wake up. I said, *Where to?*'

'Just a sec. I forget the name of the place.' Eddie pulled the Artquake invitation card out of his front pocket and held it up.

The cabbie took it and propped it against the steering wheel as he drove. 'Sorry, bud,' he said after a moment, 'you missed the boat. It was from six to eight, it says here. It's now –' he tapped reproachfully on the dashboard clock '– 9:04.'

'No, no, no. The party, the party, the party.' Eddie grabbed the card out of the driver's hand and examined it. 'At the Old York Factory. Eight-thirty.'

'Okay, that maybe you can still make.' Ostentatiously, he checked his mirrors, then jerked the car into a violent, screeching U-turn that whipped Eddie sideways. The steering wheel whizzed through the cabbie's one-handed grip when they straightened up on the other side of the street and headed back in the direction they'd come from.

Eddie rolled down his window and stuck his head and shoulders out, gobbling at the rushing air. Then he felt himself being yanked back inside by a hand that had taken a firm hold on his collar.

'Hey, smarten up!' the driver yelled. 'You could get yourself killed.' He held on to Eddie all the way to their destination, every so often glaring suspiciously at him.

When they pulled up in front of the Factory there were quite a few people on the sidewalk, but at first glance Eddie didn't recognize any of them. When he shifted in his seat in order to get out his money, the driver finally loosened his grip on his jacket.

'Three-fifty,' he said, not unkindly.

Methodically, Eddie thumbed through the bills in his wallet. It seemed essential, suddenly, to ascertain exactly how much cash he actually had. He found an unusually colourful and pleasing array of ones, twos and fives as well as a couple of twenties.

'Three-fifty,' the cabbie repeated.

Eddie nodded absently. He was calculating. *Fifteen per cent of three-fifty is … fifteen per cent of three is … three times fifteen is … hold it, hold it … forty-five.* Yeah, forty-five. *Now then, fifteen per cent of fifty is … let's see, let's see … five times fifteen is … is … is … fuck it.*

'Three-fifty!' the driver said again, as if he hadn't heard a word Eddie had thought.

Fifteen per cent of three was – wait, what was it? Three times fifteen is forty-five. Three times, no, five times fifty is … No, no, no … three times fifteen…

And just around that point, somewhere between fifteen and fifty, but after forty-five, the driver suddenly lunged for his wallet. Even though Eddie tried his best to hang on to it, the guy pried it out of his hands without much difficulty. But before he had finished pondering the possible implications and permutations of yelling for help from the crowd of strangers on the street, the cabbie extracted two two-dollar bills, waved them under Eddie's nose and handed the wallet, otherwise intact, back to him.

Then he reached over and shoved open the passenger door. 'Out,' he said. 'And take my advice, buddy, lay off the sauce.' Eddie had barely got both feet on the curb when the driver slammed the door shut again and roared away.

'HEY, EDDIE!' Bob was still half a block away from the Factory when he spotted O'Hara standing on the sidewalk. The kid was in the crowd waiting to go in, yet somehow visibly not of it. He seemed to be in some kind of a daze, not distressed exactly, but a little goofy, and his hair was windblown. When Bob came up to him and spoke his name again, more quietly, he slowly turned around. For a moment Eddie seemed not to recognize him, but then he smiled – almost too radiantly.

'Hey, Bobby!'

'Are you going in?'

'Sure, sure.'

As they started to climb the stairs, Eddie stopped and put his hands on either side of the door frame, bracing himself. 'Wow,' he said softly, as if the sight of the restaurant's interior was stunning. Or intimidating. For whatever reason, he seemed hesitant about going in and even took a step backward, lurching into a well-dressed couple on the sidewalk, who accepted his mumbled apology with good grace.

'Are you okay?' Bob asked, turning to look at him closely.

'Yeah. Sure. Maybe. Oh, shit.'

A backlog of people was starting to build up behind them, so Bob took Eddie's arm and gently guided him inside.

'What is it?' Bob asked, looking around at the same time for the bar. The prospect of free and unlimited alcohol was starting to relieve the smart of the rebuff he had been dealt by his old friend Max. During the solitary walk over to the restaurant, he had admitted to himself that that was what it had been. But in a quarter of an hour or so, he would be feeling sanguine and philosophical again.

Eddie put both his hands up to his face. 'Acid.'

'Huh?' said Bob. 'Oh.' Acid. LSD. A 'bad trip', perhaps? He was no expert on this kind of problem. Thanks, but no thanks; he didn't see the point of hallucinogens, couldn't fathom why anybody would want to take them. Wasn't life – oh, what the hell, let's call it 'reality', just for the sake of argument – already chaotic, unpredictable and frightening enough?

Eddie must have read his expression, because he patted him on the shoulder and said, 'Hey, hey, it's okay. Never mind. What time is it, anyway?'

'Um, a quarter after nine.'

'Shit. That means ….what's oh, what's three from nine and a quarter from twelve?'

'Huh?' Bob said again.

'I dropped at around three. I think. It should last for, let's see, maybe twelve hours, so …'

'So that means you've got nearly six more hours to go.' *And rather you than me, pal.*

'Oh, fuck.'

SHE HADN'T seen him coming this time. And now Sven Jorgensen had Jane up against the wall. Literally. He was so close that she could see every enlarged pore on his nose. She turned her head away to avoid his breath, but she could still hear him snuffling as he whispered in her ear.

'The trouble with you is you're too uptight.' Sniff. 'That stuff –' he gestured clumsily at the tumbler of vodka and orange juice she was clutching with both hands '– that stuff'll kill ya, babe.' Sniff.

He tipped his head back for a moment and squinted, as if he were trying to bring her face into better focus. Maybe he'd mistaken her for somebody else. It was possible, because he'd never been this specific or insistent before.

'But it's loaded with vitamin C.'

He didn't seem to hear her. 'Dulls the senses.' His pasty face loomed very close to hers again, and he propped one arm on the wall beside her, like some central-casting lech. 'But I'll tellya what. I just happen to have some fine acid on me at this very moment. Clear light – the *good* stuff.'

'Oh?'

'Yeah. I'd love to see you on it.' He chortled wetly. 'Wow, that'd really loosen you up.'

'I don't think ...'

'Aw, come on. Meet me outside in the alley in ten minutes. See that door right over there? That's how you get out. I'll be waiting. If you're not there in ten, I'll just hafta come'n'getcha!' He poked her playfully in the ribs, copping a quick feel as his hand moved upward and away.

Over Jorgensen's shoulder, Jane saw Eddie O'Hara and Bob Willard. 'I can't. I – I just realized I – promised Eddie I'd dance with him.'

Sven swung around to look at Bob and Eddie. Then he snorted, rearranging what sounded like a substantial volume of phlegm. 'O'Hara? Don't count on it, babe.'

'Sorry. Gotta go.' Jane ducked under Sven's arm, walked quickly over to Eddie and whispered, 'Help.'

Instead of answering, he bent down and looked deeply into her eyes. 'Wow,' he said softly, shaking his head. And smiling, more or less. He seemed to be looking her up and down, right through her and all around her. That was weird. But okay, she decided. Not entirely unpleasant. She took a big gulp of her screwdriver and stared boldly back at him, but she was never quite able to catch his eye.

QUINTIN was at a table close to the dance floor, with Tom Dale on his left. The grey-haired woman next to Tom had her back to Eleanor but was almost certainly Joan Dale; there was domestic complacency in the very angle of her neck. Max Lurie was sitting beside her. And the dark curly head bobbing up and down close to Max's was unmistakably Jenny Kosma's.

There was still one empty chair at the table, but Eleanor hung back. Without a man of her own beside her, she didn't feel brave enough to face both Tom and Quintin at the same time. Or maybe she was just not drunk enough. About ten minutes ago Jerry had dropped her off in front of the restaurant, because it was impossible to find a parking space close by and she couldn't walk far in her strappy silver sandals. So she'd come in by herself and gone straight to the bar. And then, standing alone in a dim corner, she had tried to get a grip on the situation.

Quintin had not called her again. But she had never felt for him what she had once – ages ago, it seemed – imagined she felt for Tom. Anyway, she had learned a lot since then. She understood now that Tom was too weak and fearful to match the intensity of her feelings. And she herself had changed. The afternoon with Quintin had been so odd, so far outside her experience that she could not even identify the emotions appropriate to it. She ought to be ashamed, probably, but she wasn't. Her behaviour had been so reckless, so out of character, that she felt like a completely new and different person. The woman who lay down on that bed at the Windsor Arms had dared everything and feared nothing. And what Eleanor really longed for was the chance to be that woman again.

She was contemplating a return visit to the bar when Jerry appeared on the far side of the room. He seemed to be looking for her. She stepped quickly behind a pillar, but when she peered around it, she saw with mingled horror and delight that her husband was taking the empty seat at the Margrave/Dale table. It took her less than a second to decide that she had no choice but to join him. Pausing just long enough to deposit her half-finished drink on the nearest unoccupied table, she hurried across the room.

EDDIE HAD the foreground pretty much nailed down now. It was more or less holding together, most of the time. But man, things were really happening in the background. And it was a long, *long* way back. An infinity-of-mirrors deal. A background you'd never get to the bottom of. If it even *had* a bottom. And lots of funny things were lurking in its depths. There was always the possibility that something weird would spring at you from some distant corner. If a background had corners.

His brain seemed to be operating on two levels simultaneously. On one, he was wallowing in infinite sensations, exquisitely aware that things could get out of hand at any moment. Yet he didn't feel any fear, just a kind of bemused excitement. On the other level, a hectoring skepticism kept reminding him that his present insights, however brilliant, were fuelled by the acid and might well be totally illusory.

Like, for instance, the chick from Gonzaga's who was coming at him.

Jane. Had something actually changed in her attitude? Was there an unprecedented flirtatiousness in her manner, or could it be a perceptual distortion caused by the acid? Maybe he was starting to imagine that *everybody* was putting the moves on him. Mrs Zeffler for instance, that day at the Embassy. He'd just seen her a minute ago in the deep background, peering out from behind a pillar. A very phallic pillar. *Was* he suddenly becoming irresistible to women? In that case, he ought to be looking for Daisy. She had to be here somewhere, right? He found it impossible to focus on the question. He was far too distracted by the throbbing kaleidoscope around him, in which the Gonzaga chick's serious, imploring face was just one tiny, insignificant detail.

'WHERE THE HELL did you get to?' Jerry muttered as soon as Eleanor was seated. He had to pull up a chair for her from the next table, but she managed to wedge it in just where she wanted it: between her husband and Quintin Margrave.

'Oh, I've just been wandering around, looking for you,' she replied sweetly, smiling experimentally at the others. They all, even Jenny Kosma, nodded noncommittally in return. Considering the noise from the dance floor, introductions all around would have been difficult, and anyway, everyone present knew who everyone else was.

Just as she had expected, Tom Dale assiduously avoided her eye. But otherwise he appeared at ease. Well, with his wife at his side, he had no reason not to feel safe, did he? In the state of semi-intoxication Eleanor had achieved during the short time she'd been on the loose in the Factory, she was able to view the situation as more piquant than horrific. With a single casual glance to her left, she could study the profiles of both Tom and Quintin, lined up like a mini Mount Rushmore and lit intermittently by the pulsing strobes. And how different they were: Tom, fatherly but still handsome in the style of an Arrow shirt advertisement, clean, kindly and benign; Quintin, unhealthy and foreign, with the long-nosed, narrow face of a medieval serf, ironic, sallow and risky.

When Jerry got up – at last – to get them some drinks, Eleanor turned boldly to Quintin. He met her glance straight on. Beneath the table, his knee, or perhaps it was only the fabric of his trousers, bunched up where his leg was bent, came gently into contact with hers. Neither of them made any reference to their teatime tryst; but how could they have, under the circumstances? Then Jerry was back with a full glass in each hand, and the others at the table seemed determined to hang on

Quintin's every word. Still, from the intensity in his eyes when they met hers, she was sure that he recalled their strange encounter as vividly as she did – and wanted another. If only there were some way for them to be alone.

Jerry had brought Manhattans, and although Eleanor didn't really care for them, she gulped hers down. She had to be ready for Quintin's next move, whatever it might turn out to be.

IT WAS ONLY after the Zefflers had joined the group that Tom understood how much he had been dreading the moment when he would have to meet Eleanor again. But once the first awful minutes of terror and remorse had passed, he recovered quickly. With both Joan and Jerry there, no allusions to the brief grappling in the studio or the near miss at the hotel would arise. No matter how nutty Eleanor might be, they both had too much to lose if there was a scene. And after observing her covertly, he was sure he had nothing to fear. She was behaving perfectly naturally; in fact, she was paying no attention to him at all.

Well, that was quite a switch, after she had (there was really no chivalrous way to put it) thrown herself at him. So what did *he* have to feel guilty about? Absolutely nothing, he decided, taking his wife's hand under the table. Joan smiled at him, and he realized that he actually deserved some credit for having resisted the blandishments (a mercifully imprecise word) of a woman as attractive as Eleanor. Yes, he'd stuck to his marriage vows, in the face of extreme provocation. For Mrs Zeffler was nothing if not provocative. Why, she'd started making eyes at Margrave the moment her husband had left the table.

Damn it! Had the woman no shame? First himself; then, if he wasn't mistaken, young O'Hara, right on Bloor Street in broad daylight. She'd even vamped that sad sack Willard, he thought, suddenly remembering that he'd seen them together at the Roof bar. And now it was Margrave's turn. Margrave? Oho. Now there, said Tom to himself with satisfaction, the lovely Eleanor was barking up the wrong tree.

WHEN THEY arrived at the restaurant, McNab confidently led the way to a table near the area cleared for dancing. But after only a few minutes, it was obvious to Bruno that the truly desirable seats were at the adjacent one. Margrave was holding court there, attended by Dale and his wife, the Zefflers, the Kosma girl (how had she managed that?) and (most galling of all) Max Lurie. Jumping up, Howard went to stand behind Margrave's chair and managed to engage him in conversation for a moment or two. But there was no seat available for him and, defeated, he returned to this obviously secondary table. And then, when Bruno saw Bob Willard approaching, he decided to get away as soon as he could. If he could not join the select company where he belonged by right, he preferred to be alone. Five minutes after Willard took the chair next to Howard's, Bruno got up and walked away.

He stood in a corner and watched the dancers, contemptuous yet half envious of their willingness to make fools of themselves in public. But since he could not imagine himself among them, he soon grew bored. Alone, he roamed through the restaurant, reluctant to light anywhere for long. Keeping a wary eye out for O'Hara, he prowled, watching and listening, taking advantage of his relative anonymity. Most of the people in this crowd didn't know him. Yet. But he might pick up some valuable information, and he hadn't come here expecting to enjoy himself.

WIN HAD had to summon all her imperiousness to compel her husband even to enter the place. Eliot had insisted on stopping at the house to call his answering service for messages, no doubt hoping against hope for some eleventh-hour reprieve that might send him to the emergency room rather than to the Old York Factory.

So the party was in full swing by the time they arrived. Confronted with the noise, the crowd (many of them dressed quite outlandishly, even Win admitted that) and the flashing lights, Eliot immediately placed one hand on his forehead and claimed to feel a migraine coming on. And Winifred reflected that hypochondria was a particularly unattractive trait in a healer.

'Oh, all right,' she said after they had sat silently for a quarter of an hour at a table as far removed as possible from the dance floor. 'Why don't you go home?' His manfully resigned expression brightened then, and he reached over to pat her on the shoulder.

'Do you really think *you* ought to stay, dear?' he said, suddenly solicitous though already on his feet. 'You can't be enjoying this any more than I am.'

'No, but as an artist I really ought to stay for at least a little longer. *Pour encourager les autres,* you know.' Even as she spoke the words, she realized that they did not quite fit the situation. Never mind, Eliot wouldn't have recognized the reference anyway. Smiling, she said, 'You run along. I won't be late. But don't wait up for me.'

They kissed, and Eliot began to make his way along the perimeter of the huge room. Winifred turned in her chair to watch him and waved just as he reached the door, but either he didn't see her gesture or chose to ignore it. When she was certain he was gone, she picked up her half-empty glass and set off in search of another seat a little closer to the action. There was no reason why she shouldn't make herself known to Quintin Margrave, even at this late date. It was glaringly obvious by now that no one else – certainly not her nominal dealer, Bruno Gonzaga, or her dear friend and mentor Tom – was going to do it for her. However, she thought she had seen Margrave sitting at a table near the dance floor.

JENNY MUST have left the table when Eleanor wasn't looking. Not that she'd been paying much attention to the girl. Although, as her mind bobbed along on the stream of conversation eddying around her, she had noticed a grubby, dishevelled boy crouching unsteadily beside Jenny's chair and whispering in her ear. One of the painters in Gonzaga's stable … Jorgensen, that was his name. Perhaps he'd taken Jenny off to dance, and with any luck she would never come back.

Eleanor avoided meeting Quintin's eye too often. That might have been noticed, since he was sitting right next to her. But from the gentle pressure of his leg against hers, an exquisitely subtle contact she was almost sure was gradually increasing, she knew that they were silently communicating. And when he rose from his seat and excused himself, she understood that he wanted her to follow. She forced herself to count slowly to a hundred before getting up, muttering 'Ladies' room,' in Jerry's ear and setting off in the direction in which she'd seen Quintin go.

After searching for a few minutes, she found him. He was waiting in a dim corner on the far side of the room, partially concealed by a large potted palm. When she whispered his name, there was a quick scuffling movement and a burst of furtive laughter behind the foliage. Quintin stepped out, smiling vaguely, seemingly surprised to see her. And close beside him, smoothing her dress and clearly displeased by the interruption, was Jenny Kosma.

❚ Chapter Sixteen

NO ONE had ever called Willard a mean drunk. Alcohol actually made him more affable and he'd always, in a small way, prided himself on that. But neither of his wives had been willing to give him any credit for it, even though they both complained about his allegedly hangdog tendencies when sober.

O'Hara had been almost rude to the Gonzaga girl. After she'd gone, Bob asked him why he didn't just go ahead and dance with her, and he said with a shudder that the paisley print on her dress was way too scary. So they found a table against the wall where Eddie just sat gazing at the passing scene while Bob had a couple of drinks. Then, once full-blown conviviality hit him, O'Hara's goofball demeanour and non-consecutive conversation started to pall, and he set off in search of livelier company.

The table he wanted to join was full, but Howard McNab, seated at an adjacent one, waved him over and he supposed he could have done worse. Soon after he sat down, Bruno Gonzaga, who had been sitting with Howard, abruptly got up and left. That was a relief – not that Bob felt in the least guilty about the little sleight of hand he had helped Eddie pull off concerning *Back Flip*. But the guy always seemed to have a bee in his bonnet. For one thing, he was possessive about the girl who worked for him, the one who had accosted Eddie near the restaurant entrance. She was a cute kid, and Bob had had several enjoyable conversations with her, but Gonzaga had always hovered disapprovingly during those visits. He was definitely not the guy you'd pick for a drinking companion. Howard, on the other hand, was tolerable, at least after you'd had a few.

As McNab droned on, Bob's eyes were irresistibly drawn to the group at the next table. Eleanor was there, just a few feet away, unattainable and lovely. And he couldn't help noticing all the comings and goings at their table. Just as Bob arrived, Jerry Zeffler, who had been seated next to his wife, got up and left. Not long after Jerry returned bearing drinks, Jenny, who'd been sitting opposite Eleanor, slipped away. Margrave was the next to go and then – it couldn't have been more than a couple of minutes later – Eleanor rose and began to walk a little unsteadily across

❏ 172

the crowded room. *You may see a stranger....* Bob watched her until she was lost in the crowd.

When he next glanced over, Joan Dale was leaving. She gave her husband a peck on the cheek and trotted off in the general direction of the coat check. That left only Max, Jerry and Tom at the table. Bob toyed with the idea of taking one of the vacated chairs in the hope that either Jenny or Eleanor would come back. But then Max and Jerry both got up and left, and Tom was sitting all alone. That was surprising.

ONCE THE DOOR had shut on the noise of the party, the washroom was almost quiet. It also appeared to be empty. That was a relief; Win Beecham had been coming out as Jane went in. She scuttled to the nearest cubicle to relieve the nearly unbearable pressure on her bladder, then lurched over to a basin to wash her hands, peering into the gold-framed mirror above it as she dried them. Her face was pleasantly indistinct in the flattering glow of the pink light bulbs above the row of sinks. And despite a slight encroachment of frizz close to the scalp, her hair looked okay.

Though Eddie had refused to dance with her, she didn't take it personally. At close range it had been obvious that he was *on* something, and she had soon found other partners. Dream or no dream, she wasn't going to change her policy of only being interested in men who had shown some interest in her. Then she saw that a fashionably dressed but not quite young woman had emerged from one of the stalls and joined her in front of the row of mirrors.

'You're Gonzaga's girl, aren't you?' the woman asked. 'His *secretary,* I mean.'

'I'm his assistant, yes.'

It was Mrs Zeffler. The dress she was wearing was made of pale blue silk with a swirling paisley pattern of shimmering multicoloured sequins, and it must have cost a fortune. Her silver-blond, chin-length hair was enviably straight and her body was still slim and youthful.

But Mrs Zeffler was not entirely pleased by what she saw in the mirror. 'You don't really think it will ever happen,' she said.

'Pardon?' Jane realized that the woman beside her was, like herself, rather drunk.

Eleanor turned her head to one side, and then the other, squinting critically at her reflection. 'It happens one day at a time, that's the awful thing. But it's not consecutive ... or do I mean cumulative ... it's one day this week, three days the next, maybe just two days the next....'

Jane took out her compact and concentrated on powdering her nose. But Mrs Zeffler continued to talk.

'Sometimes you look quite normal, and you forget all about it. There are those who seem to think I am still at least *viable*,' she went on, making a series of experimental moues. 'But tomorrow, who knows?'

'Oh, but you look great –'

'I thought this was one of my good days,' she said, 'but now I'm not so sure.... At first, you think it's just tiredness, or maybe not being loved enough. But then, when those two bad days a week get to be four, you know that four out of seven ain't good. Pretty soon you'll look that way every day. And you know – God, you know it – that soon you'll definitely be o-l-d! Over the hill, out to pasture, ready for the bone yard.' She smiled grimly at Jane's reflection. 'And that goes for you, too, in about twenty short years. You and your little dog too.' With that, she tossed back her smooth, shiny hair, slung the chain strap of her silver lamé evening bag over her shoulder and stalked out of the washroom.

That Wicked Witch of the West routine was pretty bizarre, Jane thought, swaying slightly. Though really, with the gold-framed mirrors, it was more Snow Whitish. Or maybe Grayish ... as in Dorian? But that was a painting, wasn't it, not a mirror...? She leaned closer and examined herself for signs of decay. However, without her glasses and blessed by the kindly pink lights, she still looked okay.

'OH, DEAR,' said Winifred softly. It was almost a moan.

Tom could not see her expression, because his face was buried in her neck, just behind her right ear. One of her earrings pressed against his cheek. He had approached her from behind, in much the same way as Eleanor Zeffler had crept up on him that day (it seemed years ago now) in the studio. It was, he now saw with utter clarity, the coward's way. But a few moments ago it had seemed the wisest tactic for a man only ninety-nine-per-cent sure of his welcome. The deed would be done impetuously, irrevocably, without the awkwardness that would inevitably attach to a preliminary, face-to-face acknowledgement of what was about to happen. And that single percentage point of doubt, the last remnant of the social insecurity he had long ago vanquished, would have no inhibiting effect.

All well and good, in theory. And he had been so sure that Win would

be welcoming, probably even grateful. But now, paralysed by the ambi-
guity of her words, he hardly dared lift his head.

Oh, dear.

Did that mean *Oh, darling, at last*?

Or was she really saying, *Oh, I wish you hadn't done that*?

If only Joan hadn't left. She ought to have seen that he was way out of
his element in the roaring, throbbing dimness, punctuated by the blinding flash of lights and the shrieks of revellers trying to make themselves
heard over the racket that passed for music. Though he didn't blame her
for wanting to escape; the scene was more like a battlefield than a cele-
bration.

Before Win sat down at his table, he'd been alone for a few blessed
minutes, nursing his drink and wondering if Max, who had got up to
circulate, would consider that he'd stayed long enough at the party. Jerry
Zeffler was at the bar getting refills. Perhaps, before they returned, he
should make his getaway. As he pondered that question, he watched the
dancers. Young women, probably quite respectable by day, became
brazen floozies the instant they stepped onto the floor. Although the
couples never touched each other, their movements were an explicit
pantomime of the sexual act. The girls' crude thrustings, strikingly like
the bumps and grinds of burlesque dancers, were matched by their partners. Though, Tom couldn't help noticing, the males moved with much
less confidence and panache.

Yes, there was no doubt about it; the girls were far more uninhibited
than the boys. And the less said the better about the few older fellas who
were out there, making damn fools of themselves. God – even Quintin
was writhing around like an idiot with young Jenny opposite him. Most
of the dancers, mercifully, were not as old as Margrave, and although
some looked vaguely familiar, he could not put names to many of them.

And there was McNab goggling at the girls, but from the sidelines,
thank God. The very thought of watching him cut loose on the floor was
enough to make you cringe. Sheepishly, Tom recalled his own half-
hearted resolution to undertake a therapeutic fling with some uninhibited young creature. Lord, he'd never be able to handle one of those
wild-haired, ecstatic maenads. Wouldn't have a clue where to begin.

Howard seemed to have noticed that he was alone and began to move
in his direction. It was at that moment that Winifred had pulled out the
chair next to him and placed her glass – gin and tonic, it looked like,
from the slice of lime – on the table. When he glanced over to where

McNab had been, he had disappeared. He must have changed his mind, then.

'Dreadful, isn't it?' Win said, nearly touching his ear with her lips in order to make herself heard over the din.

'Awful,' he replied, putting his own mouth close to her ear. He could smell her perfume. She'd worn the same one for as long as he could remember, and the familiar scent was soothing.

They were silent for a few moments, sipping their drinks. But as they exchanged smiles of silent commiseration, he'd felt a sweet swell of emotion. In the intermittent chiaroscuro of the strobes, she looked quite lovely. He could almost see the flower face he remembered from his youth superimposed on her middle-aged features. Or perhaps it was only the affectionate complicity in her eyes that made her so appealing. Winifred was not overawed by his present eminence. She knew the real Tom Dale. Understood him.

Well, so did Joanie, but sometimes it was tiresome to be known completely. With Win, despite their long acquaintance, he felt there was a great deal still left to say, things he'd never had a chance to tell her. They'd been young together, full of hope and ginger. In their own way and time, they were free spirits, not unlike the kids out there on the dance floor. He even remembered Win, at some long-ago party, jitterbugging to beat the band. Oh, there were banked fires under that cool exterior.

Impulsively, he reached over and took her hand. She turned towards him with a startled expression, then looked away. And after a few moments, she gently withdrew her hand from his. But she was pleased, he could have sworn it. Her profile, a pale cameo against the writhing bodies on the dance floor, was serene. And a ... a *Gioconda smile* (he unearthed the phrase with pleasure) was partially visible on her face. So when she stood up and left the table a few minutes later, touching him lightly on the shoulder to let him know she was going, he had got to his feet as well.

He'd waited for her outside the ladies'. Emerging, she'd smiled, a little surprised to see him. Then, without a word, he had followed her up the stairs that led to main part of the restaurant. And when they reached a shadowed, secluded landing, only dimly illuminated by a stained-glass wall sconce shaped like a butterfly, he'd made his move.

SOME SORT of commotion was taking place just below them, around the turn in the staircase, so (fortunately) out of sight. Despite her natural preoccupation with the sensation of Tom's lips nuzzling her neck, Win couldn't help overhearing two male voices, talking urgently. She thought she could identify Max Lurie's as one of them.

The voice that was probably Max's was incredulous. 'What the hell are you talking about?'

'I hear they're really going at it,' the other voice said. It sounded like Jerome Zeffler, the lawyer.

'There's actually a crowd gathered?'

'Yeah. Some of the kids are really egging them on, too.'

Tom lifted his head from her neck, and they both listened.

'Oh, for God's sake.' That was Max, definitely. 'I guess we ought to do something? You know, step in…?' He seemed rather reluctant.

'Okay, let's go,' said the second voice in a stout-fellow tone. And yes, it *was* Zeffler.

A split second before the two men rounded the corner on their way up the stairs, Tom released her and stepped back. Win quickly turned to face him so that it would appear that they had been engaged in a friendly, casual conversation.

Max looked relieved when he saw Tom. 'There's a fight going on,' he muttered. 'I think we'd better break it up.'

Tom started to laugh but then seemed to realize that Lurie was serious. He glanced apologetically at Winifred and said, 'Excuse me for a moment,' just as if he were politely breaking off that imaginary conversation. He patted her briefly on the arm, and started up the stairs after the other two, nearly running.

JANE LEFT the washroom and returned to the party just in time to see Eddie reach over and take a swipe at Bruno's head. O'Hara's red hair and Gonzaga's bulky, black-clad body were unmistakable, though they were twenty feet away from her. She reached into her purse and took out her glasses.

Eddie looked kind of silly, slapping clumsily at Bruno's smooth black skull. After a momentary hesitation, Bruno reacted, not striking back with those enormous fists but somehow with the weight of his whole body forcing Eddie into a staggering waltz of retreat. A look of astonishment crossed Eddie's face, as if he had expected Bruno just to stand there and be slapped without retaliating. But then, executing a jerky box step, he regained his footing and went at Gonzaga again. He had just placed his hands on Bruno's chest and started to push when Jane's view was blocked by the crowd that suddenly materialized around the two men.

A woozy buzz of excitement arose, and Jane remembered that almost everyone present was either drunk or stoned, many of them both. Everybody seemed to think the whole thing was some kind of impromptu performance piece staged by the artist and his dealer, a pantomime representing the eternal conflict between creativity and commerce.

When Eddie was heard to yelp in pain, an appreciative murmur swept through the crowd and a moment later, in response to a grunt from Bruno, there was a smattering of applause. Jane expected some of the spectators to step between the combatants or drag them apart, the way they always did in movies. But the mob in front of her only pressed forward for a better view.

Then she saw Max Lurie and Jerry Zeffler elbowing their way through the bystanders. She understood from the conversation around her that the collector-and-dealer duo had pitched in. There was a general craning of necks as the spectators explained to each other in thrilled undertones that there was a lot of symbolic potential in the newcomers' arrival. An artist, a collector and two dealers who just happened to be rivals, duking it out …

Hey, far out. Wow, what a show.

And then … *hey. Hey, look! Here comes Tom Dale, of all people.*

Jane turned to see him, more red-faced than usual, brush past her and push his way into the crowd. Then, from the groans of disappointment that arose around her, she gathered that Lurie, Zeffler and Dale, rather than joining the fray, had somehow brought it to an end.

HE HADN'T REALLY intended to hit him, didn't even make a fist. But just seeing Gonzaga set off a wave of paranoia, and the words Bruno muttered, though in a language Eddie didn't understand, carried a meaning that was crystal clear. From out of nowhere, he found himself slapping ineffectually at Bruno's head with his open palms, the way some hysterical chick might strike out at someone stronger than herself. At first, he was distracted by the motion of his own hands, an endlessly multiplied fluttering that was like a Futurist painting, the Balla with the dog's tail, or that spiral-staircase thing.

Then Gonzaga rebounded like a humanoid punching bag with an extremely low centre of gravity. A stubborn, solid weight that pivoted wildly on its heavy base but would never topple. Eddie stumbled backwards and for a moment lost his balance. When he regained it, he could think of nothing else to do but apply himself doggedly to pushing back at the squat black pillar that still stood swaying in front of him.

He became aware of a muttering, a murmuring, a crush of bodies all around them. Even if he had wanted to retreat, there was no place to go; he was surrounded on all sides by a dull roar. *Keep it down to a dull roar,* his old man always used to growl when things got too noisy around the house. He could almost hear him saying it right now. Then he heard his own voice and the sharp yelp it let out seemed to come from a very distant place. An enormous hand had closed around his forearm, and the pain was sudden and sharp. His arm was twisted behind his back, his whole body arching, then lurching after it. He kicked out blindly and connected with something. And a nice round fully packed guttural sound came from whatever, whoever, he'd hit.

'Hey, hey, hey,' a vaguely familiar voice was saying. 'Take it easy. Everybody just calm down.'

At that point, Eddie felt a determined but not hostile arm slip around his chest, dragging him right into the dull roar itself, which he now saw was only a mass of goggling faces, each one exactly like a cloth poppy, the kind you get on Remembrance Day, only with eyes, nose and mouth squeezed in where the black centre ought to have been. All the poppies were turning towards him now like flowers to the sun in one of those time-lapse nature movies, and he tried to stop to take it all in. But the arm that was now clamped around his shoulder propelled him through the nodding mass of pink and red blossoms and he saw the stems parting ominously to let him pass.

THE FIRST THING Winifred did after Tom disappeared up the stairs was to return to the ladies' room to tidy herself up. But when she looked at her reflection in the mirror, there was no sign of dishevelment. The ruffled sensation she felt was purely mental, then. She smoothed her hair and straightened the cowl neck of her dress anyway. Then from her purse she took out the small black faille pouch that held her gold compact, opened it, flicked up the little hinged flap that held the loose powder in place and applied the puff delicately to her nose.

The touch of Tom's lips, fixed limpet-like to the nape of her neck, had at first evoked in her a triumphant sense of vindication. *Well, my goodness, what on earth have you been waiting for?* she had been tempted to say, but hadn't, of course. Really, she had been so flustered that she couldn't quite remember what she *had* said.

And then, almost at once, that initial reaction had been replaced by a definite feeling of exasperation. For, after giving the question of her relationship with Tom a great deal of – perhaps too much – thought, she had finally concluded that it was far more gratifying to have him as a friend than as a lover. Despite her fundamental contempt for the posturing of the male sex, Win was fully aware that men controlled the world, especially the particular one she now wanted to conquer. Any female who was sufficiently attractive, docile and charming (she skirted the ticklish question of age) could be a great man's mistress, but only a truly exceptional woman could be his respected colleague. So she was much better off – rarely privileged, actually – in her current relationship with Tom.

Well, not really *current* of late, considering the infrequency of their meetings over the last few months, but still … that was the basis on which she had resolved to renew and continue their acquaintance. And now there had been this absurd scene, which sooner or later would require some response from her if she wanted to maintain her friendship with him. If that was even possible now. Love unspoken was one thing, love offered and rebuffed another matter entirely.

When she looked out the ladies' room door, no one she knew was in sight. She certainly had no desire to join the crowd around the unnamed pugilists. Heavens, she'd seen quite enough tonight of men and their bellicosity, their ill-timed lunges…. She made her way quietly up the stairs, retrieved her wrap from the coat check and slipped out onto the street. There were a number of taxis cruising along the curb, waiting for the theatre a few doors down to let out. She was able to summon one merely by raising her hand.

'DID YOU HAVE a coat?' the semi-familiar voice asked as its owner continued to frog-march him towards the exit.

Eddie had to think that one over. 'Nope.'

'Okay. You wait right here. Don't move. Stay with Tom.' With that, the owner of the voice disappeared. Eddie felt another hand, gentler than the first, take hold of his left arm. He turned and found himself looking into Tom Dale's mild azure eyes. 'Hey, how are you?' he asked him.

'All right.'

A brief silence ensued; then the other guy was back, latching on to his other arm. It was Jerry Zeffler. From the depths of the profound weariness that had descended upon him, Eddie heard him say, 'Okay, I've got a cab waiting. I'll take over now.'

Take over what? Not that Eddie really cared; he was too tired. All he wanted to do was lie down somewhere. But Dale was resisting. 'No, no, no – I'm leaving anyway, I'll see him safely home.' His grip on Eddie tightened.

Zeffler wasn't letting go either. 'No, Tom, I'll handle this. You go and see how Max is managing with Gonzaga.' He started to yank Eddie towards the door.

'Absolutely not. I insist.' Tom was still a contender, and it seemed to Eddie that his keepers were going to tear him in two. But they only dragged him outside and bundled him into a taxi that was waiting at the curb. For one awful moment, Eddie thought he recognized the back of the driver's head, but when the cabbie turned around to look suspiciously at him, it wasn't the same guy.

Through the closed window, he watched Dale and Zeffler argue soundlessly. Then Tom apparently gave up, and Zeffler climbed into the back seat next to Eddie. He told the cabbie to go to Morris the Hatter's on Spadina, and they were off.

▪ Chapter Seventeen

HE MISSED the whole damn thing. Bob only heard about the fight when Tom Dale, looking somewhat the worse for wear himself, reached the table where he and Howard were still sitting. By that time it was over, combatants separated, crowd dispersed, all passion presumably spent. But he really ought to have been there, in O'Hara's corner.

Tom sat down only long enough to polish off one drink, which Bob couldn't help noticing he raised to his lips with a slightly shaky hand. While he described how he, Jerry and Max had taken the pugilists in hand, his eyes darted nervously around, as if he expected some new fracas to erupt at any moment. Then, once his glass was empty, Tom got unsteadily to his feet.

'Oh, by the way,' he said, 'Jerry's taken O'Hara back to his studio in a cab. If either of you run into Mrs Zeffler, could you tell her? Jerry said he'll see her at home. He left her the car – it's just around the corner on Simcoe.' Then he bolted for the door.

'Don't worry. I'll make sure she gets the message,' Bob called after him.

MAX LURIE KEPT putting his arm around Bruno's shoulders, and Bruno kept shrugging it off. 'Take it easy, now,' Lurie said again, as if that was the answer to everything.

After the fight, Max had led him through the gawking crowd to an empty table, telling Bruno how much everyone admired his restraint, how it was clear he could have flattened the kid with a single blow if he had really let go. Well, that was true enough. But all Bruno wanted now was to be left alone, to be rid of this affable fool, the last person (except O'Hara) he would ever think of confiding in. The man was his rival; he could not trust him. How was it possible that Lurie thought otherwise?

'Okay,' Bruno said. 'I'm okay.' Finally he gulped down the glass of brandy that Lurie had pressed into his hand and shoved back the chair into which he'd forced him. At that moment McNab – another one who had to be watched carefully – rushed up, eager to hear the whole story of the fight.

'Max can tell you everything,' Bruno said in a flash of inspiration, and he was able to slip away, pretending he was going to the washroom. Instead he went directly to the exit and hurried along the street to his car, aware that his forehead was still damp with sweat, even in the cool night air.

Once he was safely in the driver's seat, he felt calm enough to take out his handkerchief and mop his brow. The iron band that rage and humiliation had clamped around his chest was slowly beginning to loosen. But the nausea took him by surprise. Holding one hand over his mouth, he fumbled for the handle and swung the door open. He leaned out over the gutter, but nothing came up. He sat motionless behind the wheel for a minute, then put the car in gear and carefully drove away. In less than a quarter of an hour he was at the Gonzaga, letting himself in the back door that led directly to the workshop.

ELEANOR DECIDED not to return to her table right away. After collecting a fresh drink at the bar, she prowled around the far reaches of the restaurant for a while. Michel Bontemps, the creator of the translucent pink bubbles on the wall of her daughter's room, asked her to dance and, judging by the stares of the people on the sidelines, they made quite a striking couple. As they frugged energetically, Eleanor looked for Quintin and Jenny but didn't see them, alone or together. When after only three dances Michel bowed and kissed her hand in an elegant farewell that was clearly non-negotiable, she was only slightly miffed.

She continued to glide about, sitting down from time to time at various tables and never feeling unwelcome. When she found herself next to Sven Jorgensen, right out of the blue he offered to 'turn her on'. Pointing at the exit to the lane at the rear of the building, he suggested she meet him out there in five minutes. After only about three minutes of reflection, she decided that she would.

It occurred to her as she pushed open the door marked Fire Exit that Jorgensen might try something out in the alley. But she needn't have worried; Sven was not alone. Jenny was with him, and they were already passing a joint back and forth. Even Eleanor knew that was what it was. When they turned to look at her she saw alarm, surprise, relief and then amused condescension move across their faces in slow, stately succession.

'Far out,' said Jorgensen. He grabbed Eleanor's arm and pulled her closer. 'Here y'go, babe,' he added, holding out the little gnarly cigarette.

As she lifted it delicately to her lips, both Sven's and Jenny's eyes were on her. And when she doubled over in a coughing fit, they burst out laughing.

'Take it easy, lady, don't eat it!' Jorgensen said, snatching the joint from her and putting it to his own mouth. 'Get some air in with it, like this.'

Next it was Jenny's turn, and then Eleanor got another chance. That time she did better, though she still found the acrid smoke quite unpleasant. She was just about to try once more when Sven barked, '*Hey*,' and held his hand out for the joint. Jenny snickered at this.

As the cigarette grew smaller and smaller, Sven and Jenny became ever more vigilant that it be passed around fairly. They groaned in unison when on her fifth turn, Eleanor accidentally knocked the tiny projection of ash off onto the ground. By this time, they were holding the … roach, that was it, in a kind of eyebrow tweezer.

'Methinks it's high time that milady returns to her own kingdom,' Jenny suddenly announced in a silly, high-pitched voice, and Sven did not make any protest. *Ah,* thought Eleanor, *they want to be alone.* Well, fine. Perhaps Jenny would stop pestering Quintin. She handed the tweezer thing back to Sven, executed an ironical curtsy and yanked open the door leading into the restaurant. And the moment she was inside, the whole episode began to seem hysterically funny.

ZEFFLER'S PARTING request that he pass on a message to Eleanor, of all people, had brought Tom back to earth with a thump. The uproar caused by the scuffle between O'Hara and Gonzaga had driven all his recent follies from his mind, but at the mention of Eleanor's name they materialized before him, like a damning Soviet-realist frieze, life-size and in full colour. Or perhaps it was only a comic strip. There he was in his studio, attempting to remove the underwear of the wife of the man who had stood facing him on the sidewalk just a moment before. Next panel: meeting her at a hotel for the purpose of adultery. The memory of these wrongs, committed against a fellow he now saw was a fairly decent sort, shamed him. Providence, in the unlikely shape of Howard McNab, had saved him once, but had he learned his lesson? Oh, no. Instead of blessing his luck and getting back to work, he had blundered into another, even more perilous entanglement, with Winifred.

He kept a wary eye out for her as he slipped back into the restaurant, but she had vanished. ·So had Eleanor, and though he was honour-bound to deliver Jerry's message, he couldn't bring himself to go looking for her. Seeing Willard and McNab, he decided to sit at their table just long enough to try to think things through. They were eager to hear about the fight, and he filled them in on how cooler heads had prevailed. Then as he downed his final nightcap, he realized that he could discharge his duty to Jerry by passing the baton, as it were, to one of them.

That done, he was free. *Hallelujah.* Joan had taken the car, and he had to walk several blocks before he found a taxi, but that didn't matter. During the long, expensive journey to Hogg's Hollow, he did some really serious thinking. About Eleanor and Win, yes, with all the required resolutions to behave better in future, but mainly about the fourth in the *Kite* series. He'd start on it first thing tomorrow morning. Max had declared that the first three were the best things he'd ever done, and that was saying something. But he was probably right.

When he finally crept into his bedroom, he found Joan deeply asleep, snoring slightly. He slipped out of his clothes, dropped them on the floor beside the bed and slid naked under the covers. The bed was warm, and he felt a faint stirring, nothing that he even considered doing anything about, though he did put a hand down to touch himself gently. For a few minutes he lay there, inhaling the familiar, pleasantly yeasty aroma of his wife's body. Then he joined her in a sound, dreamless sleep.

EDDIE FELT Zeffler's eyes on him all the way home, but did his best to ignore him. There was something zingy about the guy, an excess of energy that seemed to bounce around in the cramped shell of the cab. When they finally pulled up in front of Morris the Hatter's, Eddie grabbed the door handle as quickly as he could, but he wasn't fast enough. By the time he managed to drag himself out of the taxi, Zeffler had paid it off and was standing on the sidewalk next to him.

'That your pad?' he asked, pointing up at the bay window above the darkened shop.

'Yep.'

'Got your key?'

Eddie shrugged. It was in one of his pockets. But he didn't feel like getting it out right then. What he really wanted to do was sit down on the curb for a while, digging the night air, the timeless beauty of the El Mo palm tree and the endless row of streetlights marching off down Spadina into infinity.

'Well, do you have it or not?' Jerry said, holding his hand out.

Eddie dug around in his pockets. Finally he located it and, ignoring Zeffler's outstretched palm, brushed by him, fitted it into the lock and opened the door. He briefly considered darting up the stairs and bolting the upper door behind him before Zeffler could follow. But again he was too slow. So here they were, standing side by side in the studio.

'What time is it?' Eddie asked.

'You don't have a watch?'

'Nope.'

'Ah, now that's the real artistic temperament,' Jerry said, beaming at him. 'It's —' he shot his shirt cuff and consulted his own timepiece, a gold Rolex ' — a quarter to twelve.'

'Twelve midnight?'

'It's dark outside, isn't it?'

'Yeah.' *In that case,* Eddie thought as loudly as he could, *why don't you go home?*

But Zeffler showed no sign of hearing. He plonked himself down on the threadbare maroon cut-velvet armchair that Eddie had got from the Crippled Civilians and looked around happily. He even waved Eddie into the straight-backed wooden chair beside it, as if he were a genial host rather than an unwelcome visitor.

'You know, this is great,' he said.

Eddie nodded absently. He was looking at the trio of *Cloud* pieces and feeling he was just on the edge of figuring out what was wrong with them. Now, if he could only ...

'As a matter of fact,' Zeffler went on, 'I've been meaning to talk to you about something. Alone. I want to ask you a question, man to man, but first I want to explain why.'

Alone ... a question ... man to man? Hmm. Ominous words. And the expression on Jerry's face was serious. Suddenly Eddie's brain flashed on his afternoon at the Embassy with Mrs Zeffler. As far as he could recall, absolutely nothing sexual had taken place. But who knew what a jealous husband might *believe* had happened? Or what Eleanor might have told him? He *had* got her — or at least allowed her to get — sloppy drunk in a crummy joint where under normal circumstances she would never have gone. Then he had casually, gratefully handed her over to Bob Willard ... who, Eddie suddenly saw with lysergic hyperclarity, had a feeble, dribbly middle-aged thing for her. Anyway, his own attitude towards Mrs Z had not been one-hundred-per-cent pure. She wasn't bad-looking for her age, and a Mrs Robinson–type deal had even seemed a definite possibility at one point. But, hey, keep calm – it had to be the acid telling him Zeffler could see into his head right now and know what he was thinking. He couldn't … *but what if he could?*

Jerry reached into the breast pocket of his suit jacket.

Eddie braced himself.

'Ever had one of these?' Zeffler asked, holding up two dull silver cylinders. 'Monte Cristos. Here, try one.'

'Thanks.' When Eddie unscrewed the top of the tube, the smell that emerged was delicious. Inside its little aluminum space capsule, the cigar was nestled in a sheet of cork. Interesting. Nice texture. When he next looked up, he saw that Zeffler was running the cigar back and forth under his nose, so he did the same. Jerry showed him how to snip off the end with a little guillotine gadget, and with the leaping, torch-like flame of Jerry's Zippo, they lit up. The idea, he explained, was to keep the ash intact as long as you could.

Once the fragrant smoke began to drift upward, Eddie felt more at home. Well, fuck it, he *was* at home. More *relaxed,* then. And Zeffler's attitude now seemed pretty friendly.

'Art,' he said. Then he said it again. 'Art.' He smiled. There was a pause. 'It's the only thing that gives life meaning, isn't it?'

'Probably.'

'Some people aren't really capable of understanding that. Or appreciating it, you know?'

'Um.'

Eddie watched, fascinated, as Zeffler's lips formed a fish-like O, from which a delicate whorl of smoke emerged.

'You know my wife, don't you?'

Shit. Here we go. 'Well, yeah. But nothing –'

'She's a beautiful woman.' Puff.

'Oh, yeah, but –'

'And fairly intelligent.' Puff. 'Well, reasonably.'

'Yeah.'

'But sometimes you wouldn't know it from the way she behaves.'

'Um.'

'Don't let it go out, man!'

Eddie sucked furiously at the cigar he had forgotten he was holding and after a moment, evidently satisfied with his efforts, Jerry continued, 'As I was saying, Eleanor sometimes causes me –' he tipped his head to one side and then the other with a pained expression '– problems.'

'Problems? You mean she...?'

Abruptly, Zeffler got up and started to pace around the room. Eventually he stopped in front of *Nebula II,* the largest of the *Cloud* pieces, and stared at it. Then he turned and fixed Eddie with a baleful look. 'But you know, I think you have made a serious mistake. Yes, I have to say it: this is wrong. *Wrong.*'

'But I didn't ...'

'Now, you may think you know what you're doing.'

'Oh, no I don't. I never even ...'

'This is not right for you.' He gestured towards the wall, and Eddie realized that it was the *Cloud* Series he objected to.

'You have a point there. Actually,' Eddie went on, all too eager to agree, 'I'd just decided to scrap those. Maybe they're too intellectual –'

'When you're right, you're right,' Zeffler broke in. 'Think colour, man, colour. That's your bag. That's your groove.'

Bag? Groove? 'I guess so.'

'And I want the first look at whatever you do next. I mean *first.* Do you understand me? If we can come to a friendly arrangement, it would help me deal with Eleanor.'

Deal with ... 'How?'

'She thinks I spend too much on the collection. Really gives me a hard time. Says we should be putting in a pool instead, maybe a new kitchen ... you know, the kind of things women care about.'

Eddie didn't know at all, but he nodded sympathetically and puffed away on his cigar in what he hoped was a convincingly man-to-man way.

'But when I saw *Back Flip* again tonight, I got an idea.'

'Uh-huh?'

'It's a fabulous piece, even better than I realized. And it should have been mine. Bruno pulled a fast one on me, you know.'

'No kidding.'

'Yeah, I had it reserved on the night of the opening, but then he told me there had been a *misunderstanding,* that another buyer got there first. And now I find out he was keeping it for himself.'

'Yeah?'

'Well, you figure it out.' Puff. 'He knew it was going to be in the show, right? Going to London and all?'

'Makes sense.'

'And that means its value will skyrocket.' Puff. 'So right there and then I said to myself, the hell with Gonzaga!' Puff. 'Which brings me back to the question I wanted to ask you, man to man.'

Eddie took another hit from his Monte Cristo. 'Ask away.'

'I mean, maybe I'm wrong here, but after what happened at the Factory tonight, I assume you and Gonzaga are finished. And I don't blame you for wanting to rough him up. I felt like going over and socking him myself when I saw him sitting right at the next table with McNab and Willard.'

Eddie moved his head in a vaguely rotating, non-directional way.

'Well, anyway, I was thinking ... maybe you and I can work together without involving anybody else. No middleman ... no dealer's commission ... but a fair price. That way we both win, right?'

'You want to buy directly from me?'

'That's it. Maybe quite a few pieces.'

Eddie screwed his face into a parody of deep thought. After what seemed to be an appropriate length of time he said, 'Okay.'

'Fantastic. Let's shake on it.' Zeffler seized his hand, then began to pace again, puffing even more enthusiastically on his cigar. 'I can't wait to see what you do next. After these, I mean,' he added quickly, glancing at *Nebula III*. 'But, man, you know what? There'll never be another *Back Flip*.'

AT FIRST I *thought it was just a pile of old clothes.* Isn't that what people who find bodies usually say? But Bob knew right away that this was no pile of old clothes – for one thing, it moved, and for another, it groaned. And the clothes themselves were much too spiffy.

He'd only poked his head out the exit that led to the back alley because fifteen minutes earlier he'd spotted Eleanor coming in through that door. She had been laughing, and while Tom Dale described the fight, his mind had kept drifting back to that laughter. Whatever Mrs Jerome Zeffler had been up to in the alley was strictly none of his business, but he couldn't help being curious. Besides, he now had a message to give her. So instead of following Howard to the table where Bruno Gonzaga was recovering under Max's care, he strolled over to the fire door, quietly eased it open and took a look.

Even in the semi-darkness he recognized the suit right away. It was the same pearl grey Savile-Row-via-Carnaby-Street number Margrave had been wearing the first time Bob saw him, that afternoon at the Roof bar. The one he'd had on tonight. Another groan, mixed incongruously with a faint giggle, rose from the form lying crumpled on the ground.

Bob called out softly, 'Are you all right there?' A dumb question, but they were the first words that came to mind and he had never really met the guy, so it was hard to know what to say.

'No, actually.'

'What happened?'

'Slight altercation.'

Bob moved closer and bent over him. Margrave's knees were drawn up to his chest, and one hand was wedged between his legs. His other arm seemed to be twisted behind his back. His face, which he turned slowly towards Bob, was scraped raw on one side, and a doozy of a shiner had already started to bloom around his left eye.

'Your face ...'

'Must have hit the wall as I went down ...' Margrave let out a slurpy sound, a cross between a laugh and a sob. 'But never mind that. I've been bashed in the privates, I fear.'

Now it was Bob's turn to giggle inappropriately. 'You mean to say she actually kicked you in the balls?'

'She?'

'Eleanor. Mrs Zeffler.'

'How on earth did you ...'

'I saw her come back in through that door about fifteen minutes ago.'

'Oh, no no no. Not her.' Margrave's lips twisted into a weird little smile. 'Young lad. Strapping fellow. Viking type. Great blaring neon things.' He groaned softly and added, *sotto voce*, 'Stella-ish.'

'Jorgensen, you mean?'

'Um. That's the name. Ought to have put something of his in the exhibition, I s'pose.'

'Sven roughed you up because he didn't have a piece in the show?' It occurred to Bob that he ought to be helping the injured man, not pumping him for gossip, but this was really too good to pass up.

'Not precisely.' Margrave managed to drag himself into a half-sitting position. 'I say, could you pull me up?'

'Sure, come on.... But watch your arm; it could be broken. See if you can move it.'

Margrave cautiously wiggled his wrist. 'All right, it seems.'

Then, as he got to his feet, he staggered and Bob instinctively lunged forward to catch him. By draping one of Margrave's arms over his shoulder and holding him firmly around the waist, he was able to move him to the door. He had to prop him up against the wall for a moment while he got it open and then dragged him through it.

'Discretion, my dear fellow ...' Margrave mumbled. ''Drather not be seen in this condition. D'you suppose you could effect an exit by some means fair or foul...?'

'Well, I guess I ...'

'Get a taxi. I'll pay for it.'

'Oh, don't worry about ... that's all right ...'

Margrave put a hand up to his forehead, which was unscathed, and smoothed back the lock of greyish blondish hair that flopped down over it. 'Just get me out of here. *Quickly.*'

'Okay ... sure.'

They resumed their shuffling progress and had almost reached the street exit when a willowy, glittering figure flitted into their path. It was Eleanor, in her sequined dress. Bob started to open his mouth to give her the message from Jerry, but she didn't even glance at him. She was staring, wide-eyed, at Margrave. 'What have they *done* to you?' she shrieked, then rushed forward to seize Quintin's free arm and wrap it around her neck.

▮ Chapter Eighteen

THERE WAS ONLY ONE word for the place: squalid. Eleanor herself wasn't the world's greatest housekeeper; Jerry often complained that she was far too lax in her supervision of Mrs Yablonsky, her reliable though charmless cleaning lady. But, my God, how could anybody *live* like this?

She tried to keep her dress from touching anything in Robert Willard's disgusting little kitchen. The sink was piled high with dirty dishes, most of which looked as if they'd been there for quite some time. She could hardly wedge the flimsy aluminum kettle under the faucet. Finally she got it half full and put it to boil on one of the front burners of the narrow, grease-coated gas stove, which she actually had to light with a match. In one of the musty cupboards, she found a cracked white china teapot. When she lifted the lid, its interior was stained dark brown from what looked like decades of steeping. Oh, well, she supposed the boiling water would deal with anything that might be alive in there.

She could hear the voices of Willard and Margrave in the next room, where Quintin was stretched out on the sagging chesterfield. He had adamantly refused to be taken back to his hotel, even though Eleanor had offered slip upstairs with him and make sure he was all right. He said what he really needed was a 'restorative' cup of tea, and since Quintin was in no condition to be seen in public, Bob had made the counter-suggestion that they go to his place on Tranby. They'd had a terrible time getting him up the stairs to the apartment; he whimpered every step of the way. And then, since she was the sole female present, the duty of making the tea naturally fell to Eleanor. Nevertheless, she was in quite good spirits.

Her first, horrified reaction to the sight of Quintin's bruised and bloody face had quickly given way to less noble emotions once she recovered from the shock. She nearly succumbed to a fit of the giggles as she dashed out of the Factory and around the corner to get the car. At least – at last – something was *happening.* Quintin needed her help and his injuries provided the perfect excuse to leave the increasingly dull party. She rather enjoyed feeling sorry for him, although his reluctance to continue or even acknowledge their past intrigue still rankled. So did his pursuit of the hateful Jenny. If some outraged rival, more than likely Jorgensen, had decided to teach him a lesson – well, he had asked for it. You couldn't just toy with people's emotions and expect to get off scot-free.

The kettle began to whistle. Nobody in the living room seemed to hear her shriek of pain when for an instant her bare hand closed around its metal handle. It was only as she was running cold water from the tap over the burn that she noticed the filthy oven mitt hanging from a cup hook on the wall near the stove. When she brought the teapot, with three bags of Red Rose steeping in it, back to the living room, both men looked surprisingly cheerful. Willard had pulled an unravelling wicker armchair up close to the sofa and was flipping slowly through a large pad of paper, and Margrave was murmuring judiciously over it.

'Gestural,' he said. And as she left the room again to get cups she thought she heard him pronounce a odd word that sounded like 'twombly'.

Quintin sent her back again for sugar and milk. By some miracle, there was a usable carton in the fridge. But after she returned with it and a crusty dime-store glass sugar bowl, he complained that the tea was now far too strong, and asked, politely enough, for more water.

When she entered the room for the fourth time, they were still talking.

'... pretty busy with teaching, 'Willard said. 'But maybe I will ask Max to take a look at this stuff. Yeah, I think I will.'

She poured tea for the men and then, holding her own mug in her uninjured left hand, perched on the slippery Naugahyde hassock that was the only seat available.

'You're with the Lurie Gallery?'

'Yeah ... Max and I stay in touch. We've known each other for years. Decades. But I haven't shown anything for some time....'

'I see, I see.'

Eleanor was starting to feel invisible. She cleared her throat. 'I own a couple of Robert's paintings, you know.' The first person singular pronoun was audacious. But somehow 'we' didn't seem quite possible in the circumstances. The two men's heads swivelled reluctantly in her direction. '*Forest* and *Earth to Earth.* Both from 1955, I think. Do you remember them?' The question was directed at Bob.

'Sure.'

'Ah,' said Quintin. 'I may have seen them when I visited the Zeffler residence.' He glanced at Eleanor. Aware that Willard was looking at him with the pathetically avid expression of a dog who anticipates a treat, she shook her head ever so slightly. Quintin couldn't have seen the Willards, because for the last six weeks they had been leaning against the wall in the basement storage room. 'Well, perhaps not. It was such a brief visit.'

Bob shrugged. 'Oh, well, you didn't miss much. I was in my Nicholson/Pasmore phase at the time. And I'm sure you've seen all *that* before.' He got up and carried the pad of paper he and Margrave had been looking at into a small, very messy space off the living room. For few moments, he could be heard shuffling things around in it.

Eleanor seized the opportunity to whisper, 'What happened? Who beat you up?'

Margrave grimaced. 'Friend Jorgensen.' He looked a little sheepish now.

'I knew it! You should have stayed away from Jenny.'

Eleanor was aware that Bob had come back and was sitting in the wicker chair. But Quintin still directed his words to her.

'Jenny? Oh, no. Not my type at all. Insufficient differentiation, you see. Neither here nor there, not quite this or that. I speak purely in the formal sense, for the young person you mention is incontestably female, I have no doubt.'

'But –'

Margrave smiled. 'No, my dear, when so inclined, I much prefer something … more elegant. But of course you know that.'

Eleanor acknowledged the compliment with a smile of her own, although she wished he would be more discreet in front of Willard, who she suddenly remembered had a reputation as a gossip.

'Well, I doubt that Sven knows it,' she replied. 'Besides, he was stoned.' She felt she had pronounced the last word with the required knowing casualness. 'He must have thought you were propositioning his girl. If she is. *His* girl, I mean.'

'*Propositioning?* A ponderous but useful locution. The North American dialect is fascinating. Nouns always trying to become verbs. Though I do see what you mean. In point of fact, however …' He paused and looked in a pleased way at Bob, who had just chortled softly into his tea.

Eleanor realized that she was hopeless at figuring out when Quintin was joking and when he wasn't. Perhaps when he seemed most condescending he was only being ironical, in that deadpan English way of his.

'In point of fact,' he repeated, looking her straight in the eye, 'it was not she who interested me. Whom I *propositioned*, as you would have it. It was the young man himself. But alas he did not take at all kindly to my suggestion. Odd, how frenzied and punitive his type are apt to become about such matters. So protective of their manly virtue. Though I often think that constitutes quite a large part of their tremendous allure.'

SHE HADN'T been able to see much of what happened, but Jane did find out from the people around her that Bruno and Eddie had finally been subdued and led off in opposite directions. Her first impulse was to make herself scarce, just in case one or both of them might expect commiseration or first aid. So she skulked on the sidelines until the coast was clear. By that time it was after midnight and the place was rapidly clearing out.

The evening had been a disappointment. Navigating the noisy, indistinct space, she had felt, once she was drunk enough, both liberated and confined. It was distressingly easy to believe that no one was watching her, so it didn't actually matter how she behaved, or looked. But that anonymity also hung around her neck like a dead weight. In the blurred darkness beyond her range of vision, Jane knew that real life was going on at a fever pitch. But she felt she didn't know how it – life – really worked. Not the way other people did, anyway. Favours, debts, signals were being exchanged; she understood that much. But she, Jane, had nothing to barter with – no connections, no advantages, no achievements. All she had was herself, body and soul, two commodities whose value fluctuated unpredictably.

And all she really wanted was the undivided attention of – at least – one charismatic and physically attractive man. That had not come to pass. She hadn't seen Eddie again until the fight began; Barnaby had yet another unknown girl on his arm and even Sven seemed to have given up on her, thank God. She had danced with a few people, but they were all too dull, too ugly (there was no point in mincing words when talking to yourself, was there?) or already identified as not interested in females. She had encountered only one possibility, a borderline case, neither absolutely repulsive nor irresistibly magnetic. However, there was something about him, a kind of pattern in which, even without her glasses, she recognized a strangely compelling resonance. He was an American – a draft dodger most likely – who, she now remembered, trailed Eddie with almost canine devotion. He'd appeared late in the evening, when she was ready to see possibilities that might have been invisible earlier. To compromise, in short. Not that she considered for a second going home with the guy then and there. Jane never did, with strangers. She still felt it was bad form to succumb to what ten years earlier would have been called a 'pick-up'. But when he asked for her phone number, she wrote it down on a cocktail napkin. And then went home alone.

WHEN YOU unexpectedly attain your heart's desire, is there always an instant when you ask yourself if you really want it? Bob actually felt himself take an involuntary step backwards as Eleanor Zeffler ... came at him. *She came at me in sections.* He'd always liked that line. It sounded like the caption of a Thurber cartoon, but he thought it was from an old Fred Astaire movie – and now, finally, he had occasion to use it. He didn't, though, because Eleanor was completely serious. He had never noticed that she had much of a sense of humour, but it was hardly the first attribute a man looked for in a woman.

Seeing Eleanor in his very own cramped and threadbare habitat had quite literally brought home to him the absurdity of the fantasies he been having about her. Perched on the tan fake-leather hassock in that glimmering blue dress, she was as out of place as a ... as a ... flamingo in a hen house. Or something. Even as Quintin Margrave's polite interest in his work stirred up long-stagnant reservoirs of hope within him, he'd decided to renounce, once and for all, any designs on Eleanor. Any fool could see they were just as futile as Margrave's attempt on the manly virtue of Sven Jorgensen – though he had to admire the guy's bloody-but-unbowed reaction to the violent rebuff he had received. That came with the territory, probably. Maybe he ought to consider himself lucky: however much he had cringed at the prospect of a humiliating rejection, he'd never had to worry about Eleanor clobbering him.

After Margrave's revelation there wasn't a lot to be said. Eleanor was visibly flustered, but that was understandable in a woman who lived such a sheltered bourgeois life. And who probably had difficulty conceiving of anyone being impervious to her own beauty. Finally, after a few awkward moments of silence, Margrave had simply pulled the tattered blanket with which she had covered him up to his ears and turned sideways on the sofa. 'I think a brief nap may do me good,' he murmured before closing his eyes.

Bob and Eleanor had exchanged glances then. They had achieved a strange kind of comrades-in-arms friendliness during the unexpected events of the last hour. He jerked his head towards the kitchen, but she shook hers with an expression of distaste. So they had ended up in his bedroom, just like that.

'Well, I guess he's here for the night,' Bob said. 'You might as well go ho –'

That was when it happened. 'But I don't want to go home,' she said in a girlish yet sultry voice he had never heard her use before. Then she moved very close to him and he took that tiny step back. She didn't seem to notice, but touched his face with her hand. 'It's still quite early, you know.'

'True.' By the alarm clock on his bedside table, it was just after midnight. One of his own hands somehow came to rest at her waist. The fabric of her dress was pebbly on the surface, but silky and pliant beneath. He was suddenly aware of her perfume, the same scent he had inhaled in the Plaza Roof elevator, the one Lorraine used to wear. And of the smooth strand of hair that had fallen over her right eye. And of the way her breasts were nearly brushing against his chest. He tried to remember when he had last changed the sheets. Her fingers on his cheek were soft, but there was something cool and hard there, too. When he took her hand and brought it to his lips, he found that she was wearing a ring made almost entirely of diamonds. And when she winced as he kissed her palm, he noticed the angry red stripe that ran across it.

'I burned it on your kettle.'

'Oh, *no*.' He blew gently on the wound and she closed her eyes and threw her head back as if in ecstasy. The next moment their arms were around each other, their lips came clumsily but accurately together, and they more or less toppled sideways onto the unmade bed.

His momentary hesitation must have been only the conditioned reflex of a man too accustomed to disappointment. And though in the brief renunciation period he had dismissed her as a cold-hearted tease, he soon found out just how wrong a guy could be. But he had never been so delighted to admit a mistake.

Oh yes, delight was the operative word here. Naked, she was neither distant nor frigid. And she made a lot of noise. At first he tried, ineffectually, to shush her, but she only smiled muzzily at him, apparently not giving a hoot if Margrave heard them. And if she didn't care, why should he? To be capable of provoking those sighs, groans and cries in a woman like Eleanor could only be a source of pride and pleasure. Even if the whole world had been listening.

THE KNIFE POINT, freshly sharpened on the bench stone in the workshop, was only a centimetre from the canvas when Bruno paused, feeling tears spring irresistibly to his eyes. He had mulled over the act for nearly an hour, then spent the better part of another sorting through his carving tools, feeling it was of the utmost importance that he select the right one. There were dozens in the workshop: knives, gouges, chisels, scrapers, rasps, rifflers. Each had its own specific purpose. Some would puncture roughly, some cruelly rip and tear, and some could slice a tightly stretched, smoothly painted canvas swiftly and cleanly into ribbons. Finally he chose a knife he had brought with him from the old country, one with a gently curved blade and a wooden handle worn smooth by use. He rarely used it nowadays, but he liked to keep it near him as a reminder of the ever more rapidly receding past.

Then he had gone slowly down the stairs to the basement. After laying the knife carefully on the floor, he dragged *Back Flip* out of the cupboard, propped it against the wall and gently peeled off its brown-paper wrapping. He had not seen the painting since the night he had decided to keep it. And even in the poor light cast by the bare sixty-watt bulb over his head, it was clear that it was far superior to the feeble imitation hanging in the Artquake show.

It was a terrible thing he was about to do, but there was no other way out; his enemies had left him no choice. He could no longer allow two versions of *Back Flip* to exist. In order to gain indisputable possession of the copy, along with all the advantages that owning it would bring, he had to destroy the original. But he would not roughly, brutally despoil it. No, he had decided instead to cut the canvas neatly into small sections that could be stuffed into a garbage bag and disposed of in the next morning's collection. The stretcher could easily be dismantled and stored in the workshop as scrap wood.

He briefly considered saving one small piece of canvas in each colour as a memento, then rejected the idea. All traces of the painting had to disappear. Then there would be no way for Eddie the traitor, who believed he was so clever, to prove it had ever existed. Bruno smiled at the thought of his own superior guile, even though he felt tears running down his cheeks. Slowly, deliberately, he moved the knife forward until the tip of the blade was touching the canvas. With only the slightest pressure from his hand, it would begin to cut.

WHEN ELEANOR got home, the porch light was on and so was the ceiling fixture in the downstairs hall. But the upper floors of the house were dark and silent. It was just after two o'clock. She opened the door of Becky's room a sliver and listened for a moment to her daughter's steady breathing. In the dimness she could just make out the pale pink *Coordinateurs* hovering like huge gum bubbles over the bed. Rebecca had only recently been allowed to stay at home alone in the evening, and her parents had promised to be back before midnight. Eleanor quietly closed the door again and went on down the hall to the master suite.

Because no lights were burning upstairs, she was not worried about Jerry's waiting up for her. He had probably been asleep for a couple of hours. In the morning, she would be able to waffle without much difficulty about what time she got home.

She went quickly to the bathroom to wash up. But when she came out in her nightgown and felt her way to the bed, she discovered it was still neatly made. There was no sign of her husband in the guest room either, or the TV room on the ground floor. The Lincoln was in the garage, because they had taken the Mustang, which she had driven first to Willard's – *Robert's* – place and then home.

She returned to the bedroom and got under the covers. Lying there, wide awake behind closed eyes, she reviewed the events of the evening. She had smoked marijuana for the first time in her life. To be honest, she couldn't see what all the excitement was about, but at least she had done it. She had finally succeeded in having an actual affair, even if it was only with Bob Willard. And she had discovered that Quintin Margrave was a … fairy.

Well, at least Quintin's disclosure – *Sven Jorgensen?* – explained certain things that she hadn't understood before. Or did it? Though her flesh positively crawled at the thought of what had taken place just over two weeks ago at the Windsor Arms, she could not make any coherent connection between that event and this new information. Even as he revealed his humiliating secret, Quintin had still felt quite free to condescend. As if it was all a great joke, one of life's little ironies – and Eleanor had received the impression that the joke was on *her*.

Thank God Willard – Robert – had been there. She had always known, without much caring one way or the other, that he wanted her. So as she clung to him for comfort she also felt she was doing her good deed for the day. To her relief the rumpled, flimsy sheets on his bed had been fairly clean. The sex itself was not unpleasant. She hadn't faked, just amplified her responses a little, and it had been obvious that he could hardly believe his luck. And if Margrave had overheard them – so what?

At some point, still only fitfully dozing, she heard the front door slam. Jerry – at least she assumed it was Jerry and not some axe-wielding burglar – made no effort to be quiet as he climbed the stairs. Or when he entered the room, crossed to the bed and flicked on the light on the nightstand. Then he loomed unsteadily over her.

'You awake?'

She blinked ostentatiously and rubbed her hands over her face as she sat up. 'I am now. What time is it?'

'Late.' He consulted his watch. 'Nearly three. Boy, I really lost track.' His Countess Mara tie was loosened and his normally immaculate hair was mussed.

'Where were you, anyway?' She paused, then decided to risk adding, 'I was worried.'

'Well, after the big brawl – did you see it?'

'You mean the fight between O'Hara and Gonzaga? No, I missed it. I must have been in the washroom.' Actually, she calculated with some satisfaction, she had probably been outside in the alley at the time, toking up with Sven and Jenny. 'But I heard people talking about it.' Robert had mentioned it as they lay entwined, afterwards.

'Then I guess you heard that Max, Tom and I had to break it up. I thought I'd better get Eddie out of there as soon as possible. Gonzaga is a maniac, but I figured Max would know how to handle him, being in the same line of work.'

'Uh-huh.'

'Well, anyway, I took Eddie home in a taxi and once we were at his pad, we got talking. And talking. *And* talking. Bright kid. Great ideas. We had a very fruitful discussion and I gave him a little advice about his future direction, which I think he appreciated. Not just as a patron to an artist, although we did come to an arrangement about that, too. But like two pals, two buddies, y'know. We smoked a cigar – I don't think he'd ever had one, I mean a decent one, before – and then ...'

'Mmm?'

'Don't ever tell Becky about this, promise?'

She nodded.

'Eddie and I smoked a little grass together!'

She decided that a sharp intake of breath would be the most convincing reaction. 'Really?'

'Yeah!' Jerry grinned beatifically. 'Then we listened to some blues and after that we went out on Spadina and took a walk around. And then we just ... *goofed* on the streetlights.'

'Goofed?'

'Yeah, y'know, just took it all in, grooved on the scene ... *man*, it was beautiful.'

Eleanor knew her sour expression was unbecoming. But really – trust Jerry to try to outdo her, even when he didn't know there was anything to outdo. She had never for an instant considered telling her husband about her own little experiment with pot. She'd been certain he'd be horrified, for one thing. She would have bet money that he'd pounce on it as the most conclusive evidence to date of her incorrigible silliness. Not to mention the position in which she'd put *him*, an officer of the court, with her reckless public use of an illegal substance. And yet here he was, crowing about his pot smoking, as if he'd just had some kind of spiritual experience. He certainly seemed to have enjoyed it more than she had. Phooey.

He pranced off to the bathroom, and through the open door she could hear him singing, in a deep, raspy voice quite unlike his usual one, 'Someone is wreckin', wreckin', my *love* life ...'

There was a pause during which he brushed his teeth ... chuffa-chuffa-chuffa. Gargle. Spit. Gargle. Spit. Then after a few moments, 'Who *do* you luuuv ... who *do* you luuuv ...' accompanied by the unmistakable, prolonged sound of copious urination.

Eleanor switched off the bedside lamp, rolled onto her stomach, pulled the covers up over her head and prayed for sleep.

▪ Chapter Nineteen

AWAKE. AWAKE. AWAKE. The word was like a dreadful drumbeat in her skull, a throbbing pulse that with every thud generated a new, convoluted, stimulating and yet indistinct idea. Win Beecham opened her eyes, which were already gritty with exhaustion and, leaning on one elbow, peered at the luminous dial of the clock on her night-table for what must have been the dozenth time since she had got into bed. Three-thirteen. That meant she had been lying there, sleepless, for three interminable hours and could not reasonably get up until another four had passed.

Well, she *could,* of course. Nothing actually prevented her from going upstairs and trying to transfer some of those insistent images and emotions to paper. But no – the studio was a refuge reserved for serene contemplation and creation; it would be wrong to contaminate it with these futile, knotted thoughts. In any case, she was far too groggy and irritable to work. And if she didn't sleep for at least a few hours, she simply could not imagine how she would get through the next day.

She sat up, pummelled each of her three pillows in turn, then lay down again on her left side, with one hand under her cheek. There was no hope of catching up on lost sleep tomorrow. She had never been able to nap in daylight; she was too high-strung for that. Then she remembered that she couldn't even go to bed early the next night, because she had to attend Eliot's annual Medical Society dinner dance at the Royal York. Weary though she now was of such gatherings, she hated the prospect of appearing grey-faced and dull-witted in that company. Many of the guests would be out-and-out meritocrats, the sort of people who in former days could never have become physicians, or physicians' wives. It was bad enough to feel that her lineage was irrelevant, her physical appearance just a little too faded to compel the admiration once taken for granted. But even worse was the fact that her husband's colleagues were indifferent to her artistic achievements. They listened with only minimal politeness and perhaps even scepticism to her attempts to broaden the range of conversation. And as for their simpering, overdressed wives ...

Stop it, stop it, stop it! These were just the sort of corrosive ruminations that had been swirling around in her head for three hours. She turned over, throwing off the stifling bedclothes that had become tangled around her, to lie spread-eagled, flat on her back. At midnight, when she had still hoped to sleep, the party last evening had not seemed a complete failure and the recollection of Tom's embrace had been rather pleasant. She'd felt she was entitled to savour it just a little before working out just how she would graciously dispel the awkwardness it might create between them. But now, in the hour of the wolf, she saw that she'd been as good as dead when the touch of Tom's lips brought her back to life like some post-menopausal Sleeping Beauty.

And what purpose could that artificial reanimation possibly serve? The kiss had been unsettling but futile; it had only created complications without compensating benefits. She changed position again, ending up on her right side with her knees bent, arms folded in front of her.

It came to her then that there had there been a touch of condescension in Tom's manner when he said goodbye to her before going off with Zeffler and Lurie. He had patted her on the arm as one might a dear old lady – some maiden aunt, perhaps – in a gesture of kindly dismissal. Could that be how he really saw her? Oh, it was *all* unbearable. With a gulping sound like a half-suppressed sob, she rolled onto her stomach and pressed her cheek firmly into her goose-down pillow, determined not to look at the clock again until the sun came up.

AT SEVEN SHARP, when the Rancho opened for breakfast, Bruno went over there and ordered a coffee and a toasted Danish. He had developed a taste for this strange Canadian confection, a sweet iced fruit bun (he liked the cherry ones best, but blueberry was all right too) fried on a big, greasy iron griddle beside the eggs and bacon that other customers ordered but that he still, after all these years, did not find appetizing as the first meal of the day. He decided to 'eat in' as Stavros, the proprietor, suggested and took a seat at the counter. Leaning on his elbows, he finished his cigarette and sipped his coffee, which tasted subtly different in the thick white china cup, while he waited for the Danish to be ready.

He had not gone home last night, but just after three o'clock he telephoned his wife so that she would not worry. It was hard to tell from her voice or words whether she had been asleep or awake, but she asked him no questions, perhaps suspecting there was another woman involved. That, at least, was easier for her to understand than the reasons, only partially known even to himself, that he occasionally stayed overnight at the gallery. Then he had dozed for a couple of hours on the folding cot he kept in the workshop and awakened, not refreshed exactly, but with thoughts that were less agitated and disordered.

In the end, he had not been able to do it. The knife point, which curved delicately downwards like the beak of a bird of prey, had only pierced the canvas a millimetre when he pulled it back with a roar of frustration and anger. He stood very still and listened for a moment then, thinking that someone might have heard his cry. But all was silent in the dim basement, the empty gallery above it and the deserted street outside. Quickly, trembling, fumbling, he had covered *Back Flip* again in its torn brown-paper wrapping and slid the painting back into the closet before he could change his mind.

Later, upstairs, lying wide awake on the thin, lumpy mattress of the cot, he had thought and thought, his head rolling from side to side with the effort of forcing his mind to overrule his emotions, and finally a plan came to him that allowed him to sleep.

THE SMELL of bacon frying brought Tom gently and pleasantly to consciousness. At his age, it was close to impossible to leap out of bed singing, but he would have if he could have. He didn't even glance at the clock. He had slept long enough, and well. The idiocies of the previous evening were not forgotten exactly, but they seemed distant and inconsequential as he swung his legs over the side of the bed and felt with his toes for his slippers, fairly confident that Joan had placed them there as usual. And so she had. He was still naked, but his tartan Viyella robe was also within easy reach, draped neatly across the striped boudoir chair just a few feet away.

He was not hung over, because although he had drunk quite a lot the night before, the drinks had been well spaced out. A hearty breakfast would be just the thing to set him up for a productive day in the studio. And by God, he was raring to go. In the bathroom, he ran a hand over his chin, then decided not to bother shaving. The white stubble became him, somehow. *Thomas R. Dale, grizzled patriarch of Canadian art....* He grinned at his reflection in the mirror, absolving himself of guilt for whatever he had done last night, just as he now felt sure dear old understanding Winnie already had.

Anyway, neither she nor anyone else would be waiting for him in the studio. Behind its locked door there was only freedom and solitude and the large, square primed canvas that would in a day or two (or maybe sooner) be *Kite IV*. Once he really got going, he forgot everything – and never mind how cornball this might sound – everything except the constructive elation of making through his own independent effort something greater than himself that was nobody's goddamn business but his own. Other people's desires or expectations could be inconvenient, but only if you let them get to you.

He decided on over-easy for his eggs and shouted the information down the stairs to Joan. When he took his seat in the breakfast nook already dressed in his painting clothes, she gave him a surprised look.

'You're up early,' she said as she placed his plate in front of him. 'It's only eight-thirty. Didn't you get home late?'

'Not very.' He took her hand and brought it briefly to his lips. 'It was pretty dull after you left.'

JANE SQUINTED at the clock. It seemed to be saying that the time was 9:34. She must have rolled into bed without taking off her makeup, because her eyelashes were stuck together in a tangle of tiny Fabulash fibres. She managed to pry them apart with her fingers, then reached over and dragged the clock closer. How could it be so late? She must also have forgotten to set the alarm. As a result, she had under thirty minutes to get up, get dressed and travel halfway across town to the gallery. And she'd *better* make it more or less on time, because who knew what kind of mood or condition Bruno might be in today, after all that uproar last night?

With a groan, she staggered to her feet and dragged on a brassiere and a sweater that happened to be lying on the floor beside the bed. Still naked below the waist, she dashed to the bathroom, then back to the bedroom to grab a pair of tights from the dresser and a skirt from the closet. She moaned when she looked in the mirror. Her trusty prescription sunglasses and a scarf would camouflage the full horror of her appearance enough for the subway ride, but as soon as she arrived at work she'd have to sneak down to the bathroom in the basement to put on fresh make-up and try to do something with her hair. Panting, she rushed back to the bathroom to get the curling iron and stuff it in a tote bag and to the bedroom to jam her feet into shoes. Then she hurtled along the hall, down the stairs, out the door, off the porch, onto the street, where she set off at a ragged run for the Bathurst subway station.

OVER BREAKFAST, Jerry was noticeably less chipper. His face was creased and pale, his expression disagreeable. He had a meeting downtown at ten-thirty, so there was no question of either of them sleeping in. Eleanor, though just as badly rested as her husband, had to pretend to be reasonably alert because she had not let on how late she herself had got home. After seeing Becky off to school, she rustled up a soft-boiled egg and some whole-wheat toast for Jerry, who was watching his diet.

He looked at the food doubtfully, choked down a few bites of the toast and then buried his nose in the morning paper while he drank his coffee. Under normal circumstances, Eleanor would have been annoyed by that, but this morning she found silence preferable to the risks of a crabby cross-examination. On the other side of the table, hidden by the business section, which Jerry had spread open like a screen between them, she spooned her corn flakes into her mouth as quietly as she could.

She didn't really feel much worse than she had most mornings when Rebecca was small, when after three weeks the baby nurse left and Eleanor herself had had to get up several times a night. For a couple of years, too. So this wasn't that bad, really. When she had finished her breakfast, she went back upstairs to take stock of her appearance, privately, in the bathroom. Pretty grim, but probably reparable with a couple of hours of morning sleep, once Jerry had left the house.

Then she'd sit down and try to figure out whether she ought to see Willard again. The main point in his favour was that he clearly adored her. Her experiences with Tom and Quintin had given her a new appreciation of adoration, and perhaps at her age Robert was the best she could do. Actually, he was kind of cute – if you enlarged the definition a bit. And he was, at least nominally, an artist. Why, she'd lived with two of his paintings for years. What a coincidence. Once she was feeling a little more human, she'd go down to the basement and take another look at them with the new perspective she had gained from their … whatever it was, last night.

When she heard the front door slam and the garage door grind open and then closed, she lay down on the bed in her dressing gown. Quintin – she actually shuddered at the thought of him – had treated Robert with a surprising amount of respect, so it was remotely possible that he was an underrated, unrecognized genius, the kind Jerry was always hoping to discover just before everybody else did. But that didn't make sense; a man couldn't be an undiscovered genius and a has-been at the same time, could he? Maybe, just as she had believed right up until midnight last night, Willard really *was* a complete schnook. But strange as it seemed, she could hardly wait to see him again.

THE STREET DOOR was unlocked, but Bruno was nowhere in sight when Jane arrived at work. She was less than fifteen minutes late. An unidentifiable shuffling and the faint sound of a throat being cleared emanated from the alcove as she sat down at her desk, having slipped down to the basement only long enough to hang up her coat on the rack at the bottom of the stairs. She responded by rolling a sheet of letterhead into the typewriter and tapping out *the quick brown fox jumps over the lazy dog* a few times to signal that she was both present and industrious.

Half an hour later, Bruno had still not emerged. After examining small segments of her face and hair in the mirror of her pressed-powder compact, Jane had discovered that things were even worse than she'd thought. She could wait no longer; any minute now, someone might come into the gallery and see her. As quietly as she could, she went down the stairs to the washroom, carrying the curling iron. She had only been in there for a moment when she realized there was no electrical outlet in the cramped plywood cubicle, which contained only a toilet and a small wall-mounted hand basin with a mirror over it. And then she heard footsteps approaching the door at the top of the stairs. When she opened the washroom door a few inches and peered up, she caught a glimpse of a hefty black-clad figure stepping quickly away from the open doorway.

It was impossible, with Bruno hovering at the top of the stairs and no electricity, to make herself really presentable. She slapped on some powder and blusher and applied new eyeliner and mascara, but without the curling iron, nothing could be done about her hair. It sprang out at right angles from her scalp in uncontrollable, grotesquely shaped curls instead of hanging down smoothly as it should have. Finally she gave up and returned to her desk.

Bruno was standing by the window, staring out into the street. When he turned around, she noticed that he looked pretty haggard – at least, as haggard as someone with his build and complexion *could* look. There were dark circles under his eyes, his hair was messy, and it was obvious that he had not shaved.

'Big party last night,' was all he had to say.

'It sure was,' Jane replied.

Neither of them mentioned the fight with Eddie, or even *Back Flip*. Then Bruno returned to the workshop, and Jane busied herself straightening the contents of her desk drawers.

An hour or so later, he reappeared and said that he had to go out. As soon as she was absolutely certain he was gone, she slipped downstairs again. She had seen an extension cord somewhere in the broom closet. If she could find it, she might be able to plug her curling iron into the floor outlet under the desk that powered the electric typewriter.

BOB STAYED in bed as long as he could, contemplating the wondrous fact that on Fridays he did not have any classes until mid-afternoon and replaying in his mind the stupendous events of the previous night. When his bladder finally commanded him to arise and walk to the bathroom, it was well past eleven. Even then, he could hardly bear to drag himself out of the soft, warm sheets. They still held a faint memory of Sortilège, along with other, less rarefied odours that also reminded him of Eleanor.

She had left at some point in the wee hours; he didn't know exactly what time, but he did remember that she had got up and dressed with what seemed like remarkable speed and efficiency. Insisting that he stay there in bed, beached and blissful, she had begun to make her way silently to the apartment door with her silver sandals dangling by their slender straps from her hand. When she went into the living room to retrieve her coat and purse, she must have tiptoed past the sleeping form of Margrave, who by then could be heard snoring noisily on the chesterfield....

Oh, hell; he had forgotten all about Margrave. After he had finished at the toilet, he covered his nakedness prudently with a towel and stepped quietly into the hall. He looked into the living room, vaguely apprehensive about what he might find in there. It was empty. The blanket that Margrave had used was folded neatly on the sofa, and a small white rectangle that looked like a business card was sitting on top of it. He went over and picked it up. It was Margrave's card, identifying him as the chief curator of the Spitalfields Gallery of London. 'Nine o'clock,' was written on the back in a spiky, confident hand. Then,

My dear Robert,

Please accept sincere thanks for your assistance and hospitality and my apologies for any inconvenience caused. I must be off, for my plane for London leaves at noon or thereabouts.

Q. M.

P.S. Kiss the fair Eleanor on my behalf!

'I shall without fail do that very thing, old man,' Bob said aloud. 'You may absolutely count on it.' Then he tossed the card back onto the sofa and went into the kitchen to forage for breakfast.

THERE WERE TWO cigarettes left in the package. Otherwise, Eddie would have had to get up, get dressed and go out to get some. As he waited for the kettle to boil, he lit one, then strolled into the studio. From the window, he observed that regular, everyday Friday-afternoon life was in full swing out on Spadina. His brain, too, had returned to normal – a little shell-shocked, sure, but fully rational with all neurons intact and firing. After Zeffler had left, he had crashed for ... oh, it must have been more than ten hours, because it was after one o'clock now. Still, he could recall at least some of the events of the previous night.

The fight with Bruno, and everything that had led up to it, was kind of blurry. *Back Flip* had been in the exhibition; he didn't have to worry about that any more, and once Artquake '67 hit London – *England*, baby – he'd really be in the big time. But there had been something not quite right about it; he couldn't quite recall exactly what. Why had he taken that first fatal swipe at Gonzaga? It was way out of character for him, a peaceable guy if ever there was one – anybody could tell you that. Maybe he ought to go back and have another look at the show, just to make sure everything was okay.

He glanced speculatively at the *Clouds*. They could be easily painted over, so at least those pricey stretchers wouldn't be totally wasted. It might be a kick to see what he could do with those shapes. Yeah. And if he played his cards right, he might even find a buyer for them. Last night, Jerry Zeffler had been almost insanely enthusiastic, and he'd made it clear that he really hated Bruno. He'd kept saying Gonzaga had 'pulled a fast one' on him. Eddie had been sorely tempted to tell him that the piece in the exhibition was not the original, to assure him there were more than enough *Flips* to go around. But he'd held back, knowing even under the lingering influence of the acid that it would be wiser to keep his mouth shut.

Finally, Eddie had plied Zeffler with a little medium-quality grass and played the new Superblues album he happened to have on the turntable. By that time Jerry had forgotten all about his wife, and Eddie was pretty sure he wasn't going to be accused of making a pass at her, so everything was cool. Zeffler had actually used that very word with obvious relish. And he'd even offered to help Eddie with any legal problems he might encounter in separating himself from Gonzaga.

Later, the two of them had gone out for a little walk around the neighbourhood, because Eddie was feeling kind of claustrophobic as the acid wore off. The idea was to get rid of Zeffler at the same time. But the guy wasn't so bad, really.

Jerry had pointed out one of the old rag-trade buildings and said that his father had started out there, way back in the thirties. The old man did well enough for his son, the first Zeffler to be born in Canada, to go to law school, even in the Toronto of the early fifties, with all the 'restrictions' and quotas of fine old traditional bigotry. Eddie could certainly dig that – his own parents, only partially lapsed Catholics, had always got a bit testy when the Glorious Twelfth and the Orange Parade rolled around each year. Especially in the days when the mayor himself was a member.

It was late when they finally arrived back at the studio door. After a lot of handshaking and backslapping that was fairly heartfelt on both sides, Jerry had flagged down a passing taxi and headed home. And Eddie had hit the sack.

RECLINING IN the barber's chair, Bruno went over in his mind the list of supplies he would need: lumber for the framing, plywood, two-inch nails, primer, white paint. He had all the measurements in his pocket, jotted down on a square of scrap mat board. Once he was shaved and his hair had been washed and returned to its customary neatness, he would drive over to the lumberyard on Mount Pleasant and buy all these things. He might have to stop somewhere else for the paint. But it was not a big job. After a proper night's rest tonight in his own bed at home, he'd start work very early on Saturday morning, before the gallery opened for business. Then, if he did the painting on Saturday night after closing time, he could move everything back into place on Sunday afternoon, well before Jane arrived on Monday morning. There was no reason for her to know anything about his plan. It would be better if she didn't, because he was beginning to have serious doubts about her loyalty. She had stayed much too long in the basement that morning. There was no time to waste.

He kept an electric razor in the workshop, but today he felt he was entitled to the luxury of a professional treatment. The barber's soothing stream of talk flowed over him, though he did not pay much attention to what the guy was saying. He spoke of hockey teams, football games and the day's headlines – safe and reliable topics that most of the shop's customers probably found fascinating. They held no interest whatsoever for Bruno. And the barber would probably have been mystified by the thoughts of the man whose jaw he was now covering with fragrant white foam.

Pride, honour, power, ambition ... the treachery of false friends. Surely these were universal preoccupations, even here. They were just not talked about. Perhaps the barber, so full of trivial everyday facts, would understand Bruno's state of mind if the story of *Back Flip* had been recast as a tale of carnal love and betrayal. Suppose a man's wife is the love of his life and his most prized possession. Say another man, who pretends to be his friend, steals her away – and yes, that was exactly what O'Hara had done, *stolen* the painting from its rightful owner. The angry husband's first impulse is to hurt them and destroy them both, his former friend and his beloved. But if he is truly wise, he remains calm and purposeful. Mastering his rage, he finds a way to keep his beloved safe from harm and still possess her.

THERE WAS just enough milk left in the carton for one bowl of Wheaties, Breakfast of Champions. *Ha.* Well, considering what had happened last night, Bob felt like one. After downing it, along with two cups of strong black coffee, he took a long and invigorating shower, emerging only when the supply of hot water gave out. If the towel he dried himself with had smelled less musty (he resolved to make a trip to the laundromat as soon as he had time) he'd have felt like an entirely new man.

He decided to get dressed before telephoning Eleanor. Though he was eager – longing, in fact – to see and touch her again, he felt curiously reluctant to call her. Was it because last night had been so perfect that he was afraid to shatter its lingering spell? Yeah, that had to be it. He looked up the number in the phone book while he drank his third cup of coffee and had a cigarette. But as he weighed the ethical and practical implications of telephoning his new mistress at her matrimonial home, he remembered that he had always sworn he would never do this sort of thing.

Margie, wherever and whoever she was now, could have given him some tips on the finer points of phone etiquette during an adulterous affair. For example, when the husband answers, do you: a) hang up at once; b) pretend it's a wrong number; c) greet him and, winging it, invent some plausible pretext for calling; or e) none of the above?

Bob thought back, trying to identify possible occasions when one of these options might have been used on him by his second wife's lover. It was nearly three years ago, but he did remember an unusual number of hang-ups, and there had been the occasional late-night query about supposedly mislaid scripts. Maybe if he'd been paying more attention ...

He stubbed out his third cigarette of the day and pulled his still partially buttoned shirt, the same one he had worn last night, over his head. Shorts, pants, belt, socks, shoes, wristwatch on the arm, cigarettes in the pocket, matches. Hair combed, teeth brushed ... okay, he was definitely going to make the call ... *right now*.

∎ Chapter Twenty

THE PHONE rang three times before Jane answered it. Whether at home or at work, she never picked up the receiver on the first ring. That might give the impression that your life was pathetically uneventful or that business was embarrassingly slow. Bruno, who agreed with her reasoning, approved the practice.

He had returned from his errands shaved and with his hair tidied up and could now be intermittently heard shifting unidentified objects from one place to another somewhere in the far reaches of the workshop. She herself had just got back from lunch. It was one-thirty, which meant that there were only four and a half hours left before she could lock the place up and go home.

'Bruno Gonzaga Gallery.'

'Jane?'

'Yes?'

'Hi. It's Jim.'

'Oh, hello.' Jim Watkin. The draft dodger she had met last night. She had only a vague idea now of whether or not she liked him. It had been dark and noisy at the party, and she had drunk quite a lot.

'Say, Jane, I was thinking that maybe we could go see a movie tonight.'

'Okay.'

'What time do you finish work?'

'Six.'

'Okay, I'll come by the gallery at six.'

'Okay.'

Oh, why not? Her hair looked all right. She had managed to locate the extension cord, though it had taken some digging. She might have found one more easily in the workshop but felt a little nervous about venturing into it when Bruno wasn't there. He probably didn't actually have it booby-trapped, but she wouldn't put it past him. That was why it was so strange that he had stored the painting downstairs. With hindsight, Jane realized that it had probably been there for quite a while, although she'd never noticed the large paper-wrapped object at the back of the cupboard. Under normal circumstances, she opened the door only briefly and reluctantly, to get out the cleaning stuff.

But as she'd rummaged around for the cord, which she eventually found coiled up on the floor, she had delved deeper into the closet. And she saw that the paper on the big flat package at the back was loose. It looked as if it been unwrapped, then quickly and carelessly recovered. Shoving the brooms, mops and buckets out of the way, she moved closer to it. And then, through a slit in the paper where the reapplied tape had failed to stick, Jane saw a sliver of startlingly familiar blue.

IT ALL CAME BACK to him when he read the wall label. He remembered everything: the sudden unease of seeing it for the first time, then the galloping paranoia that had driven him to cower in the men's room. And finally the clumsy, spaced-out, ineffectual tussle with Bruno. Eddie sat down on the nearest bench and covered his face with his hands.

Somehow, some way – without even knowing it existed – Gonzaga had become the owner of *Back Flip* number two. It was right there in black and white. That was what Zeffler had been so steamed up about. First Bruno had made the real *Back Flip* disappear, and now he had claimed the copy. And. it was horribly clear that he, Eddie, now had absolutely nothing, except the totally irrelevant distinction of having painted them both.

What would happen if everybody found out? That might be a much more serious problem than the one he had tried to solve by making the copy. At least when the real – or at least the first – *Back Flip* was missing, he had still believed that by withholding it Bruno would end up thwarting his own ambitions just as much as Eddie's. Cutting off his nose to spite his face. But, fuck it, wasn't that the very surgical procedure he, Eddie, had just performed on himself? Man oh man, what a dope he'd been.

BY THE TIME he finally called, it was really too late for them to get together that day. Becky would be home from school in less than two hours. Besides, Robert said, he had to teach a class in the afternoon and wouldn't be free until after five o'clock. Tomorrow was Saturday and the next day, inexorably, Sunday. That meant that Eleanor couldn't see him again until Monday at the earliest. But between now and then stretched all the tedium of a domestic weekend. Driving Becky to her riding lesson in Caledon early on Saturday afternoon, spending two hours watching her canter around the track, or paddock, or whatever the hell it was called. And afterwards, Jerry's weekly ritual, which could not be varied short of plague or pestilence: dining out at Scala or Mr Tony's or Gaston's or the Restaurant at the Three Small Rooms. Then on Sunday night, she would serve dinner at home to the in-laws. The preparations for that, both culinary and psychological, were always elaborate. So – two full days of unrelieved gloom to be endured, unless she could think of some excuse to sneak out tonight.

WILLARD WASN'T at the Pilot. Funny, Eddie had been sure he would be – Bob almost always showed up there on Fridays. Jim Watkin was coming out the door just as Eddie arrived, but for once he didn't want to stop and talk. He was in a hurry. He hadn't seen Willard, and neither had anybody else.

But Eddie *had* to talk to Bob about the *Back Flip* thing. The guy had been around the art scene a long time; if anybody knew what could be done, he might. And he was the only person besides Eddie who knew about the copy. Shit, without Willard's encouragement he would never have done it. You could almost say it was Bob's idea. Okay, maybe that was going a bit far, but he'd certainly glommed on to the plan with eagerness and delight. Yeah … *yeah!* He'd egged Eddie on, treating the chance to outwit Gonzaga and Margrave like a joke. Sure – easy for him, a guy who had already had his chance and blown it.

The longer Eddie stood on the sidewalk outside the bar, trying to decide on his next move, the more sinister Willard's absence seemed. And the more he thought about it, the more he realized that Bob's behaviour at the Artquake opening, even viewed through the fisheye lens imposed by the acid, had been kind of suspicious, too. They'd arrived together, Eddie remembered, but once the party got under way Bob had abandoned him. Then, according to Jerry Zeffler, Willard had actually sat down at the same table as Gonzaga. And during the fight with Bruno, where had Eddie's pal and co-conspirator been? Making himself extremely scarce.

Bruno had always said that Willard was angling to join the Gonzaga. Eddie had never believed it, but maybe Godzilla was right. The real question was, would a has-been like Willard be so desperate to get a show that he'd actually sell out a fellow artist?

He knew Bob lived over on Tranby, so he started to walk west along

Yorkville. It was still early, and there was not much happening; the Mousehole, the Mynah Bird, the Riverboat were just opening for business. At Avenue Road, he turned north, and at that moment remembered he didn't know Willard's exact address. He stopped in at Webster's to check the phone book. Then, once he had the house number, he dashed across the wide, roaring canyon of traffic to the west side and headed straight there.

From the street, lights were visible in the upper flat, and through the thin material of the curtains Eddie could even see figures moving about. 'Willard' was scrawled on the scrap of paper thumbtacked above the upper buzzer. *Dis mus' be de place.* The street door was unlocked, so he didn't bother ringing the bell. He took the stairs two at a time and paused on the landing at the top: music was playing inside the apartment, some tuneless bebop stuff, and he could also hear Bob's voice. He seemed to be talking – with false modesty, naturally – about some work he'd recently done. After listening for a few seconds, Eddie started pounding on the door.

Into the silence that immediately fell on the other side of it he yelled, 'Willard, I know you're in there. Open up, you bastard!'

There was no reply, only the monotonous honk of the saxophone and then an agitated whispering that got fainter and fainter as Bob and whoever was with him tried to pretend they weren't there at all.

ELEANOR HAD BROUGHT along a bottle of Krug, obviously filched from the matrimonial cellar. But, Bob asked himself, why start quibbling now over such moral trifles as drinking another man's champagne behind his back? Still, he did wish he'd had something more suitable to pour it into than a couple of yellow-and-blue-striped juice glasses. Eleanor didn't seem to mind, though.

She had called him back almost immediately that afternoon, saying she'd thought of a way to get out of the house after all, and they'd agreed to meet at his place at six-thirty. There were a few moments of awkwardness right after he let her in. Both still stone-cold sober, both dragging behind them the bulky, mismatched baggage of their daily lives, they were slightly shy with each other on this evening after the night before. But once they'd downed a glass or two of bubbly, their smiles started to become goofy with pleasure rather than embarrassment. Still, they both seemed to have tacitly agreed not to rush things. For atmosphere, Bob put on a record: Johnny Griffin's first LP. It was old now, and scratchy, but it still represented everything cool, modern and sophisticated, as far as he was concerned.

Meanwhile, carrying her topped-up glass, Eleanor had wandered into the sunroom and picked up the pad of sketches that Margrave had looked over last night. 'Tell *me* about these,' she said in a voice that was both reproachful and seductive.

He had just begun to when somebody started banging on the apartment door. They stared at each other and Bob put a finger to his lips. Then, a moment later, a voice shouted, 'I know you're in there. Open up, you bastard!' The voice was familiar, but he couldn't immediately place it, and the actual words coming from the other side of the door were so chillingly appropriate for a wronged husband that Bob nearly panicked.

Eleanor just stood there with naked fear in her eyes.

He pointed at the bedroom, then pushed her gently towards it and said as quietly as he could, 'Stay in there until I get rid of him.' Before he closed the door, he added, 'It's not Jerry.' He had just recognized Eddie's voice but had not yet had time to wonder why the kid sounded so belligerent.

As soon as he opened the apartment door, Eddie elbowed his way in. 'I want to talk to you.'

'It's not exactly a good time. I've got company.'

'This'll only take a minute.'

'What is it?' Bob said, suddenly conscious that Eddie was almost a foot taller than he was.

'Okay, I'm going to ask you a simple question and I want a straight answer. Did you tell Bruno about the copy?'

'No. *No.* Why would I? And what makes you think I did?'

'Well, according to the wall label, he owns it. "Collection of Bruno Gonzaga". That's what it says. And what I'd like to know is, how did *he* know before the show opened that the painting was there? Or that it even existed?'

Bob thought for a second. 'Burnham. He must have called Gonzaga when it turned up on the loading dock with no information.'

'Yeah? But why would he call Bruno instead of me?'

'Well, as far as Burnham knows, Bruno's your dealer. He's supposed to look after these kinds of arrangements for you. *Flip* was in your show there.'

'I made all the arrangements with Margrave myself.'

'Maybe he never bothered to mention that to Burnham. Quintin's a pretty important guy, y'know. Wouldn't concern himself with mundane details like the wording on wall labels.'

Eddie fixed him with a challenging, sceptical stare, and Bob forced himself to return it without flinching. But why *should* he flinch? He didn't know what the hell the kid was driving at and anyway, he had nothing to hide.

Except Eleanor.

Eddie pushed past him into the living room. He glanced around suspiciously, as if he were trying to sniff out a reason for Bob to be lying. When his eye lit on the champagne bottle and the two half-full juice glasses, his face stiffened.

'Celebrating?'

Bob shrugged, trying to convey a clear message that even if he was, it was none of O'Hara's business. Then Eddie picked up the pad of drawings that was lying on the coffee table and started flipping through it. 'Not bad,' he said. 'New stuff?'

'Just some ideas I've been fooling around with.'

'When did you do them?'

'Oh, a couple of – why?'

'Have you shown them to anyone?'

'Well, I ... yeah.'

'To Bruno?'

'*Bruno?* Why would I...? *No,* I showed them to ... oh, never mind.' He wasn't going to tell O'Hara about Margrave being at his place, or anything else that had happened after the Artquake party.

Eddie stepped back into the hall and went towards the closed bedroom door. Bob was right behind him, so they both heard the big old-fashioned iron key being turned on the inside, locking it.

'Who's in there?'

'What?'

'I said, *who's in there?*'

'Whoa, pal. What makes that your business? And, by the way, what's with the cross-examination?'

'I just want to know what's going on, that's all.'

'Nothing. Nothing that concerns you, anyway. And maybe you should leave now.'

'Okay. I'll leave. But watch yourself, *pal,* because I just figured out what's happening here.'

'Great. Maybe someday you'll tell *me.*' He opened the door with a flourish and waved his unwelcome visitor onto the landing. 'Bye now.'

Eddie only snorted contemptuously. Then, without another word, he turned and went down the stairs. *Strange,* Bob thought. *Really, really strange.*

JANE REALIZED now that something about Jim Watkin reminded her of her first – what could she call him? – crush, infatuation? So maybe that accounted for what was happening. She and Stephen, the first comely male with intellectual pretensions Jane had ever met, had been marooned together on the arid atoll of high school, back in the days when she was still naïve enough to expect that her true love would be someone very much like herself – though different in certain crucial respects. However, Jane and Stephen were neither alike nor meant for each other. She only found that out after a physical consummation that failed to induce quite the nirvana she had been banking on. And when he was never heard from again, she resolved to write the night, and him, off to experience.

So … if she remained susceptible to Stephen's 'type', that merely demonstrated the ineluctable nature of the unconscious, which come to think of it sounded eerily like something he himself might have said. But at least it was one way to explain why Jane had got to where she was: naked and restless beneath the large, pale, labouring body of Jim Watkin.

He raised himself slightly on his elbows, but his eyes stayed tightly shut. Though his breathing was noisy, she had no idea what plateau he was on or what peak he might be approaching. From the moment he had clambered on, there had been a total absence of communication, and a great deal of time seemed to have passed. At the beginning she had gamely made all the usual noises denoting enthusiasm and delight, but as far as she could tell they had gone unnoticed as Jim set off on an arduous and solitary journey. Jane herself had turned back in discouragement somewhere in the low foothills. She wondered if there was anything she could do to get his attention.

Bored, she began to analyse Jim's resemblance to Stephen. It boiled down to his Prince Valiant bob and soft, adenoidal voice. But in contrast to Stephen's almost too studied knowingness, Jim affected an *aw-shucks-ma'am* style. He even wore suspenders, for God's sake, and plaid shirts and steel-toed work boots. Averting her eyes from these items, which had been dropped in a heap on the floor beside the bed, she stared balefully at Jim's ear. He, still galloping, galloping, paid her no never mind.

I might as well be a dead body, she thought. She sighed theatrically, then let herself go utterly limp. Her head lolled and her arms slipped from Jim's shoulders and fell at her sides. Her legs, which had been wrapped encouragingly around his buttocks, slid down to lie lifelessly on the bed. As her eyes closed, she wondered if a small death rattle would be in order, and if so, what one sounded like.

Jim gave no sign of noticing that the girl beneath him had just expired. Perhaps he mistook her limpness for an orgasmic swoon, because the pace of his headlong charge towards the finish line increased. And it was only a few moments later that with a final, frantic thrust and a grateful gasp he reined in his froth-covered steed and collapsed on her, apparently unconscious.

While he rested up, Jane also lay still, composing various scenarios in her mind. She was starting to feel a little sheepish. What was Jim feeling, what would he say – would he be worried about her, or just embarrassed by his selfishness? More to the point, what would *she* say? That she now knew you couldn't just substitute one person for another and hope that it might work out better this time?

At last he stirred, rolled off her, stretched. Without a word, he reached for his clothes. Jane watched silently as he pulled on his droopy, greyish underwear, his silly red-and-white-striped socks, his plaid flannel shirt, and his jeans. As he slipped the ridiculous suspenders over his shoulders, he glanced at her with a hangdog expression. Had he just become aware that his clothes made him look uncannily like L'il Abner?

Jane sat up, holding the sheet over her breasts. Now she was actually feeling remorseful. She ought to explain herself somehow. 'You know, I –'

Jim looked up from lacing his boots. He reached over and pressed a finger gently on her lips. Then he said, 'Jane … it just didn't happen for us, did it?'

'Well, I –'

Again he shushed her, this time placing one finger against his own mouth and shaking his head. 'I'd say we just aren't sexually compatible, that's all. And when that somethin' special is missin' … chemistry, maybe you could call it … well, there's really no point in tryin', is there?' With that, he got slowly to his feet, shaking his head ruefully. 'So maybe it's best we just say goodbye now, Jane.'

The complacent, more-in-sorrow expression on his face was infuriating, but she only nodded and sat there silently as he left the room and went along the hall to the living room to retrieve his coat, then let himself out of the apartment. After she heard him clomp down the stairs to the ground floor, she jumped out of bed and ran naked to the window. It took considerable force to wrench open the casement, which was caked with layers of old paint and decades of accumulated grime.

By the time she got it open he was halfway down the block, moving rapidly with a peculiar bouncing lope that seemed designed to telegraph spontaneity, high spirits and a candid receptivity to new experience. Covering her breasts with her hands just in case some innocent passerby should look up through the nearly leafless branches of the trees, Jane leaned out and screamed after him, *'Goodbye now, Jane!'* But Jim must have been out of earshot, because he didn't turn around.

ELEANOR SUPPOSED she would be seeing quite a lot of Rachel Weiner in the coming weeks. Her old school friend, who now lived in Ancaster, missed the city and was socially impulsive. She was also having a complicated marital crisis and would be needing Eleanor's support and counsel on short notice and at odd and unpredictable hours. Jerry hadn't remembered her at all at first, but like most husbands he took very little interest in his wife's friends unless they were fair of face, bubbly of personality and adequately deferential to himself. Rachel was none of these things, as Eleanor described her. Also, she was slightly overweight and prematurely wrinkled as well as a little argumentative because of her increasingly unhappy domestic life. But a good kid, nevertheless.

With ill-concealed distaste, Jerry had waved away any further details about Rachel and her no-goodnik husband, obviously relieved that at least Eleanor hadn't invited this unappetizing person to the house. So relieved he even remembered that he *had* met her, years and years ago. Nor did he complain about the way his wife had dashed out to meet her old friend at ten to six on Friday night, leaving a foil container of *paupiettes de veau aux champignons* from the Vieux Paris in a low oven for her family's dinner.

After Robert's telephone call that afternoon, Eleanor had tried to think of a friend who might cover for her and realized that she didn't have one. Oh, she had friends, but none that she cared to confide in. They had all read *The Feminine Mystique* and nearly all claimed to find their lives stultifying, but not one of them, Eleanor believed, had the guts to do anything about it. And they might well turn on the first of their number who did.

But good old Rachel understood. Considering her substandard looks and the loser she had married, she was in no position to judge Eleanor, anyway. Most important, the fact that there *was* no such person as Rachel made her nearly foolproof as cover; how could Jerry ever check on his wife's whereabouts with someone who didn't even exist?

If Rachel *had* been real, Eleanor thought as she drove home from Willard's, they probably would have gone to the Grill at the Three Small Rooms, a cosy spot favoured by well-heeled women dining in pairs. The fillet of trout with dill sauce they served was delicious. But since the Zefflers were regulars in the adjoining Restaurant, she decided to take her distressed imaginary friend to the Coffee Mill, where their non-appearance would not be noted by anyone of importance. Besides, it was much cheaper and the coffeehouse was only a couple of blocks from Robert's apartment.

When she got home, Jerry was in the den watching the *Tonight Show*. His eyes never left the screen during Eleanor's brief report on Rachel's current emotional state. That was kind of depressing; only a husband with no interest whatsoever in his wife could be so eager to believe in an entirely fictional friend. She had a sudden urge to tell him the truth, to watch his head jerk in her direction and to see the stunned expression on his face, but she controlled it without difficulty.

However, if she had been in a position to repeat the conversation she had overheard between Willard and O'Hara, that would probably have interested him more. She hadn't really understood what they were talking about, but she did pick up the name *Margrave* and the words *Back Flip*. Wasn't that the painting Jerry had wanted, the one Bruno Gonzaga had tricked him out of getting?

She remembered how her husband's satisfaction with *Tusk* had evaporated the moment he found out from Howard McNab that Quintin had chosen *Back Flip* for the Artquake show. Being in the exhibition meant an immediate increase in its value as well as prestige for the lender. At the opening, as he took in the full significance of the credit line, she saw his lower lip begin to protrude, like that of a two-year-old wavering between tantrum and tears. It would have been so gratifying to have his 'eye' validated, and Gonzaga had as good as stolen that satisfaction from him. Jerry had managed to cover his full disappointment in public, but not from her. And maybe there was more to the story.

She had not asked Robert about it because the moment O'Hara was gone, she flung open the bedroom door and they fell upon each other without a word. And afterwards, hanging half off the bed and grinning like idiots, they had agreed that sudden terror, once relieved, was an amazingly powerful aphrodisiac. Then it had been time for Eleanor to go home.

After a final, lingering glance at the back of her husband's head, she left the den and went down the hall to the kitchen. The foil pan that had held the *paupiettes* still sat on the counter, and a saucepan that had obviously been used to reheat rice was in the sink, half filled with murky, greyish water. She tossed the empty container in the garbage can under the sink and wiped off the countertop but decided to leave the pot until tomorrow morning. Then she took the back stairs up to the large bathroom, locked herself in and turned on the taps in the tub.

The tiny bathroom in Robert's apartment was just as disgusting as the kitchen. When she could no longer put off using the toilet, she had hovered an inch above the seat, unwilling to bring her flesh into direct contact with its surface. It was strange, then, that she so willingly brought it into far more intimate and prolonged contact with the grubby flat's inhabitant. Love (or whatever this was) was not supposed to be logical, but all the same, entering that mouldy-looking shower stall was absolutely out of the question. And even a husband as complacent as Jerry might start to get suspicious if she took a bath each and every time she came back from a counselling session with Rachel. What she needed was a bidet, like the one they'd had in their bathroom at the Georges V in Paris. They had to be available somewhere in Toronto. We really ought to get one, she decided as she peeled off her clothes and stepped gracefully into the tub.

▮ Chapter Twenty-one

JUST BECAUSE they're out to get you –

'Ow! Fuck it!' Eddie kicked the boot, if that was what it was, aside with his bare foot and stumbled on down the hall. He had never got around to replacing that burnt-out bulb.

– that doesn't mean you aren't paranoid.

But he wasn't, no way, no how. When he reached the front room, he went to the window, pulling the quilt he had wrapped around him up over his shoulders. It was like a fucking meat locker in here. That old bastard Swartz was probably trying to freeze him out. Why, he couldn't figure; he paid the rent regularly, but maybe there was somebody else ready and willing to pay more.

He stared down into the street, which was as close to empty as it ever got. Cars were still passing, roaring by instead of crawling along the way they did during the day. As he watched, an almost empty bus came bar-relling down the road, lurched to a halt at the stop just below his window, then started up again with a grinding roar.

He hadn't been able to sleep. After walking home from Willard's place, he'd smoked a leisurely joint but still felt lonely and bummed out. Sometimes he wished he had TV. Back at D'Arcy Street, Sandra had an old black-and-white set that had provided many hours of harmless fun. Watching the *Dean Martin Show* or maybe *The Flying Nun* might have relieved the sense of impending doom that had dogged him all the way from Tranby Street. Instead, as he lay alone on his foam pallet, the evidence of a conspiracy just went on accumulating in his mind.

Okay, maybe it was a *little* far-fetched to think that Bruto had really been hiding in Willard's bedroom. Godzilla would more likely have shown himself, if only to gloat over the fast one he and Willard had pulled on the chump O'Hara. Or maybe not. Both of them were more devious than Eddie had ever guessed. So maybe Gonzaga *was* listening silently behind that closed door.

What was really scary about this was how each initially ridiculous suspicion grew more plausible as it tumbled over and over in his mind like a sock in a laundromat dryer, picking up a dusting of credibility, like lint, from all the others. But then just about everybody Eddie knew had been behaving strangely over the last week or two.

First of all, there had been Gonzaga's refusal to say who had bought *Back Flip*. Not to mention his even odder readiness to hand over the cash for it. And what about that weird chick Mrs Zeffler, who'd as good as kidnapped him off the street? Maybe she'd been about to tell him something. Then, suddenly, Willard had showed up and taken her away. Coincidence? Maybe.

Concentrate. Take it in sequence.

Lister's slimy waffling, while not out of character, was suspiciously excessive. Suppose something bad had happened to the original piece … damaged, stolen in transit … and suppose Bruno knew about it? So he was looking for a way to replace it. Yeah. So far, so good. Then there was the copy … and that trail led right back to Willard. The idea of making a second *Flip* had been nothing more than that, an idea … until Bob had started egging him on. Had Bruno put him up to it, having lost the real one? And Willard had been pretty obliging about delivering the copy, after more or less commissioning it.

Then what about the eerie silence of Alan Burnham, who was supposed to be setting up the show in which he, Eddie, was an exhibitor? Eddie had a phone, right? Okay, he wasn't in the book yet, but there was always directory assistance. And he had done a little checking on Mr Quintin Margrave. According to the desk clerk at the Windsor Arms, he'd taken off early on the day after the Artquake opening. Fled back to England. Now that was something to think about. Wasn't it? Well, maybe.

Even Jim Watkin was avoiding him now. Watkin – the guy he'd been trying to shake off for months – had brushed by him with hardly a word at the entrance to the Pilot. Inside, the first person he saw was Jorgensen, the guy who gave him the bog acid that had screwed him up on the night of the opening. And there was malice – maybe even cunning – in Sven's piggy little eyes.

'Willard?' he'd said. 'Nah, haven't seen him, man.' Then, as Eddie walked away he shouted after him, 'You looking to slap *him* around too?' That witticism provoked some blubbery laughter from the bunch of juiced-up clowns at Sven's table, but Eddie pretended not to hear it.

And then, as he scanned the room fruitlessly for Willard, there they were again: Daisy and Barnaby Asshole Keeler. Not that he thought either of them had anything to do with the mess he was in. No, he wasn't that far gone. Anyway, who the hell wanted Daisy now, after Keeler had had her?

On his way back to the bedroom, he kicked the boot – or its mate – right up into the air. It ricocheted off the wall and hit the floor with a satisfying thud. Then he turned around and kicked it again, this time sending it all the way down to the end of the hall.

'*HE SAID, "You were like a statue. I thought I'd never be able to bring you to life."*

'"*I was afraid you wouldn't too," I said. "But you made it all right for me."*

'*He said, "You feel all right about it now, don't you, my sweet?" His voice has a particular way with endearments – irresistible.*

'"*It was wonderful," I said; I seemed to realize suddenly … wishing we were back now in the room, and it could all be again.…*'

Jane leaned over and put the book on the floor beside the bed. It was nearly one o'clock, and she thought she might finally be able to fall asleep. When Jim was completely out of sight, she had gone straight to the kitchen and made herself an egg and some toast. It was still early then, not even ten-thirty. The movie they'd seen, *Pierrot le Fou,* had finished by nine, and since she had paid for her own ticket (Jim had made no move to do so), she certainly wasn't going to suggest going out for dinner. Maybe he had eaten earlier. Or maybe not; Jane was so ravenous by the time they got to her place that she had put out some cheddar and Saltines on a plate, and Jim had quickly gulped down more than his share. So, she calculated, the sexual encounter that followed this makeshift meal had taken less than twenty minutes all told, suspenders down to suspenders up.

After she had eaten, she put the plate and frying pan in the sink. Then she went into the living room and crouched before a small, cream-painted wooden bookcase, one of the few items of furniture that she had brought with her from home. Jane had already read all the books it contained, quite a few of them more than once, but that didn't matter. Knowing how the plots came out reduced her enjoyment only slightly. Most of the repeat reads were novels written between the wars by upper-class Englishwomen, purchased and read by Jane's mother long before Jane was born. But she liked their thick, deckle-edged paper, their wide margins and elegant, old-fashioned type. The sufferings of their heroines at the hands of the cads they inevitably fell for was elegant, too. Maybe it was only the briar patch of social gradations in which all the characters lived that made their lives so interesting. But still, the cads themselves, while just as cruel and elusive as the men Jane had to deal with, really had a way about them.

Take Rollo, the upper-class cad in the book Jane had just placed on the floor. Though the conventions of 1936 made it necessary to imply rather than describe this, he was apparently a whiz in bed. And he also gave costly and perfect gifts – like the emerald ring and the gold cigarette case that the heroine Olivia would later have to pawn to pay for her abortion. But even though he broke Olivia's heart (and you knew he was going to, right from the start), Rollo was definitely worth pining and suffering for.

Not like the men Jane kept meeting. They behaved badly out of sheer carelessness – in short, like oafs, rather than cads. Stephen, Jim, Barnaby … and Eddie, too, she realized, remembering his refusal to rescue her from Sven at the Artquake party. Not one of them would love and care for her, even for a little while. Well, there was Bertrand, but he was such a … twit.

Oaves, she thought, as she began to drift off, *oaves and fishes … cold fishes.* Gradually, blessed oblivion began to claim her, closing down successive chambers of her brain like a careful housekeeper checking every door and window before shutting off the lights. *Oaves … and knishes …* oaver and over and over and out.

BOB HAD STUCK Margrave's card into the frame of the speckled mirror over the tiny gumwood mantel in the living room. He was pretty sure Eleanor hadn't noticed it, because if she had she would probably have made some nasty remark. She had taken a real scunner to the guy. Sometimes women were even tougher on queers than men were. He wondered what she would say if she saw the reference to herself on the back of the card. It *was* a little condescending. And it did allude to the sounds of … well, whoopee … that had echoed through the house of Willard three nights before.

Bob got up from the sofa where he had been stretched out with a bottle of beer and a cigarette and went over to the mirror. He took down the card, carried it into the bedroom and tucked it away at the back of the top drawer of his dresser. He felt like an idiot doing that. But he knew that he'd soon feel the urge to look at it again. For Bob had a deep, dark secret concerning Quintin Margrave that he didn't want anyone, least of all Eleanor, to know.

On the night of the Artquake opening, while she was in the kitchen making the tea, Margrave had said, 'You're on to something here.' Then, as he handed the sheaf of drawings back to Bob, he had added, 'I'll keep in touch, if you don't mind. I'd rather like to see more of these.' And those words, however offhand, had been tumbling around in Bob's skull ever since. Cynic, scoffer, washed-up might-have-been though he was; in spite of everything he knew about himself and the world, he could not help, oh, *tingling* with something that felt suspiciously like hope.

But nothing was going to come of it. Even if he did keep working, that didn't mean he'd ever get another show at the Lurie or anywhere else. Besides, Margrave's kind words were probably due to drunkenness, exhaustion and, most important, gratitude. What better and cheaper way for a curator to repay an artist than with casual, meaningless praise? Remember, he had just rescued the man from the dark alleyway, from Sven Jorgensen's fists and possible public humiliation. And perhaps even from Eleanor.

That explained why she disliked Margrave so much: she had seen him as a possible conquest! His type was easy to misread. It was nearly impossible to tell whether Margrave was extremely polite or extremely rude – and wasn't that supposed to be the sign of an English gentleman? And yes, there *had* been something faintly embarrassing about the conversation he had overheard between those two in the car on the way to his place. God, who knew what mortification Eleanor might have had to endure if she had gone up to Quintin's room at the Windsor Arms!

It was funny; now that he had gained full and free access to the formerly unattainable Mrs Zeffler, he felt fiercely protective of her. All her faults had been transformed into virtues by their intimacy. Her vanity, which not long ago he had secretly condemned, now struck him as gallant and touching. Her flirtatiousness, which had seemed relentlessly indiscriminate, now looked like a woman's candid quest for love. If she was a little conventional in some ways … well, that was understandable, considering the life she led. He knew this amnesty would not last forever; eventually, Eleanor would start to irritate him again. But their affair would not last forever, either. That was all right, too. The only thing he didn't like, really, was the fact that for the time being he felt compelled to hang around here, waiting for her to call.

Though he was familiar with the basic facts of Eleanor's life, he found it hard to picture the details of her routine. But it seemed likely that on a Saturday evening she would be busy. He could have gone out himself, but like most lovers in the first flush of passion, he had temporarily lost interest in his usual activities. And maybe Eleanor *would* be able to get away. So, if he was going to stick around the apartment, he might as well work up a few of the things Margrave had said were promising. Why not? He didn't have anything else to do.

EDDIE MUST HAVE tossed a dozen stones at Sandra's window before she finally rolled up the rice-paper blind and peered down into the back yard, pushing her long hair back from her face and yawning. It was very early on Monday morning, just starting to get light. Finally she saw him, though she didn't look as pleased as he had expected. Shit, couldn't he even rely on *her* any more?

He'd hardly slept for the last couple of nights, staggering through the intervening days in a haze of exhaustion. After finishing work at the store on Saturday, he went straight home, unwilling to face the snickering derision of the crowd at the Pilot. Besides, he needed to think, get his act together. He couldn't do that surrounded by a bunch of jabbering fools. When it came right down to it, Willard was the only one of them he had ever had any respect for. And now he was all but certain that the guy had sold him down the river. Saturday night and nearly all day Sunday he had stayed at home, smoking and brooding. And when there was nothing left to smoke, he'd found that all of a sudden he couldn't stand to spend another moment there.

He was just about to give Sandra the finger and stomp off when she smiled and waved. Then she gestured to show that she was coming down to the back door to let him in. He no longer had a key to the house, and in his present state of mind he wasn't eager to run into any of the other residents. There had been a slight misunderstanding about the rent, or his supposed share of it, during his last month at D'Arcy Street.

At the door, he put his arms around her and they kissed. She made a face at the roughness of his unshaven cheek. Neither of them said a word, though, not wanting to take a chance on waking anybody. She pointed at his feet and he slipped off his boots, holding them in one hand. As he followed her up the narrow stairs, he put the other hand on her left buttock and she let out a muffled squeak. And as soon as they were in her room, he stripped off his clothes.

The place hadn't changed much; it was still very neat, though crammed with junk. But on her dressing table there was something new: a sort of makeshift shrine, consisting of a couple of joss sticks propped up in a pebbly amber glass vase, a purple chiffon scarf with tiny shards of mirror sewn into it and a garland of paper flowers. The last two items were draped around a framed photograph of a guru-type guy with a straggly beard and a blissed-out-like-a-fox expression on his big moonface.

Once Eddie was naked, the room felt kind of chilly. But the bedclothes were still warm when he crawled underneath them. He rolled over on his back and watched Sandra's bare torso appear as she slowly raised her paisley-printed shift like a curtain. When she pulled it off with crossed arms over her head her breasts rose, too, then dropped into place again. She didn't look at him as she folded the shift neatly and placed it in the top drawer of the dresser. But when he threw back the covers to show her his own body's reaction, she clambered quickly onto the bed and straddled him. Inch by inch, with exquisite slowness, she lowered herself over, onto and around him. Once she was securely in place, he pulled the sheet up again to make a warm, fragrant, billowing tent above them.

BRUNO SLEPT LATE on Monday morning and awoke more refreshed and at ease than he had felt in a long time. With the problem of *Back Flip* solved and the painting safe, he was able to relax. At least, as much as a man who felt it necessary to maintain eternal vigilance against bad luck and ill wishes could ever relax. In retrospect, his inability to destroy the real, the first *Back Flip* looked like an act of courage rather than a failure of nerve. And the fact that he had now, through the strange workings of fate, also laid claim to the copy, showed that he must have made the right decisions all along the way.

Part of his pleasure came from the dream from which he had just awakened. Usually when he dreamed, he found himself persecuted and pursued. But this time there had been no breathless agitation, no head-long flight or futile quest, no anger or fear. He'd been seated behind a large desk, its surface made of some highly polished and costly wood – ebony, perhaps – in which it was possible to make out the reflection of his own face. On the other side of it, facing him, sat Margrave, Burnham and McNab. The sheer size of the desk meant that they were very far away. But distance alone did not account for the smallness of those three heads, lined up like apples above its sharp dark edge. Though he could not recall any words being spoken, he knew that in his dream these supposedly powerful men had been supplicants, humbly seeking his favour.

He chuckled at the absurdity of those tiny heads but still savoured the sweetness of their subjugation as he rolled over and reached out blindly for his sleeping wife. When he pushed aside her nightdress and slid his hand between her thighs, she stirred and groaned softly, though whether in pleasure, protest or resignation, he could not tell. But what did it matter which it was? She was his wife and he was her husband. The relationship between them was understood by both and could never be ambiguous, he thought with a surge of tenderness, taking care not to crush her as he eased himself into position.

SHE HAD TO tell him. Jane had made her mind up about that. Oaf or not, Eddie was entitled to know what she had found in the basement. If the painting wrapped in brown paper was *Back Flip*. But how *could* it be, when she'd seen it hanging in the Artquake exhibition just a few days ago? Maybe the canvas downstairs was a copy. But why? And how? And *who?* Eddie had never been back to the gallery, at least as far as she knew, since the day he had stormed out of it. And if, as the wall label said, Bruno owned the painting at the Art Gallery, why would *he* make a copy – if that was what it was – and put it in the cupboard?

The street door was still locked when she got to work on Monday. After she'd let herself in, no one replied to her shouted greeting. She decided to find out what was in that package. If Bruno came in while she was downstairs, she could always pretend that she was merely getting out the floor mop like a truly keen and trustworthy employee.

The smell was noticeable even from the top of the stairs. Fresh paint, and perhaps the lingering aroma of sawdust. That was odd. But even odder was what she found inside the cupboard. Its dingy interior had been painted white and a set of shelves had been attached to the back wall with brackets. Jane couldn't really see the point of those shelves; apart from a gallon jug of Mr Clean, a giant-size box of Dust Bane and a couple of unopened cartons of gallery letterheads, they were empty and they somehow made the cupboard seem a lot smaller. On one of the walls, spring clamps with rubber rollers on each side had been installed. In them the mops and brooms were ranked, heads up, in a tidy parallel row, like soldiers on parade. The usually dusty cement floor had been swept clean. Everything was neat and orderly.

But there was no sign at all of the large package that might – or might not – have been *Back Flip*.

WIN DID NOT want to look – or, heaven forbid, *be* – young again. She simply wished to look like *herself*, to see in the mirror the face that until quite recently had always gazed calmly back at her. And for Tom to see it, too. She fluffed more powder onto her nose, but it still looked flabby, undefined, not like the small, straight, delicate one she used to have. That appeared to be gone for good. And the silvery-blue stuff she had just applied to her eyelids only made her look ill. It also threw every crease and wrinkle into high relief, without doing anything at all to bring out her eyes. Secretly, she had always considered them her best feature: large, expressive, grey-blue, the windows of her soul.... What on earth was happening to them? Now each time she looked they seemed to have grown smaller, their colour less true, as if they were gradually fading and sinking into the softening flesh of her face.

When she was young, her upbringing had made it difficult to address the question of physical beauty, in particular its presence or absence. One was suitably grateful that one was not misshapen or ill-favoured, but vanity was bad form. To think about one's appearance, other than to ensure cleanliness and neatness, was rather common. There was none of the intensive face-painting that young women of every class relied on nowadays. One made do with what nature had given. If she remembered correctly, a little powder, a touch of lip colour, had been permitted once a girl was eighteen but never before. And even in adulthood, rouge was treacherous: an intensely hued, waxy goo that was much too easy to go overboard with. Think of those vain old ladies, their eyesight obviously gone, with neat scarlet circles on their cheeks like Edwardian dolls. Mascara, too, always had a distinctly tawdry aura. It came in a dry black cake that had to be moistened with water – or saliva! – and applied with a fiddly little brush.

Though perhaps it was really the skill required to apply these enhancements that had seemed suspect and déclassé. Make-up, if done expertly, was, well, *actressy;* it suggested self-regard and premeditation. And who could say what other cool calculations and dubious experiences? Today's cosmetics – pale, transparent lipsticks and rouges, mascara wands, nearly colourless powders – were much easier to cope with. Young girls probably still felt artless and candid, even if they were as luridly painted as Nefertiti.

Win reminded herself that it was essential to avoid the appearance of coquetry when she knocked at Tom's door this afternoon. For what was her purpose in going to his studio?

To clear the air.

To show him that she, a good sport, had taken the incident at the restaurant in her stride.

To let him know that although she still valued his friendship immensely, a romantic relationship was ... well, quite out of the question.

But on the other hand, she did not want to be entirely unappealing as she conveyed this message. Tom had to look at her with regret and longing; otherwise, there would be no gratification in renouncing him. If he accepted her tactful rebuff cheerfully, she might just as well have allowed herself the diametric and possibly more intense pleasure of surrender.

The blue eye shadow looked ridiculous. She wiped it off with a moistened tissue. She had never used much eye make-up (only a touch of brownish mascara, once she was safely married) and there was no point in starting now. But the glimmery, pale pink cheek powder she'd fluffed on with a brush was subtle and becoming, hardly like rouge at all. Her skin was still quite good, anyway. And the rose-coloured lipstick did help somewhat, bringing out what was left of the blue of her eyes by contrast.

She pulled open the middle drawer of her dressing table and removed a worn brown leather jewel case. Her pearls were very fine ones, old, large, well matched and well cared for. When she took them out of the case and held them against her cheek, she saw at once that they were far more flattering to the complexion than any cosmetic yet invented.

■ Chapter Twenty-two

AS SOON AS Jerry had left for the day and Rebecca was safely off to school, Eleanor went straight to the broom closet to reconnoitre. If she was going to continue to be a regular visitor to Robert's flat, something would have to be done about the standards of cleanliness there. Installing a bidet in her own bathroom would not make it any easier for her to use the toilet at Robert's, and she could hardly avoid peeing every time she was there. For a moment she had considered paying Mrs Yablonsky – no, that would have been insane, considering how the woman loved to talk, but maybe some other cleaning lady – to go to Tranby Street and whip the place into shape. Perhaps in time she would persuade Robert to hire somebody himself, though she suspected that might be difficult. In the back of her mind skulked the embarrassing suspicion that he probably did not have the money to do so. She hadn't the faintest idea how much a part-time art teacher would pull in, but common sense suggested it couldn't be much. So she would just have to take care of the situation herself.

Pine Sol, Dutch Cleanser, Windex … Aerowax? No, she wouldn't be waxing the floors; she wasn't *that* crazy. She dropped the other stuff, along with a box of J-Cloths and some rubber gloves to protect her manicure, into the canvas bookbag she had dug out of the closet in Becky's room and tucked the sponge floor mop under her arm. Mrs Y wasn't due at the Zefflers' until Friday, and she'd replace everything before then. There was a bottle of toilet cleaner in each of the bathrooms; she took one of those, too. She thought she remembered seeing some kind of toilet brush, misshapen and brownish, at Robert's. It would have to do.

She left the cleaning supplies in the front hall and went upstairs to shower, make up and dress. She'd wear something casual, something suitable for cleaning – the green corduroy pants, maybe. With a chartreuse poor-boy scoop-necked sweater. And black boots. On top, her new pea jacket. The whole outfit had a hippie look, which was quite appropriate because Robert's place was just across the street from Yorkville. She ran a brush through her hair and rapidly made up her face;

just the minimum: eyeliner, mascara, powder, blusher and pale lipstick.

When she looked at herself in the mirror, she wondered why she had been worrying about her looks going. They weren't, at least not yet. Either that or her acrobatics with Robert were having remarkably rejuvenating effects. Maybe it was like drinking gelatin for your nails. Now, if she could just figure out a way to deodorize and bottle it, she'd make her fortune....

IT MUST HAVE BEEN the rattle of the loose old doorknob that woke him. The first thing that struck Eddie when he reluctantly opened his eyes on the daylight coming through the rice-paper blind was the sensation that he was floating somewhere in space. That, he realized almost immediately, was because Sandra had a bed with a mattress, a box spring and legs. There was even a headboard. Since he'd moved to Spadina, he'd got so used to seeing the usual mess of discarded clothes, beer bottles, coffee cups and ashtrays on the floor when he awoke that he'd almost forgotten real beds existed. So this was good. And now that he'd caught up a little on his sleep, well, he could at least *deal* with the sight of Sandra's face peering around the edge of the half-open door.

As soon as she saw he was awake, she shoved it wide open and came in.

He yawned and stretched ostentatiously. 'What time is it?'

'Nearly eleven.' She was carrying a mug – one of those handcrafted, lopsided, drip-glazed jobs, with steam swirling out of it just like in an advertisement for cocoa – which she placed on the night table. 'I made some tea.'

'Okay. Thanks.'

'Want something to eat?'

'Sure.'

'Oatmeal?'

'Yeah. Fine.' As she started to leave, he added, 'Is anybody, you know, around?'

'No. Everybody seems to be out. The coast is clear.'

'Good.' When she was gone, he slipped out of bed and sprinted naked down the hall to the bathroom. And when he was done in there, he got dressed and went downstairs to the old familiar kitchen, where Sandra already had a pot of beige mush seething on the stove and was setting the table for two.

SOME INSTINCT had told Eleanor that it would be best to leave her cleaning-lady kit in the car. And when Robert opened the apartment door still wrapped in his stringy terry-cloth dressing gown, she knew she had made the right decision. As soon as she was inside, he held the robe open with both arms like some park flasher and, cackling maniacally, pulled her against his naked body.

'Eek!' she squealed, glad that she did not have a sponge mop under her arm, 'a sex fiend! Just what I was looking for!'

When she stepped back to begin removing her own clothes, he flapped the robe open again and jutted his lower torso towards her. Pointing straight at her without using either of his hands, he said in a stern voice, 'Your Country Needs YOU.'

And so the morning pleasantly passed. They took a tea-and-toast break at one, to keep their strength up. Later, when Robert finally tumbled out of bed and started getting ready to leave for his three o'clock class, Eleanor just stretched languorously and groaned that she was much, much too comfortable to move.

'Okay, honeybunch,' said Robert, leaning down to rub his cheek over her left breast, and then her right, 'why don't you just stay right where you are until I get back?'

She pulled the sheet up to her chin. 'You know I can't.'

'Yeah.' He seemed very busy all of a sudden with doing up the cuff buttons of his shirt.

'But maybe I could just let myself out?'

'Okay. The apartment door locks automatically, so just close it after you when you leave.'

'I will. Another kiss, please.' As if by accident, she let the sheet slip down to her waist again.

He stood with his hands on his hips and studied her with an expression of intense concentration, tilting his head to one side as if judiciously evaluating the pros and cons of her request. 'Oh, all right, if you *insist*.' He gave her one, then another, then one more on the lips, and then he was gone.

Crouched by the window with a sheet wrapped around her, she watched him walk down the street. When he was out of sight, she went out to the hall to get her clothes and put them on right there. She wedged a folded newspaper in the apartment door to stop it from closing completely, then dashed down the stairs to the street and along the sidewalk to the car. In less than a minute she was back in the apartment with the canvas bag that contained the cleaning stuff.

It occurred to her that once she started working, she would inevitably dislodge a lot of dust. Remembering how Mrs Y always wore a cotton kerchief printed with lurid cabbage roses and scrolls, she took the silk scarf that had been knotted onto the strap of her handbag and wrapped it around her head, tying it under her hair at the back. She felt industrious and efficient, but she couldn't help wondering how she actually looked. Not bad; after examining herself from various angles in the mirror over the mantelpiece, she decided the scarf created a rather Audrey Hepburn effect.

TOM BACKED AWAY from the peephole and ran a hand over his face. If the record player had not been turned up so loud, he might have just ignored the knock on the door. But since anyone standing outside in the hall could tell that he *was* in the studio, he'd felt he ought to at least take a look and find out who was there.

Kite IV had not taken shape as quickly or easily as he had anticipated; it was almost three o'clock. He had decided to try stoking the creative fires with a small libation and a brief musical interlude. The record he had selected, a choice collaboration between Pee Wee and Buck and a few other stalwarts, had just begun to work its magic. By the fourth number, he was back in front of the half-finished canvas, bouncing from one foot to the other, summoning up the lyrics of 'Lulu's Back in Town', and teetering enjoyably on the very edge of inspiration.

'Gotta get my old tuxedo pressed ... gotta something something on my vest....' But then, in the brief silence that fell as that song ended and before the next began, he could no longer fail to hear the delicate but determined tapping on the door.

It was Win. It had taken him a moment or two to recognize her, perhaps because of the flushed anticipation on her face. That expression immediately alerted him to potential danger. He took another swig from the glass he was holding and put his eye to the spy-hole again.

She was all dolled up: a pearl choker was visible above the collar of what appeared to be a silk blouse, approximately the colour of whipping cream, which rose in turn from beneath a well-tailored (from what he could see of it) elephant-grey wool coat. And above it all, her face was pleasantly, almost girlishly, pink with that mysterious agitation. Apparently unaware that she was being observed, she closed her eyes, pressed her rose-painted lips together, took a deep breath and straightened her shoulders. Tom felt a mild but genuine twinge of curiosity and a faint stir of excitement. He rarely accomplished much on Mondays, anyway, and today had been pretty much par for the course. He transferred his nearly empty glass to his left hand and held it behind his back while with his right he turned the knob on the deadbolt lock. Then he swung the door open and bowed her inside.

She walked past him with a gliding, self-conscious gait that, like the exalted expression he had observed through the peephole, was both ominous and intriguing. He followed her and managed to catch her coat one-handedly as she let it slip off her shoulders, then went to hang it up on the tree in the corner. When he turned around, she had already taken a seat on the couch. She crossed her legs, which were still pretty good, smoothed her skirt down over her knees, taking her time about it, and then looked up at him expectantly, as if he had paused in the middle of a sentence.

But he had said nothing, except the usual mumbled, automatic things: 'Well, hello there; let me take that for you....' And now, for the life of him, he couldn't come up with the next line. He just stood staring at her, more aware of the tune that was just ending on the record player than of his duty to engage the woman sitting in front of him – an attractive one for her age, at least from this distance – in significant conversation.

Suddenly he became conscious of the empty glass that was still in his hand. He raised it convivially. 'How about a little drink, kiddo?'

With a faint smile, she shook her head. After a moment, still smiling, she said, 'I think it's best that I stay sober.'

'Well, I hope you don't mind if I indulge.'

She nodded, though she looked none too pleased.

When he came back with a fresh drink, she was still wearing that mysterious and unsettling expression. And he was still utterly unable to produce the words it seemed to be asking for. So, after taking a quick gulp from his glass, he put it down on the low table next to the couch. Then he took both of her hands in his and pulled her, a little more roughly than he had really intended, to her feet.

AT FIRST, Eddie couldn't quite put his finger on what was odd about the situation. Finally he realized it was just the fact that he was alone with Sandra, vertical and fully clothed. The moment he sat down across from her at the kitchen table, he had felt uncomfortable. The silence around them seemed deafening.

During the year he had lived at D'Arcy Street, he had found his way to Sandra's bed for an hour or so maybe once every two weeks. And that was really the only time they had spent alone together. They'd never gone out on what could be termed, even loosely, a 'date'. As far as he could recall, they'd never even walked down the street together. In the house, there were usually lots of people around. Meals were communal, parties crowded and noisy. And neither of them had ever made a big deal of the fact that they occasionally had sex. He didn't even know – or care, for fuck's sake – whether anybody else in the house was aware of it. Hey, for all he knew, some of the other guys could have been making it with Sandra, too. Maybe they still were.

Although, cautiously meeting her eyes as she placed his bowl of oatmeal in front of him, he didn't think so. Sandra was looking at him in a way that seemed different, somehow. All lovey-dovey. Definitely mushy. When she handed him his spoon, she bent down and kissed him on the cheek. She'd never had the nerve to do that kind of thing before.

Without intending to, he found himself smiling back at her. Man, was it even remotely possible that he had the same shit-for-brains look on his own face? If he didn't pull himself together, she was *really* going to get the wrong idea.

YANKED unceremoniously from her seat, Win was too startled even to think of protesting, let alone resisting. She only laughed (it came out, unfortunately, as a nervous giggle) when Tom pulled her into his arms – though not into an embrace, exactly. He seized her, instead, like a dance partner: one hand still holding hers out to the side, the other placed firmly on the small of her back. And like a compliant automaton she assumed the corresponding posture, raising her free hand to his shoulder. For an instant they stood with their bodies and faces close together but not touching. Then the music started again and suddenly they were off, moving across the large room in a neat, well-synchronized foxtrot.

The tempo of the music blaring from the record player was rapid, but though she still felt dazed, Win had no trouble keeping up. Tom was very easy to follow. In fact he had always been quite masterful, even slightly overbearing when he led. She thought all at once of some long-ago event at which they had taken the floor and elicited some good-natured clapping from those on the sidelines. Back then, 'ballroom' dancing, as it was called nowadays, was simply dancing, an essential social skill for both ladies and gentlemen.

She glanced sideways at his face and saw that he was smiling, though rather absently, not looking at her. Then, with his eyes still fixed on something in the distance, he put his cheek against hers. And he began to sing.

SANDRA'S EYES sparkled with indignation as Eddie told her the whole stinking story. If anything, she seemed more outraged by it than he was himself. It felt good to let it all pour out. How Gonzaga had first tried to stiff him on *Back Flip,* and then made it disappear to keep him out of Artquake; how Mrs Zeffler had tried to seduce him in the Embassy; how Bob Willard had tricked him into making the copy (he didn't yet know exactly why, but he had a pretty good idea); how Sven Jorgensen had stuck him with bog acid; and how Bruno had not only stolen the second *Flip* but had also, without provocation, tried to punch him out at the opening.

'I really thought the guy was trying to kill me. He came at me out of nowhere, like a fucking maniac. Which he *is.* Normally, I could have taken him easily, but I could barely stay on my feet because of that prick Sven ...'

Sandra's expression was so sympathetic that he almost felt like telling her how loverboy Keeler had practically yanked Daisy right out from under him. But she probably wouldn't have liked hearing him talk about another chick right now. They were back in her room, curled up in bed with their arms wrapped around each other. Voices had started to float up from downstairs, which meant that the other guys had arrived home for supper. And come to think of it, he was hungry himself; the only thing he'd had to eat since the previous night was a bowl of Sandra's sludgy back-to-the-land gruel.

He nuzzled her neck, then her shoulder. She smelled pretty good. 'Hey, do you think you could find us something to eat? And bring it up here? The thing is, I'm still not crazy about the idea of running into *them* –' he pointed towards the floor – 'after ... um ... they stole all the food I left in the fridge when I moved out.'

'Sure. I could bring some cheese and crackers up here, I guess. Maybe some fruit or something.'

'Bring lots. And maybe some weed, if you can.'

'Oh, there's some up here. Remember, in the Santa box?'

Sure he remembered. The round cookie tin, probably from the forties, with a corny apple-cheeked Santa guzzling an ice-cold Coke in front of the fireplace. Sandra loved that kitschy stuff; she was into a heavy Rosy the Riveter trip. You never knew when it would be safe to take her out in public. She might just decide to put on a little hat with a veil or some bedraggled cocktail dress she'd dug up at the Crippled Civilians.

THE PROBLEM WAS in the upper right quadrant. From the far side of the studio, Tom suddenly saw the obvious: an ill-advised smudge of ochre was keeping the whole thing earthbound. Get rid of that and it would be clear sailing. Or clear flying. He touched his cheek to Win's again and smiled with genuine pleasure. Sometimes a distraction from the task at hand could be just what you needed. He knew exactly how he'd fix up *Kite IV*, as soon as she was gone.

He held Winifred more firmly around the waist and swung into a turn that sent them skittering back across the floor again. Dancing with her like this made him think of old times – good ones, on the whole. The words of the old chestnut Buck and Pee Wee were playing, 'I Would Do Anything for You', hovered just beyond his grasp. Wasn't it Prez who said you had to know the words before you could really play a standard? A clear acknowledgement, to Tom's way of thinking, that the interplay between voice and horn, content and form was always reciprocal....

Wait, now ... wait, he had them.

'I would swim the ocean wide, I would cross the Great Divide, I would do anything for you,' he sang, dipping Win gently backward, then pulling her up again. 'I'd gladly give a fortune just to see you smile and hear you say "I love you" every little while ...'

Form and content. Now that was something kids these days didn't always get.

'In my heart there's ecstasy ... long as you de-dum with me ...'

Whereas, because he'd put in his time as an illustrator, he knew his instinct was not *just* instinct at all, it was solid know-how *plus* instinct, a very different kettle of fish....

'... I would do most anything for you.'

Now Pee Wee was launched into his first solo. Win and Tom started to jitterbug like a couple of crazy kids. At arm's length, undulating with one finger stirring the air in time to Russell's inspired noodling, she looked almost like the girl he remembered from those dear dead days.

And by God she could still dance. Her strange, exalted expression had been transformed into one of intense concentration, and now the flush on her face was certainly the result of their exertions.

After Buck's second solo, Tom pulled her close again, wondering if she and Dr Whatsit ever danced like this. Not likely. Or was her husband a lawyer…? Whichever. During the piano, bass and drum solos they vamped awhile, both of them slightly out of breath now, but when the final choruses of the melody began, they swung back into action again, recrossing the room with rapid steps to end up where they'd started. And as the final note rang out, they collapsed right back onto the sofa, both laughing like lunatics at their own exhilaration and foolishness.

SANDRA HAD BEEN RIFFING for some time (who knew how long?) about freeing herself from material possessions before Eddie started to tune in to the fact that she actually had some. Quite a lot, too, if he'd heard right. He lifted his head from the pile of pillows stacked against the headboard and stared at her. She was sitting cross-legged at the far end of the bed.

'Wait a sec. Your old man just gave you a cheque for two thousand bucks? Is that what you just said, or is this stuff stronger than I thought?'

'Yeah. I just *told* you, he was giving me this lecture about becoming more responsible and all that. A real young lady, just like Daddy always dreamed I would be, with a first-class honours degree in history.' She giggled at that for a minute or ten, then went on, 'And I said, like, how do you expect me to learn to be responsible if you keep me on a monthly allowance, like a little kid?'

'So?'

'So, he said, "Just to prove I do trust you, I'm going to give you your whole term's allowance in one lump sum." And I said, "Daddy, I am just so touched by that." And y'know, I really was.'

'Yeah?'

'Oh, *yeah*. Because now I have enough bread – oh, *more* than enough – to get to India. I'm gonna sell all my stuff –' she gestured vaguely around the room '– and that should bring in another couple of hundred, I guess….'

'You're *serious* about this Maharishi shit?'

'I'll be out of here in a week or two at the most. Maybe sooner.'

For a moment, Eddie couldn't think of a thing to say. He was fucking stunned. He'd just about got used to the idea that he and Sandra were together now. So her life would start to revolve around him. That was what chicks always wanted, wasn't it? And then – just when he was starting to see the possible advantages, she tells him she's about to leave the country for a long time, maybe permanently. This tidy, cosy room, this comfortable bed, where he had just resigned himself to having to spend a lot of time, would no longer be available. The lid of the Santa box would snap permanently shut. He'd have to go back to his own freezing dump on Spadina, broke, alone, friendless, unfed, unloved.

All that must have shown on his face, because Sandra reached over and stroked his cheek. 'Don't be sad. I didn't know how to say it before but ... I was just thinking ... maybe you could come with me. I've got more than enough dough, and somebody even told me that it'd be safer if I travelled with a guy. You know, in India and Nepal. With my blond hair and all.'

Well, light brown. Let's not exaggerate. Eddie closed his eyes and frowned, as if he was thinking it over. He was just about to tell her what a dumb idea it was when he got a flash of himself in a snow-white dhoti, wearing a garland of fragrant pastel blossoms around his neck and holding a monster spliff packed full to bursting with dirt-cheap but top-quality weed. Sandra was by his side. And maybe one or two other better-looking chicks. It was warm. The living was easy. And best of all he was far, far away from Toronto, and from everybody and everything that had been royally bugging him lately.

Sandra was still talking. 'You see, the problem with all of us in the West – you, too, Eddie – is that we're so hung up on the fantasy of material success. In order to know true inner peace, we have to renounce those false gods and relinquish everything we once held most dear. Destroy the material things that tether us to earth ...'

Suppose he *did* just disappear in a puff of smoke ... that would be the end of his troubles. Maybe. The only problem it wouldn't solve was the fact that thanks to Willard's machinations, he had become a forger. He hadn't done anything illegal by copying his own stuff, but who knew what crazy interpretation people might put on it – especially while he was out of the country and unable to tell his side of the story. No, no – he couldn't take off for India leaving that unresolved shit behind. Willard might squeal on him, too, if he saw something in it for himself.

But Bruto had somehow got his big fat paws on the copy. Probably he had the original, too. The bastard. And in a couple of weeks, the show would be shipped off to London. Fuck it! Margrave was no fool; he might eventually think there was something funny about the piece, even if the real one never surfaced. But whatever happened, Godzilla would reap the glory. Eddie could just picture him lumbering around the Spitalfields Gallery, wallowing like a hog in his role as an international art figure.

Though maybe there *was* something that could be done.

It was pretty simple, really. The thing was only a copy; he could always make another one, if necessary. When he got back from India.

■ Chapter Twenty-three

WIN WAS STILL a little out of breath when the door of Tom's studio closed gently after her. They had parted quite amicably, with promises to meet again soon, but she wondered if they ever would, except by chance. And perhaps it was best that way. She tucked her handbag under her arm, smoothed her hair and tightened the belt of her coat. Then she started slowly down the two flights of stairs to the ground floor, holding on to the banister and placing each foot with care.

In the midst of that frenzied dance, it had dawned on her that Tom was not the man she had thought – or perhaps only imagined – he was. It even seemed that he was becoming rather dotty, though the word sounded odd applied to a person of Tom Dale's gender and eminence. He'd never been prone to impulsive, inappropriate acts. But what else could you call his recent behaviour? She had rather enjoyed dancing with him, but Tom had made it quite impossible to talk seriously about his intentions towards her.

She felt sure now that he had none, for when the music stopped and they collapsed laughing on the sofa, it would have been the ideal moment for an ardent, passionate embrace. But Tom had merely pulled his handkerchief out of his pocket and wiped the perspiration first from her brow, then from his – an oddly intimate but unromantic and some-what presumptuous act. And that chaste commingling of the sweat from their respective brows would likely be the only physical union they would ever achieve. His friendly but noncommittal conversation after that was baffling. At certain moments he had almost seemed not to know precisely who she was, and she began to receive the strong impression that he was eager for her to go.

By the time she was within sight of her car, she was starting to feel the relief that follows a narrow escape. It was terribly sad, of course, but the truth was that poor old Tom was becoming more and more ... dotty. Really, there *was* no other word for it.

AS HE UNLOCKED the apartment door, Bob briefly entertained the hope that Eleanor might still be dozing in his bed. She wasn't. The bed was neatly made and the room seemed oddly bare. He noticed that the jumble of shoes he usually kept beside the dresser for easy access had been cleared away, and when he looked in the closet, there they were, lined up in a tidy row on the floor. The top of the dresser itself was bare. He pulled open the top drawer and discovered that all the loose change, ticket stubs, half-used matchbooks, unidentified keys and detached buttons had ended up there. Lucky, then, that he had shoved Margrave's business card right to the back.

The bedside table, too, had been cleared off. The stack of *New Yorkers* and *Esquires* that normally teetered next to it had been reduced to two fairly recent issues. The triangular brown glass ashtray that sat next to them was empty and it actually appeared to have been washed.

What the hell?

There was a powerful smell in the bathroom, but not the usual kind. It was a harsh, antiseptic odour overlaid with a synthetic woodsy scent that conjured up a majestic forest of plastic pines. The old pedestal sink had been wiped clean of whiskers, shaving scum and toothpaste smears. The toilet lid was closed and both of the towels were hanging, precisely folded, on the rack behind the door. However, when he lifted a corner of one of them to his face, he found that it still smelled musty.

In the kitchen, the tiny linoleum-covered countertop had a powdery look. The residue of Dutch Cleanser. He knew that was what it was, because there was a canister of the stuff sitting next to the sink. But the greenish stains in the pock-marked porcelain were still there and the tap over it was dripping slowly, just the way it always had. A blue cloth made of some strange perforated material drooped from the central rod of the flimsy pivoting rack on the wall just over the sink. And on each of the other two prongs a bright yellow rubber glove was positioned with the metal rod in its index finger. They looked like a pair of hands arrested in the act of applauding. 'Bravo,' said Bob, pushing the two rods together so that those yellow palms came floppily into contact with the damp cloth between them.

The kitchen floor was still sticky in spots, and when he opened the door to extract a bottle of beer, he saw that the fridge was undisturbed. Well, that was a relief; she hadn't completely flipped. It came as no surprise that Eleanor's attempts at housecleaning were inept and haphazard because (praise the Lord) she was hardly the domestic type. But why the hell had she ever taken it into her head to do this at all?

Even after he'd finished a cigarette and half of the beer, he still wasn't sure what was going on. But he knew didn't like it. If he had wanted to be looked after he would have stayed with Margie – well, if she hadn't walked out on him. But then he had never really felt comfortable with the ever-tightening noose of domesticity around his neck, so sooner or later something would have had to give. Anyway, forget Margie. This is Eleanor we're talking about. And the whole point about Eleanor was that she wasn't his wife, and he didn't want her to be.

She wasn't supposed to have anything to do with the daily grind. She was its antithesis – a bird of paradise, a glamour-puss, a trip to the moon on gossamer wings. A goddess who would float through his drab existence, gilding it with delight ... and then go home to a life about which he preferred to know as little as possible. Not, repeat *not*, a slapdash washerwoman in yellow rubber gloves.

WHERE OR WHEN, exactly, he had taken the wrong turn, Tom could not recall. It was goddamn embarrassing to find himself somewhere in the general vicinity of home without knowing in which direction to go. He stopped the car on the unpaved shoulder of the road and tried to concentrate. His mind must have been so full of *Kite IV* that he had missed a crucial landmark somewhere.

Overcome by weariness, he'd unwillingly left the painting unfinished and headed for home. It was nearly seven, so he was hungry, too. Darkness was falling quickly now and the houses, tucked cunningly into the hills and dales of Hogg's Hollow, were far apart and screened by hedges and trees. Here and there lights flickered through their branches, but Tom couldn't quite picture himself trudging up the flagstone path to one of those quaint, secluded doorways and asking whoever answered where his own house might be. Besides, for the life of him, he couldn't put his finger on the actual *name* of his street, despite the fact that he'd lived there for ... well, years and years. Maybe if he just turned the car around and headed back in the direction he'd come from, he'd encounter the spot where he'd made his first mistake. The problem was, he discovered as he started to retrace what he'd thought was his previous route, the roads were so winding that in the dusk it was well nigh impossible to decide which fork to choose. *Damn it.* This was ridiculous. There was plenty of gas in the tank, so he was just going to keep driving around until he passed his own house. He was certain he'd recognize *it* when he finally ran across it, as surely he would before long.

'NO!' TOO LATE, Eleanor realized the word had come out louder than she'd intended. Even Becky turned her head slightly in her mother's general direction. Eleanor took another gulp of wine and stared fixedly at the plate of food in front of her.

Jerry's fork paused in its way to his lips. 'What do you mean, *no*?'

'Nothing ... I must have been thinking about something else.'

'Yeah? What?' He glanced at Becky, looking for confirmation of his exasperation, but she kept her eyes on her own plate. Lately she seemed to have made up her mind to pretend that her parents did not exist or that she herself was elsewhere.

Mercifully, Jerry went back to sawing at his steak. 'Anyway, why shouldn't I give Willard a call?' He popped the slice of meat into his mouth and continued, chewing, 'If I remember correctly, *you* were always the one who thought he had something going for him. You didn't want me to get rid of *Forest* – or was it *Earth to Earth*?'

'The green one.' Now her voice was too quiet.

'What?'

'It was *Forest*.'

'Well, now it turns out that maybe you were right.' His tone implied that such unexpected perspicacity was in itself a kind of betrayal. 'Anyway, I dropped into the Lurie on the way home, just to see what was cooking. And Max told me in confidence that Quintin had told *him* that he – I mean Margrave – had seen some stuff at Willard's studio that was quite promising. Totally different from his old work. Although I didn't even think Bob *had* a studio any more.'

Eleanor only shrugged, fearful of saying another ill-modulated word about either the stuff or the studio.

'So I figure, maybe this time we can get in on the ground floor. I can tell you one thing: I'm sure as hell not going to get screwed over again the way I did with *Back Flip*.' He glanced over at *Tusk*, which took up most of the wall opposite his chair.

'Max hasn't even seen any of it himself yet. He sounded pretty sceptical. I got the impression he gave up on Willard a long time ago, but that could just be a tactic to put me off the scent. Anyway, he claims that when he was on the phone to Margrave in England about the Dales he's sending to the dealer over there, Margrave brought up the subject of Willard. He was surprised, naturally.... By the way, did you know that Tom is going to have a commercial show in London that'll be on at the same time as Artquake?'

'Can I be excused?' Becky had already pushed back her chair.

'*May* I be excused,' said Eleanor automatically, but she nodded. Becky picked up her plate and glass and took them out to the kitchen on her way upstairs.

There was a brief silence before Eleanor exclaimed, 'A London show?' Isn't that great!' Maybe if she showed enough enthusiasm for this entirely predictable development, he'd forget all about Bob Willard and his new work.

'Well, that's always the way these things happen. Tom and Margrave get chummy while Margrave is here, Margrave the big shot puts in a good word where it counts for his new pal, and presto, Tom's got a London dealer. And *that's* why −' he began to speak slowly and distinctly, as if addressing a person of limited intelligence or imperfect hearing '− it's absolutely imperative to act quickly.'

'Act ... quickly?' she repeated like a parrot.

'Willard hasn't shown anything for years, and I'll bet he and Max have never had a contract anyway. They go way back to the old Gerrard Street days when nobody ever thought of such a thing. So I might be able to pick up a few pieces before Willard even shows any of the new stuff. That is, if it's any good.'

'If it's any good.' Oh, Polly *really* wants a cracker.

'Well, honey, he was always your boy. Remember, you picked out the two pieces of his we bought way back when. With my guidance, of course.'

'Did I? I'd forgotten that.' And yes, she had, strange as it seemed. And she couldn't even remember what Robert had looked like then.

'So maybe you should come along, give me the benefit of your expertise.' He chuckled at this original though clearly preposterous idea, and began to hack another piece off the slab of meat on his plate. 'Or maybe I'll just drop in on him one of these days. He lives down on Tranby; I checked the phone book last night. That'd be just north of the Park Plaza, wouldn't it?'

'*I* don't know. Why would I?' Again her voice was too loud, and as she shoved her uneaten food around on her plate she could feel her husband's irritable glance passing slowly over her like the searchlight from a prison watchtower.

As soon as Jerry was settled in front of the TV, Eleanor slipped upstairs to the bathroom and took a Valium. Then she crept down the hall to the extension phone in the bedroom. She had never before telephoned Robert in the evening; in fact she hardly ever called him at all. It would have made sense for her to do the telephoning, since he lived alone, but some vestigial pride kept her from doing so. She felt almost faint with impatience and anxiety – the tranquillizer had not kicked in yet – as she dialled the number and then listened to the phone ring and ring and ring and ring unanswered.

THE INSISTENT tapping on the glass startled him, but for a moment or two Tom wasn't sure whether he had been asleep or merely lost in thought. He was suddenly aware of darkness and cold … so yes, perhaps he *had* been dozing. He was slumped slightly sideways on the seat, and when he pulled himself into an upright position, he found his right arm was numb. It started to fizz with pins and needles when he tried to straighten it. As he turned slowly towards the sound that had woken him, he caught sight of a large, pale face peering through the side window. Its mouth opened to issue some incomprehensible command as the beam of a powerful flashlight swept over the interior of the car. Tom felt a stab of fear, nearly whimpering with it as he rubbed his useless arm. Then he noticed the uniform.

He rolled down the window with his left hand. 'Something wrong, officer?'

'Well, you tell me. Are you all right in there?'

'Perfectly.' He wasn't absolutely sure that was true, but it didn't do to act helpless in a situation like this. In a minute he'd figure out how he'd come to be parked on the side of a country road in the middle of the night. The cop was courteous so far, and fairly respectful, but contrary to the cliché, he did not look especially young to Tom. He was no apple-cheeked bobby, that was for sure. This fellow was heavyset and vaguely middle-aged, like a policeman from a 1930s movie comedy, the kind that always strolled up behind Jean Arthur or Cary Grant on the sidewalk, swinging his baton behind his back, and put the kibosh on their screwball antics.

'Got your licence with you?' he asked in a cajoling voice, as if he were talking to a lunatic or a child.

'Certainly.' Tom pulled out his wallet and handed over his driver's licence.

The cop trained his flashlight on it for a couple of seconds and seemed pleased with what he read there. Then he handed it back. 'Mr Dale, do you know your wife has been looking for you all night?'

'All night? What time is it?'

The cop checked his watch. 'Eleven fifty-three, sir. She's been very worried.'

'She worries too much,' Tom said stoutly as he slipped his wallet back into his pocket. 'You know how women are.' He wanted to ask where the hell he was, but thought better of it just in the nick of time.

'Tell you what, Mr Dale,' said the policeman in that same Mary Poppins tone, 'why don't you just hop in my car and I'll drive you home?' He reached in through the open window and released the lock, then swung the driver's door wide.

'But ... I can't leave....'

'Don't worry. You and Mrs Dale can pick up your car tomorrow.'

'Where ... we must be miles from ...'

'Believe it or not, you're less than half a mile from home. Hogg's Hollow can be confusing that way. All these twists and turns. We'll be there in a jiffy, sir. It's just around the corner.'

As soon as Tom had set one tentative foot on the ground, the cop took him by the arm and bundled him into the passenger seat of the patrol car parked close behind his own. He heard all four of its doors click locked around him, then watched as the policeman went back to Tom's car, taking his time about it. The overhead light came on as he opened the door and leaned in to retrieve the keys.

'Don't forget to lock 'er up,' Tom called out, but then he saw that the cop was already doing so. He probably couldn't have heard him anyway, because all the windows of the squad car were tightly closed.

WITH LOVE and squalor. As she struggled to wakefulness with the sense that she had been deeply asleep for only a minute or two, Eleanor heard those words as if they had been spoken aloud. For one awful moment she feared she had said them. But when she listened carefully in the silent room she could hear her husband beside her in the darkness, snoring softly. There was a faint pearliness in the curtains that suggested dawn was not far off. She closed her eyes again without much expectation of sleeping.

Love and squalor. The words rang a bell somewhere in the back of Eleanor's mind. Was it the title of a book? No, a story. 'For ... Somebody, with Love and Squalor'. Salinger, wasn't it? Wherever it came from, it summed up her present situation perfectly.

But even more than squalor itself, Eleanor hated housework. The existence of Mrs Yablonsky had allowed her to forget that in recent years, but less than an hour of dusting and scrubbing on Tranby Street had brought it all back. As for love, it was hard to say. Right now it did not seem to matter as much to her as she had been led to believe it would. But love was what she had been searching for, wasn't it, first with Tom, then with Quintin, and now with Robert? Love that was capricious, unnecessary, freely given and received?

But the prospect of Jerry visiting Robert's flat had suddenly stripped the word and the act of all frivolity. The very thought filled her with galloping terror. Supposing Jerry (who, whatever his shortcomings, was no fool) somehow sensed what had been going on in the bedroom adjacent to Willard's grubby little sunroom studio? She could well have left something recognizable – a scarf, a bracelet, an earring – in the apartment.

Or suppose Robert, who was obviously crazy about her and probably (though he'd never actually said so) would like her to leave her husband and move in with him, took it into his head to make a clean breast of things? In other words, what if she were forced to abandon her present existence and plunge, as if diving from the top of a cliff, into a new life where everything – but *everything* – would be different?

JOAN WAS MAD at him, he could tell. Well, maybe not really mad; annoyed. Nettled. She was trying not to show it, but the sweet forbearance with which she treated him, as if he were some kind of invalid or imbecile, was starting to nettle him, too. Even though they'd collected his car this morning from the cul-de-sac where that busybody cop had made him leave it, she was insisting that if he wanted to go to the studio he'd have to take a taxi.

Ridiculous! He'd only lost his way last night because of fatigue (he'd been working flat-out all day) and the sudden, unexpected dusk that had fallen. The days were getting shorter now, and the small, badly illuminated street signs in this pseudo-bucolic neighbourhood were awfully hard to read. After he'd rested for a few minutes, it had seemed easiest just to leave the car there and let the cop give him a lift home.

With a perfectly good car sitting in the garage, there seemed to be no reason on earth to pay for a taxi. Joan was being irrational, but he didn't have either the time or the inclination to argue with her; he had to get to the studio. In some sliver of time tucked between sleeping and waking this morning, he'd seen – actually *seen* – the solution to *Kite IV*. He was trying now to keep that vision bouncing softly in his head without concentrating too hard on it, because there was always the danger of draining the thing of freshness and vigour before you even had a chance to try it.

So he humoured Joan and let her call a cab for him. When at last it pulled up in front of the house, Tom just gritted his teeth and waited patiently while she came out with him and gave the driver precise directions to the studio. He got into the front seat beside the driver as he always did in cabs, shoving aside the map book that lay open on it. He exchanged a comradely smile with the guy, and said, gesturing at the street directory, 'I get lost in this neighbourhood myself, sometimes.' As they pulled away, Tom caught a glimpse of Joan in the rear-view mirror. She was still standing there, with a very funny look on her face, not unlike the expression she'd worn when Nancy went away to summer camp for the very first time.

MUCH TO Jane's surprise, Jim Watkin showed up at the Gonzaga on Tuesday afternoon, shortly after she got back from lunch. His demeanour was friendly but casual, more or less the same as it had been before last Friday evening. It was as if the awfulness of their ... date ... had never happened. Or he hadn't noticed that it had happened. But she had to be at least civil to him, because she couldn't leave her post. She was trapped, until he decided to leave.

He had brought along a copy of *Ramparts* with an article about draft resistance that he considered she ought to read. Every so often he glanced, apprehensively it seemed to her, towards the back of the gallery. But there was nothing to worry about; Bruno was out and had told her he wouldn't be back for a couple of hours. It wasn't until Jim himself was finally gone too and she was alone and reading, not the article that he had suggested but a book by Elizabeth Bowen, that Jane suddenly realized what he had come for.

He wanted to get a show at the Gonzaga. That was why he was always following Eddie around. He hadn't been *afraid* that Bruno was in the back, not at all – he'd been *hoping* he was there and would come out so they could talk about Art, specifically Jim's. And most likely that was the only reason he had decided to give her a tumble. His heart had never really been in it. Now that Eddie was on the outs with Bruno, and a man without a gallery, Jim could no longer use him as a contact. Jane, wowed by his sexual technique, was supposed to fall madly in love with him and insist on putting in a good word for him with her boss. What an idiot.

THAT EVENING, Win felt exhausted, both mentally and physically. Though for no good reason, really. As usual, she had spent the morning in the studio, though inspiration had remained elusive. In the afternoon, after lunch with a trio of old friends from the garden club days, she dropped in at one or two galleries in the Yorkville area, but there was nothing of any interest to be seen. She did not enter the Gonzaga. She had paused for a moment before its plate-glass window, but put off by the sight of some long-haired lout lounging near the reception desk, apparently deep in conversation with the gormless girl who sat there, she had decided against going in.

Not long after dinner, she told Eliot she was going to bed early. However, once she was in her own room, she only sat down in the small upholstered chair near the window and stared out into the dark, ambushed by melancholy. Perhaps she ought to go upstairs and try to paint her way out of this sudden anguish, but that had never been her method. She had always been the emotion-recollected-in-tranquillity type … and at the moment she had far too much of the former, and far too little of the latter.

The calm of the last two days had disappeared, and it seemed to Win that she might never recover it. It was as if the loss of Tom had stealthily stolen all optimism and certainty from her.

She had recognized the signs. Ever since Monday, the day they had danced, memories of her own father's mental decline had been intruding, no matter how she tried to banish them. Not dotty – *senile*. That was the word. And there was nothing, absolutely nothing, that could be done about it. The best one could hope for was that it would not go on for long; that the afflicted person would not suffer too much humiliation but would die soon and quickly. She clearly remembered her shock at overhearing her mother say those very words about Father. And that thank heaven he did not really understand what was happening to him.

Now that he was drifting beyond her reach like a rowboat that had slipped its moorings, it seemed to her that Tom had been her last chance at happiness. Because who but an old friend, who had known her when she was a beauty, would find her desirable now? Pearls or no pearls, she was physically past it. Who – except Eliot, in his phlegmatic way – would love her now? Who would believe in her talent as an artist? Perhaps even belief in oneself was an attribute of youth. This afternoon she had been too cowardly to face the crude, inarticulate man who was supposed to be her dealer. And this morning, in the studio, playing with all those top-quality pigments and handmade papers, she might as well have been Marie Antoinette churning butter in her *hameau*.

Yet only a few hours ago, she had still felt pleasantly superior to the other women at the luncheon table. Sometimes she even thought that was the only reason she bothered to keep up her friendships with them. Their utterly unexamined lives had always seemed so inferior to her own. From the moment of her marriage to Alex – oh, no, long before that; think of those art classes with Lismer – she had been immersed in the larger world of culture and ideas. The life of the mind. Of creativity and inspiration. But what good had it done her, finally?

Those other women were preoccupied with the practical, conventional side of life – their gardens, their houses and cottages, their children and grandchildren – and maybe that was sensible rather than pathetic. Perhaps it was a boon to be placidly unmoved by art, literature and music. Did any of them ever lie awake at night, writhing in despair at the unbearable sadness of life ... the *lacrimae rerum?* And, she wondered as she fumbled blindly in her pocket for her handkerchief, did they ever find themselves wiping away real, wet, bitter tears, shed for departed youth, dashed hopes and a love that would never be?

∎ Chapter Twenty-four

IT WAS WEIRD. As he headed back to his place, it seemed to Eddie that he'd been away from it much longer than three days. So much had happened since he'd tossed that handful of pebbles at Sandra's window early Monday morning. He'd actually spent most of the intervening time dozing and smoking in her comfortable bed. But mentally he'd done a real turnaround, finally got his head straight.

He zipped past the window of Morris the Hatter's without seeing, or (he hoped) being seen by Mr Swartz. It was nearly nine o'clock and the shop was closed, but sometimes the old guy was still in there after business hours. The next month's rent was due in a couple of days, but Eddie wasn't planning on paying it. Or giving any notice, either. He'd just stay here one more night, get organized, take care of the essentials and tomorrow do the deed. After that he'd hide out at Sandra's until it was time to split for the Subcontinent. It had turned out that nobody at the D'Arcy Street house actually gave a shit whether he stayed there; hardly any of the old group were left and those that remembered him didn't seem to care about the minor hassles when he'd moved out.

Everything was all set up for the following afternoon; Sandra knew exactly what she had to do. But he was almost sorry he'd mentioned the Augustus John, because it turned out to be her *absolutely favourite* painting and he then had to listen to some long, complicated story about how one of the Marchesa Casati's footmen had suffocated after she had him painted gold, et cetera, et cetera. Anyway, the main thing was that Sandra was willing to help out. Then as soon as his passport came through, they could split. She already had one, from the term she'd spent in Switzerland when she was at Havergal.

Right now, though, he had to get rid of the fucking *Cloud* series. He was going to leave the other, good pieces at his parents' place while he was gone, but there was no point in storing the duds. However, if he just abandoned them in the studio, who knew where they might end up? Godzilla might even get his fat mitts on them. Besides, when he got back, he'd almost certainly have all kinds of new ideas; everybody said that India and Nepal would really blow your mind.

It turned out to be kind of a blast, actually, slicing those dull grey surfaces to ribbons with the old X-Acto and then taking the stretchers to pieces with a claw hammer and his bare hands. A real Creator/Destroyer trip, and come to think of it, not a bad way of warming up for the main event at the Art Gallery tomorrow. Once he'd reduced the last *Cloud* to a pile of monochrome rubble, he shoved the whole mess into a bunch of big green plastic garbage bags, which Sandra had sent with him. He even tied them up neatly with the twisty things provided. Then he dragged them down the hall and with a series of war whoops hurled them all out the kitchen window into the alley below.

IN THE CLEAR light of day, Winifred recovered her equilibrium. As soon as she awoke on Thursday morning, she began by reminding herself a little sternly that she was not a quitter or a whiner. Perish the thought. She was an artist and therefore sensitive, but defeatism was alien to her nature. Where would this country be today if generations of Beechams and Overtons and Newsomes had not squared their shoulders in the face of adversity and simply got on with it? (Well, perhaps not the Newsomes; much as she had loved him, Alex's background had not been quite as distinguished as her own.) Most likely her forebears would never have needed the sort of silent pep talk she was now giving herself, but one has to pay a certain price for having a highly developed aesthetic sense. Very well, she would pay it.

Although she sat down as usual after breakfast to write in her journal, she decided not to go into any detail about her fears for dear Tom. She merely set down, in general terms, some thoughts she had had the previous night about the inevitability of loss in human existence. However, as an illustration of this theme, she included one or two childhood memories of Father, whose mental and physical decline had been all the more pathetic because of his innate, rather leonine dignity and exalted position in the world of jurisprudence.

She closed the slim calfskin-bound book and as she slid it back into the drawer, her eye wandered to the corkboard over the desk. The garish Op Art invitation to the François Mazzano opening was pinned up on it, along with a number of other current announcements. She had not planned to attend, but all at once she felt she must. She had been avoiding the Gonzaga Gallery and its brutish proprietor for far too long. She was a Beecham, by name and nature, and she knew her duty. It was time to reenter the fray with all flags flying.

THE PHONE CALL did come as a bit of a surprise.

'Well, yeah,' said Bob, 'I *have* been working up a couple of ideas.…' Even he could hear the apology in his voice. Nothing irritates successful people more, he'd often noticed, than a pitiable failure who unexpectedly turns himself around. Shaking the ladder always annoys those perched on the higher rungs, because nobody likes having one less person to patronize.

'Yeah, Margrave did have a look at my stuff.' He tucked the receiver between his jaw and shoulder as he got out his cigarettes and lit one. 'What? No, I didn't mention it, but … no! Why would I want to keep it a secret?'

Though he *was* reluctant to describe the sequence of events that had brought Margrave to his place after the Artquake party. So what if Quintin had found Sven Jorgensen inexplicably alluring? It was a miracle – and interesting, come to think of it – that Sven himself hadn't already spread the story all over town. But there was no reason for Bob to talk about it now, especially since Margrave was repaying his insignificant kindness in such a remarkable way. And there was also the small matter of Eleanor's presence in the flat that evening.

She had phoned first thing Tuesday morning – so early that he was just taking his first sip of coffee – nearly gibbering with anxiety. She'd tried to reach him all last evening, she said. And the way she fished shamelessly for information on his whereabouts the night before only confirmed his feeling that it was time to back off a little. He didn't want her cleaning his apartment and he didn't want to account for his movements every minute they were apart. It was unlikely her husband was 'on to' them, as Eleanor seemed to fear, though Jerry's renewed interest in his work wasn't quite plausible, either.

'Don't worry about it,' he'd told her. 'I'll handle it if he does come. No, you didn't leave anything here. What? Yes, I'll double-check. Really? Well … okay, we can cool it for a bit, if that's really what you want, sweetie. Yeah. I know. I understand. All right, I *promise* I won't phone you.' Though he'd pooh-poohed Eleanor's fears, he braced himself. But Zeffler didn't call or show up that day or the next.

And now here was Max on the phone, pretending to be cut to the quick because he hadn't been the first to see the new work. 'Of course I was going to show them to you.' It was true; the idea of looking for a new dealer had never even crossed his mind. Until now. 'Sure. Yeah, why *don't* you drop in sometime and take a look? Right now, if you want to.

Tomorrow? All right. I've got a class at two but I'll be back around four. Okay. Oh yeah, I guess I'll see you at the Mazzano thing tonight. Bye.'

It was a fairly safe bet that the Zefflers would not be attending the opening. The night Eddie had barged in on them, Eleanor had mentioned how mad Jerry was at Gonzaga about the *Back Flip* debacle. He was tempted then to tell her about the copy, but decided not to. O'Hara had trusted him and even if the kid was flipping out, Bob still felt he ought to keep it quiet.

Eddie, Quintin, Eleanor ... they all had something to hide. But how the hell had he, an innocent bystander if ever there was one, become the repository of their secrets? Well, at least he was pretty sure none of them would be at the Gonzaga Gallery tonight. But some comely young creatures might be. These days he was really limbered up in the love department, and he was free to play the field now that the thing with Eleanor was cooling off. Lots of good-looking girls hung around the art scene. And there was always Gonzaga's girl – what *was* her name? She had to be there whether she wanted to or not.

BRUNO was different lately. His energy seemed boundless, and that was really starting to get on Jane's nerves. She almost missed the brooding, inscrutable boss she had found so unnerving when she first started the job. But at least the new, annoyingly ebullient Bruno was away from the gallery more often. Sometimes he was gone for hours. She wouldn't have been at all surprised if he'd been sneaking down to the Artquake exhibition, just to hang around and moon over *Back Flip*.

He'd clipped an advertisement for the show and an enthusiastic review of it by a woman art critic out of one of the newspapers and pinned them on the bulletin board near the entrance. He also put up a glossy black-and-white installation shot of the painting taken at the Gonzaga. When ordered to do so, Jane had grudgingly typed up a label to be placed beside it that was identical to the one at the exhibition. Bruno had also ordered an 8-by-10 print to be made from the colour slide, but it wasn't back from the photo shop yet.

The title of the newspaper article was 'Canadian Art Comes of Age'. The writer, Elsie Brooks, was a likeable middle-aged woman who out of sheer good will approved of almost everything she saw. However, her piece did not mention either Eddie or *Back Flip* specifically.

Howard McNab's more judicious account of the exhibition appeared in the other paper a few days later. It was called 'Almost Grown?' Jane knew he was trying to be cute, demonstrating that he, though an intellectual, was also tuned in to popular culture. Or maybe just that there was no subject under the sun that he didn't know absolutely everything about. And probably Chuck Berry *had* been the latest thing when Howard was a teenager. That would make him only a few years older than she was. *Ugh.* He seemed much more ancient than that. Howard's review was essentially a rebuttal of Elsie's Centennial cheerleading, but it didn't mention *Flip* by name, either. Seated at the alcove table, leaning on one elbow with a cigarette burning unnoticed in his hand, Bruno had read it slowly and suspiciously. When he'd finished, he *huh*-ed furiously and in reply to Jane's innocent question, told her not to put it up on the board.

But even during Artquake, life and business had to go on at the Gonzaga, and Bruno had been busy since early morning. He and François Mazzano were hanging Mazzano's show, which was to open that night. Installations usually took place after hours, when Jane was absent, but the shipment of paintings from Montreal had been delayed, so it all had to be done at the last minute.

François, a second-string Op-abstractionist, was in his forties, but still handsome. He seemed unusually relaxed about the hanging of his show. At regular intervals he shook Bruno off and wandered towards the front of the gallery. Sometimes he even sat down on Jane's desk for a cigarette break and, to his credit, perched on the opposite side of the desk, not right next to her like must-touch-flesh McNab. Furthermore, unlike Michel Bontemps, Mazzano seemed to have no objection to conversing with her in French. And before long there was clear evidence that he, like others before him, found her imperfect grammar and Jane Birkin accent quite appealing.

On his third break, right out of the blue – unless she had missed something because of his Quebec accent – François invited Jane to come and visit him in Montreal. He even jotted down a telephone number at which he urged her to call him upon arrival. It seemed odd, however, that he didn't just ask her out to dinner, or even for drinks, right here in Toronto after the opening. A bird in the hand …

But Jane had pretty much given up trying to figure men out. If Mazzano – a strange name for a Frenchman, theoretically, although she supposed his ancestors could have been from Corsica, or maybe just Marseilles, like Jean-Paul Belmondo's – had simply tried to make a date with her, she would very likely have accepted, even though he was almost an old man. However, the idea of travelling for six hours on the train just to go to bed (this was understood) with a complete stranger, really made no sense to her at all. Maybe the invitation was just a type of rhetorical flirtation, not unlike Bertrand's air-mail declarations, and not meant to be taken seriously. Either that, or one or both of them were crazy.

She accepted the piece of paper with the phone number on it and put it carefully in the top drawer of her desk, saying *'Pourquoi pas?'* with a demure smile so as not to offend. This seemed to please François, because he then got up, blew her a kiss and returned to work with what looked like renewed vigour.

THEY SPLIT UP a couple of blocks from the gallery. Since Eddie didn't have a watch, Sandra had dug one up for him somewhere – a lady's Timex, but what the hell – and they synchronized it with her little fourteen-jewel Bulova. He'd wanted to smoke a little weed before they left to ease his jitters, but Sandra had argued that could be a serious mistake when precise timing was of the essence. The caper was scheduled for 5:15 p.m. exactly. Closing time was five-thirty and that meant that the guards would likely be semi-comatose, just counting the minutes until they could lock up and go home. Get in and out fast, that was the plan – just like in *Topkapi* or *How to Steal a Million.*

At 5:14 by the Timex he stepped through the front door. He was just passing one of the Old Master galleries when he heard the voice. It was a man's, saying words that were only partially intelligible.

'Abomination … something … vipers' … another mumbled phrase … 'The beast …' And as this hysterical but rhythmic chanting began to rise intermittently to hoarse shouts, Eddie also heard the sound of running footsteps. He really felt like turning around and heading for the exit but forced himself to continue walking and quietly skirted the room where the commotion was. The noise gradually died away as he reached the Artquake space. It was completely deserted; there was not a single art lover or guard in sight.

BRUNO WAS GETTING annoyed with François Mazzano. He was not a painter of the first rank even in Quebec and should have been more grateful to the Gonzaga Gallery for taking him on. But he didn't seem to consider exhibiting in Toronto of any importance. He was paying more attention to Jane, who must be half his age, than to the hanging of his show. She encouraged him, of course. But even Mazzano's lechery seemed half-hearted, as if nothing in this alien city was quite real to him.

The installation was finished less than an hour before the time indicated on the invitations as the start of the opening. Bruno had sent Jane home at five so that she could be back at seven sharp to greet the guests. His own clean white shirt and freshly pressed suit were hanging, covered in plastic, on a hook in the workshop. Mazzano had gone back to the place where he was staying with a woman friend, a few blocks away on Park Road. But it was no wonder it had taken so long to hang the guy's exhibition, considering how uninterested the artist himself seemed to be in the process.

In a way, Bruno could understand how François felt about Toronto. During his first few months here, he had also been stunned and nearly paralysed by the sheer sprawling ugliness of the place. But he, Bruno, had put his shoulder to the wheel and the past behind him and finally got over it. Besides, Mazzano, despite his name, was a Canadian, born here, so he really had no excuse for acting as if he had just arrived from a far more civilized country.

Maybe it was just the Expo that made these Montreal guys act so superior. For a couple of months at least, they were at the centre of the universe. There was even a crazy man in Quebec who believed the whole province ought to secede from Canada – he'd actually stood right up in the local parliament to say so. And the English, innocent fools, not knowing which way to turn, were taken in by it. Some of them, Bruno noticed, were indignant, resenting such troublesome echoes of the past, while others, even more deluded, were racked with guilt because they'd happened to emerge as victors from a simple accident of history. Imbeciles, every one of them, French and English both. Didn't they see what they had here? A chance to let go of the past instead of gnawing endlessly on it, yanking it this way and that like two dogs with one bone.

He had finished the hamburger and coffee he had brought back from the Rancho and was just about to plug his electric razor into the socket under the work table when the telephone rang. The sound, raw and strident, echoed stereophonically through the otherwise silent gallery. Both extensions were ringing, the one on Jane's desk at the front and Bruno's own at the back.

Still holding the razor with its cord trailing behind him, he advanced on the phone in the workshop and stared at it, as if by close observation he might discover the identity and motive of the caller. He really didn't want to answer, and decided not to. Finally, after it had rung twelve times, it stopped, and Bruno was glad of that. It would have been unlucky, he believed, if it had gone as far as thirteen.

TOM HAD no intention of answering the door. This time he wasn't even tempted to sneak over and use the peephole to find out who was knocking. He didn't need or desire company. He finally had *Kite IV* just where he wanted it, and he had just sat down and taken the first sip of his celebratory drink when the pounding started. He mouthed *Go away* at the deadbolted door, glad that there was no music playing to reveal his presence.

'Tom!' A male voice, vaguely familiar.

Oh, just get lost, whoever you are.

'Tom, open up!'

'Bugger off, will you!' Oops – had he said that aloud?

'Tom? Was that you?'

Damn it. He had.

'It's Max, Tom. Just thought I'd stop in and see how you're doing.'

Max? He couldn't remember the last time Max had dropped in at the studio without warning.

'Tom! I know you're in there, open the door.'

'All right, all right.' He placed his glass on the floor and got to his feet. 'Keep your shirt on. I'm coming, I'm coming.'

When he opened up, Max paused on the threshold and looked him over as if he expected to find something seriously amiss. Apparently satisfied that all was well, he clapped Tom familiarly on the back and strode into the middle of the room. He glanced at the four *Kite* canvases on the walls. Then he began rubbing his hands together like a stage villain and turned to his old friend with an ingratiating smile.

'You've been busy, I see. Wonderful stuff.'

Tom shrugged. Surely he and Max were beyond this kind of fatuous small talk. 'To what do I owe this rare pleasure?' he asked in as cheerful a tone as he could muster. As he waited for Max to reply, Tom walked over to the sink and raised an empty and more or less clean glass questioningly at his dealer. When Max shook his head, he put it back where he'd found it.

'So,' said Max, 'I was in the neighbourhood....'

Tom shot him a sceptical look but he ignored it.

'...and I wondered if you could use a lift back uptown.'

Uptown, downtown, all around the town, Tom hummed under his breath. 'Well, as a matter of fact, I don't have the car today. Some kind of … engine trouble.'

'Yeah, Joan mentioned that.'

Oh, did she now?

'So she suggested that the three of us meet at the Mazzano opening. Then you two could go home from there.'

There was some sequence of events in this arrangement, some form of collusion that didn't sit well with Tom, but at that moment he couldn't pinpoint exactly what it was. Still, he really ought to make it up with Joanie. He'd had the feeling she was mad at him this morning. Or was that yesterday? Whenever it had been, she was acting a little testy.

He retrieved his glass from the floor and drained it. The idea of a ride home (he'd have preferred to skip the stop at the Gonzaga, but beggars can't be choosers) was suddenly quite appealing. He hadn't even thought of how he'd get back tonight … a taxi was the logical answer, the easiest … but gad, the hellish cost of it. Not that he really had to worry about money, but still … and it could be bloody hard to find a cab in this less than elegant neighbourhood.…

'Tom? Shall we get going? It's nearly seven.'

Max seemed to be waiting for an answer. 'Sure. Great,' said Tom. 'I'll get my …' He waved at the row of hooks near the door to show what he meant.

'Coat?' suggested Max, helpful as always.

'That's it. Be right with you.'

FRANÇOIS HAD a woman with him. An elderly one – she must have been at least thirty-five, Jane calculated, erring on the high side out of sheer pique – and a superannuated beatnik. Her long black hair, threaded here and there with grey, was piled up on top of her head, and huge silver hoop earrings bobbed against the funnel neck of her mud-toned hopsack tunic as she talked and laughed in an absurdly overanimated way. Not that Jane had taken Mazzano's come-on seriously for one second, nor did she have any intention of taking him up on his invitation to Montreal, but she still felt like a dope for listening to him.

It figured that Jim Watkin would turn up, but their tacit agreement to pretend that the other night had never happened seemed to be holding. The appearance of Win Beecham was unexpected, though. She hadn't been to the gallery since the opening of Eddie's show. The Zefflers came, too, and it occurred to Jane that lately Mr Zeffler had not been dropping in as often as he used to. Neither had Bob Willard, but tonight he'd been one of the first to arrive. And it was possible that she was only imagining it, but every time Jane looked up Willard seemed to be standing quite close to her, trying to catch her eye. She ignored him.

Jenny, Sven, Jiri, Howard McNab ... they all filed in. There were also some unidentified middle-aged types: potential buyers, theoretically. And when Tom Dale and Max Lurie made their grand entrance – another surprise – Bruno moved purposefully but without undue haste towards the door.

He waylaid the two men and greeted them with what seemed to Jane unctuous formality. As he led them towards the alcove they passed quite close to her. She saw that Tom Dale's head swivelled in the direction of Mrs Zeffler, who was planted at her husband's side in the centre of the gallery. And he kept looking back at her as Bruno almost strong-armed him into the alcove and commanded him to have a seat. Lurie was permitted to enter the inner sanctum too, an act of magnanimity that must have been difficult for Bruno, but a worthwhile trade-off for the opportunity to be seen in intimate yet public conversation with Canada's foremost abstractionist.

AS ELEANOR'S EYES met Bob's, they managed to say very clearly, *Act natural; don't blow it.* But she had barely finished delivering these commands when Jerry stepped around his wife and took Bob familiarly by the arm. Zeffler's expression suggested that he'd found the very person he'd been looking for.

Whatever had made him think that the Zefflers would not be present tonight? Just because Jerry claimed to be mad at Gonzaga didn't mean he was about to forgo the pleasure of playing the influential collector at every art-related event he might deem worthy of his attention.

'I've been hearing some very interesting things about you,' Zeffler said in an insistent, slightly chiding undertone that amid the general hubbub of conversation could only have been heard by the three of them. If Bob had not been forewarned by Eleanor, those words would have been real heart-stoppers.

'It seems you've made friends in high places,' Jerry continued. 'Quintin Margrave is quite a fan of yours, you know.'

Yes, there it was: the barely suppressed annoyance that a designated failure might be about to rise from his own ashes. Along with the implication that he, Jerry, had a direct line to the director of the Spital-fields Gallery.

Bob shrugged and smiled noncommittally.

'But I've always liked your stuff ... we've got a couple of your early pieces, you know.'

'Yep.' He went on grinning affably.

'The little lady here was the one who picked them out.'

They both turned their heads to gaze benignly upon Eleanor, who did not return their glances. At that moment she appeared to be trans-fixed by the sight of Tom Dale bearing down on her with a broad and remarkably goofy smile on his face.

IT HAD BEEN all Tom could do to get it down, the pinkish swill that somehow managed to be sickly sweet and acrid at the same time. But he figured he might never get away if he didn't drink at least one thick-rimmed glass of it. The burly guy in the black suit wasn't much of a conversationalist, but he looked as pleased as punch to be sitting there between Tom and Max. He seemed reluctant to let them leave the table, but after a few minutes Tom got to his feet, saying, 'Excuse me. There's someone over there I want to speak to.'

She was absolutely radiant tonight. Looking much better than the last time he'd seen her. He felt the same sudden, unnerving vagueness about her name as he had the other afternoon at the studio, but never mind. He knew her, had known her for a long time; she was his type; the kind of woman he'd always thought of as a thoroughbred: willowy, sleek, long-legged, dressed with unfussy elegance.

The string of pearls around her neck brought back the memory of their wild dance together. It almost made him laugh aloud with plea-sure. And as he got closer to her, he thought of the hidden, fragrant places, just below where those pearls now hung, where his lips had once – at least once, and not so long ago it suddenly seemed – been pressed in illicit rapture.

'I would do most anything for you.'

She took his outstretched hand with what looked like surprise. But she was happy to see him, he was sure of that. If the two men, one of them a painter who'd been around since the old Gerrard Street days – what the hell was his name? – hadn't been standing right next to her, he might have kissed her then and there.

It was only when the better-dressed of the two men put his arm proprietarily around her that Tom realized that that one must be her husband. But wasn't old ... Alex ... yes, Alex ... dead? Years ago, surely. But this husband, who had now seized Tom's hand, was probably someone he ought to recognize, too. God, it was getting harder and harder these days to keep track of all the people who wanted to be his best pal. He smiled as pleasantly as he could, but he felt a vague, queasy sensation that could very easily have become panic. And no doubt it would have, had it not been for the blessed sight of Joan hurrying towards him through the crowded room with a look of love and worry on her dear, familiar face.

▌ Chapter Twenty-Five

BRUNO shut the door after the last stragglers and locked it. There was only one lonely, indecisive blue dot visible in the whole exhibition, but even so it seemed to him that the evening had gone well. The crowd had been larger and more distinguished than Mazzano's status warranted, and that could only reflect the increasing prestige of the Gonzaga Gallery and its proprietor. Maybe the fight with O'Hara at the Artquake party had actually enhanced his reputation.

Tom Dale's arrival had been an especially welcome surprise. The sight of the painter's ruddy, affable face as he sat sipping wine in the alcove was so pleasant that it even made Lurie's presence less hateful. It also more than compensated for the annoyance of Win Beecham's nearly constant hovering. He wondered if he had misjudged the relationship between Dale and Beecham. Dale hadn't paid any attention to her, and he'd looked delighted when his plain little wife showed up. Or maybe there *had* been something going on, but Dale had decided to put an end to it. In any case, Bruno didn't have to bother with Win Beecham any more, that was clear.

Calmed by these reflections and the glass or two of wine he had drunk for conviviality's sake, Bruno felt almost no anxiety when the telephone began to ring again. He answered it quite casually on the fourth ring.

'Mr Gonzaga? Alan Burnham here.'

He sat down at the desk before replying. 'How are you? And please, you must call me Bruno.'

'Bruno. And you must call me Alan.'

There was a brief silence, which for tactical reasons Bruno did not break.

'Well, Mr – er, Bruno ... I'm afraid I have some slightly, well, actually pretty unpleasant news. There's been an ... incident ... here at the Gallery.'

AN INTERESTING evening, all told. With Eleanor unexpectedly on the scene, Bob had not been able to make any time with … Jane, that was her name. Instead, he'd been forced to play the affable eunuch. In Jerry's presence he felt it was wiser not to be even nominally flirtatious with Eleanor. Since they actually were lovers, the sort of gallantry that might have appeared natural and even flattering to the husband of an acknowledged beauty was out of the question. To the guilty parties at least, it would have seemed like a dead giveaway.

He left the Gonzaga early and walked home, shivering penitently in the chilly late-autumn air and thinking about what he'd become. An adulterer, a cold-blooded, wily dissembler who could greet his mistress's husband with a calm, public smile. The smiler with the knife. And boy, it was amazing how easy it was, once you got the hang of it.

But that was only part of the problem. He'd even become cynical about his own emotions. The old Bob – the *young* Bob – the impetuous, romantic fool he was sure he had once been, would have at least *wanted* to punch his rival out, crush and obliterate him, though he might not have had the courage to do it. But now, as he stood beside Jerry Zeffler, he felt nothing more than a lukewarm, apologetic comradeship. He and Zeffler were simply sharing her, really. Each of them was providing Madame with a quite distinct service.

Well, maybe not entirely. Eleanor's demeanour in bed had largely confirmed the suspicion that he'd had way back when: that she had not been sex-starved when their affair began. She was enthusiastic, and he certainly wasn't going to complain about that, but she seemed to take her own pleasure for granted. No sea-changes or eurekas there, as far as he could tell. And no gratitude, either – not that he was expecting any.

So what was she doing with him, really? Looking for variety? Diversion? Revenge for some peccadillo of Jerry's? Or maybe just a chance to slum? He found he could consider all those possibilities without rancour, which in itself was depressing. And in return for whatever it was she got out of the affair, she gave him … what, exactly? Sexual pleasure, of course, and the related, but not quite synonymous satisfaction of possessing such a superior specimen. He'd be a liar if he didn't admit that without her beauty, Eleanor would not have interested him much. He had never yet fallen in love with an ugly woman, and with one or two regrettable exceptions, had avoided sleeping with any.

Still, he'd always managed to convince himself that the women he'd loved were sweet – and intelligent, too. Well, they'd chosen him, hadn't they? Somehow, with Eleanor, that delusion had never quite taken hold.

Perhaps it was only that he was old and jaded enough to like their arrangement just as it was: provisional and temporary.

ELIOT'S LIGHT was on when Win passed his room on her way to her own. It was still early, not even ten o'clock yet. She tapped lightly on the half-closed door and spoke his name softly before entering. He was propped up on a pile of pillows, reading. As she walked towards the bed, he marked his place and laid the book on the bedside table, then looked at her over his glasses. 'What was it tonight?' he asked.

'An opening at the Gonzaga. François Mazzano. Rather dull, actually. All the usual tiresome people.'

At times, Eliot's complete lack of interest in the art world was a blessing. Now, for instance, it meant that she was spared having to recount the events of the evening in detail. Oh, he would have risen to the occasion, becoming righteously indignant on her behalf when she described how Gonzaga had fawned on Tom Dale while refusing to meet her eye. And as for François Mazzano, whose response to her friendly artist-to-artist overtures had been almost condescending, Eliot would likely have had something choice to say about uppity *habitants*.

But she knew that if pressed Eliot would also say that all these undeserved and (in his view) trivial slights simply proved that she did not belong in that demimonde and would be far better off accepting her natural, her privileged place in the world. She was a talented amateur painter, an accomplished gardener, an all-around woman of refinement. And not least a devoted wife.

So she could never have mentioned the evening's worst moment of all: watching poor Tom leer like an oversexed teenager at the Zeffler woman, even as her husband stood grinning at her side. Fortunately Joan had arrived just in the nick of time.

Still, on some level, Eliot must have understood that things had not gone as she would have liked. When she sat down on the bed, he reached over and began to stroke her head and then, more forcefully, the nape of her neck. His large, strong, competent fingers slid upwards into her hair and began to massage her scalp. She moved closer and laid her head on his shoulder. He smelt of 4711 cologne with a very faint undercurrent of hospital antiseptic, a familiar and in Win's opinion pleasing combination. She had always appreciated strict cleanliness in men.

After a few moments during which neither of them said anything he removed his glasses, placed them on the bedside table next to the book and began to undo the buttons of her blouse. She got to her feet just long enough to remove the rest of her clothes, letting them fall where they might, then slipped quickly under the covers and into her husband's arms. When he pulled her against him she was immediately made aware that he had already kicked off his pyjama bottoms.

IF JOAN DALE had not horned in at the crucial moment, Eleanor thought, she might somehow have managed to signal to Tom that she was ready to forgive him. She had seen in his eyes that he wanted her to. The words he had murmured – almost sung – as he took her hand, *I would do anything for you*, still thrilled her.

She turned over in bed and tried to get into a comfortable position facing away from Jerry, who had just begun to snore. Perhaps the entire mix-up about her rendezvous with Tom at the Park Plaza had been just that, an unavoidable snafu that neither of them had quite known how to make right. And now ... well, now that she had more experience in such matters, she understood that Tom was not a practised philanderer. What had happened between them that day at the studio had probably shaken him just as much as it had her. Maybe he had simply been too shy to show up at the house for drinks with Margrave. Just because he was brilliant, successful and famous didn't necessarily mean he was sophisticated or blasé when it came to love. As a matter of fact, she found that boyish, ingenuous side of him enormously appealing. Youthfulness, Eleanor told herself, pressing the pillow over her ears in a futile attempt to muffle the rhythmic wheezing now coming from the other side of the bed, was not a matter of age at all, but of a person's entire attitude towards life. It was just too bad that certain other people she could name – and not just her husband – weren't more like him.

The truth was, Robert's cynicism and cowardice were beginning to get her down. Not that she had ever really *wanted* him to challenge Jerry for her hand, though it would have been nice if he'd at least made a gesture in that direction. And he rarely had a good word to say for anybody. From the way he acted, you'd think that his having failed at his chosen calling only meant that he was more principled than those who succeeded.

Well, at least he wasn't a fairy; he'd proved that to her satisfaction. So to speak. However, apart from the reasonably pleasurable afternoons and, occasionally, evenings they had spent in bed over the past few weeks, what was she really getting out of the affair? They never did anything or went anywhere else – out to dinner, for instance. They couldn't. Even Capriccio, a restaurant over a store on a dull and unfashionable stretch of College away out near Grace Street was not really safe, because Jerry and his friends had just 'discovered' it. Or that was the reason they agreed on when she once suggested they go there. Eleanor also suspected that Robert simply couldn't afford even a modest place like that.

She was starting to get really fed up with Rachel, too. It sounded completely crazy, but an imaginary person was actually depressing her. Maybe it was just that the Rachel cover story was in danger of wearing thin. Jerry, knowing she was hardly an emotional philanthropist, must wonder why she spent so much time with a person of so little charm. And why she always took a bath after seeing her.

The condition of the bathroom at Tranby Street was still a problem. She had not been able to think of any way to clean the mouldy shower stall without actually getting into it. Besides, she had the distinct feeling that now Robert *had* her, he did not value her quite as much as before. At the Gonzaga this evening, hemmed in on one side by her husband and on the other by her lover, she had told herself fiercely that she would dump them both in an instant if Tom Dale would only say the word.

WITH ONLY MINIMAL regret, Tom left the vast, sun-filled room whose gleaming windows soared to a high ceiling that was tinted blue like the sky outside. It must have been on the top floor of a fairly tall building, because no other structure, only an expanse of that clear azure, was visible through the glass. And he knew that the completed *Kite V* was there, though he had not quite succeeded in catching sight of it. He knew, too, with deep contentment, that it was good; the last of the series and the best thing he'd ever done, without a doubt. The room gradually faded from view, but still he felt the boundless confidence that had filled him while he was in it. His own messy but functional studio suited him just fine, thank you, and it was time to get to work.

When he opened his eyes, everything was dark. He found he was not reclining on the leather couch as he had expected but instead seemed to be in bed, under the covers. He sat up, feeling puzzled about something he could not quite name, and shoved the sheet and blanket aside with one hand. Gradually the outlines of the bedroom took shape in the dimness, and he could make out a sleeping form next to him. He leaned closer. It was Joan. His wife. He ought to have known that. She mumbled softly in her sleep and rolled half away from him as he peered at her, but she did not wake.

He slid his legs sideways and put his feet on the floor. As quietly as possible he made his way across the room to the closet, pulled out his tweed jacket and put it on. After feeling around for a while on the floor of the cupboard, he located a pair of shoes and slipped his bare feet into them without stopping to tie the laces. Then he went out into the hall and started down the stairs.

Before he had even reached the landing, he heard quick footsteps behind him. The hall light came on. Turning, he saw Joan's face, still blotchy and creased from sleep but with that querulous look that lately seemed to be her only expression. She was close enough now to grasp his arm.

'What are you doing? Where are you going?'

He shook himself loose. 'To the studio.' What was the matter with the woman?

'But it's the middle of the night. And look at you. You're not dressed.'

To placate her, he glanced into the mirror over the squat, pseudo-Jacobean chest on the landing. His old sport coat hung open, revealing his striped pyjama top, and beneath it his pyjama pants with the front placket gaping indecorously. He twitched the pants closed and buttoned his jacket over them. 'I didn't want to wake you, but I've got work to do. Sorry.' He turned then and started to go down the stairs, but Joan was right behind him.

When she took hold of his arm again, he pulled away, more violently this time. She held on. For a moment they struggled silently, and it seemed that they might fall together down the stairs.

'You can't go,' she said. 'You don't know what you're doing or where you're going. You're not yourself.'

Well, he couldn't help chuckling at that. 'Who am I, then?' he asked in a teasing voice, kidding her along. It seemed like a reasonable enough question, but when he looked at her for an answer, he saw that the old girl actually had tears in her eyes. Because of him. He stopped trying to get away and instead reached out and put his arms around her.

SO MUCH FOR ebullience. On Friday morning the gloom level at the Gonzaga was higher than it had ever been. Bruno had not shown his face when Jane arrived, and an hour later he was still hiding in the workshop.

She wasn't feeling too hot herself. The opening last night had been a real drag, all things considered. Once again she had ended up going straight home afterwards. Alone. Oh, towards the end of the evening Sven had lurched in her direction and mumbled something about going for a drink at the Pilot, but she had ignored him.

It was eleven o'clock now and she had a right to some coffee. When she looked into the workshop to ask if he wanted any, Bruno had the front section of the morning newspaper spread out in front of him on the framing table. That was unusual. For a moment or two he didn't even seem to notice her standing there, but continued to turn the pages, scanning each one with a look of intense concentration that actually furrowed his brow. When she spoke, it took a moment for her voice to register. Finally, he glanced reluctantly towards her with a dazed expression, then reached into his pocket and tossed a dollar bill over for the coffees.

It was a nice day, brisk but sunny. And at least it was Friday. An hour later, on her lunch break, instead of going back to the Rancho to eat, Jane walked over to Harridge's to look at clothes. She couldn't really afford to buy anything. She had her week's pay in her purse, but all of it was already earmarked for necessities like rent and food. Or should have been. Still, she reasoned, girl cannot live by wieners and beans alone, so she ended up spending fifteen dollars on a navy blue silk *fond de robe*, imported from France. As she hurried back to work, stopping to pick up a take-out sandwich on the way, she was feeling better. If something – or someone – good did by some miracle happen to her, she would be ready.

A CUCKOO'S EGG in the nest; that was what it had always been. And he had been too quick to accept it as his own. Now it was slashed, cut to ribbons by some unknown vandal. But Bruno had not been able to find any mention of it in the morning paper. While Jane was at lunch, he slipped out to the corner store and bought the two afternoon papers, but there was nothing in them about the 'incident', as the curator had called it, either. So he still had a little time to plan a course of action before the situation became public knowledge. And before Burnham could find a replacement for *Back Flip* in the exhibition. For he had realized that that would almost certainly happen.

Yes, looking back, claiming ownership of the false painting had been a miscalculation, made in haste and confusion and under duress. And all the more regrettable because the original, the real one, had always been truly his, if possession meant anything at all. Possession ... nobody could question that. He still had the original; that was the secret weapon that would confound his enemies. He stopped pacing for a moment, just long enough to stub out his cigarette in the ashtray on the work table. He had hardly taken a puff of the next one, however, before he saw that things were not quite so simple.

Naturally, he had felt no deep attachment to the painting that had been hanging in the exhibition. It was only a symbol, a representation of the original. He chuckled, thinking that last night, on the telephone, Burnham must have been puzzled by his composure when he received the news. No doubt he would have been even more surprised to discover that the Artquake *Back Flip* was a copy. A fake. But Bruno was not yet ready to tell him so, or to reveal that he had the real one tucked away for just such an emergency.

But ... but. What good was the original to him when as far as anyone who mattered knew, the painting he was supposed to own no longer existed? According to Burnham – Alan – *Back Flip* was a total loss, and like nearly all contemporary works of art, impossible to repair. The curator had assured him that the Art Gallery's insurance policy would fully cover Bruno's financial loss. Still, what was that – less than a thousand dollars? Even though he'd set the replacement value as more than twice the actual selling price (and three times what he'd handed over to O'Hara), such a small sum was nothing, compared with the true worth of a painting that would have lifted him and the Gonzaga Gallery to another level of importance. And now it was ... *cut to ribbons*. If he had been a different sort of man, Bruno might have savoured the irony of that. But he'd always considered irony a pointless indulgence, the consolation of weaklings and malcontents.

He had to think clearly. He didn't have much time. The copy had been a snare placed in his path by O'Hara, of that he was sure. There might be others. He must be very careful now not to be caught again.

'WINIFRED?' It was a woman's voice, cultivated and, at the moment, rather tremulous, but not one that she immediately recognized.

'Yes?'

'It's Joan Dale.'

'Joan. Why, hello.' Surely it wasn't possible that some whisper of scandal about Tom and herself had only now reached his wife's ears. Not now, when there would never be anything to tell. 'How are you?'

'Not very well, I'm afraid.'

'Oh, dear.' Win reached across her desk to the antique lustre bowl that contained the collection of subtly coloured, unusually shaped stones she had gathered from the shores of Go Home Bay over the years, and selected one. Its delicately mottled, blue, grey and beige surface was cool, smooth, soothing against her palm. 'What is the matter?'

'Well … this is so difficult to say. To talk about.' Joan's voice quavered, and somewhat to her surprise Win felt pity mingle with her apprehension. She ran her fingers over the stone's almost velvety surface, then tested the weight of it in her hand while she waited for Joan to continue.

'Winifred … you were at the Mazzano opening last night, weren't you?'

'Yes.'

'I wasn't able to speak to you then but … well, actually, I wanted to talk to you privately. About Tom.'

'Yes?' It was the only possible thing to say.

'Did you notice then – or *have* you noticed before – that he is acting rather strangely these days?'

Although at last she was beginning to see where the conversation was leading, Win decided to be cautious. 'What do you mean by *strangely*?'

'Well, he's become terribly forgetful. He got lost on his way back from the studio last week. A policeman had to bring him home, if you can imagine it. Sometimes he doesn't recognize people he ought to know. He's awfully irritable, too. And last night at the Gonzaga – well, since you were there, you probably saw it – he actually seemed to be making … well, overtures … to Mrs Zeffler. You see, he's become rather *libidinously disinhibited*. That's what Dr Crerar calls it. Quite a mouthful, isn't it? Not that I mind that at all when it comes to me. Tom and I have always got on very, very well in that department….'

Oh, stop bragging. Win felt her sympathy for poor drab little Joan evaporating. 'What are you saying, Joan? That you think Tom is getting senile? Is that what you mean?'

When she finally answered, Joan's voice was wobbly again. 'I don't know what to think. He actually tried to leave the house in the middle of the night in his pyjamas on Thursday. He insisted he had to get to the studio. The only way I was able to stop him was by –'

'What does this Dr Crerar of yours say?' *Some crusty old ignoramus who'd been looking after the Dales for years, no doubt.*

'Well, he's one of these new, up-to-date fellows. Can't be more than thirty-five, and he's very up on the psychological side. Rather too much so for me at times, but in any event he says Tom is far too young to be getting senile. He's only fifty-four. But of course you know that; you and he are the same age, aren't you?'

'Yes.' *And you're five years younger, lest we forget.* 'We've been the dearest of friends for ages and ages. Since childhood, you know.' *Long before* you *were even thought of.*

'Yes. Well, Dr Crerar puts it down to something he calls the male crisis of middle life. It's rather like our Change. He says that with this sexual revolution going on, some older men feel they have missed out. They try to compensate. And there's Tom's artistic temperament, too. The furore of creation – a sort of brainstorm. The doctor believes it will pass.'

'I see.' Maybe it was best for poor Joan to go on deluding herself. She would have awful things to face in the coming years, if Tom did end up like Father. 'Well, who knows, perhaps it will.'

'So you *do* understand. It's *such* a relief to hear you say that.'

Win was silent for a moment. Then she said, 'What do you mean?'

'Well ... I was rather afraid that Tom might have said or done something inappropriate to you. You know, made some kind of ... advance. Something he said to me the other night while we were ... well, at a particular moment he spoke your name and someone else's, all jumbled up together.'

'Really.'

'Yes, he seemed somehow to have confused you with the Zeffler woman, which made me wonder, you see. But he said it in the heat of –'

'Heavens, Joan. You mean he actually ... how awful for you. But I can assure you that never by word or deed ... and even supposing ... naturally I would not take such a thing seriously for one moment. Not for a single second. Or take offence in any way. I value dear Tom's friendship far too much. And yours, too.'

'I know you do. We really ought to see more of each other.'

'Yes. Let's, very soon.'

'Let's. Goodbye, Winifred.'

'Goodbye, Joan. Do take care of yourself. And Tom.'

'I will.'

'Goodbye, then.'

'Goodbye.'

EDDIE'S PASSPORT was ready on Friday, so he dragged himself out of the sack at eleven and went down to the government office to pick it up.

In a way it was a relief to be away from Sandra. They'd spent almost every waking, not to mention sleeping, hour together for almost a week. He'd been staying off the streets and steering clear of his studio, because the last thing he wanted was to be asked how he felt about the destruction of *Back Flip*.

The night before, even during the hour it had taken to load the last three pieces from his Gonzaga show into Sandra's brother's old station wagon for transport to Eddie's parents' basement, the phone in the studio had rung several times. He didn't answer it.

Since neither he nor Sandra could drive, the brother had brought the car over himself, and Eddie figured that must mean he was now Sandra's official boyfriend. Scott, a supercilious Ph.D. candidate in geophysics, had made it crystal clear that Eddie was nowhere near good enough for his sister, especially after eyeballing the ancestral O'Hara seat – a Rexdale bungalow. But at least they'd got the job done without running into Mr Swartz, and there was no reason Eddie could see to go back to the place on Spadina ever again.

JUST BEFORE DAWN, calculating that at this hour he might catch the traitor off guard, Bruno found himself dialling Eddie's number. But just as the phone began to ring, he replaced the receiver quickly. If he started talking to Eddie, he might be forced to admit that he had lost control of the situation, that he didn't know what was going on. He did know, as a matter of absolute truth, that he would rather die than reveal that. Nevertheless, it gave him some pleasure to imagine O'Hara rudely awakened, startled by a sound he might not have had time to identify, then maybe tossing and turning, unable to get back to sleep after the interruption. Why should he, Bruno, be the only one to suffer?

And he was suffering. Though he had stretched out on the cot in the hope that inspiration might miraculously flood his brain as he slept, he did not lose consciousness for a second. He only lay rigid, as rage – or was it dread? – pressed down on his chest like a thousand-pound boulder. When he got up again, nearly staggering with anxiety and fatigue, the weight did not lift. Now it seemed to be within him, spreading slowly to his left arm and then upwards to his throat. For a moment he felt it might suffocate him, and he groaned. He made his way over to the shaving mirror and stared into it as if he were beginning to doubt his own existence. Beneath the black stubble that had reasserted itself with what seemed even greater speed than usual, his face was haggard, and slick with cold sweat. His hands felt clammy. He pulled out his handkerchief and wiped his forehead and temples.

When he got to the alcove he collapsed into his chair, leaning one elbow on the table and keeping the other crooked at his side. In the silence, his breathing sounded oddly loud and laboured, like the noise a cornered animal might make as it searched vainly for a means of escape. Grimly, for what seemed the thousandth time, he reviewed his dilemma: O'Hara, Burnham, the real painting, the false one. The real one was safe. The false one was gone. But the original was now completely useless, its value stolen first by the existence of the fake, and then by its destruction. If only he had denounced the false *Back Flip* from the very first ...

The real, the fake, the fake, the real.... He had to concentrate on the real one. Maybe even now, if he simply presented it to Burnham, sent it anonymously perhaps, there would be no questions asked. And if there were ... well, he could always pretend not to understand them.

He heaved himself to his feet, grimacing with the effort, and staggered back into the workshop. It took only a moment to find the crowbar he used to open shipping crates. Clutching it in his right hand, he burst through the alcove and out into the rear gallery at a ragged, lurching trot. He was just approaching the central partition when he felt the unexpected blow come out of the darkness. A crushing, twisting, grinding, relentless force bent him backward, then forward, and nearly lifted him off his feet. He flailed, swinging the crowbar around him with all his remaining strength, but his assailant was too quick, darting behind the partition before he could even catch sight of him. Bruno's weapon flew from his fist and landed with a clattering crash somewhere in the darkness. Then he too was falling.

It was only when his cheek slid painfully across the rough black concrete floor that he understood there had been no intruder. The blow had come from within himself. He tried to get up but could not. He realized he was utterly alone in this silent, empty place lit dimly by the pale light of dawn that now, instead of growing brighter, was beginning to fade.

▮ Chapter Twenty-six

THE SOUND that Jerry let out was half groan, half grunt. It began low in his throat, then rose very slightly and finally ended with an incredulous squeak that conveyed dismay and glee in more or less equal parts. His half-full coffee cup crashed onto its saucer and he reared up in his chair, flapping the newspaper at Eleanor.

'Did you see *this?*'

Well, she couldn't have seen anything in the morning paper, because he always commandeered it as soon as he came down in the morning. She was on the other side of the kitchen, anyway. It was Saturday, and even though Becky was still sleeping, Eleanor was mixing up pancake batter.

'No, what?'

' "*Vandalism at Art Gallery.*" That's the headline. *"Just before closing time on Thursday afternoon at the Art Gallery of Ontario, an abstract painting entitled* Black Ship *by local artist Edwin O'Hara –* " typical, they get everything wrong "*– was slashed with a sharp instrument by a person or persons unknown.*" '

'Oh, my God!' said Eleanor, with much more emotion than she felt.

' "*The picture, part of the contemporary exhibit –*" exhibit! "*– Artquake '67, was attacked while no guards were present.*" Where the hell were they – on their goddamn coffee break? *"The guard assigned to the room was absent due to two other, nearly simultaneous disturbances in the adjacent Old Master galleries.*" '

'What on earth is going on down –'

But he had only paused for breath. ' "*A man, described by police as mentally unbalanced and of no fixed address, was taken into custody after threatening to deface with spray paint a priceless canvas attributed to the seventeenth-century Italian master Bronzino. It has not been determined whether there was a connection between this attempt and the attack on the O'Hara painting.*" '

'For heaven's –'

'Hold it, there's more: "*In a separate but apparently unrelated incident, a young girl collapsed in an adjoining gallery. She was revived at the* scene." And get this: *"Curator Alan Burnham stated that* Black Ship *was a total loss, damaged beyond repair."* '

He slapped the paper down on the breakfast table and, in a rare moment of silent unanimity, Eleanor and Jerry just stared at each other with incredulous but not entirely displeased expressions on their faces.

SANDRA WENT OUT to get the Saturday morning paper and she and Eddie looked at it in bed. They took turns reading aloud the account of what had happened at the Art Gallery on Thursday and got a few laughs out of it, although Eddie really didn't find the mistakes about his name or the title of the painting all that funny. But at least they finally understood what all the yelling had been about in the Old Master gallery. Neither of them had hung around long enough to figure that out.

Seeing the story right there in black and white, Eddie couldn't help wondering whether it had been such a smart thing to do. Maybe he *had* let paranoia get the better of him. *Shit.* And maybe he should have talked it over with somebody other than Sandra. In retrospect, he didn't believe she really understood what he had been trying to prove. She thought it was all about spiritual liberation, and her face actually screwed up in prissy disapproval when he mentioned fixing that fucker Godzilla's wagon and flushing out the real *Back Flip,* which the bastard must have stashed away somewhere. And now he wouldn't be around to see that happen. At least not until he got back, in a month or two. Another thing that Sandra didn't really seem to *get* was that he had no intention of giving up painting, that this trip was just a temporary, head-straightening vacation.

But anyway, they were flying out that evening, late, on what he'd taken to calling Orange Crate Airlines, although Sandra didn't find *that* particularly amusing, either. It was Icelandic, actually. There would be a stopover in Luxembourg at some hour he couldn't even begin to calculate. From there they'd have to make their way to Amsterdam to pick up another bargain-basement charter to India. Sandra had looked after the arrangements, such as they were, and all she had to do now was take all their travelling clothes to a laundromat that afternoon. So, not having a thing to wear, Eddie had no choice but to stay in bed naked, smoking, reading and dozing in preparation for what would probably turn out to be two or three days without a decent night's sleep.

'YOU KNOW HIM,' Max said.

Bob shook his head. 'I don't think so.'

'Sure you do.'

It was just before noon. Outside the door of Max's office he could hear the judicious murmurs of a couple of art lovers who were working their way through the Lurie Gallery, a key stop on their Saturday pilgrimage route. He was supposed to be here to talk about plans for his show. He could hardly believe it yet, but after seeing the new stuff, Max had actually suggested a small works-on-paper exhibition, a dozen pieces at most, just to get him back in the swing. Then of course they'd immediately got sidetracked by the news about *Back Flip*.

'What's he look like?'

Max put his hand on the top of his own head. 'Wears a beret and usually an old pin-striped vest. Stinks to high heaven. Hangs around a lot down there, Allan says. He even shows up here every so often, but Marie is pretty good at getting rid of him.'

'A beret? You don't mean ... what's-his-face ... you know, the icon guy?'

'Yeah, that's him. Used to hang around the Vanguard. He was still sane back then. Well, semi-sane. Remember, he was always after me to show his stuff? Those egg-tempera icon things, red-eyed Madonnas ...'

'Egg tempera! On plywood. Or was it Masonite?'

'Cardboard,' Max said. 'He was more or less a rubby even in those days.'

'And his name was ... Ra-something. Rab ... Rad ...' Bob muttered, feeling his way back into the past like a blind man.

'*Radovic!*' Max yelled. 'I never did figure out whether it was his first or his last name, though. He was Croatian, or Serbian, something like that.'

Bob was nodding now, and smiling. 'And didn't he have kind of a thing for Betty?'

'Who didn't?' said Max softly, with a faraway look in his eye.

'Anyway ... yeah, that's the guy. A real fruitcake. I *have* seen him around, come to think of it. So he's the one who slashed O'Hara's piece?'

'Nobody seems to be sure about that. It could be he just happened to be in the next room with a spray can at the time, getting set to censor that Bronzino copy. You know the one; I think it was Blunt who palmed it off on them in the thirties or forties. The original is in the National Gallery in London.'

'Oh, yeah ... you mean the chick, the curtain, the cupid, the crone ...'

'That's it. Apparently all the guards were busy with Radovic, and there was nobody in the Artquake space. Alan thinks that was when *Back Flip* got carved up.'

'Maybe he was planning to do both of them.'

'Maybe, but that's not what I got from Burnham. All was quiet, until the guard heard Radovic casting spells in the next gallery and went to help his buddy who was on duty there. But Radovic didn't have a knife on him, and they didn't find one lying around anywhere, either. Oh, and believe it or not something else happened, too: some young girl passed out right in front of the *Marchesa Casati*.'

'You're kidding. You mean all at the same time?'

'Yep. Wiggy, eh? I feel sorry for O'Hara, though.'

Bob shrugged. 'He'll get over it. Anyway ...' He clamped his lips firmly closed before he could say, *There's plenty more where that came from.*

'The funny thing is,' Max went on casually, 'I've been trying to get in touch with Eddie for a few days, but he never seems to answer his phone.'

'You have?'

'Well, after the rumble −' they both grinned at the word '− at the Artquake party, I think it's a good bet that he's looking for a dealer. The thought crossed my mind that maybe his stuff might fit in here.' He glanced at Bob as if he were testing his response to the idea. 'I mean, when the dust settles with Gonzaga.'

But then Max's eyes moved up and came to rest on something or someone just behind Bob. When he turned to look, Howard McNab was standing in the office doorway with an unpleasantly stimulated expression on his face. He nodded briefly at Bob but addressed Max.

'Have you seen Bruno this morning?'

'Nope, but you probably know about the −'

'Yes, yes, I spoke to Alan last night and got a full report. No, the thing is, I was just going to pop into the Gonzaga and talk to Bruno for a little piece I'm working on, and I found the place locked up, no sign of life. He should have been open an hour ago.'

'Well, maybe he just −'

Howard didn't let him finish. 'And I saw, at least I think I did, something peculiar through the window. I can't decide what to do about it; would you come and have a look?'

They both followed him out onto the street. Over at the Gonzaga, the lights were off and except for the area near the window, the interior was dim. Max tried the door and found it still locked. He knocked on it, hard, but there was no sound or movement from within. Howard and Bob peered through the window, shading their eyes with their hands.

'See it?'

'Nope.'

'Look, back there – just by the partition in the middle, down at the bottom on the left side.'

Max joined them and all three stood in a row with their noses pressed against the glass, squinting into the gallery.

'Oh yeah. Okay, I see it now. It looks like ...' Bob cupped both palms at his temples, straining to make out the beige-coloured, free-form object Howard was pointing at. 'It could be ... I don't know, maybe a ...'

'... hand,' Max said.

'Yes, that's what I thought,' Howard replied.

And Bob realized that was just what it was: a hand, a large one, attached to part of a burly arm with a sliver of white shirtsleeve visible, sticking out from behind the freestanding wall that divided the Gonzaga Gallery more or less in two. The arm and the hand were lying flat on the floor and after a few moments it became fairly clear that they weren't going to move.

By this time the Saturday art pilgrims, a well-dressed couple in their forties, had joined the three of them at the window, but they didn't seem to have noticed the hand yet. Max jerked his head at Bob, and they moved a few steps away and stood uneasily on the sidewalk. Howard followed. They looked at one another, then back at the Gonzaga Gallery's window, where a small hubbub had just erupted and passersby, drawn by the continued presence of the first two rubberneckers, had begun to gather.

Finally Bob said, whispering, although he didn't really know why, 'Maybe we'd better call the cops.'

AFTER JERRY LEFT for the Gonzaga to find out what was going on, Eleanor went upstairs. She looked in on Becky, who stirred, grumbled, rolled over and pulled the covers up over her head. Eleanor withdrew, closing the door gently after her, and went on down the hall to the master bedroom.

From the bedside phone, she called Robert, but there was no answer,

❏ 284

even though she let it ring and ring and ring. It seemed that every single time she called him, he was out. Or the line was busy. She looked at her watch; it was just after noon. He didn't have any classes to teach on Saturday, so where was he? Anywhere he liked, of course; he was a grown man with an entire life that she knew almost nothing about.

She hung up and went back downstairs to the kitchen. She supposed she would have liked him to be in some sort of suspended animation during the time they spent apart. All adulterers must feel that way, she told herself as she put the unused pancake batter into the refrigerator, covered tightly with Saran Wrap. But Robert's elusiveness was especially annoying because she had decided, in the wee small hours of the night before, to end their affair. Oh, perhaps not right away, but soon. He'd be crushed, but there was no point in getting sentimental, was there? Or, what was the expression, prolonging the agony? It was not Robert she loved, but Tom, and she would have him. Somehow, she would. The thought made her feel ruthless, invigorated and more grown-up than she had ever felt before.

FOREVER AFTER, Jane would be grateful that she didn't work on Saturdays. If she had been scheduled to be at the gallery that day, she would have been the one to find Bruno, because whatever had happened to him had happened overnight. For the first time she also felt thankful for the humble anonymity of her role at the Gonzaga. If anybody had been able to remember her last name, the cops would have called her to come over with her key and open the door, so she still would have found him, though at least not all alone.

But as it turned out, neither Max Lurie, Bob Willard nor Howard McNab knew her surname. Even though she had composed and typed every letter sent out from the Gonzaga Gallery for the last six months, she had never been allowed to sign a single one. Besides, people, especially men, found it quite natural to be on a strictly first-name basis with the girls who sat behind reception desks all over the city, just as they would expect to be with ... well, a Playboy Bunny. They didn't have last names, either. *Take a letter, Miss Haigh* had gone out with the Homburg hat and the celluloid collar; Bunny Jane was doing the typing now.

Eventually, the police had found her name and phone number, along with a few others that Bruno considered essential, written on the wall in the workshop. Foul play was considered a possibility, so they asked her to come to the gallery to determine if anything of value was missing. She agreed, after making sure that Bruno was no longer there. It only occurred to her after she had hung up that if Bruno was … well, gone for good … she no longer had a job.

'THE CAMERA DEGLI SPOSI,' Howard said, as the waiter placed his second beer in front of him. 'That's what he was thinking of. He saw himself not just as a dealer, but as a patron. The Gonzagas –' he chuckled with real delight '– why, those guys really *made* Mantegna, you know. And Romano – the Palazzo del Te! God! Fantastic stuff. The Sala dei Giganti. Hallucinatory. The Cinemascope of its day. And then there was Rubens, who worked as a *copyist* for the Gonzaga family, if you can believe it.…' He paused to take a gulp of his drink.

'And "Bruno" … I suppose that was just a …' Bob waved his hand vaguely, reaching for an idea, but Howard broke in before he could grasp it.

'A metaphor of nomenclature. Bruno – *the bear*. Get it? A solitary animal. Strong, brave, untamed, majestic, intimidating; all the things he secretly longed to be. Or not so secretly, come to think of it. Yes, somehow it all fits perfectly, doesn't it?'

Bob and Max both nodded solemnly, neither meeting the other's eye. They were already well into their third round, because Howard had been doing all the talking.

After the cops said they could go, the three of them had repaired to the nearest source of alcoholic refreshment, the Pilot. At that early hour the place was nearly empty. 'Death,' Max had observed with a theatrical shudder as they sat down, 'gives a man a powerful thirst.'

When the squad car had at last rolled up, the two patrolmen in it were surprisingly reluctant to break down the door of the Gonzaga Gallery. The angle of the sun had shifted and the object on the floor was even less distinct than it had been at first. It was only a pale, amorphous mass amid the shadows. Maybe it wasn't even a human hand at all, the cops suggested, exchanging not-so-surreptitious glances that indicated their opinion of the three effete and excitable characters who had lured them out of their warm, comfortable cruiser on a cool Saturday afternoon. Maybe it was just a *piece of modern art*, the younger of the two cops said in a tone of voice that caused Howard to become first very silent, then red in the face and finally quite belligerent.

Nobody knew the last name of Gonzaga's girl, so they couldn't phone her at home, and there was no residential listing for a Bruno Gonzaga.

Eventually the cops, goaded into action by Howard's pointed allusions to the unusual eagerness of the police to intervene in the case of Eros '65, radioed to headquarters. Someone there located the owner of the building through city records, and he came over with his keys.

It turned out that he, the landlord, had never actually met the person whose name marched in black metal letters across the gallery's whitewashed façade. No, he said, his lease was with somebody called Vittorio DiFalco, whom he at once recognized as the man who now lay dead on the floor of the Gonzaga Gallery.

In due course two detectives in suits arrived, and then a considerable time later an ambulance came and took the body away. DiFalco's wife was contacted but discouraged from coming to the scene. Bob, Max and Howard all gave statements positively identifying the deceased as the man they had known as Bruno Gonzaga. Jane, the receptionist, finally showed up looking wan and apprehensive (but still kind of cute, Bob thought) and went into the gallery with the detectives. That was when the cops told the three men that they were no longer needed.

So there had never been any such person as Bruno Gonzaga. Amazing. And the kicker was that wily old Max had known it all along. That was why Bruno (there was no point in calling the poor guy Vito now) always tried to avoid him. Oh, sure, Max said casually, he knew DiFalco from way back, when he'd first had the framing shop; he had occasionally sent him some jobs. He even remembered when the partner had decided to go back to the old country and Vito had struck out on his own.

Howard was just working up a nice head of steam over the fact that Max had kept this juicy information from him for almost two years, when the group's attention was caught by a couple who were coming across the room towards their table.

The man was Jerry Zeffler, looking lugubrious yet excited, and the girl with him, around whose shoulders he had placed a protective but not quite fatherly arm, was Jane What's-her-name, the girl from the Gonzaga. *No, not fatherly at all,* Bob thought with righteous indignation, though whether it was on Eleanor's behalf or his own, he could not in all honesty have said.

THERE ARE TIMES when a well-dressed, well-groomed, sympathetic middle-aged man can be a very welcome sight. As she stumbled along the sidewalk, relieved to be out of the Gonzaga at last but also stunned by the realization that she would probably never go back there ever again, Jane at first didn't pay any attention to the guy gesturing at her through the window of the Lurie Gallery. Then, just as she was passing the door, Jerry Zeffler burst through it, and strangely enough she was really glad to see him.

'Jane!' he said. 'God, isn't this awful?'

'You mean that Bruno's dead? Or whoever he really was.'

'Marie just told me. What happened? You were in there with the cops, weren't you?'

'Yeah. But they'd already taken him away, thank heaven. They asked me a lot of questions, though. Like, did he have any enemies.'

They both started to grin at that, then both, Jane could tell from the way Zeffler's mouth twisted as he at once became solemn again, felt ashamed of themselves. She went on quickly, 'Because apparently his face was kind of bashed up on one side and they found a crowbar on the floor....' Despite herself, she gulped noisily and felt her lips start to tremble.

'Oh, you poor kid,' said Jerry, stepping forward gallantly. When he put his arms around her she did not resist, or even want to. It was a rare pleasure to be held close by a man who shaved regularly and then put on lots of cologne, an expensive brand, tart and citrusy. And, judging by the feel of the material pressed against her now tear-dampened cheek, whose overcoat was made of cashmere. A slightly guilty pleasure, also, because he was old (at least forty-five, she guessed) and married.

Jane had never, so far, got involved in adultery. Unless you counted Barnaby. But he was young, selfish, unshaven, untouched by cologne, and his wife had already left him. Anyway, he was hardly the sort of man you'd look to for comfort or protection. More of a boy, really. And what she really longed for sometimes was a man who could, and would, take care of her. One mature enough to possess, if not wisdom, at least savoir-faire. She sniffed pathetically and again inhaled the bracing aroma of Eau Sauvage.

'What you need, young lady,' said Jerry, releasing her just enough to be able to look her empathetically in the eye, 'is a stiff drink. You are twenty-one, aren't you?'

'Twenty-two, actually.'

'Perfect. We'll go to the Pilot. Marie says Max is over there right now with Willard and McNab.' She must have grimaced involuntarily at

Howard's name because he added, tightening the arm he still had around her shoulders, 'Don't worry, dear, I'll look after you.'

WHEN BOB TRIED to shift just a smidgen to ease the cramp in his left leg, the girl from Gonzaga's turned her head towards him, as if annoyed by his knee pressing against the back of her seat. But she didn't say anything. He could hardly believe it, but here he was, squeezed into the tiny rear seat of the Zefflers' Mustang again, just as he had been on the fateful night of the Artquake opening. This time Jerry was at the wheel, and the three of them were heading over to Spadina, to O'Hara's studio. Max had said he'd better get back to minding the store, and Howard had rushed off to start work on what he promised would be the definitive piece about Bruno Gonzaga and, not coincidentally, issues of authenticity in contemporary Canadian art.

Bob didn't want to go over to Eddie's place, but he felt he ought to tag along, if only to monitor the situation between Jerry and Jane. He had sensed some furtive exchange taking place when he turned away to climb into the back seat. Well, if something untoward really was blossoming there, he'd figure out later where his duty lay. It might be tricky to decide whether informing one's mistress of the pending infidelity of her husband was (on the one hand) unthinkable or (on the other) obligatory. Man, talk about your tangled web.

When they got to Spadina, Jerry eased the car into a parking spot just half a block from Eddie's place. As they hurried along the broad sidewalk, Jane kept muttering, 'I can't believe any of this.' It wasn't clear whether she was talking to them or just to herself. Bob assumed she referred not only to Bruno's death and the slashing of *Back Flip* but also to the bizarre idea, postulated by Jerry, that Eddie O'Hara might have had something to do with Bruno's demise. That was why they were here. Zeffler's plan was to get to the kid first and give him the benefit of legal counsel before the cops could put him in the hot seat for the third degree.

Even from the street they could hear the bell going off at the top of the stairs, so O'Hara couldn't be sleeping through it. But though Zeffler rang again and again there was no answering buzz to open the door. At his urging, on the theory that a young female voice would be disarming, Jane crouched down and called through the mail slot, 'It's us, Eddie! Friends!'

When the only response was silence, Jerry himself took a turn. 'No cops, buddy! You can open up. We're all on your side. We're here to help.'

Still there was no reply. They had stepped back to the edge of the sidewalk and were staring up at the bay window when a tiny old man in shirtsleeves and a black vest came running out of the hat shop beneath Eddie's studio. He stopped and stared at Zeffler for a moment and then, with a beatific smile, held out his arms to him.

'They told me you were dead!' he cried.

Jerry sidestepped out of his reach. 'I'm sorry, I –'

'You don't know me? Your old pal? Morrie Swartz? Why, we worked the machines together for years! Right down the street there.' He turned to Jane and Bob as if they might be willing to back up his story and said, pointing at Jerry, 'It's Jake – Jake Zeffler, my old friend, and he doesn't even know me!'

Jerry was smiling now and he even let Morrie put his arms around him. But he, too, spoke over the little man's head to Jane and Bob, as if they were mediums, somehow in charge of this apparition. 'Jake was my father. He *is* dead, as he said. I look something like him, I guess.'

'*Something* like him? *Exactly* like him is more like it,' said the old guy, who, by the time he released Zeffler, appeared to have recovered from his confusion and completely lost interest in old times. 'So. What can I do for the son of my old pal? You're looking for my tenant O'Hara? He hasn't been staying here for a week, and the rent was due yesterday. He came back and threw out a lot of junk into the alley a few nights ago, and then moved the rest out Thursday night. Paintings and all. A college-boy type with an old jalopy car was helping him. He thought I didn't know, maybe. He won't be back.'

Again the old man turned to Bob and Jane, probably having eliminated Jerry as a potential artist on account of the fine hand of his cashmere overcoat, and asked, 'Either of you kids looking for a nice big studio, cheap?'

'*YOU KIDS.*' Imagine him saying that. Well, to such an ancient character, whose eyesight was probably shot to hell, he and the girl could conceivably have seemed more or less the same age. Jane had suppressed a giggle at Morris the Hatter's question, but whether she was laughing at that ludicrous implication or only the suggestion that she herself might be an artist in need of a studio, Bob could not guess. However, she did promise to mention the place to anybody she knew who might be interested. Then almost immediately she said she had to split and, refusing Jerry's offer to drive her home, set off up Spadina on foot.

Zeffler watched her go with a wistful expression, but then turned back to his father's old buddy and said maybe they *would* have a look at the place, since his good friend Willard here was a painter and it just might suit him. Over the little man's head, he winked at Bob to let him know he only wanted to get inside in order to snoop. Morrie, pleased, at once pulled a heavy key ring out of his pocket and after taking his time selecting the right one, opened the door for them.

'Go on up,' he said. 'I know you. I trust you. Me, I can't make the stairs. Just close the door after you when you leave.' Turning to Bob, he added, 'If you decide to take it, you know where I am.'

Like a couple of Hardy Boys, they looked for clues, but the only thing they discovered was that O'Hara didn't live there any more. A foam mattress with a mound of tangled greyish sheets on top of it was still on the bedroom floor, but otherwise the room was empty, except for a paint-stained sweatshirt rolled into a ball in one corner and one stiff, solitary sock near the door. They went down the narrow hall to the studio itself. A few spent paint tubes, empty cans, oily rags and matted paint rollers were strewn around on the spattered floor, but there were no canvases, finished or unfinished.

Once they were back on the street, Jerry led the way around the corner and into the alley at the rear of the building. There they found some plastic garbage bags containing what was left of the *Cloud* series. Jerry grunted approvingly as he peered inside the first one and said, 'I *told* him these were all wrong for him.'

'What do you suggest we do now?' said Bob, also asking himself silently how the hell he had managed to end up in a back alley on a Saturday afternoon rooting around in garbage with his mistress's husband.

'Let's see,' Zeffler said, 'did Eddie have a girlfriend? He could be staying with her – you know, hiding out.'

'Not that I know of. The only girl he ever talked about was somebody who didn't want to have anything to do with him.'

'You don't say. I'm surprised.' Jerry consulted his Rolex. 'Well, I guess the best thing to do is go home and hope he calls me there. For all we know he might be trying to reach me right now. I told him I'd help him out with anything legal, but who knew it would come to … well, manslaughter, maybe. A spur-of-the-moment thing. Unpremeditated. I'd guess we could establish provocation, too.'

'You don't really think …'

Jerry shrugged ominously and then said, 'Oh, damn it! I hope to God he hasn't already phoned. Eleanor might have hung up on the poor guy. I made the mistake of telling her I'd smoked a little grass with O'Hara after the Artquake party. She was not amused.' He shook his head in a rueful but pleased way and added, grinning, 'That was quite a night, wasn't it?'

'Um.'

'Definitely. And, you know, just between the two of us, Eleanor can sometimes be a real…. No spirit of adventure or experimentation – not like these young chicks today.' He jerked his head in the general direction Jane had taken. 'You know what I mean? And sometimes I even think that wife of mine despises artists, painters especially.' He paused and after a brief silence went on, 'Not you, of course. No, no. Actually, we both admire your work. Love it. I've been meaning to talk to you about it, as a matter of fact.'

▪ Chapter Twenty-seven

THE WEIGHT of Sandra's head on his shoulder, the continuous roar of the engines and the unexpected effect of the two small bottles of wine he had drunk with his miniature dinner all made Eddie feel quite stupefied. Sandra had been out cold for nearly an hour, and almost all the plane's lights were off. But since he'd spent most of the preceding day in bed, he was wide awake in a groggy kind of way. Hurtling through space, suspended in the dark over a vast expanse of water, between continents, between time zones, between the immeasurable sky and the unfathomable sea, he didn't even know for sure what day it was. Was it still Saturday, or Sunday already?

He raised the porthole blind just enough to peer out. The sky was slowly brightening as dawn crept across the ocean. He pictured the little plane – there was barely room for his legs in the crevice between his own seat and the one in front of him – zipping around the blue-beige-and-green beach ball of Planet Earth like one of those corny models where a tiny jet was attached to the globe by a piece of wire. But this rattletrap charter was attached to nothing at all; he was simply zooming through the night without a safety net or a hope in hell of survival if the thing went down.

What if it did? He knew now that he'd done something incredibly dumb yesterday. Or the day before or whenever it was. He'd blown his chance to be in the London Artquake show, something that only a week or so ago had seemed like the greatest thing that could ever happen to him. He had no idea if Godzilla would – or even *could* – produce the original *Flip*. Or if Margrave, now back in England, would even bother trying to replace it with another piece. He was totally fucked.

He jerked spastically in his seat, dislodging Sandra's head from its resting place. But she only turned away from him with a sour expression and buried her cheek in the child-sized pillow she had wedged between her seat back and the wall next to the window. Everybody seemed to be asleep. Even the charter's stewardesses – who were much less cute and perky than legend might lead you to believe – had disappeared into some cubbyhole where they too were probably curled up in their wrinkle-resistant polyester uniforms. He felt utterly alone in the darkness.

THANK GOODNESS Eliot was the strong, silent type during lovemaking and always had been. Not that he wasn't ardent – there was certainly no deficiency there – but Win was grateful that she would never have to hear the sort of distasteful things Joan Dale was apparently obliged to listen to. If she had understood her correctly. Each time Win reviewed their conversation, she found it more difficult to pin down precisely what had been said. It did seem, however, that Tom was declining rapidly, whatever Joan's silly young doctor believed or Joan herself might hope.

By mutual consent, once the boys were grown, she and Eliot had given up the by now nearly meaningless custom of attending church. However, Win still tended to rise early on Sundays. And perhaps it was some vestigial religious impulse that nearly always sent her up to the studio right after breakfast. But this morning, though she had already begun a composition in black-and-white gouache, her thoughts kept returning to poor Tom.

Surely it was impossible that anything had actually happened between him and Mrs Zeffler. Win was rather offended, in fact, that Tom had spoken of herself and that woman in the same breath. True, she – Eleanor – was quite striking, if in a rather brittle style. But not Tom's type at all. Besides, imagine such a creature being interested in a man so many years older than herself. And so different in background and culture. There was nothing in the least flashy or showy about dear Tom, and there never had been. For all his brilliance as a painter, he was a simple person, of sturdy English peasant ... well, at least yeoman stock. Father a house painter, if she remembered correctly – from Sheffield, wasn't it, or Bradford? – though ambitious and canny enough to send his young son to art classes once the family had immigrated to Canada.

Besides, the woman had a perfectly good husband of her own – an almost too handsome man who was making quite a name for himself as a litigator. From all accounts, Zeffler was bright, ambitious, dynamic and, judging by his wife's wardrobe, doing extremely well financially. A potential Q.C., it was even said, though of course not at all the sort of barrister that Father would have been favourably disposed towards if he had appeared in his court. But times change and we must change with them.

So Tom was not merely – what was the word had Joan used? – *disinhibited*. He was actually having delusions. Though if he had murmured her *own* name in a moment of passion, it was understandable enough. Unpleasant for Joan, certainly – she was sorry for that – but once the mind starts to go, a person's true feelings are liable to emerge at the most inappropriate times – an *in vino veritas* sort of thing.

Once again Win gave thanks for a narrow escape. She never would have expected Tom to be, well, a talker. Perhaps using language that was quite … unpalatable. And perhaps urging his partner to reply in kind. A man could always surprise you by turning out to have some unattractive sexual proclivity, as indelible as a tattoo, that only came to light when it was too late to change your mind.

Resolutely, she returned her attention to her gouache, in which the abstracted shape of a loose garment could be discerned floating like a ghost on a turbulent background that looked rather like a cloudy sky. It would have been pleasant to imagine that the image had emerged full-blown from her unconscious, but it hadn't, really. The robe represented Father; he had been on her mind a great deal because of Tom's decline. The clouds, an admittedly hackneyed symbol of eternity. The theme was dignity devoured by time, power turned to weakness, then those tattered remnants claimed at last by death itself. Death, whose reluctant bride we must all one day become.

Yesterday, Death had swooped down on Bruno Gonzaga, a man who had seemed annoyingly vigorous just a few days ago, but whose demise she could not in all honesty say she regretted. And now it turned out that his very identity had been a fraud. A quite courteous policeman had telephoned the previous evening with the news. They were calling everyone on the list of gallery artists, he'd explained, since 'foul play' had not yet been ruled out. She'd been circumspect, since she had nothing concrete to offer in the way of evidence, but it would not really have surprised her to learn that Gonzaga had been murdered. A man like that must have made a lot of enemies.

THE MORE he thought about it, the less and less likely it seemed to Bob that Eddie could under any circumstances have split Bruno Gonzaga's head open with a crowbar. Or Vito DiFalco's, for that matter. Based on Max's account, O'Hara's performance in the ring at the Artquake party had been ineffectual at best. Apparently Eddie had only succeeded in landing a couple of open-handed slaps on the side of his dealer's head.

Then, the moment Bruno started to push him away, he'd stumbled backwards and nearly fallen on his face.

No, O'Hara had neither the technique nor the temperament to beat anyone to death, no matter how he felt about the guy. True, he had acted pretty paranoid that time he showed up at the apartment, the night Eleanor had had to hide in the bedroom. But that could just have been the result of habitual overindulgence in inspirational substances, couldn't it? The kid was a pothead, an acid head, a goofball, much too busy mapping the convoluted topography of his own brain to summon up the gumption to commit murder. Or even manslaughter, as Zeffler, instinctively plea-bargaining, had suggested.

Then there was the slashing business. As far as Bob was aware, he and Eddie were the only people who knew the painting in the show was a fake. Or a copy or a duplicate or a multiple or whatever the hell O'Hara had intended it to be. And since it *was* one of the above, Eddie couldn't have been driven to murder by the destruction of his unique and irreplaceable masterpiece. Even if he thought Bruno had done it. Though in fact Gonzaga – or DiFalco – had no more motive for the slashing than Eddie, because having *Back Flip* in the exhibition would have been good for him, too.

If the perpetrator wasn't Radovic, the old icon master, who was it? Maybe the attack had just been a random act of vandalism by some unknown nut who didn't like modern art. But the piece was hardly controversial, and it was unusual for anybody in this city to feel that passionate about art of any style – except that unavoidable hunk of municipal edification, the city hall *Archer*.

There had been nothing in the studio that provided any clue to Eddie's present whereabouts. He'd moved everything out, the old man had said. The *Cloud* series was just a pile of rubble down in a back alley; he and Zeffler had verified that. And the other paintings ... how had Morris the Hatter put it? 'A college boy type with a old jalopy car....' Like an old Chevy station wagon, for instance. He hadn't noticed the number of the house on D'Arcy Street, but he was pretty sure he'd recognize the place if he walked by it. Well, he might just do that after his afternoon class on Monday, because it was, or could easily be, right on his way home.

ACCORDING TO Jerry Zeffler, who telephoned Jane on Monday morning to find out how she was recovering from the shock, the police had now pretty much ruled out foul play in Bruno's death. Wow, that was a relief. Jane had actually wondered for a couple of minutes whether Eddie *had* had something to do with it, but she'd said nothing to the detectives about the feud between him and Bruno. She knew she had been the sole witness to the money-throwing incident. If the cops continued to investigate, somebody else would eventually tell them about the fight at the restaurant, but there was no reason for her to implicate Eddie right from the start. She was pretty good at playing dumb and, considering her eyesight, could truthfully claim to miss a lot of detail and get things all wrong. That would explain why she'd thought she'd seen *Back Flip* in the basement of the Gonzaga when it was actually in the Artquake exhibition. Fortunately, she had never told anybody about that; if she had, she really would have looked like an idiot.

But she'd never believed Eddie had killed Bruno. It was a lot easier to imagine Win Beecham whacking him over the head with a crowbar because he wouldn't offer her a second solo show than to picture Eddie doing it. Besides, there was always that nutcase, the one she had mistaken for a connoisseur on her first day on the job. He must have hated Bruno. But then, wouldn't he have been in custody on Friday night because of the attack on *Back Flip* at the Art Gallery?

Anyway, Jerry (who claimed to have his own reliable sources in the coroner's office) said the autopsy showed that Gonzaga, or DiFalco, had died of a massive heart attack. The bruise and abrasion on his face had occurred when he hit the floor, there was no blood or tissue (ugh!) on the crowbar, and the only fingerprints found on it were the dead man's own. That made sense. Bruno always insisted on opening all shipping crates himself so that he could check the contents for damage. Since there was a risk of liability, he never trusted anyone else, even the artist, to do it.

The question of Bruno's actual identity did not seem to concern the authorities very much. There was no law, it appeared, against using what basically amounted to a pen name, as long as you didn't try to defraud anybody with it. Well, Eddie might have had something to say about that, but he had disappeared, at least according to Mr Zeffler – Jerry. Besides, she and Eddie had always made fun of Bruno's ridiculously ornate and completely illegible signature, so who knew what name he had actually been signing at the bottom of all the letters Jane had laboriously pecked out over the past six months? It could just as easily have been DiFalco as Gonzaga.

Zeffler's phone call hadn't come as a complete surprise. On Saturday, while Bob Willard's back was turned, he'd asked her for her home number in case there was any news about the Bruno situation that they ought to share. She'd jotted it down on one of his business cards and in exchange he'd given her another one of the cards to keep, in case she had any information to pass on to him. But when, as their phone conversation that morning was drawing to a close, he'd suggested that they get together for lunch on Friday, she had been taken aback. It really was kind of weird how she never, ever, saw that kind of thing coming, even in cases where she'd secretly hoped it would.

THE KID who answered the door had dark hair that hung down over his forehead, nearly covering his eyes. Bob remembered then that he didn't know even the first name of the pale, long-haired girl he had seen, a month or so ago, waving from the front porch he was now standing on. Although he wasn't even one-hundred-per-cent sure that he had the right house, either. It could have been the one next door.

The kid was staring at him impatiently. 'Yeah?' he said.

'I'm looking for a girl ...'

'You don't say, Pops. Welcome to the club.'

'I mean, I think she lives here. Or maybe next door.'

'What are you, her favourite uncle?'

An appreciative cackle erupted from the hall behind the jokester and another unkempt but slightly fairer head appeared around the door. Its face immediately assumed a surprised and not particularly pleased expression.

'Mr Willard.'

'Pete.' By some miracle he had dredged up the right name, because the second head nodded. The kid had been in his life class. 'Well, hi there.'

'Hi,' said Pete. 'What are you doing here?'

'I'm looking for a friend of mine who I think lives in this house. She's, oh, about twenty, and she has long light brown hair, and ... oh, yeah, she has a brother who has an old Chevy station wagon. A two-tone, green and –'

'You mean Sandra?'

'Could be. Is she around right now?'

'No, man. She and Eddie split last night.'

Bingo. 'Know where they are, or when they'll be back?'

Pete turned for guidance the other kid, who seemed to be marginally the brighter of the two.

'Why would we want to tell you?' he demanded.

'Actually it's Eddie I'm looking for, not the girl. He could be in trouble and I'm trying to help him out.'

'This guy's a teacher, man, from OCA,' Pete muttered. 'Used to be a painter.'

'Yeah?' The dark kid's expression became even less cordial than before. But after a moment he shrugged and said, 'Well, nobody can catch up to them now, so I guess it doesn't matter. They're in India, meditating, and they may never come back. Got it?'

Then, without waiting for a response, he closed the door. A second later Bob heard it being locked. Funny, neither of them had even bothered to ask what kind of trouble Eddie was in. And he hadn't thought to inquire if by any chance Sandra had a thing about the Marchesa Casati.

JANE KIND OF liked the restaurant on the top floor of the Park Plaza. The way the tables were lined up in two rows reminded her of the dining car on the train she had taken out west when she was a kid. So did the starched white tablecloths and napkins, the heavy hotel cutlery with its dull, pock-marked finish, the large footed goblets of ice water and the oval silver dish of celery hearts, carrot sticks and black and green olives sitting on a bed of ice cubes.

There were windows along one side of the room. She and Jerry Zeffler were seated next to them, and before she took off her sunglasses, Jane glanced out over the Annex streets far below. But despite the dowdy comfort of the place – or rather because of it – she knew that this was not a restaurant where a man would take a girl he was trying to impress, or wanted to risk being seen with. Only two other tables were occupied.

'I called Quintin in London as soon as I heard about *Flip*,' he said. 'I got to know him pretty well when he was here. And he wants *Tusk* over in London next week. Said he'll make room for it no matter what.'

'That's great.'

He was having the steak sandwich, she the chicken salad plate, and they were sharing a bottle of red wine. They had had drinks in the bar before lunch, too – martinis. Rollo would probably have ordered champagne for himself and Olivia. And Rule's, the restaurant where they went in *The Weather in the Streets*, was dark, womb-like, cosy – at least that was the way the author described it. Jane had been in London, but hadn't known anyone with enough money to take her to Rule's. The Plaza Roof restaurant, on the other hand, was almost too bright. And Jerry Zeffler did not seem quite as attractive as he had on Saturday afternoon. Leaning towards her across the table, he looked even older than forty-five.

'So. Jane. What are you going to do now?' He swirled his wine around and around in the glass and then drank some of it.

'Oh, I guess I'll have to find another job. Maybe in a bookstore or a library; that's what I did before I started working at the Gonzaga.'

'Gotta pay the rent somehow, eh?'

'Yeah.'

'Do you share with anybody? I mean, a roommate? Or maybe a live-in boyfriend?'

Getting right to the point. The answer to the second question would reveal, two for the price of one, her receptiveness to sexual activity and whether any human obstacles lay in the way of immediate consummation. Same-day, if possible. He had already mentioned, as he ordered the wine, that he was taking the rest of the afternoon off. What had ever made her imagine that this might be a long and sophisticated courtship?

'I used to have a roommate, but she left.' She kept her eyes on her plate. 'No other live-ins, so far.'

'Hmmm.'

Probably he would wait until they were post-coital to ask if she and her girlfriend had ever fooled around together. That seemed to be an amazingly common preoccupation of older men. Sometimes she even thought these guys rushed through the act itself just in order to be able to ask the question. And they really didn't want to believe her when she told them the idea had never entered her mind. Or Debbie's either, as far as she knew.

'Drink up,' he said, pouring more wine for both of them. 'This is quite good stuff.'

She was aware that he had raised his glass to his lips, but still she did not look up. A glance of suggestive complicity would almost certainly be waiting for her when their eyes met.

'Yep,' she went on briskly. 'So I have to get another job right away. And as a matter of fact I have an interview at the ... at the ... university library this afternoon.' Finally she got up the courage to look at him. 'Oh, do you have the time?'

He shot his shirt cuff and glanced at his watch. Then he poured the rest of the wine into his own glass and drained it. 'Ten after two.'

'Wow, I'd better get going. I'm supposed to be there at two-thirty. Can't be late. I've got to make a good impression, because I really need that job.'

Seeing what might have been shame or maybe even sadness on his face, Jane felt a twinge of remorse. But she had to get out of there, and this was the only way she could think of to do it. It wasn't as if she could just say, Look, I'm terribly sorry, but the thing is … I just don't think I want to sleep with you after all. God, that would have sounded *really* stupid.

TOM NOW HAD a regular arrangement with a taxi driver who picked him up in the morning and took him downtown. The same guy every day, which made it almost like having a chauffeur. Joan packed him a lunch, which he usually remembered to eat. And then, when it was time for supper, the same driver picked him up and – *Home, James* – took him back to Hogg's Hollow.

It worked out pretty well, except when James (which wasn't his real name, but the guy didn't seem to mind) arrived before he was ready to go. The first time it happened, Tom persuaded him, with the offer of a drink or two, to hang around until he was done. But when they finally did get home, Joan was hopping mad, and from then on James politely refused the Scotch, saying he preferred to keep his job.

Anyway, on the whole, it was a reasonable set-up. The car … well, why bother with it any more? That was what Joanie said. She frequently – perhaps every day? – showed up at the studio, letting herself in with her own key, and they'd have lunch together. He shooed her out right afterwards, though. It was impossible to paint with her hovering over him and fussing. She'd asked him to promise that he wouldn't open the door to anyone except herself and Max, who also had a key. In reply, he had grunted noncommittally, hoping she would take that as a yes, but reserving the right to do as he saw fit.

Max had also taken to dropping in regularly to see how he was getting on with the *Kites*. Once or twice Tom had been forced to tell him to back off and quit rushing him. There was even a possibility that the show might be at the public gallery, as a kind of retrospective. If they tightened up security, Max said, he might be willing to consider it. It seemed there'd been an incident there in which a painting got damaged, though Tom wasn't clear on the details. Anyway, it hadn't been one of his, so that was all right.

But Max had his own way of fussing. He kept saying Tom's style was changing, but what the hell was wrong with that? An artist's got to keep evolving, whether his dealer likes it or not. Otherwise, he'd still be doing the kind of stuff he'd started out with at the old Vanguard, intentionally crude antidotes to the upbeat commercial slickness he'd had to slide around on all day at the office.

The old Vanguard. Odd, how those long-ago days seemed so much more real than the large, flat expanses of time he had to fill in now. Sometimes he found himself standing in front of the half-finished canvas that was supposed to be the last *Kite* piece, frozen in a kind of panic about the way everything was just melting away to nothing. He was afraid to tell anyone – Max, Joan or even James – how he really felt, and he probably couldn't have explained it anyway.

Though at other times he thought he might be able to. But they were all, every one of them, much too obtuse to understand what he'd have to say. Watchful, too, scrutinizing his simplest actions for some sign of ... what? Recalcitrance, rebellion, insanity? Maybe all they really wanted was to make sure he kept working. Kept producing. So they all could go on living off his life's blood. Well, he was trying, damn it.

Better to keep what he now knew secret, anyway; it was something that nobody in their right mind would willingly hear. Because more and more it seemed to Tom that from beginning to end, life itself was nothing but confusion, sadness and forgetting. Oh, occasionally – during a particularly fine solo by Prez or Tatum, for instance – he still felt the world might have some logic and meaning. And there were flashes of brightness that shifted and shuffled at random, like the geometric confetti of an old ... what was it called? A tube with mirrors and bits of paper inside it. Sometimes, with a piercing, nearly unbearable pleasure, he saw a pattern that made sense but then suddenly it would lurch into an incomprehensible jumble. And down the road a piece, still fairly distant but getting closer each day, there seemed to be an area of vaporous obscurity in which no reliable landmarks were visible. Though sometimes he thought he could make out the figure of a lovely woman, nameless, ageless, not Joanie but comfortably familiar, who stood waiting amid the shifting mists.

N O W   T H A T the dates for the Lurie show were set and he actually had a deadline, Bob could no longer postpone getting to work. Old friend or not, Max would never give him another chance if he blew this one. Besides, Marie had let it slip that the main reason for his good luck was the cancellation, at short notice, of a previously scheduled exhibition by an artist with whom the boss had had a sudden falling-out. Well, never mind; he laid in a supply of Arches paper, gritting his teeth at the cost, and circled around it for a few days, daunted by the insidiously luxurious surface of the stuff.

But at last he began, and discovered that in the doing itself, the ideas started to come. Soon it seemed he had too many, every one angling imperiously for attention. But that was probably because he was so unaccustomed to the fever of creation. However, his current studio, which had been just fine when he was an artist only in theory, was now, in practice, completely inadequate. He resolved to have another look at O'Hara's place on Spadina. If the price was right, he'd take it, cockroaches and all. It might even be cheaper than the flat on Tranby, which anyway was too crowded with the ghosts of defeat to be an auspicious setting for his new life as a successful person.

Thus preoccupied, he was a little surprised by Eleanor's telephone call announcing that she wanted to come over and see him that afternoon. She'd been trying to reach him for over a week, she said. He'd been keeping the phone off the hook for long periods in order to work. But he was not much bothered by her decree, delivered a moment or two after she arrived, that they could no longer 'go on this way'. Or even by her accompanying complaint that he unjustifiably considered himself, and even acted, superior to other people. Did he? He didn't think so, but if it *was* true, he was more pleased than embarrassed by the charge. It meant, if nothing else, that he had kept his self-doubt well concealed.

He still hadn't been able to decide whether he ought to say anything to her about Jerry and Jane. Maybe he had only imagined the sparks between those two. Anyway, Zeffler's infidelity, real or potential, was no longer any of his business, because it appeared he and Eleanor were finally, officially through. But the equanimity with which he accepted this – her – decision seemed to annoy her. She must have counted on his being angry or wounded, and perhaps for just that reason he did not rise to the occasion. However, there was more – she 'loved someone else'. Stung at last, he could not stop himself from asking if this nameless person returned her feelings.

'What difference would that make?' she shot back, surprising him again. He had never thought of her being so romantic; she had seemed almost too pragmatic. Well, good luck to the poor bastard, whoever he was. They kissed chastely, a last caress that was just as casual and meaningless as their first one, in the front seat of the Mustang, the day he had rescued her from the Embassy. But she probably didn't even remember that.

'Goodbye, then; see you around.' In unison, they murmured some nearly identical version of that banal farewell, knowing they would not be able to avoid each other forever. Then, gently, Bob closed the door after Eleanor. Maybe, he thought as he listened to the sound of her footsteps descending the stairs to the street, he had underestimated her.

IT WAS REALLY too late to retreat by the time she saw Joan Dale standing on the sidewalk right opposite the building where Tom's studio was located. But maybe Joan had not noticed her yet. Eleanor felt like jumping right back into the Mustang and getting out of there, but the street was one-way and narrow. Surely it would only attract Joan's attention if she drove right past her. Dashing across the road to the other side, Eleanor walked quickly in the opposite direction and turned the first corner she came to.

The street she found herself on was no different from the one she had left. There was nothing as far as the eye could see but tiny, peak-roofed semi-detached houses with postage-stamp front yards, punctuated here and there with small, rundown industrial buildings. No shop or restaurant was visible that might account for her own well-dressed, carefully groomed presence in the neighbourhood. She hurried on until she came to another intersection and decided to make her way back to the car by going around the block.

When she was again within sight of the Mustang, Joan was gone and the street was empty except for a couple of parked cars. After hesitating for only a moment, she walked right past her own car and on into Tom's building before there was any chance of changing her mind.

The studio was on the top floor, four dusty flights up; she remembered that very clearly as she climbed them. The grubby old wooden door on the last landing was just the same, too, studded with three separate locks, one quite new and shiny, and a peephole at eye level. But now she recognized the elegant signature scribbled across the rather tattered piece of paper thumbtacked next to the tarnished brass doorbell. She pressed her finger to the button and then, after a pause during which she could actually feel her heart beating, heard his footsteps approaching the door. There was another, briefer, pause before he opened it.

This time he did not seem at all surprised to see her. He held out his arms exactly as she had imagined he would. She only had to step into them.

'Where have you been?' Tom asked after a moment. One of his hands was already under her coat, making its way inside her blouse.

'You mean, all your life?' said Eleanor.

He didn't answer, and she wondered whether she had been too bold. But he continued to caress her, in a calm, deliberate way that this time seemed to express deep emotion rather than the lack of it. His face was still buried in her neck so she couldn't see his expression. Finally he said, 'I meant, since the last … that was quite a dance we did, wasn't it?'

'Oh, yes, God, what a mess! I thought you weren't coming, and then when I saw you in the bar I…' She sagged against him, miming the despair she had felt that day at the hotel. 'The only reason I was with Willard…'

'Bob Willard!' he cried, releasing her suddenly as if he had just figured something out. 'The other night … I knew it was him. From the old Gerrard Street days…. I *knew* it was him,' he repeated.

Oh, why had she ever mentioned that name? 'But it was really you I wanted. Not him.'

'Not him?'

'No, no. Neither of them. Always you. Oh, I wish we could start over, just as if all that never happened.'

He smiled and pulled her close again. 'Yes. Let's start all over again.'

'Just where we left off, at the Park Plaza, where we were meant to begin. Let's go now. The car's right outside.'

'I know.'

H E   H A D been looking out the window when the Mustang came slowly down the street. Joan had just left and he saw her pause to watch it pull into a parking spot halfway down the short block. When Eleanor Zeffler got out, then immediately turned and hurried off in the opposite direction from the studio, he'd felt a brief prick of disappointment. For a moment it had seemed possible that she was coming to see him. But after she disappeared around the corner, he returned his attention to

Joan, who was still standing motionless on the sidewalk with her purse over one arm and the tote bag containing the remnants of their lunch over the other.

After a few seconds she took the few remaining steps to her red Mini (a vehicle well suited to her cheerful and practical nature), opened the driver's door and tossed the larger bag into the back seat. Then she got in, put the little car into reverse and backed it rapidly down the street and into the alley that ran beside the old candy factory building a few doors down. At that point the Mini was no longer visible. Tom turned away from the window then, with the intention of pouring himself a small drink from the bottle of J&B he now kept out of sight behind the chesterfield. He had just done so when he heard a knock on the door. After taking a quick sip from his drink, he put the bottle and, after a moment's hesitation, the glass, back in its hiding place and went to answer it.

Taking her in his arms seemed entirely natural, and what he felt as he did it was a fair approximation of joy. When she mentioned Willard's name, it jolted him for a second. Of course: he was the guy with her the other night, the one that wasn't her husband. But – Willard and this lovely creature? By God, she was too good for him. He was a has-been – no, a never-was, and for years now, surely. But yesterday (or maybe it was last week) Max had mentioned, as if Tom would be pleased to hear it, that Willard was painting again and was going to have a small show next month at the Lurie. Well, maybe Max had forgotten, but his own memories of the Vanguard days were not so rose-coloured that he couldn't recall how Willard, a know-it-all hick right off the farm, had argued against his, Tom's, first one-man show there. That was not the kind of thing he'd be likely to forget, no matter how elliptical his memory might be nowadays.

But when she talked about 'starting over', he knew at once that was exactly what he wanted, too. Back up, begin again, do it all over and get it right this time. Hell, wasn't that exactly what everyone his age wished they could be granted a chance to do? This woman – Eleanor – didn't think he was past it, didn't talk to him as if he were some addled codger, barely *compos mentis* enough to eat lunch without supervision. They stayed entwined (he closed and locked the studio door with one hand, keeping his other arm around her) until they reached her car, where the bucket seats finally forced them to let go of each other.

They didn't talk much on the way, but he watched with frank

admiration as she steered and shifted, cutting confidently through the midtown traffic, so unlike Joan, whose driving was exasperatingly deliberate and cautious. As they sailed around the great oval that ringed Queen's Park like a racetrack and came within sight of the hotel itself, he experienced a burst of quite unreasonable elation. He actually laughed out loud as the car shot onto the home stretch, zipped past the Museum and flew across Bloor Street on a yellow light. Hell, he already felt like a new man. Or like his old self. Never mind which; the fog was starting to lift and everything, from now on, was going to be all right.

AS ELEANOR DROVE uptown, Tom was relaxed and cheerful. He didn't sit there rigid with feigned fear and genuine disapproval, the way Jerry always did when he consented to be her passenger. After she cut deftly in front of a Cadillac that was dawdling in the middle lane of Queen's Park Circle, Tom actually chortled and said 'Good girl.'

She'd been right – he still wanted her. Though what else *could* he have meant the other night at the Gonzaga when he whispered 'I'd do anything for you'? And somehow she'd always known that Tom was the sort of man who could take pleasure in simple things, even a drive through the city – the sort who could give her the love she craved and, yes, *deserved*. He wasn't an overbearing loudmouth like Jerry, or a cynical malcontent like … but why even think about Robert now? She took her eyes off the road for a second to smile at Tom, and he looked back at her with plain adoration.

There was a burst of honking behind them. Eleanor whipped her head around, intending to glare at the driver of the car following her, but when the honking continued she realized that the dispute was several cars back and had nothing to do with her. In the rearview mirror, she saw that the offender was a red Mini. The little car, almost like a toy among the big American sedans and trucks, popped suddenly out of its lane and nearly sideswiped the car it was trying to pass. A new chorus of outraged honks broke out, the Mini lurched back into the right lane, and Eleanor lost sight of it as she roared onto the straightaway north of the park.

Twenty feet in front of her, at the intersection of Bloor and Avenue Road, the traffic light turned from green to yellow. Tom leaned forward as if that would make the car go faster and yelled, 'Floor it – we'll make it!' And with only a fraction of a second to spare, they did.

AFTER MAKING a U-turn that Tom found frankly hair-raising, Eleanor drove into the Park Plaza courtyard on Avenue Road. She let him off under the scalloped cement canopy, then steered the car down the winding ramp that led to the underground garage. When he approached the registration desk, the clerk greeted him like an old friend. Well, he must have registered a fair number of John Smiths in his time. Tom merely winked when the guy asked if there was any luggage and quickly pocketed the key he passed across the counter.

The room was in the north wing, a quiet top-floor suite on the Prince Arthur side, or so the clerk had assured him. He was nearly halfway down the long glass-enclosed corridor when he heard the wail of approaching sirens. That urgent keening thrilled him. The sound was like a signal of the city's dangerous vitality, telling him just how far he now was from the bland safety of Hogg's Hollow. A police car, followed by an ambulance, roared into view, shot right past the hotel and continued, still screaming, in the direction of Queen's Park.

Tom walked on into the north lobby and pushed the call button for the elevator. The doors opened at once and slid smoothly closed after him, shutting out the racket from the street. All was silent then, and the only thing he could hear was the shuddering whoosh of the elevator as it carried him up.

▮ Chapter Twenty-eight

THOUGH THEY WERE on opposite sides of the room, Willard felt certain that Eleanor's glance was about to turn in his direction. He began to study the painting in front of him with every appearance of interest. And why not? It was one of his own, a piece from the series he had begun just after their breakup back in '67. *Yellow Streak.* He'd started to use those punning but descriptive titles at the beginning of his 'second career'.

Jerry Zeffler had bought it out of his 1968 show at the Lurie. However, according to the label on the wall, *Streak* now belonged to the gallery in which he was standing, the Canadian Institute of Contemporary Art. A tax-deductible gift, no doubt, bestowed on the eve of Zeffler's retirement to the Dordogne in 1992. By that time he and Jerry had pretty much lost touch.

Well, considering *Streak*'s incorrigibly *retardataire* style, he guessed he ought to be grateful that Howard, or his acquisitions committee, had accepted it. In fact, it was kind of strange to see actual paintings hanging in the elegant converted warehouse, all blond wood, grey slate and sandblasted steel, that housed the Institute. Usually the art on display here was of a more up-to-date type – video loops, large-scale Cibachromes, burlap bag or lumber arrangements, even the occasional animal by-product. Not that Bob had anything against that kind of thing. Hell, no, he'd even tried a few such experiments himself, though with precious little success. The only piece he'd been able to place in a public collection – a birchbark-and-Plexiglas assemblage, circa 1985 – was almost certain to be turfed out of the McMichael any day now. But all the same it was refreshing to see some work hanging in CICA tonight that might actually be described as beautiful, though perhaps not within Howard's hearing.

Bob sucked in his gut and straightened his spine, trying to suppress the combined stoop-and-paunch effect he had begun to notice whenever he unexpectedly caught sight of himself in a full-length mirror. Never mind; a man in his seventies could still be dynamic, productive, on top of things. Look at Picasso, for God's sake: *he* hadn't slowed down, or stopped getting chicks, either, until well beyond that age. Or take de Kooning – No, better not think of him, in view of the final years. Augustus John, then; a lusty procreator to the very end.

But Eleanor, being female, was certainly past it – if by *it* you meant romantic love or erotic passion. She had to be pushing seventy-five, anyway, whereas he himself had just clocked in the big seven-o. Well, a year ago. But, all things considered, Eleanor still looked remarkably good. She'd been the Widow Dale for – God! – it must be more than twenty years.

At least he had succeeded in outliving Tom, who had stepped off in … it had to be '78, roughly ten years after marrying Eleanor. And *that* had happened, to everyone's amazement, just a few months after the sudden death of Dale's first wife. The accident was in late '67, and then in '68, the moment Eleanor's uncontested if not amicable divorce from Jerry was final, she became Mrs Dale. But they had really had only a couple of years together – that is, years when Tom still knew who she was.

Bob often wondered when Eleanor had found out that Tom was losing his marbles, or if she had known it from the start. But though over the last three decades they had run into each other dozens of times at events like this one and usually managed to chat amiably enough for a minute or two, it had never quite seemed possible to ask her that question.

He risked another quick look. Good bones, that was it; the handsome thoroughbreds invariably aged better that the merely pretty ones. There were wrinkles, naturally, and the last time he'd got close enough, he had noticed some advanced crepiness in the neck area. At this distance, though, such signs of decay were invisible. Her hair looked more or less the same as it always had; a little shorter, less artfully arranged, but still the silvery blond shade that must have been synthetic even in the days when he had been allowed to tousle it. She had remained slim and straight, and in that all-black-with-a-touch-of-white-at-the-throat outfit, she still looked elegant in an austere kind of way. Thank God, though, that the young chicks had started to wear bright colours again; the Dutch Syndics look seemed at long last to be on its way out.

At Eleanor's side stood Thomas Dale Junior, the son she had coaxed from Tom's loins at the last possible moment, before he was utterly lost to dementia and she to menopause. Junior looked enough like Senior to quash any sceptical notions Bob or anyone else might have had about his paternity. Not that he nursed any illusions that the boy – *boy?* – he had to be thirty if a day – was his. No, no; the thing between him and Eleanor had been over for more than a year before the kid was conceived. But even now he could remember the unexpected pain he'd felt, seeing her pregnant – radiant, huge in front yet still desirable. It had seemed outrageous that even then, even when pretty much out to lunch, Tom simply could not fail at whatever he attempted.

The Widow Dale, keeper of the flame. She was not looking his way after all. Max Lurie had materialized at her side and was kissing her, in the French manner, on both cheeks. When had *that* started? Not the complicity between those two, but the epidemic of double and even triple cheek-kissing. Sometime in the mid-eighties, he thought. Eleanor and Max had teamed up much earlier, in the late seventies, soon after Tom had finally absented himself physically as well as mentally.

But long before that, Max had surprised Bob by being very much in favour of Dale's marriage to Eleanor. He could see his point. Without a wife to look after him, Tom might not have continued to paint. He was already losing it when Joan died. On the afternoon that her little Mini had veered into the path of a truck at the top of Queen's Park Circle, Tom was nowhere to be found. And when he finally turned up at the studio later that day he could not even remember where he had been. But all that had been hushed up at the time.

Now Max's wiry energy had wizened to a bird-like jauntiness, and his once dark, abundant hair was pure white and wispy. The Lurie Gallery had been closed for years, but he kept his hand in as a director of the Dale Foundation, an entity created to manage and control the dissemination of the Late Work. And there was a helluva lot of it – a huge collection of hectic, gaudily coloured canvases, quite unlike Tom's serene, assured midlife paintings. One of the latter, a gigantic piece in blue and grey-green, was hanging just down the wall from where Bob now stood. But very few of these had been left in the Widow's care. Nearly all of them been sold by the Lurie Gallery during Tom's long decline. When, as occasionally happened, a classic Dale changed hands nowadays, there was no financial benefit to its creator's heirs. Or to Max, for that matter, and maybe that was why he was helping Eleanor. But perhaps, Bob thought, suddenly feeling like an idiot not to have realized it before, it was simply because he loved her.

Max must have seen him, because he smiled and raised one arthritic claw in greeting. Bob waved back but made no attempt to force his way through the mob to the far side of the room. They'd catch each other later and exchange the old-fogy reminiscences that were unavoidable on occasions like this.

DUO! Win was quite unprepared for the surge of emotion she felt, seeing it again after all these years – the very painting Tom had just finished when she first understood their true feelings for each other. She slipped a small magnifying glass out of her purse and took a quick peek at the wall label. *Duo,* acrylic on canvas, 1967, on loan from a university gallery in the midwestern United States – that was not surprising, since many of Tom's collectors had been American. Goodness, Howard had really done his homework, because if she remembered correctly this painting had also hung in the original Artquake exhibition.

He hadn't attempted to recreate the show exactly, though. So many of its original artists had failed to live up to the potential Quintin Margrave had seen in them, while others, who for one reason or another had been left out of the 1967 exhibition, had later proved to be important. Like herself, for instance; she was represented in *67+33* by *Oleander,* a small, early tissue collage that quite clearly, or so Howard said, presaged her later, more substantial work. No, the present show was merely a reconsideration of and tribute to the optimism and ferment of that Centennial year; an 'imaginary' version, according to the catalogue, of the exhibition the British curator might have organized had he possessed the gift of prophecy. A brilliant concept, Win thought. And useful, too. Today's brash young iconoclasts simply didn't know how much they owed to the recent past.

But fortunately, as Howard often said, we Canadians no longer consider it either necessary or appropriate to import foreigners like Margrave to explain our own culture to us. We have our own vital institutions, such as CICA, established in 1995, just at the eleventh hour before public funding for the arts dwindled to a mere trickle. And our own experts, like Howard McNab himself, its widely respected director.

She could see him now on the far side of the room, moving slowly through the crowd. He was carrying, apparently with some difficulty, the chair he had agreed to bring from his office for her. Although people kept saying that her mind was as sharp as ever (a compliment, supposedly) Win found that nowadays her body tired very easily. She was nearly eighty-seven, after all. Henceforth, she feared, she might be forced to rest on her laurels, which, thanks in part to Howard, were still quite green.

The series of textile-relief pieces that had made her reputation in the late eighties might not have been properly understood but for his bold interpretation of them. Until Howard's review appeared she herself had not quite grasped the complex symbolism of the judicial robes (ordered in quantity from the same venerable firm that had supplied Father), which she had tacked, spread-eagled, onto special stretchers and then painted over with many coats of encaustic.

At once a critique of and an elegy for the tattered trappings of our colonial past, he had written (she knew it all by heart), *a thorough, yet not merciless dismantling of the patriarchy's imperial presumptions.*

It was lucky (though crushing) that Eliot had died by that time. He would have been mortified to read such words in the pages of the newspaper he had been able to open confidently for decades without fear of contradiction. And so had she been, at first. She had meant to memorialize Father, not to criticize him; the dark, roiling surfaces of the finished works represented grief, not resentment. But eventually, a woman alone in a time when being in that situation was easier and pleasanter than in any previous period of recorded history, she had come to see the acuity of Howard's reading.

The artist, he'd written, *herself a descendant of the Family Compact, interrogates its iconic remnants with clear-eyed rigour and stunning technical audacity.* At least — at last — she was being taken seriously, though the women's collective where she had first exhibited the *Robe* series was rather unfortunate — all too reminiscent of the church basements of yesteryear. But everything had been quite different once Howard got the show into a proper gallery.

However, McNab had overlooked the other subject hidden beneath all the swirling impasto, obstructive as cerebral plaque: the loss of Tom and with him the imaginary alternative narrative — it was nearly impossible to resist such locutions, finally —of her own life. No living creature, except herself, would ever see it now.

IT WAS A BIT like being at a high-school reunion, Jane decided. She'd actually attended one when she'd happened to be in town a decade ago visiting her parents. A real last-shall-be-first-first-shall-be-last scene. Generally speaking, the despised grinds of both sexes had become university professors, the jocks used-car salesmen and the cheerleaders harried housewives. The beatniks, like herself, seemed to have changed very little – at least those few, like herself, who were pathetic enough to show up.

But the 67+33 opening was even more disorienting. A whole generation of artsy-intellectual people had sprung up since her youth, so most of the people standing around self-consciously tonight were strangers to her. Though at least she could see them fairly clearly, because she wore contacts now. Every once in a while she thought she saw someone she knew, but then remembered that by now the person she imagined she recognized would be much, much older than the one she was looking at. She'd been away for nearly thirty years.

Eventually, though, some of the faces in the crowd began to morph into identifiable ones, unnervingly altered like those digitally aged pictures of missing children. The man standing next to her, for example, was ... Bob Willard! He looked like a total codger with his bifocals and nearly nonexistent hair. And the woman with him was ... God! ... Jenny Kosma, almost matronly now but, judging from her stance – feet apart and arms akimbo – still quite the tomboy.

On the far side of the room Jane spotted Max Lurie, white-haired and oddly miniaturized by age, but still animated and dapper. He was deep in conversation with ... could it be? ... yes, it was ... Eleanor Zeffler, remarkably preserved yet slightly dehydrated-looking, as if she had been buried for the intervening years beneath hot desert sands. It was obvious even now that she had once been a great beauty and still expected to be treated like one. Yet, remembering that Eleanor's husband had once, briefly, been hers for the taking, Jane was able to look at her without envy.

The person who had changed the most was Howard McNab. Outwardly at least, the years had vastly improved him. His mouldy, water-logged complexion was now almost rosy, and his greasy hair had become a close-cropped salt-and-pepper ring around a smooth, pink tonsure. He wore a charcoal-grey suit that looked expensive, and as he passed through the crowd, stopping here and there to accept what looked like praise and congratulations, he carried a Gehry popsicle-stick chair. Finally, in front of a huge, gorgeous painting that even after all these years Jane instantly identified as a Tom Dale, he halted, placed the chair on the floor and waited while a little old lady sat carefully down in it.

'Excuse me,' Jane said rather loudly to Willard, who was staring off into space. Her turned to look at her, but there was no sign of recognition in his eyes. She didn't feel like explaining who she was – or had been, all those years ago. Instead, she pointed at McNab. 'Do you know who that old lady is, the one he's making such a fuss over?'

'Sure. Win Beecham. An artist. Or at least she used to be.'

Jenny Kosma snorted at that. 'Hell,' she said, 'weren't we all?'

YEARS AGO, for tax reasons, Max had recommended that Eleanor transfer ownership of *Tusk* to the Foundation. 'Let's face it, dear,' he'd told her back in '79, 'nobody else is going to buy it. O'Hara's career was too short to make a real reputation. Nobody knows who he is any more. Or *was*. This way, at least you still get a little something out of it.'

Since she had never really grasped the mechanics of tax planning and Max nearly always knew what he was talking about, Eleanor did as he suggested, though she had grown attached to the triptych in a funny kind of way. So it was nice to see it hanging in the +33 show. She had got it as part of the settlement with Jerry, along with a few other pieces she hadn't really wanted, though naturally she didn't admit that at the time. She had not even been sure she wanted the divorce, but Tom had needed her desperately and so finally she had had no choice. But when it came to the small early Dale, *Bay Blues,* Jerry had been immovable – and not just because it was worth more than any of the other things they owned. No, he simply couldn't stand the idea of her and, especially, Tom getting their adulterous paws on it, though he hadn't hesitated to put it on the market the minute the divorce papers were final.

Tom had accepted the situation with a shrug (why, he'd just have to paint her another one, he'd said with a boyish grin), and she didn't know, or care very much, except for sentimental reasons, where *Bay Blues* was now. The only Dales that were worth anything today were the huge middle-period things, like *Duo,* for instance. And there it was, a mute but unmistakable taunt, way over on the far side of the room near the spot where she had seen Bob Willard standing a moment or two ago.

Max was circulating, and Thom (he insisted on the 'h' to stave off what he called the 'Junior' thing) had also disappeared. Well, you couldn't expect a handsome young man to spend the evening chatting with his mother, could you? Suddenly alone, and wanting to appear occupied, Eleanor strolled over to *Tusk* and made as if to check the label for accuracy. She didn't bother to dig her reading glasses out of her purse, because she already knew exactly what it said.

Edward O'Hara

Canadian, 1946–(?)1972

God, that sad little question mark!

Tusk, 1967

acrylic on canvas

Courtesy of the Thomas Dale Foundation

Tom hadn't thought much of *Tusk.* She wondered what he would think if he could see his name up there *below* Eddie's. In the sixties he'd been irritated by the way people said that O'Hara was going be the 'next Tom Dale', and when after a couple of years Eddie still hadn't returned from Nepal or Thailand or wherever it was he had gone, Tom was probably more pleased than not. Though by then it was starting to be difficult to know for certain what – or *if* – Tom really thought about anything.

After a few more years it turned out that Eddie was probably dead, one of the many victims of the Indo-French serial killer, Charles Something-or-Other. The skeleton of the girl he was travelling with, whose parents had enough money to send someone to investigate, had eventually been found in Katmandu in the early seventies and identified through dental records. Most likely O'Hara had met the same end. And maybe it was only the tragedy-of-a-young-life-cut-off-in-all-its-promise thing, just as Howard had said in his little memorial piece for *artscanada,* but from then on Eleanor had a kind of melancholy fondness for *Tusk,* the only painting of Eddie's that she and Jerry had ever owned.

It had taken a lot of finagling to get it into the London showing of the original Artquake '67 exhibition as a replacement for the other O'Hara that had been slashed by some vandal. A homeless person, she thought she remembered. They were called rubbies in those days. That was just after Bruno Gonzaga died, but long before anyone had even started to worry about Eddie. The A G O curator at the time – what was his name? – had been recalcitrant, saying the triptych was too big. Furious, Jerry had contacted Margrave directly and after some expensive long-distance telephone conversations he had agreed, since the Spitalfields show was going to be hung quite differently and they had the space.

Eleanor wondered later if Quintin had really just wanted to see *her* again. When they were in London for the opening (nothing on earth would have kept Jerry away) he joined them one night for dinner at Mirabelle. All through the meal, he played shoes-off footsie with her, and even though she knew by then that Tom would be the real love of her life, and naturally she was still disgusted with Quintin, she had astonished herself by not only allowing but enjoying it.

IF HE MOVED quickly, Bob calculated, he'd make it to the other side of the room while the Widow Dale was still alone. And wasn't that big three-part piece she was looking at with such close attention an early O'Hara? Not that there would ever be any *late* O'Haras. God, he hadn't thought about the poor kid in years; it was too depressing. The last time he'd spoken to him was the night Eddie burst into the place on Tranby, full of wild accusations, while Eleanor cowered in the bedroom. And after that, he'd never seen O'Hara again.

He was just about to start moving towards Eleanor when he felt an elbow jab into his ribs and heard Jenny mutter, 'Shit. Here he comes. Fuck.' She had started swearing quite freely again now that the girls were grown up. With a grimace, she jerked her head in Howard's direction. He was only about a dozen conversations away and gesticulating in a manner that indicated he was on his way over to talk to them.

Bob had almost mastered his aversion to McNab now that Howard was firmly in a position of power. He respected the work the guy had done over the years. And he really was grateful to him for putting *Yellow Streak* in this show, particularly since there had not been a Willard in, or anywhere near, the original Artquake exhibition. But even though Howard hadn't laid a finger on her for decades, Jenny still considered him an out-and-out cop-a-feel creep. She didn't need to be civil to McNab, because she didn't paint any more; she was into crafts – ceramics, to be exact – these days. Strange, Bob thought sometimes, how he had ended up with another potter, though a far more determined and professional one than Lorraine had ever been. Of course if Jenny hadn't been determined, he wouldn't have married her in the first place.

Back in '69, he'd imagined that like every other dolly-bird of the era, she would know the address of a good abortionist and be more than happy to avail herself of his services. But no. She'd *wanted* the baby. He was astonished, not only by the fact that tough-talking, tomboyish Jenny would so easily and carelessly get herself knocked up (oh, all right, he'd had something to do with it, too) but that she was so tearfully sappy about it. It wasn't, she admitted, that the Pill had failed; she hadn't been taking it and actually had been longing and trying to get pregnant for ages. Mike Orley – he of the towering phalluses of steel – had been shooting blanks, which was one of the reasons they'd broken up in 1966. So it was Bob's problem and not hers, Jenny had stated calmly in between those out-of-character boo-hoos, if he'd just assumed she was on it and had failed to take any responsibility for contraception himself.

And so, reader, he married her, despite the difference in their ages, which when you thought about it was kind of flattering to him. Besides, he'd just proved that Thomas R. Dale was not the only one who knew how to pop a bun in the oven. Overall, three decades and daughters later, he and Jenny were precisely as happy, no more and no less, than he had expected they'd be. At fifty-five she was still in good shape, quite capable of diapering him in his dotage, if it came to that.

'Okay,' she suddenly barked, 'I'm going to the can.' And a moment later, Howard McNab was standing right beside him, wearing a mysterious grin.

WOULD SHE REALLY want to live be a hundred or whatever gigantic age Win Beecham must be by this time? Jane hadn't made up her mind about that yet, although she herself had now reached the point where death no longer seemed quite so reassuringly conceptual.

Even tonight there were ghosts at the feast: Bruno for one, Tom Dale for another and poor, poor Eddie. He'd been dead for years and years, apparently, though she had only heard about it a few days before. But lots of people – her contemporaries – had begun to die lately, from all the usual diseases or just plain, unforeseeable bad luck: oops, wrong car, wrong road, wrong flight, wrong lover. And like every other woman of her age, told to search her own body for the first signs of creeping death, she felt dutifully around each month, heart in mouth, for its stealthy spores.

So far she had been lucky. And in general as well as specific terms, her good fortune seemed to be more a matter of what she had avoided finding than what she had found. Until very recently, she had continued to think of herself as a romantic adventuress. But maybe she had actually been too cautious. The men she had attached herself to had been steadily employed and faithful, for she'd finally realized that in the long term she would never survive the easily predictable cruelty of the creative types she was always drawn to, moth to flame, when young. And surprisingly, some of the straight arrows had quite a strong grasp of female anatomy, or at least an earnest willingness to learn. They had their own nasty little ways, though, some far more crazy-making than simple infidelity or substance abuse. But at least none of them had ever hit or left her.

She had not had, or wanted, children, a renunciation made easy and discreet for years – no, decades – by the dear old Pill. Even now, despite the neurotic fears of young women today, oral contraception still seemed to Jane like a beloved childhood friend she would simply not hear denigrated, whatever misdeeds he or she might later have been discovered to be guilty of. Oddly enough, bullied into getting tested by Fred, who late in life suddenly wished to be a patriarch, she had discovered in her mid-forties that she was not fertile after all. Though maybe that was just a case of mind over matter. But it was only now, when it was quite safe to do so, that she had begun to experience some very feeble twinges of regret.

Until recently, the very idea of Motherhood – an unholy state that turned carefree, impudent girls into harried, dishevelled, selfless and sexless women – had revolted her. Anyway, she would certainly have failed at it, because she suspected she was incapable of placing someone else's welfare and contentment above her own. Well, not for very long, anyway. Both her husbands – ex-husbands now, by more or less mutual consent – had told her as much, and perhaps they were right. Still, she had never really been able to see why they expected her to be unconditionally unselfish and supportive, when neither of them would for a moment have considered doing it themselves. Besides, being loved (at least for a while) despite her unwillingness to behave like a real wife had always seemed to Jane an achievement in itself.

Pushing forcefully off from her second marriage like a swimmer, she had shot cleanly out of the American college town where she had spent nearly ten years as the wife of a professor of mathematics, then paddled back to Toronto. As Frederick, their house and all its contents receded into the distance (a U.S.-dollar cash settlement had been the logical solution), her former life seemed utterly ridiculous and she wondered how she had ever imagined she would be happy in it. But such are the necessary delusions of Love, in which despite everything she still believed. Not as a panacea – she was much too old and battle-scarred for that – and anyway her consciousness had been irreversibly raised, fish-and-bicycle style, in the seventies. No, love was not a solution to anything; it was merely the greatest and most thrilling experience that life could offer.

She had just enough to live on, but Jane felt she ought to keep busy while she waited for lightning to strike again. She'd always had jobs – jobettes, jobules – wherever she'd gone, all of them ill paid and arts-related. But now, in Toronto, she'd found that she was too old to get, or want to do, the kind of thankless low-level work that she would have taken on thirty years ago. There really *were* no jobs like that any more – young girls now actually expected to be promoted from such positions and were in turn required to take them seriously.

Back in Minnesota and still nominally married, Jane had looked, to herself, more or less the same as she always had. No great beauty (why tempt fate by exaggerating?) but not bad, either. Her face was a little fuller, true, but even scrupulously factoring in the soft focus of presbyopia, she was still ... presentable. *Sortable,* that French boyfriend of hers from the sixties had once said in a teasing voice that promised she was much more than that.

Mustering the courage to leave Fred, she had assured herself she ought to be able to manage at least one more serious affair before she was done. Before she was *really* over the hill – a place that like death itself had always, until recently, seemed miles away and highly theoretical. But some subtle change must have overtaken her on the voyage home. No viable candidates for the last affair had appeared, and she could tell from the reactions of bus drivers and waiters that she had left the zone where youth and comeliness grant certain automatic privileges. Even Bob Willard had looked at her without a flicker of interest a few minutes ago. No one, it was now becoming clear, would ever again praise her merely for existing.

'AN AMAZING CASE of synchronicity, don't you think?' Howard demanded as soon as he had closed the office door after them. 'I mean that it should surface at this precise moment in time.'

At first Bob hadn't been able to figure out why McNab, still smiling, had led him into his inner sanctum, especially when there were so many other more important people milling around the joint. But now, looking at the painting propped against the bookshelf, all he could think was *Perhaps the dead do speak, in their own language.*

'I thought you might be interested in seeing this,' Howard was saying. 'You and O'Hara were quite close at one time, weren't you?'

'Not really. But how –'

McNab sat down behind the desk and waved Bob into a chair opposite him. 'A foreman on a renovation project brought it here this afternoon. They're redoing the space where the Gonzaga Gallery used to be – though not for the first time, which is the amazing thing – it's been a book shop, a clothing store, and has had, I believe, several other incarnations over the years. In this latest it's to be yet another coffee emporium.'

'Where was –'

'In the basement, behind a false wall in a closet. It must have been there since '67 when the Gonzaga closed. A bit of urban archaeology, you might say. Naturally the workmen who ripped out the wall and found it were very disappointed when they learned they hadn't discovered, and I quote, "a priceless old master" that would make them all rich when sold at auction. Anyway, they decided to show it to the foreman who, it so happens, worked on the CICA conversion and thus picked up some half-baked notions about "modern art". He came straight to me, still imagining the find might be worth something, cash on the nail, no questions asked.'

'Unbelievable – on the very afternoon this show was opening! But I guess there wasn't time to –'

'He was quite crushed, I think, when I had to tell him it was a forgery.'

'A forg –' For an instant Bob was afraid his face might betray him and reveal the furious reshuffling of memories going on inside his head. But Howard McNab hadn't got where he was today by paying attention to the expressions of the uninfluential.

McNab's voice was slightly impatient now. 'Yes, yes, a crude pastiche. You do remember, don't you, that the original was slashed during the Artquake exhibition in 1967? Beyond any hope of restoration – you can't *imagine* the conservation headaches we have with those sixties things. And that Gonzaga owned it?'

'Sure. But …' For some reason – though in retrospect, he could not think of any good one – Bob had never told a soul, not even Jenny, about the *Back Flip* caper or his participation in it.

'So this –' Howard cocked his head at *Back Flip* with a faint grimace of distaste '– was clearly a desperate attempt by Bruno, or I should say *Vito,* to recoup his investment. He was quite a skilled craftsman, but no artist – amazing how people think all they need to do this sort of thing is masking tape and a roller – or even a master forger. Though I must say

321

the signature on the back is reasonably convincing. But the colours are completely wrong. I remember the piece perfectly, because as you may not know – I was never credited – I actually wrote the Artquake catalogue. And here's something really odd: there's a tiny slit in the canvas – see it, right there in the centre? – as if Gonzaga had started to mimic the damage done to the original. Why, though? That, I must confess I don't understand.'

Neither did Bob, so he only shrugged.

'However, as it happened, he dropped dead before he could even try to make use of the copy. Remember the day we found him? Though how he ever hoped to convince Allan or myself that there was something fishy about the other canvas and this one was the real thing, I can't imagine. Even with O'Hara out of the country and unable to intervene. But of course he – I mean Bruno – was in the final analysis a simple man, despite that penchant he had for self-aggrandizement and mystification.'

'Well...'

'Imagine it: Bruno and Eddie, comrades and adversaries – remember that incredible fist fight? – and both of them gone so long. Rather poignant, isn't it?'

'Definitely.'

'You know, when I think of O'Hara – and Gonzaga, too, in some respects; he was only thirty-six when he died – I'm always reminded of what Pound wrote after Gaudier-Breszka's death in the Great War. He talked about the difficulty of disentangling "promise" from "achievement" when an artist dies young and how one must be careful not to confuse the tragedy of that interruption with the merit of the work.'

'Didn't you say something along those lines in that obit you did on O'Hara?' *Though without crediting the old collaborator, if I'm not mistaken.*

'I may have.'

'I thought so. But what are you going to do with it? *Back Flip*, I mean. You are planning to keep it, aren't you?'

'The copy? Oh ... I don't know.' McNab glanced at the painting again. 'Perhaps in some sort of study collection. I recall from my student days that the ROM keeps a number of fakes on hand for educational purposes. We at CICA might do the same. The thing is a document of sorts, I suppose. Its very existence is a testament to the persistence of romanticizing ideations around art.' His expression was brightening. 'And useful, possibly, for interrogating the socioeconomic history of the art marketplace and decoding certain pervasive doxa attached to what Marx so aptly termed commodity fetishism.'

'Worth a thousand words, at the very least,' Bob said as he got up, but Howard didn't seem to have heard him.

Out in the crowded gallery again, he was struck by the sheer number of people he didn't know. He stood in a corner for a few minutes and watched them. Then he decided to go and find Max, because all of a sudden he was seized by an urgent longing, as insistent as hunger or thirst, to talk about old times.

▮ Acknowledgements

The quotation that opens scene 2 of chapter 21 is from *The Weather in the Streets*, by Rosamond Lehmann (London, Collins, 1936). A Virago paperback was published in 1981 and is still in print in the UK.

A number of songs are briefly quoted throughout the text. They are: 'A Sailboat in the Moonlight' by Carmen Lombardo and John Jacob Loeb, 'Exactly Like You' by Dorothy Fields and Jimmy McHugh, 'I Wish I Were Twins' by Edgar De Lange, Frank Loesser and Joseph Meyer, 'I Would Do Anything for You' by Claude Hopkins and Alex Hill, 'Lulu's Back in Town' by Harry Warren and Al Dubin, 'Who Do You Love' and '(Someone Is) Wrecking My Love Life' by Ellis McDaniel (Bo Diddley).

Anne Denoon was born in Toronto. During the 1960s, she studied art history at the University of Toronto, and returned in 1980 to complete her degree. For most of the 1970s, she lived in France, the Netherlands and England. She has worked in both public and commercial art galleries, and from 1986 to 1995, was a frequent contributor of reviews and articles to *Books in Canada*. *Back Flip* is her first novel.